"Why am I in a room?"

"They're keeping you overnight for observation." She tapped her forefinger to her own forehead. "Concerned about the brain trauma."

"I'm fine."

"So you've said. If the MRI comes back clean, you'll be good to go. I think it's scheduled for tonight."

Kyle felt bad for keeping her from her life.

"You should go." That didn't come out right, and the thought of her leaving him alone twisted his gut with fear. What was wrong with him? Maddie was nothing more than a paramedic he occasionally ran into at the hospital.

"Oh, so you're dismissing me?" she said in a strange tone.

Had he offended her? "I meant you don't have to stay and babysit me."

"I came with you in the helicopter, so I'm waiting for a ride." She redirected her attention to her phone.

Good to know that she wasn't hovering at his bedside because she cared about him, that he wouldn't have to worry about her developing feelings for a man who had no interest in love.

Love? He was surely suffering from brain trauma.

Hope White
and
Christy Barritt

Deadly Mountain Refuge

Previously published as *Mountain Ambush*
and *Mountain Hideaway*

H HARLEQUIN® LOVE INSPIRED®CLASSICS

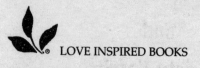

LOVE INSPIRED BOOKS

ISBN-13: 978-1-335-52385-3

Deadly Mountain Refuge

Copyright © 2019 by Harlequin Books S.A.

First published as Mountain Ambush by Harlequin Books in 2017 and Mountain Hideaway by Harlequin Books in 2016.

The publisher acknowledges the copyright holders of the individual works as follows:

Mountain Ambush
Copyright © 2017 by Pat White

Mountain Hideaway
Copyright © 2016 by Christy Barritt

www.Harlequin.com

Printed in U.S.A.

CONTENTS

An eternal optimist, **Hope White** was born and raised in the Midwest. She and her college sweetheart have been married for thirty years and are blessed with two wonderful sons, two feisty cats and a bossy border collie. When not dreaming up inspirational tales, Hope enjoys hiking, sipping tea with friends and going to the movies. She loves to hear from readers, who can contact her at hopewhiteauthor@gmail.com.

Books by Hope White

Love Inspired Suspense

Hidden in Shadows
Witness on the Run
Christmas Haven
Small Town Protector
Safe Harbor
Baby on the Run

Echo Mountain

Mountain Rescue
Covert Christmas
Payback
Christmas Undercover
Witness Pursuit
Mountain Ambush

Visit the Author Profile page at Harlequin.com.

MOUNTAIN AMBUSH

Hope White

When I am afraid, I put my trust in you.
—*Psalms* 56:3

This book is dedicated to ER doctor Jim Keen,
Fire Chief Chris Tubbs and
Deputy Fire Chief Rich Burke
for their help and patience.

ONE

I'm going to die.

The text shot adrenaline through Dr. Kyle Spencer's body. In less than a minute he'd packed his gear and was heading into the mountains.

Can't make it down on my own.

Spence sprinted up the trail, his muscles burning from the strain of carrying the pack across his shoulders. He couldn't think about that now, couldn't be concerned about his own discomfort when Gwen Taylor was stranded in the mountains, cold, immobile and most likely terrified.

He had to get to her.

He'd read desperation in the teenager's eyes when she'd been brought in with a drug overdose a few weeks ago. No matter how hard she'd tried to push people away, Spence's gut told him she wanted help, she didn't like using drugs and alcohol to manage her depression, and the overconsumption had been an accident.

Her last text message had confirmed his suspicions: I don't want to die.

He'd given her his cell number in case she had any questions after she'd been released from the hospital. That wasn't his usual practice, but he occasionally felt it necessary. Now he was glad he'd given it to Gwen.

Spence called to speak with her, calm her down, but she didn't answer. Had she taken drugs with her into the mountains, planning to end her life, but changed her mind and had injured herself?

Wiping sweat from his forehead, he inhaled the crisp scent of mountain air and hoped the search-and-rescue team was close behind. He'd left a voice mail for his friend Police Chief Nate Walsh, alerting him to Gwen's situation. He wasn't sure how long it would take Search and Rescue to assemble, but Spence couldn't wait for his team. Gwen could be seriously injured.

An image of his little brother sparked across his mind. His boots slipped on the wet ground and he skidded toward the edge of the trail. Arms flailing, he caught hold of a nearby tree branch and stopped his momentum. He paused and took a calming breath before continuing up the trail.

The memory of his brother's injuries had disrupted Spence's concentration. It had happened twenty years ago, yet felt like yesterday. He resented the distraction. He couldn't let his personal failure affect his ability to save Gwen.

Helping people, saving lives, lessened the guilt about Bobby's death. Maybe if he helped enough patients he'd be able to release the torturous thoughts that kept him up at night. And maybe, God willing, he'd find peace.

God willing? It was simply an expression. Spence didn't believe in a God who could let his brother die at only eight years old.

A gust of wind shoved him against the mountainside but he held his ground, slowing down a bit to ease the resistance. Spence was no good to the team if he ended up needing to be rescued himself.

The sound of a woman's scream echoed across the mountain range. He hesitated.

Listened.

The wind howled back at him.

Had he imagined it?

A second ear-piercing scream sent him into action, running uphill against the blustery wind. Hyper-focused, Spence controlled his breathing for maximum efficiency and sidestepped every rock and tree root popping up on the trail.

He rounded a corner and spotted Gwen flat on her back, motionless. Rushing to her side, he felt for a pulse. It was weak. Blood oozed from her scalp and her skin was cool and pale.

The first sixty minutes after a patient suffered a trauma were critical to her survival. That was why ER doctors called it the golden hour.

I don't want to die.

Spence automatically did his ABCs: airway, breathing and circulation. Her breathing seemed labored, which meant an occluded airway and that intubation would be necessary.

He pulled out his phone to call for help. They'd need a helicopter rescue, no question.

Something smashed against the side of his head and he flew backward, hitting the ground. Spence struggled to make sense of what was happening. Firm hands grabbed his jacket collar and dragged him toward the edge of the trail.

And the steep drop down the mountainside.

Through the haze of a possible concussion, Spence wondered if his attacker was a drug dealer, one of Gwen's troubled *friends*? Had he sold Gwen drugs she may have overused, and the criminal didn't want to get caught and go to jail?

"I don't care what you've done," Spence said. "Just let me take care of Gwen."

The guy pressed what felt like the barrel of a gun against the back of Spence's head.

"You're done taking care of people," the man threatened, and continued dragging him across the hard ground.

Anger seared its way up Spence's chest. This couldn't be his last day on earth. He hadn't saved enough lives, wasn't anywhere close to earning redemption.

Spence fought off his attacker, reaching for the guy's arm.

The man pistol-whipped him. Pain seared through Spence's brain.

The ledge loomed closer...

"Listen to the sound of His glory," a woman's voice echoed.

Momentarily distracted, the assailant loosened his grip.

Spence grabbed his wrist and yanked hard. The attacker lost his balance, stumbled and fell to the ground.

The gun sprang from his hand.

Spence dived on top of him and pulled his arms behind his back, wishing he had something to bind his wrists.

A gasping sound drew his attention to Gwen. Her airway was closing up. Not good. He had to get to her before she stopped breathing altogether.

The attacker swung his fist backward and nailed Spence in the jaw. The guy scrambled out from under him, jumped to his feet and began kicking Spence in the ribs.

Spence rolled, hoping to get to the gun before the attacker did. But his head snapped back and slammed against a rock. More stars sparked across his vision.

A shot rang out.

This was it. The end.

Yet Spence didn't feel the burn of a bullet ripping through his flesh.

He didn't feel much of anything as he stared up at the gray sky.

I'm coming, Bobby. I'm coming...

"Freeze!" Maddie McBride ordered the attacker.

Maddie obviously knew her way around a gun better than this birdbrain who was kicking the stuffing out of Dr. Dreamboat.

As she aimed the weapon at the attacker's back, she heard her father's voice from childhood: *never aim a gun at something you aren't prepared to destroy.*

Well, this might be the day she destroyed another human being. Not something she wanted to do, but she might not have a choice. Her priority was to save the doc and the injured female on the ground.

The guy stood very still for a few seconds, and then kicked the doc again.

"I said freeze, turkey, or the next one's going in your back."

He slowly turned, and she swallowed a ball of fear knotting in her throat. Talk about creepy-looking. The guy wore a black face mask that covered everything but his dark gray eyes. More like black—they looked black as coal.

"Not another step," she said, but even Maddie could see her hands were trembling from the adrenaline rush.

"You wouldn't shoot me." He took a step toward her.

Maddie fired off a round at his feet, coming dangerously close to taking off his big toe in those ridiculous blue sneakers.

He jumped back, his eyes darkening even more.

She didn't have the patience for this, she really didn't. She'd been on a hike, saw the text go out, and decided to stop by and offer medical assistance.

Things got a lot more complicated.

"Down on your knees," she said. "Interlace your hands behind your head."

She calmed her breathing. If he lunged at her, she'd have to shoot him. Time froze in those few seconds.

She thought a smile curled his lips.

Her finger braced against the trigger.

Then he spun around and took off.

"Hey! Get back here!" She fired a shot into the air.

The guy instinctively ducked, and tripped. He hit the ground, rolling...

Over the edge of the trail into the abyss below.

She rushed to the edge and looked down into the lush green forest. There was no sign of him or any movement at all. Great, now they'd have to send a second team to rescue that jerk.

At least he was no longer a threat and she could concentrate on the injured doc and unconscious female. Maddie engaged the safety and shoved the gun into her waistband.

"Hey, Doc, you okay?" She knelt beside him.

He blinked and looked up at her. His eyes were bloodshot and glassy. He struggled to sit up.

"Whoa, whoa, take it easy."

He waved her off and sat up, shaking his head as if to clear the cobwebs. Glancing beyond her he said, "You shot him?"

"Yeah, I shot him," she quipped, then read his worried expression. "Doc, I'm kidding."

He didn't look convinced.

"I fired to get his attention and he fell off the trail." She handed him the gun. "Hang on to this in case he comes back."

His eyes widened as he stared at the gun.

"Or maybe not." She tucked the gun back into her waistband and shucked her backpack.

"You shot at him?" Dr. Spencer was frowning at her.

Really? She'd saved his life and he was judging her for discharging the weapon?

"What's the status of the victim?" Shoving his judgment aside, she went to the female lying motionless on the ground. "Hang on, I know this girl." As a paramedic, Maddie and her partner Rocky had rushed this girl to the hospital for a drug overdose a few weeks ago. "This is—"

"Gwen," he offered.

"What have we got, forty, forty-five minutes left?"

She glanced at Dr. Spencer for confirmation. He was looking around as if trying to figure out how he'd ended up out here. Oh boy, maybe it wasn't judgment she'd read in his eyes a moment ago as much as confusion. Could Dr. Dreamboat be suffering from a head injury courtesy of the masked creep?

She clicked on her small flashlight and checked his pupils. The man had the bluest eyes she'd ever seen. "Do you know where you are, Dr. Spencer?"

"Of course I do. I'm fine." He batted her hand away and went to Gwen, as if Maddie's offensive question had snapped him into action.

Good. He was okay. He had to be okay so he could help her treat Gwen.

Dr. Dreamboat, as the ladies in town called him, was not only a skilled doc but he had a charming bedside manner that made young women, old women, pretty much all women line up to date him.

Not Maddie. She wasn't buying Dr. Spencer's smooth charm and overconfidence. No one was that perfect. Besides, Echo Mountain was a temporary stop for the cosmopolitan doc, and she belonged here, with her friends and family.

"You need to keep her head steady," he said.

"Are you sure—?"

"Occluded airway. I don't see a better option."

Maddie was about to offer to take over, but the doctor seemed suddenly confident about doing an intubation in the middle of a national forest with a heavy wind swirling around them. Maddie positioned Gwen's head just right.

"Ready?" he said, making eye contact.

"Are you?" she said.

The doctor ignored her question and used a laryngoscope to hold the tongue aside while inserting the endotracheal tube. Done properly, this would allow air to pass to and from the lungs.

Maddie realized she was holding her breath. It seemed like it was taking forever.

"I think..." His voice trailed off.

Gwen's skin suddenly looked better, pinker, and her chest began to rise and fall.

"Whoa, what happened?" a man said.

Maddie recognized her cousin Aiden's voice behind her but she remained focused on the patient. Although employed as Echo Mountain Resort Manager, Aiden also volunteered for search and rescue. Boy was she glad SAR had officially arrived.

"Spence?" Aiden said.

"Occluded airway. Had to intubate," Dr. Spencer said. "We need..." He hesitated before saying, "A helicopter."

"I'm on it." Aiden called it in.

Maddie studied the doctor. He seemed a little off and not acting like his usual charming self.

"Someone needs to monitor her pulse and..." He glanced at Maddie.

Her breath caught in her throat at the confused look in his eyes.

"Bag her," Maddie offered.

"Yes, bag her," Dr. Spencer said.

SAR volunteer Luke Marshall knelt and monitored Gwen's pulse, while local firefighter Sam Treadwell helped her breathe using the vinyl bag.

"Helicopter is on the way, Doc," Aiden said. "Why does Maddie have a gun in her jeans?"

Dr. Spencer glanced at Maddie as if he wasn't sure.

"A guy in a black ski mask attacked Dr. Spencer," Maddie started, hoping the doc would join in. He didn't, so she continued, not taking her eyes off him. "I got the guy's gun and he ran. Fell off the trail over there." She pointed. "They'll want to send another search team, with police officers."

"Why'd he attack you, Spence?" Aiden asked.

The doctor shot him a confused look. Maddie's skin pricked with goosebumps.

"That's the twelve-thousand-dollar question," Maddie recovered. She felt protective of the doc, probably because she owed him a debt of gratitude for protecting her cousin Cassie last year from mob thugs.

"What are you doing out here?" Aiden asked Maddie.

"I was hiking and saw the text. The guy was crazed, Aiden, beating Dr. Spencer like they were mortal enemies."

Aiden narrowed his eyes at the doctor, who was also a good friend. "Who was he, Spence?"

"I," Dr. Spencer started. "It doesn't matter. We need to focus on getting Gwen to the hospital." He stood and wavered.

Maddie jumped to her feet. She and Aiden caught him as he went down. Kneeling beside the unconscious doctor, she took his pulse.

She glanced up at her cousin. "It's too slow. We need to get him to a hospital!"

TWO

"*Bobby!*" *Spence peered over the edge onto the cliff below. His younger brother's body lay motionless, his eyes closed. Spence had to get to him, but he had to get help.*

Spence glanced down the trail. No, he couldn't abandon his brother.

"*Help!*" *Spence shouted. "Somebody help!" His voice echoed back at him.*

The wind whistled through the dense forest. He didn't know what to do.

"*You know what your most important job is in the whole world? Take care of your baby brother,*" *his mom said on a weekly basis. Bobby was a trouble magnet, everyone knew it. But still...*

Spence shifted onto his stomach hoping to climb down to the ledge where his brother had landed. With a solid hold of a tree branch, he lowered his left foot to a knot in the mountain wall.

The branch snapped.

And he fell the remaining ten feet onto his back. The wind knocked from his lungs, he struggled to breathe as he stared up at the pine and cedar trees filling his line of vision. He forced himself to breathe, rolled onto his hands and knees and looked at his brother.

"*Bobby?*" *he gasped.*

He hadn't a clue what to do, how to help him. What had he seen on that medical show Mom always watched? Spence tipped Bobby's head back to keep him from swallowing his tongue. He grabbed his brother's wrist and felt for a pulse.

"Where is it?" he muttered, trying the other wrist.

Panic coiled in his gut.

"Bobby! Wake up!"

"Wake up!"

Spence gasped and opened his eyes, struggling to get his bearings. The lush trees and whistling wind were gone.

His brother…

Was gone.

A ball of pain knotted in his throat.

"Breathe," a woman said.

He blinked, and Maddie McBride's round face framed with rich auburn hair came into focus. She offered an encouraging nod and squeezed his shoulder.

He glanced past her and realized he was in a hospital room, but he wasn't the attending physician. He was the patient.

"You're okay," she said.

There was something in her voice that didn't sound so sure. Her green eyes studied him with concern.

"Who's Bobby?" she asked.

Right, he'd been sucked down into the childhood nightmare. He shook his head and closed his eyes, hoping she'd leave him alone with his shame.

"Are you in pain? Want me to call the nurse?"

"No and absolutely not." His response was more clipped than he'd intended, but he didn't want to be here, didn't want to be a patient.

"Okay then," she said with that same note of sarcasm

she'd used in the mountains. "Do you remember how you got here?"

"I…" He shook his head. Had they carried him down?

"What's the last thing you do remember?"

"Some guy assaulted me. Then you—" He opened his eyes. "You shot him?"

"No, I fired off a round to make a point. And—" she paused before continuing "—you're welcome."

He must have looked puzzled.

"For saving your life?" she prompted.

He nodded. It all seemed so unreal.

"How's Gwen?" he asked.

"Much better. Breathing on her own. You did good work out there, especially considering your condition."

"My condition?"

"Yeah, your brain trauma," she said as if it was the obvious answer. "Intubating with a concussion? Gutsy."

She started to slip her hand off his shoulder and he caught it in his own. He wasn't sure why, but the feel of her warm skin eased the panic in his chest. Her bright green eyes widened and her head tipped slightly.

"I… I think…" He struggled for the right words, wanting to thank her for coming along when she did, and for being here to wake him from the torturous dream.

A knowing smile eased across her lips. "How about I get you some water?"

She slipped her hand from beneath his palm and took the plastic pitcher to the sink. He sensed she knew that he struggled to find words, to make sense of the thoughts jumbling around in his brain.

Man, his head hurt. Maybe he *should* call for the nurse. No, the last thing he wanted was for hospital staff to think of him as broken and unable to do his job. He needed to appear strong, even if he felt weak. He wanted respect, not pity from his peers.

"What happened to the man you shot?" he asked.

"Shot at," she corrected, walking back to the bed. "They're still searching for him." She handed him a cup of water. "Chief Walsh said when they find him they'll charge him with assault and question him about what happened to Gwen."

"She texted me, wanting my help, but I assumed she was alone."

Maddie's brow furrowed. "Poor kid. She seemed so lost when we brought her in."

Lost. Exactly how Spence felt right now. Confused, fragile and powerless. Not a feeling he was used to.

"How's the head pain?" she asked.

"About a two."

"Uh-huh." She narrowed her eyes. "I saw what happened, remember?"

"Wait, that sound… You were singing?"

"That sound? Wow, thanks."

"I didn't mean—"

"It's fine, I know I'm no Carrie Underwood. I figured singing would distract the guy long enough for you to get the upper hand. Well-done, by the way."

"Thanks."

"But then, how did he get the advantage?"

He struggled to remember. "Gwen was gasping for air. Guess I got distracted." He sipped his water. "Why am I in a room?"

"They're keeping you overnight for observation." She tapped her forefinger to her own forehead. "Concerned about the brain trauma."

"I'm fine."

"So you've said. If the MRI comes back clean you'll be good to go. I think it's scheduled for tonight."

He felt bad for keeping her from her life.

"You should go." That didn't come out right, and the

thought of her leaving him alone twisted his gut into a knot. What was wrong with him? Maddie was nothing more than a paramedic he occasionally ran into at the hospital.

"Oh, so you're dismissing me?" she said, in a strange tone.

Had he offended her? "I meant you don't have to stay and babysit me."

"I came with you in the helicopter so I'm waiting for a ride." She redirected her attention to her phone.

Good to know that she wasn't hovering at his bedside because she cared about him, that he'd have to worry about her developing feelings for a man who had no interest in love.

Love? He was surely suffering from brain trauma.

"Huh," she said, eyeing something on her phone.

"What?"

"A text from my cop brother. They can't find the assailant who attacked you." She sighed. "Terrific, now there's a psycho running around town. Makes me wish I woulda shot him."

"You're kidding," he said, his voice flat.

"Yes, Doctor, I am kidding. Did you ever have a sense of humor or was it beaten out of you in the mountains?"

He was about to shoot back a smart remark when Dr. William Danner breezed into the room. "There he is, the superhero not looking so super." He stopped short and glanced at Maddie. "What are you doing here?"

"I came in the helicopter with him." She crossed her arms over her chest as if daring him to challenge her.

Danner, a few years older than Spence, had a razor-sharp tongue he used to intimidate much of the staff at Echo Mountain Hospital. But not Spence and apparently not Maddie, either. She narrowed her eyes at Danner as if challenging him to pick a fight.

Spence never could understand guys like Danner. Instead of leading with compassion, he ruled with intimidation. The guy was a bully.

"What's my prognosis, Doctor?" Spence said, hoping to divert him from ripping into Maddie. The thought bothered Spence.

Danner redirected his attention to Spence, no doubt a bigger and more interesting target. For some reason Danner considered Spence his competition and would use any means necessary to come out the victor. Yet weren't they after the same thing? Helping patients?

"Besides the head injury, where else were you injured? Ribs?"

"Minor bruising. I'd like to be discharged," Spence said.

"Is that right?"

Spence realized by the slight curl to Danner's lips that he was enjoying being in control of Spence's life a little too much.

"I lost consciousness," Spence said. "It happens after a head injury. I'm fine."

Danner checked Spence's pupils. "Be that as it may, Dr. Carver wants MRI results before you can be released."

"I can always discharge myself."

"You could, which would only prove that your head trauma is clouding your judgment. Is it clouding your judgment, Kyle?"

No one had called him Kyle since his relationship with Andrea had exploded into pieces. He preferred not to be called Kyle because it brought back too many memories. Danner obviously sensed this and used it as a weapon.

"He seems pretty sharp to me," Maddie offered.

Without looking at her, Danner responded. "And who, pray tell, are you to offer a medical opinion?"

"Hey," Spence snapped. "She saved my life out there."

"I didn't realize you two were…" Danner's voice trailed off.

"We're not," Maddie said firmly.

Nurse Heather Warren came into the room. She was in her forties with a round face and warm smile. "I have the medication you ordered, Dr. Danner."

"What medication?" Spence asked.

"Sedative for the MRI," Nurse Heather said.

"I don't need that."

"And I don't need you messing up the imaging department's schedule because you have a claustrophobic meltdown," Danner said.

"Who says I'm claustrophobic?" Spence snapped.

"Hey, what's going on in here?" Dr. Ruth Carver said, entering the room.

Spence was glad to see his friend, the one person Danner wouldn't challenge. Ruth was the hospital administrator who'd hired Spence over a year ago. They had served on medical committees and had become friends over the years, and when there was an opening at Echo Mountain Hospital, she contacted him about joining their team. The timing had been perfect, a few months after his ugly breakup.

Dr. Danner handed Ruth the clipboard. "He's all yours. I have patients who need me." Danner marched out of the room.

"Jerk," Maddie let slip.

Nurse Heather bit back a smile.

"Leave the medication," Ruth said to the nurse.

"Yes, Doctor." Heather did as ordered and left the room.

Ruth looked at Spence. "I'm sorry I couldn't get here sooner. The board president cornered me. How's your pain?"

"About a two."

"At least a six," Maddie offered.

"I said a two," Spence countered.

"But you meant a seven."

"I can speak for myself. I don't need medication and I want to be discharged."

Ruth narrowed her eyes. "You're not acting like yourself, Spence."

Which they both knew was another symptom of brain trauma.

"I'm fine," he said.

"Spence, you live alone out in the country," Ruth said. "If I send you home without MRI results and it's worse than a mild concussion and you lose consciousness, I'd never forgive myself. Please don't fight me on this," she said with pleading brown eyes.

Ruth and her husband, Cal, both in their fifties, had been gracious to Spence when he moved to town, having him over for dinner a number of times and treating him like family.

"Sorry," he said. "I guess I'm proof that doctors make horrible patients."

Relief eased across Ruth's face. "Good, now that that's settled, take the sedative so you can relax for the MRI. It's very mild."

If he was his own patient he'd be following Ruth's protocol without question. He swallowed the pill and sipped water to wash it down.

"They'll be up shortly to take you to imaging." Ruth glanced at Maddie. "Are you staying?"

"Until my ride shows up."

"You mean Rocky?"

"No, my cousin Bree."

"Oh, I thought your boyfriend would pick you up."

"My boyfriend?"

"I assumed you and Rocky were a couple, but kept it quiet because of work policy."

Spence noted Maddie's confused expression. Not guilty for putting her job at risk by dating a fellow employee, but she seemed confused by the question as if the thought of dating Rocky had never crossed her mind.

"Rocky and I are good friends, that's all," Maddie said.

Ruth nodded, but didn't look convinced. "Well, it's nice of you to stay with Spence. I didn't realize you two were friends."

"We're not, but she saved me," Spence said.

"Saved you?" Ruth said.

"Maddie showed up and distracted the guy from throwing me down the mountain."

"Oh dear." Ruth glanced at Maddie. "You are certainly a brave young woman."

Maddie shrugged.

"That must have been terrifying," Ruth said.

"It all happened pretty fast."

Ruth turned to Spence. "Who attacked you?"

"I don't know. He was wearing a mask."

Ruth's pager buzzed and she glanced at it. "I've gotta run. I'll check in later."

"Thanks," Spence said.

Ruth left the room and Spence gazed out the window into the dark night.

It was clear that Maddie was hanging around because she felt sorry for him. After all, Spence had no family, no dutiful wife. Not that the women in town hadn't auditioned for that role many times during the past year. He'd never step into that bottomless pit again.

Never trust a woman with his heart.

If he eventually considered marriage, it would be a partnership of familial obligation, not romantic love. Was there a woman out there who'd be open to such a life? It would be nice to share a home-cooked meal and conversation with someone, and he'd enjoy having a travel buddy, someone who liked to hike as much as he did. His guy friends were great, but they had other commitments—Nate with his job as police chief and new romance with Cassie McBride; and Aiden, who managed a resort and a relationship with his concierge, Nia Sharpe.

Deep down, Spence knew true love was an illusion. His parents had split only a few years after Bobby's death, and his own fiancée's betrayal had nearly destroyed him. Yet there were days when the thought of a solitary life spiked melancholy through his chest.

"Five bucks for your thoughts."

He snapped his attention to Maddie. "What?"

"You were far, far away." She frowned and raised three fingers. "How many fingers do I have up?"

"Knock it off. I'm fine."

"So you keep saying." She slid a long strand of copper-streaked auburn hair behind her ear. "Why do I get the feeling you're not being totally honest with Dr. Carver?"

"You're accusing me of what, exactly?"

"Wanting to get out of here sooner than later. I get it, I do. I was hospitalized for a migraine last year." She shuddered. "The experience made me more compassionate with my patients, that's for sure."

More compassionate? She'd always seemed to have a gentle and consoling way with patients whenever she wheeled them into his ER.

"You need to be straight with Dr. Carver so she can help you. That's what you always tell your patients, right?"

"Sure. Thanks for the advice," Spence said, wanting to shut down this topic of discussion. "You really don't need to hang around."

A flash of hurt sparked in her green eyes. He hadn't meant for that to happen. The concussion was obviously making him irritable. He opened his mouth to apologize, but she spoke first.

"My ride isn't here and I'd rather not hang out in the

lobby to be interrogated by fans wanting an update on Dr. Dreamboat." She redirected her attention to her phone.

"Dr. Dreamboat?"

"You know they call you that," she muttered.

"I didn't—"

"Hi, Dr. Spencer." Oscar Burke, a twentysomething orderly pushed a wheelchair into the room. "What are you doing here, Maddie?"

She didn't look up from her phone. "Waiting."

"For what?"

"The ski lift."

"Huh?"

"Never mind. My work is done here." Without making eye contact, she turned and left the room.

He sat up, wanting to call her back and say something, express his thanks again.

Apologize for his rude behavior.

"She's a weird duck," Oscar said.

"Why do you say that?"

"Bossy one minute, friendly the next."

Which actually sounded like Spence tonight thanks to the head injury.

"You ready for your MRI?" Oscar said.

"Yes." Spence got out of bed and shifted his feet onto the floor. When Oscar reached out for the assist, Spence motioned him off. "I'm fine."

Maddie was right. He kept repeating the words, but even Spence knew it wasn't true. He sat in the wheelchair and Oscar adjusted the footrests.

The MRI was one more thing to check off the list. The radiologist wouldn't see anything alarming and Spence would be released in the morning.

As Oscar wheeled him to the elevator, Spence closed his eyes, giving hospital staff the message that he wasn't in the mood to talk. Unfortunately, Oscar couldn't see Spence's face.

"That was some fight you got into on the trail, huh?" Oscar said.

"It was."

"Good thing you shot at the guy and scared him off."

Spence was about to correct him, to say that Maddie had fired the weapon, but didn't want to encourage further conversation. They successfully avoided hospital staff as Oscar wheeled him into the elevator.

Spence sighed with relief. Relief? He was usually outgoing, not the type of person to avoid social interaction.

The elevator doors closed. "Head hurts, huh?" Oscar asked.

"Yes." Spence nodded and rubbed his temples.

"I'm sorry."

"Why? It's not your fault," Spence snapped. "Sorry."

Again, that was not like him. He chalked it up to the hammering in his skull that wouldn't quit. It would make anyone cranky. Perhaps he should ask for a pain reliever to help him sleep tonight.

Then again, sleep would only bring more nightmares, and besides, they were careful not to overmedicate patients suffering from head trauma.

Spence focused on relaxing for the MRI. Being in that enclosed space wasn't the most pleasant experience with the banging, knocking and buzzing sounds filling the tube.

When they got to imaging, Oscar handed Spence off to an MRI tech named Kurt. As Kurt helped him onto the table, Spence could tell the medication was taking effect. He felt relaxed, and even a little light-headed.

"Music choice?" Kurt asked, handing Spence headphones.

Spence stretched out on the table. "Classical."

"Okay. I can hear you so if you have any concerns while the procedure—"

"I won't," Spence said. He wanted this done, over. He wanted to go home to his remote cabin.

As Spence lay still, arms by his sides, the tech slid the table into the tube. A moment later, classical music drifted through the headphones. He'd try to find a peaceful place in his mind, a calm place. He'd always found peace in Echo Mountain National Park surrounded by majestic evergreens, pine and cedar trees—a blanket of green spanning the mountain range.

Green like Maddie's eyes.

That's why she'd been able to calm him down, because her eyes reminded him of the one place he could find comfort.

The hammering sounds of the MRI scan started to interfere with the calming effect of the music. His thoughts drifted to this afternoon's rescue, finding Gwen and the brutal attack. Should he have performed the complicated procedure on her considering his brain trauma? Of course. Gwen was okay now, breathing on her own, Maddie said as much.

Maddie, his defender. She'd saved his life.

The medication caused him to drift deeper…deeper.

He wasn't sure how much time had passed when silence filled the tube. Were they done? Had Spence slept through the forty-five minute procedure?

Heavy metal music blasted through the headphones, sparking a migraine that clawed its way through his skull.

"Ah!" He ripped off the headphones and fought the nausea rolling through his stomach.

The table slid out of the tube.

He was surrounded by darkness.

"Kurt?" he said, his voice weak.

Spence rolled off the table and stumbled across the room. The door, he needed to find the door.

"Kurt!"

"He can't help you," a voice whispered.

Spence whipped around. "Who's there?"

"It's time to pay for your sins."

THREE

Maddie motored down the hall, checking email on her phone. She didn't want to be cornered by female staff members for an update on Dr. Perfect Spencer, nor did she want to perpetuate the story that he'd fired off the warning shot to save Maddie. That bit of untruth had been spreading like the flu ever since they'd arrived at the hospital, but Chief Walsh asked Maddie not to discuss details of the case. So rather than correct the chatterboxes and tell them she had saved Dr. Dreamboat, Maddie had to play the helpless waif.

Anyone who knew Maddie knew she was a determined woman who did not need protecting. But it was too easy for people to assume Dr. Spencer had been the protector since he was the confident and commanding type.

He didn't seem very commanding just now. Fear dulled his normally bright blue eyes. His lost expression, combined with his messed-up hair and bruise on the side of his forehead, made him seem almost…fragile.

Kind of like Maddie after she'd been abandoned. Again.

She shook off the thought. Even a capable man like Dr. Spencer would be rattled after being assaulted by a lunatic in the mountains. Yet Dr. Spencer had been so worried about Gwen that he had managed to ignore his head injury long enough to successfully intubate her.

"Amazing," she whispered to herself. Even if she didn't particularly care for the doc's overconfidence and bravado, she could definitely appreciate his skills. She hoped those skills wouldn't be affected by his head injury.

She stepped outside into the misty rain and paced the hospital's front walkway. Pulling her rain jacket closed in front, she struggled to forget the image of the doctor's expression as he'd gripped her hand resting on his shoulder. As a paramedic, she recognized the expression—fear mixed with vulnerability—because she'd seen it on her patients' faces.

Yet this was different. It was vulnerability, sure, but an edge of confusion dulled his eyes. She'd seen that look on Aunt Margaret's face when Uncle Jack had suddenly died of a heart attack years ago. The same look had pinched Dr. Spencer's forehead when he'd awakened from his nightmare calling out a name: *Bobby*. Maddie suspected Dr. Spencer had lost someone close to him and that emotional wound had yet to heal.

Aunt Margaret said the only thing that kept her going after her husband's death was the support and love of family. Maddie glanced back at the hospital. Dr. Spencer had no family, at least none in Echo Mountain. Instead, he was surrounded by a hospital full of admirers, people who propped him up on a pedestal and adored him. They completely bought into the Dr. Charming act he performed every time he showed up for work.

Would they be able to see past their admiration and realize how scared he was? Would he let them see past his normally affable demeanor into the devastation brewing beneath the surface? Probably not, but Maddie had already been there, heard his cry for Bobby and saw the terrified look in his eyes.

She imagined that was how she looked when Dad had left, then Mom, and then Waylan.

Her cousin Bree pulled up in her SUV. Perfect timing. Maddie needed to snap out of her pensive mood.

Maddie started to reach for the SUV door, then let her hand drop to her side.

Bree rolled down the passenger side window. "Hey, what's up?"

"I'm not sure."

"Are you getting in?"

Something told her to go back inside and check on the doctor, even if he was snappy and asked her to leave again. Being there could help him feel safe, and she owed him that for what he did for Cassie. That's all, there was nothing more to it.

"I'm sorry, but I think I'd better stay," Maddie said.

"Are you sure? I mean, you're here so much as it is," Bree said.

"Yeah, I need to check on somebody."

"You've really got to stop getting emotionally connected to your patients, sweetie. Boundaries, remember?"

"You're right, but this one…" Maddie sighed. "It's Dr. Spencer. I won't be able to sleep unless I know he's okay."

"I heard some guy attacked him. But wait, you don't even like Spence."

"I know, but he helped Nate save Cassie last year and, well, he seems kind of broken."

"Maddie," her cousin said.

"What?"

"When are you gonna stop trying to fix people?"

"It's my job, remember?" Maddie teased.

"That's not what I meant and you know it."

"This is different."

"He's got an entire hospital of people to take care of him."

"They don't know what's really going on. Please don't be upset with me. I'll catch a ride with Rocky when he gets off his extra shift. I just—" She glanced at the hospital, and then back at her cousin. "You always say to follow your instincts."

"It's true."

"Sorry I dragged you out here."

"No need to apologize. Had to pick up something for Mom anyway."

"Give her my love."

"Will do." Bree winked and pulled away.

Maddie felt a smile curl the corner of her lips. She had the best family in the world, even if her parents weren't included on that list.

Maddie reentered the hospital and headed for imaging where they'd taken Dr. Spencer. For some reason she wanted to be there when he finished.

As she stepped into the elevator her phone vibrated and she glanced at a text from Rocky, fellow paramedic and rumored love interest. She was still a bit stunned about that assumption.

You okay? Heard rumors, Rocky wrote.

A-OK. No worries, she responded.

Heard the doc shot some guy.

"Really?" she muttered. Oh, how she wanted to share the truth with her friend, but she would not ignore a direct order from Chief Walsh. He must have his reasons for asking her to remain mute on the subject.

Grapevine's been busy, she responded.

The elevator doors opened to the lower level and she glanced up.

Into a pitch-black hallway.

No lights, no emergency lights, nothing. Yet no alarms had gone off and everything was business as usual upstairs.

She stepped out of the elevator.

A crash echoed down the hall from the imaging room.

Maddie texted Rocky that there was trouble and to send security ASAP. Maybe she was overreacting—she hoped she was overreacting.

"Get away from me!" Dr. Spencer shouted.

Maddie snapped her penlight off her keychain and made her way down the hall. Maybe not such a good idea. She should wait for help to arrive. Surely it wouldn't take security more than a few minutes to—

Another crash, then "Stop!"

She dropped to her knees and crawled toward the imaging area. The desperate tone of the doc's voice drove her forward. As she edged closer, she took slow breaths to calm her racing pulse.

She turned the corner and aimed her penlight into the office.

The technician, Kurt, lay motionless on the floor. She scrambled to his side and felt for a pulse. Strong and steady. He was alive, but completely out. She pried open his eyes. Pupils were dilated. Had he been drugged?

"What do you want?" Dr. Spencer shouted.

A low mumble responded to the question. She glanced at the tech, then at the window into the MRI area. If the attacker was bold enough to drug Kurt, he might do much worse to Dr. Spencer.

She scanned the office for something to use as a weapon. Unfortunately hospitals were not rife with defensive tools. Fine, she'd rely on her self-defense training.

"Let go of me!" Another crash was followed by a slam against the window.

Adrenaline shot through Maddie's body. She shouldered the door open and realized that by doing so, she'd made herself as vulnerable as the doc. She arced the beam of her flashlight across the room.

Suddenly someone shoved her face-first against the wall. She kicked the top of his foot, hard. He released her and took off down the hall, the squeak of his shoes echoing as he ran.

"Yeah, run, you jerk!" The outburst escaped her lips.

"Hey, you! Stop!" a voice called outside from the office.

Security must have arrived. Good, she could focus on the doctor. She took a few deep breaths and turned.

"Dr. Spencer?" she said.

No response.

She aimed her flashlight and spotted him on the floor in the corner.

"No, no, no," she muttered, rushing across the room to him.

When she touched his shoulder, he jerked away as if he'd been stung. "I said don't touch me!"

A shudder ran down her spine. This kind of raw fear looked all wrong on the doc.

"Dr. Spencer, it's me. It's Maddie." She aimed the flashlight at her own face and offered a bright smile. Then she redirected the beam at the doctor. He was curled up, looking away from her.

"It's okay," she said. "You're okay now."

She reached out again and tentatively placed her hand on his shoulder. "Remember me? Maddie McBride?"

The emergency lights clicked on, bathing them in a soft glow.

"Doc?" she prompted.

He slowly turned to look at her. "Maddie? Of course I remember you. How could I ever forget you?"

Whoa, not exactly the response she expected. His eyes looked glassy, and not totally focused.

"Did that man hurt you?" she said.

His eyes widened with fear.

"Don't worry, he's gone." She smiled. "Are you hurt?"

He shook his head that he wasn't, looking at her like he adored her. This wasn't right. The amount of medication he'd been given for the MRI shouldn't have made him this loopy.

"What did he say to you?" she asked.

"Maddie!" a male voice called.

"In here!" She glanced over her shoulder.

Security guard Ted Graves stepped into the room. "Is he okay?"

"Seems to be. Someone needs to examine Kurt. I think he's been drugged."

Ted called it into his radio.

Dr. Spencer squeezed Maddie's hand, still resting on his shoulder. She looked at him.

"You saved me…again," he said. He brought her hand to his lips and kissed it.

Oh yeah, he'd been overmedicated all right. Which meant someone breached the hospital's drug protocol and gave him a higher dose than intended so that he couldn't defend himself.

A man cleared his throat in the doorway. She glanced up at Chief Nate Walsh.

"Everything okay?" he said.

"He doesn't seem to be physically hurt, but I suspect Dr. Spencer was given higher dose of the sedative than was ordered for the MRI. Did you catch the attacker?"

"No, he escaped," Chief Walsh said. "Did you get a good look at him?"

"Lights didn't come on until after he'd left," Maddie said. "We need to get Dr. Spencer back to his room."

"No." Dr. Spencer squeezed Maddie's hand. "I can't stay here. He'll find me."

Maddie glanced at Nate. "What should we do?"

"I'll assign an officer to him 24/7."

Maddie looked at the doctor. "Does that work?"

He nodded, but didn't look so sure.

"If you want, I can stay, too, okay?" she said.

With a sigh, he nodded and closed his eyes.

To say Spence was disappointed when he awoke the next morning just as Maddie was leaving his room was an understatement. He reminded himself that he shouldn't depend on her so much, especially to feel safe. The brain trauma must be causing anxiety, that's all. It's not like he specifically needed Maddie's caring nature to feel grounded. It could be anyone kind enough to offer comforting words.

If that was true, why hadn't he felt grounded when Nurse Bethany came to check on him, or Nurse Tanya?

He felt smothered by the staff and utterly frustrated on so many levels. Dr. Danner seemed to enjoy holding Spence hostage, yet every minute spent at the hospital as a patient made him feel more broken, and more anxious because someone got to him here last night.

He appreciated both Maddie's presence, and the police protection. Without them he wouldn't have slept at all.

Ruth gave him the good news that the intruder hadn't interrupted the MRI, and his scan indicated a mild concussion.

The discharge couldn't come fast enough. Whatever trouble he'd stumbled into out in the mountains seemed to have followed him back to town. What else could explain the attack in the MRI department last night? He didn't want to put staff members in danger by staying in the hospital another minute longer than necessary.

Chief Nate Walsh offered to give Spence a ride. Nate was a good friend and Spence didn't feel he had to watch his words around him, or keep up the charming pretense.

"We're doing everything we can to find the guy," Nate

said eyeing Spence in the rearview mirror of his cruiser. "You don't remember anything he said, do you?"

"Not really, no."

Spence racked his brain trying to remember something from the encounter last night. Between the head injury and the overmedication, it was all still foggy.

"Do you remember *anything* from last night?" Nate asked.

"Like what?"

Nate shot him a look through the rearview mirror.

"What?" Spence said, curious.

"Do you remember Maddie finding you?"

In a rush, the scent of coconut rushed through his mind. A memory...

The feel of his lips pressed against her soft skin.

"Oh no," Spence said.

"So you *do* remember?" Nate teased.

"I really kissed her hand?"

"Yep."

"I didn't mean to."

"You sure about that?"

Spence glanced out the window.

"Don't worry, buddy. She knows you were under the influence of a powerful drug. She didn't take it seriously."

Good, because the last person Spence wanted to offend was the woman who'd saved his life. Twice.

As Nate pulled onto Spence's property, he noticed two cars parked out front.

"Who's here?" Spence said.

"Probably locals filling your fridge."

Spence got out of Nate's cruiser and was greeted by Cal, Dr. Carver's husband. "How ya feeling, buddy?" Cal reached out and shook Spence's hand.

"Hanging in there, Cal. What's going on?"

"The McBride clan asked if they could stock the fridge.

Since we've got your spare key, I let them in. Hope that's okay."

Nate shook hands with Cal. "That's nice of you, Cal. But I think Spence is a little wiped out to have company."

"No problem. Could you manage five minutes, Spence?" Cal asked. "To say thanks and all that?"

"Of course," Spence said. He didn't want to seem ungrateful, or rude.

Acting unusually curt would cause Drs. Carver and Danner to question the severity of his brain injury. Although his injury didn't look serious on the scan, brain injuries were all different and unpredictable. TBI victims could experience mood swings, or personality changes, which was what his doctors would be looking for.

Spence had always worn a smile as his armor, but today his head hurt and his body ached. He wanted to relax without having to smile or make pleasant conversation.

"Your assistant is supposed to start tonight," Cal said.

"Assistant?" Spence questioned.

"Ruth hired someone to help you out until you're fully recovered," Cal said.

"That's not necessary."

"Perhaps not, but she doesn't want to take any chances. She found someone to check in on you for the next week or so, until you're up and running at your usual 120 percent."

Spence suspected it might take longer than a week. Two or three perhaps? What if he never cleared the clutter from his brain, and had to give up practicing medicine? He fisted his hand, frustrated at the thought of not being a doctor, not saving lives.

His life would be, in a word, over. Panic overwhelmed him.

Get it together, Spence. He pulled himself back from the edge. He'd be okay; he had to be okay. He was just exhausted.

The men went to the cabin and Cal swung open the door.

Margaret, matriarch of the McBride clan, was directing her daughter, Cassie, on building a fire.

Cassie glanced over her shoulder, dropped the kindling and ran into Nate's arms. "Hi, Chief. I could use your fire expertise."

Spence noticed Nate's face light up as he hugged his girlfriend.

"With pleasure, dear," he said, teasingly.

"Dr. Spencer, it's so good to see you up and around," Margaret said.

"Thank you."

A light, melodic sound echoed from the kitchen. Spence glanced across the cabin. Maddie stood at the counter with her back to the group, singing along with a song playing through her earbuds.

"And I always knew…with your love…"

"Maddie?" her aunt Margaret said.

"I could do anything…"

"Maddie!" her aunt tried again.

Cassie grabbed a piece of kindling and tossed it at her cousin to get her attention.

Maddie shrieked and spun around, wielding a chopping knife like a weapon. She glanced at the utensil in her hand and scrunched her nose. Removing the earbuds, she offered a smile, blushing. "Sorry. Got lost in the music. Hi, Doc. Hi, Chief."

"Maddie, nice to see you," Nate said.

"I didn't know there'd be four for dinner." Maddie glanced over her shoulder at the vegetables she'd been chopping.

"Actually, I've got an appointment," Cal said.

"I won't be staying for dinner, either," Nate said.

"Hey, my cooking isn't that bad," Maddie joked.

Joked. Smiled. Cooked. Spence enjoyed the moment, however fleeting.

"It's not your cooking, coz," Cassie said. "Chief promised me dinner at Mackey's Dim Sum tonight."

"Nice," Maddie said with envy in her voice.

Spence suddenly wanted to take Maddie out to dinner.

Okay, now he was really losing his mind.

"Well, I'm off," Cal said.

"Could I have the spare key for the officer who will be keeping watch?" Nate asked.

"Sure, Chief. Spence, your assistant should be checking in at eight. Well, have a good night, everyone." Cal handed Nate the key and left.

"Your assistant?" Maddie asked.

"Dr. Carver hired someone to keep an eye on me," Spence explained.

"Ah," Maddie said, and went back to chopping vegetables.

Something felt off, Spence wasn't sure what. He and Maddie hadn't spoken about what had happened in the MRI room, and they probably should. At the very least he should apologize for kissing her hand.

"I brewed some herbal tea from Healthy Eats," Maddie said. "It's especially good for healing. Would you like a cup, Dr. Spencer?"

"Maddie, you're in my home, making me dinner. Call me Spence like everyone else."

"Yes, sir."

"And no sir stuff."

"Okay, Spence."

It sounded strange coming out of her mouth, unusually intimate. Nate helped his girlfriend build the fire, and Margaret assisted Maddie with dinner preparation.

"So tea, yes?" Maddie asked.

"Yes, thank you." Spence wandered to the living room sofa and collapsed.

"We'll be out of your hair in a few minutes, Doctor," Margaret said.

"Thanks."

The cabin had an open floor plan along with two private bedrooms, so Maddie was never out of Spence's sight. For some reason he liked being able to watch her auburn ponytail dance across her shoulders as she moved back and forth from the refrigerator to the sink.

This had to stop. He ripped his gaze from Maddie in time to see Nate kiss Cassie on the cheek.

"I'll pick you up at seven," Nate said.

"I'll be ready." When Cassie hugged him, Spence had to look away.

The love shared between those two was palpable. Spence had accepted the fact he wasn't meant to experience romantic love, but some days he ached for what he was missing. No, it was the head injury messing with him, making him moody, that's all.

"Come on, Ma." Cassie motioned to Margaret.

"But I'm not done helping—"

"I can finish," Maddie said. "I think the chief has to ask me some questions anyway, so I'll stick around a little while."

Margaret grabbed her purse and smiled at Spence. "You're in our prayers, Doctor."

"Thank you, Margaret," he said.

"Don't be late," Cassie said to Nate.

"Am I ever?"

"That means no police emergencies, either." Cassie winked and shut the door behind her and her mom.

"If only that were up to me," Nate said softly. He joined Spence in the living room, sitting on the sofa. "How ya feeling, buddy?"

"Better, now that I'm home."

Nate glanced across the cabin. "Maddie, can you take a break? You should hear this, too."

Spence didn't like the sound of that. He didn't want Maddie to be threatened by the danger stalking him.

When Maddie joined them, Spence noticed a few strands of hair had escaped her ponytail, framing her face. He snapped his attention from her and looked at Nate.

"We went through video footage from the hospital and came up with this." Nate flashed a photo on his phone of a man in a black jacket with a cap pulled low over his forehead.

"It's the same guy from the mountains," Maddie said.

"How can you be sure? You can't see his face," Nate said.

"His shoes squeaked. I heard it in the mountains, and again after he shoved me against the wall and ran out of the MRI room."

It felt like someone punched Spence in the gut. "He shoved you against the wall?"

"I'm fine, and he is too apparently. Obviously survived the fall off the trail. Do you have any better images?"

"Unfortunately not." Nate pocketed his phone. "He disappeared right in front of security."

"How is that possible?" Spence asked, growing more frustrated.

"We're not sure," Nate said.

"What about Kurt? Did he remember anything?" Maddie asked.

"Nothing usable," Nate said. "The attacker got him by the throat and stuck him with a syringe. As he was losing consciousness he said he saw a gorilla."

"Whoa, that was some drug," Maddie said.

"What we can't figure out is why he came after you at the hospital, Spence," Nate said. "At first this looked like you randomly stepped into trouble when you went to help Gwen. Now I'm not so sure that's all it is. I hate to ask, but can you think of anyone who'd want to hurt you?"

"Hurt me?" Spence scoffed. "Dr. Dreamboat?"

Nate and Maddie weren't smiling.

"What?" Spence challenged, anxiety trickling across his nerve endings.

"You're being awfully cavalier about this," Nate said.

"As opposed to what, launching into full-blown panic?" Which was exactly where he was going. Then he remembered the emails.

"What is it?" Nate said, eyeing him.

"Nothing."

"It's something if it made you frown like that," Maddie said.

"I started getting emails about a month ago. Nasty emails."

"Nasty, as in threatening?" Nate pushed.

"You could say that, but anyone can send an email. That doesn't mean they'd concoct a plan to come after me."

"We'll need to look at those emails," Nate said. "In the meantime I've assigned an off-duty officer on the cabin until we find the assailant."

Frustration bubbled up in Spence's chest. "Yeah, right. We don't even know what he looks like." Spence stood. "I need an aspirin."

"I can get it."

"No," he snapped at Maddie. "You need to leave."

"Spence?" Nate questioned his friend's abruptness.

"Look, if you're right and I'm in danger then I don't want Maddie anywhere near me."

"But—"

"Thanks for making dinner, Maddie," he interrupted her. "Please let yourself out." Spence marched into his bedroom and shut the door, feeling like a total jerk, but he truly didn't want to put Maddie at risk.

Besides, he craved peace and quiet to calm the annoying anxiety taunting him. He struggled to accept the fact that he could be a killer's primary target. He'd tried joking it off because the thought of someone coming for him in his current, damaged state was more than he could process.

His head ached and his world seemed to be teetering on rocky ground. All he wanted was time alone to regroup. Instead Maddie was here offering to get him aspirin; cooking him dinner.

Blinking those adorable green eyes at him.

Singing heartfelt songs about love.

He stumbled toward the bed and flopped down on his stomach. It was rude to walk out on Nate and Maddie like that, but he didn't have another ounce of energy to continue the conversation. Hopefully she'd pack up her things and leave.

Go home.

Where she'd be safe.

An hour later Maddie had finished the food prep, done the dishes and set the table for Dr. Spencer's dinner. There were no more excuses to hang around.

He'd given her a firm order to leave, which meant technically she was trespassing.

Something niggled at her brain as she headed for the door. Hesitating, she glanced at his bedroom door, wondering if she should check on him before she left. His assistant wasn't going to be here for another hour.

A soft knock echoed from the front door. She cracked it open and greeted off-duty police officer Red Carrington.

"Hi, Red."

"Maddie. The chief wanted me to make sure you were okay in here."

"The chief should be focused on his date."

Red frowned in confusion.

"He's out with my cousin Cassie."

"Ah, right. How's the doc?" Red glanced over her shoulder into the cabin.

"I was actually going to check on him before I left. Did you want some coffee or dinner? There's plenty of food."

"Nah, I brought a sandwich from home. I've got the key to the cabin to lock up after you leave."

"Great, thanks. Just give me a few minutes."

"Take your time."

She shut and locked the front door, grateful to Nate for assigning an officer to Dr. Spencer's cabin. No matter how aloof he seemed, the doc knew he was in trouble and it had to terrify him, especially in his current state.

Heading for his room, she decided she'd take his pulse and check him for a fever, not that she expected him to have one. If he seemed okay, she could leave with a clear mind and calm heart. She wouldn't be up all night worrying about him.

Really, Maddie? She wondered how she'd become so attached to the doc and figured it was twofold: she could never repay him for saving her cousin Cassie's life, plus, Maddie was a fixer at her core. If she saw someone in emotional turmoil, she did everything within her power to help ease his pain.

Whether he wanted to admit it or not, Dr. Spencer was certainly in trouble.

She turned the doorknob to his bedroom, relieved that it wasn't locked. "Dr. Spencer?"

The room was dark except for the shaft of light streaming in from the living room behind her. The doc was stretched diagonally across the bed on his stomach.

She considered her options. She didn't want to turn on the light and rouse him from much-needed sleep. He got little sleep last night in the hospital thanks to nightmares that plagued him until about 3:00 a.m. It was a good thing she'd stayed to awaken him from the terror each time he'd called out the name *Bobby*.

Maddie went to his bedside, knelt and took his pulse. Solid at sixty beats per minute. She placed her palm across his forehead. It was cool to the touch, not warm and clammy. Still, should she wake him to check his pupils?

No, if Dr. Carver suspected it was more serious than a mild concussion she wouldn't have discharged him. Maddie pulled the comforter across the bed to cover his body. He looked so peaceful. She sighed, glad he wasn't thrashing about, tortured by nightmares.

Since there was nothing more she could do for him, she decided to scoot. If Spence awakened and found her hovering, he'd surely be cross. She'd leave the doctor in the capable hands of Officer Carrington.

As she made her way to the front door, she considered taking a personal day off work tomorrow. She had plenty coming, actually enough days to piece together a nice trip somewhere. A vacation would be perfect right about now, especially after the craziness of the last twenty-four hours.

She opened the front door and froze.

The driver's side door of Officer Carrington's car was open but he was nowhere in sight.

"Red?" she called out.

A gunshot echoed across the property.

FOUR

Maddie darted inside the cabin and slammed the door, her heart hammering against her chest. Was it the masked man from the mountains? Had he tracked Dr. Spencer home, waiting for the best moment to attack?

Officer Carrington must have seen the guy stalking the cabin and went after him.

She hoped. She prayed. She also prayed that Red had been the one to fire the shot, perhaps a warning shot, to get the guy to stop. Yeah, she knew how well that did *not* work when she'd fired a warning shot. On the off chance the masked attacker neutralized the police officer, she had to focus on protecting herself and the doctor.

Since his curtainless living room windows exposed them to the world, she clicked off all the lights. Snapping the small flashlight off her keychain, she aimed the beam and made her way into the bedroom.

She pulled her phone out of her pocket and called emergency.

"9-1-1, what's your emergency?"

"This is Maddie McBride. I'm at Dr. Kyle Spencer's cabin and I heard gunfire outside."

"We have an officer posted on the premises."

"He's not in his car. Send help, and notify Chief Walsh ASAP."

Someone pounded on the front door, obviously not Red because he had a key to the cabin.

"He's trying to get in," she said to the operator. "I have to go."

"Maddie, please stay on the line."

Shoving the phone into her pocket, she crouched beside Dr. Spencer. She could only focus on one thing at a time, and right now her priority was to keep herself and Spence alive.

She clicked on his nightstand lamp. Shades covered his windows, probably so he could sleep after getting off a night shift at the hospital.

"Spence, wake up." She gave his shoulder a gentle nudge.

More pounding echoed from the front door.

"Spence?" When that didn't work, she decided to use his full name. "Dr. Kyle Spencer, wake up."

The doctor moaned and blinked his eyes open. "What, where am I?"

Her breath caught in her throat. Did he really not know he was in his own bedroom? Or was he disoriented because she'd awakened him from a deep sleep?

"What is that racket?" He rolled onto his back and threw an arm across his eyes as if he intended to fall back asleep.

"You can't go back to sleep. Someone's trying to break in."

"What?" He sat up abruptly and gripped his head with both hands. "Ah, man." He looked at her with bloodshot eyes. "What are you still doing here?"

"Yell at me later. Do you keep any weapons in the cabin?"

"I'm a doctor," he said, as if that was explanation enough.

"So no weapons then."

"Is it the same guy?"

"Unless you have other enemies we don't know about."

He shot her a look, then said, "We can sneak out through the window." He wavered as he crossed the room, looking like someone who'd been overserved at the local pub.

Maddie knew that running wasn't an option. With Spence in his current state they'd be easy prey in the wilderness. At least inside the cabin they could hold their ground.

His started to open the window.

"Don't," she said. "I've got a better idea. I saw chili powder in your kitchen earlier."

"Chili powder?"

"Come on." She motioned to him.

Instead, he stared at her.

The pounding stopped. Which was not necessarily a good thing. The guy could be gearing up to bust his way through the door with an ax. She'd noticed one on the front porch, probably for chopping wood.

She dashed out of the bedroom and whipped open a kitchen cabinet. Spence came up behind her, opened a drawer and took out a butcher knife. He glanced at her, the knife clutched in his hand.

"He could just as easily use that on us." She grabbed chili powder and flung open the cabinet beneath the sink. "Here, you take the fire extinguisher." She handed it to him. "Spray him in the face and whack him over the head with the tank. Got it?"

"Spray and whack, sure."

There wasn't much confidence in his voice. He was probably still groggy from sleep, or the head injury, or a combination of both.

She'd have to rely on her own strength and determination to get them out of this dangerous situation.

Tapping echoed from the bedroom. The guy was trying to get in through the bedroom window. She encouraged the doctor to crouch behind the kitchen island, out of sight. "Stay down."

She spotted a hiking stick propped against the wall by the front door. After temporarily blinding the attacker with the chili powder, she'd use the stick as a defensive weapon. Karate class would come in handy tonight.

She would position herself behind a large leather armchair, the perfect position from which to make her attack. On her way to the hiding spot, she opened the front door to confuse the intruder, making it look like she and the doc had fled—a risky move if there was a second assailant but good strategy if the guy was alone.

She'd be ready either way.

A crash echoed from the bedroom.

Heart hammering against her chest, she ducked behind the chair, gripping the stick in one hand and the chili powder in the other. No one entered through the front door, which was certainly a good sign. It meant they were dealing with only the one intruder who had breached the bedroom window, most likely the same guy who'd attacked the doctor in the mountains and shoved her against the wall in the hospital last night.

Maddie waited, calmed her breathing and prayed to God for help. She wasn't a violent person by nature, but needed to do what was necessary to protect herself and the doc.

The wooden floorboards creaked as the guy made his way through the cabin.

"Doctor?" he said. "Where are you?"

Silence rang in her ears.

"Get out of my cabin!" Dr. Spencer ordered.

What? She'd told him to stay hidden, out of sight. Did his brain injury cause him to forget her instructions? Maddie peered around the chair she was using as cover. The intruder was stalking Dr. Spencer from the other side of the kitchen island.

"You need to come with me," the guy said.

"Why, so you can kill me?" Spence was gripping the fire extinguisher to his chest, but not pointing it at the guy.

The guy was tall, broad-shouldered, wearing a black jacket but no mask, which meant he wasn't worried about being identified because he planned to kill the witness to this attack.

He planned to kill the doctor.

But Spence wasn't the only witness.

The assailant drew a knife. "One way or another, Doc."

Maddie jumped out of her hiding spot. "Hey!"

The guy turned to her, more irritated than anything else. He had a full beard of dark hair and piercing brown eyes.

He started toward her.

"The cops are on the way," she said, clutching the hiking stick.

She had to make him drop the knife.

He took a step closer. "You weren't supposed to be here."

If only he'd get close enough. She fingered the container of chili powder in her other hand.

Spence suddenly grabbed him from behind.

"No!" she cried, fearing the bearded guy would slash him with the knife.

The guy elbowed Spence in the ribs and the doctor released his grip, dropping to his knees.

As the stranger turned his attention to Maddie, she lunged...

Hurling chili powder into his eyes.

The guy cried out and made a wide arc with the knife. Gripping the walking stick with both hands, she nailed him in the gut. He pitched forward, faltering as he tried to get away from her.

She smacked him again, and again.

Flailing his arms, he couldn't see her well enough to hit his mark. She had no problem hitting hers.

"Out of here!" she shouted, delivering firm strikes to his ribs, arms and shoulders, forcing him backward. He stumbled out the open front door. She slammed it shut and flipped the dead bolt.

She rushed to Spence's side. "Are you—?"

"Fine," he said.

"Come on." She grabbed his arm and led him into the bedroom. "We need to block the window!"

She didn't think the intruder would try another attack, not with blurred vision from the chili powder and bruised ribs, but she couldn't be sure. Spence helped her shoulder an armoire in front of the now glassless window.

Shutting the bedroom door, she scanned the room, grabbed a chair and wedged it against the handle. Even if the intruder got in through a living room window, he wasn't getting into the bedroom.

Backing up against the empty wall where the armoire had been, she took a deep breath and reminded herself it wasn't over until the police arrived.

She had to be ready for whatever happened next.

Spence shifted onto the edge of the bed. Silence stretched between them, the sound of her heart pounding against her eardrums.

"You're a ninja," Dr. Spencer said.

She glanced at him. "What?"

"The way you used my hiking stick as a weapon. You're a ninja."

"And you're an idiot," she let slip.

He looked up at her with a confused expression.

"I told you to stay hidden, but you jumped up like a jack-in-the-box and announced yourself. What was that about?"

"I was trying to distract him, so he wouldn't hurt you."

Maddie was speechless. Even in his injured state, Dr. Spencer was trying to protect her?

"I had a hard time figuring out how to activate the extinguisher, sorry," he said.

"We should keep quiet and listen."

"I doubt he'll come back. You gave him at least three broken ribs by my count."

She didn't respond, trying to stay in the present, and not relive what had just happened. With full concentration on the now, she could effectively catalog every sound that tweaked her eardrums.

"Thanks for saving my life," he said, "again."

She didn't want his thanks. She wanted him to get better so he could defend himself. She wanted him to use his common sense. He was in no condition to protect Maddie from harm. It was pretty obvious she didn't need his help, or anyone else's for that matter.

"Where'd you learn that stuff with the stick?" Spence asked.

"Martial arts class."

"Guess I should sign up."

"How can you be so aloof?" she said.

"Not sure how the alternative would help."

He was right, although Maddie still couldn't calm her racing pulse. Her phone vibrated and she answered with one hand, while gripping the stick with her other. "Hello?"

"It's Nate."

"The guy broke in. We forced him out, but he might still be on the premises."

"Officer Carrington called in suspicious activity and went silent."

"I heard a gunshot. I haven't seen him since then."

"I'm en route, along with another cruiser. Two minutes tops."

"Thanks."

The fact that help was close eased the tension in her

shoulders. Taking a deep breath, she said a prayer of thanks for giving her the strength to snap into action so quickly.

"What's wrong?" Spence said.

"Why do you think something's wrong?"

"You're humming."

"I am?"

"Yes."

"Sometimes I hum when I pray."

"You're praying?"

"Yep. A prayer of thanks that we outmaneuvered that jerk."

"A prayer of thanks," he said in a soft, puzzled voice.

"Don't you pray?"

"Never given it much thought."

"That's the beauty of it. You don't have to think about prayer. You just do it."

"Does it help?"

"Absolutely."

She sensed he was processing her explanation. It didn't surprise her that Dr. Spencer wasn't one for prayer. He was a physician, a profession prone to big egos. Some docs didn't feel the need to look outside themselves for guidance, comfort or emotional peace.

"I'm sorry," he said.

"For not listening to me? I get it, you're used to giving orders, not following them."

"Not that. I'm sorry I dragged you into all this."

"Hey, I chose to respond to the call in the mountains."

"But not to do hand-to-hand combat with a psycho in my living room."

"It's good to know I still have my skills. Now shush, we need to listen."

This whole apology and conversation moment in his bedroom felt unusually raw and authentic. She sensed his guard was down, probably because of the head injury, or because of the threatening encounter with the bearded guy. At any rate, a connection was developing between herself and Dr. Spencer, a connection that made her uncomfortable on so many levels.

Maddie had no interest in romance, especially not with a charming city doc she knew would grow tired of country life and flee town soon enough. And Maddie didn't plan on leaving her hometown of Echo Mountain. This was where she belonged.

A crash echoed from the living room. She straightened.

"He broke another window. Determined, isn't he?" she said, positioning herself between the door and Dr. Spencer. She gripped the hiking stick with white-knuckled fingers. If the guy made it into the bedroom, she wouldn't hold back. She'd deliver a full-on assault, the goal being to knock him out.

Could she really do it?

She heard Spence rifling through drawers behind her.

"What are you doing?" she whispered.

"Looking for a weapon."

"I got this."

"I can't sit here and do nothing," Spence said.

Someone jiggled the nickel-plated door handle.

She adjusted her grip on the stick. "Got anything heavy, like a paperweight or rock or something?"

"I've got a salt lamp."

"Get it and stand on the other side of the door. If he breaks in, I'll lure him into the room and you whack him in the head with that thing."

He glanced at the salt lamp in his hand with a distasteful expression. Maiming, killing, was not in his makeup.

Nor was it in hers. But before he'd abandoned her, Dad had taught her the importance of survival, a good thing since that kind of determination could very well save her life tonight.

She and the doctor waited for the assailant's next move. Although Spence seemed fragile, he gripped the eight-inch oblong lamp with resolute focus. She sensed that he, too, would do what was necessary to survive.

"Dear Lord, give us courage," she whispered.

The door handle rattled again, followed by a smacking sound, as if someone was kicking the door.

"And the strength to do what is necessary," she continued.

Whack, whack.

Sirens wailed in the distance, sending a rush of relief through Maddie's chest.

The intruder pounded one last time on the door, probably in frustration, and she heard footsteps echo across the living room.

"He's leaving," Spence said with surprise in his voice. He put down the salt lamp and went to open the door.

"No." She blocked him. "Not yet. Let's wait until we know it's safe."

"Right, okay." He leaned against the wall, blinked a few times and lowered his head.

"Are you light-headed? Dizzy?" She propped the stick against the wall and gripped his arm.

He shook his head and wandered back to the bed. "I'm—"

"Don't say it." She sat beside him on the bed. "We both know you're not fine. Neither am I."

Her phone vibrated. "Hello?"

"We're pulling up now," Chief Walsh said. "Is he in the house?"

"I heard him flee the cabin, but we're staying in the bedroom to be safe."

"I'll let you know when it's clear."

"Thanks." She redirected her attention to Spence.

"This is happening because of me, because I did some-

thing that's made me a target, and now you're a target."
He caught her gaze for a brief second and then began pacing the room.

"Come on, this isn't your fault," she said.

He paced, rubbing his hands together, growing more agitated. Another symptom of the brain injury?

"What if Officer Carrington is hurt and Gwen doesn't recover?" he said. "What if she dies?"

Maddie had to stop this frantic spin. "Hey, her injury wasn't serious. She's breathing on her own, remember?" She blocked him from pacing to the other side of the room. "Spence?"

"What do you think happened to Red?" he said.

"He's a savvy and strong officer. He'll be okay."

"What if he's wounded? I need to get out there and offer medical assistance."

"Stop." She placed her open palm against his soft cotton T-shirt. "Remember what they taught you in SAR? Don't become another victim the team has to rescue. Let's wait until we get the clear signal from Nate, then we'll see if Red needs medical assistance."

He turned and paced away from her. She sensed if the armoire wasn't blocking the window he'd climb out and search the property for Red. He wasn't unstable exactly, but he was definitely a tangle of emotions, especially guilt. That seemed irrational, making her question his condition. At times he seemed confused and agitated, and other times he could be totally calm, like when he'd asked her about karate and prayer.

She considered his decision to jump out of hiding to defend Maddie. Was that irrational or sensible? She could make an argument for both sides. It was irrational to expose his location, yet his motivation was pure, born of his protective instinct.

His actions exposed his good heart in wanting to protect Maddie.

Don't go there, Madeline.

"You think I'm crazy, don't you?" he said in a soft voice.

"Why would you say that?"

"The look on your face."

"I was thinking about something else."

The thought of falling in love and being devastated again, because that's what would happen. There hadn't been enough excitement to keep Waylan in town, and there certainly wouldn't be enough to keep a man like Kyle Spencer in Echo Mountain.

He placed a hand on her shoulder. Shocked by his touch, she looked up into his blue eyes.

"I am truly sorry. About everything," he said.

"Stop apologizing. None of this is your fault."

He studied her like he didn't quite believe her words, but wanted to desperately. She also sensed he wanted something else. A hug?

Don't do it, Maddie. The intensity of their situation was causing a visceral, emotional connection, nothing more. It wasn't real.

"I can't help it," he said. "I hardly know you and yet you've saved my life what, three times now, and in doing so you've risked your own. You didn't sign up for all this. You're just a paramedic."

The sting from his insult must have shown on her face because he put out his hand in a soothing gesture.

"Wait, that didn't come out right."

"Spence! Maddie! Open up!" Chief Walsh called from the living room.

She removed the chair from the door and flung it open. "Good to see you, Chief." With purposeful steps, she crossed the living room to the kitchen.

Just a paramedic? He made it sound like she had an insignificant job in a small, boring town.

The doc's tone reminded her of when Waylan tried talking her into quitting her job claiming she could do so much better. Really? So much better than helping people who were in crisis? She might not be a doctor like Spence or a software engineer like Waylan, but she felt like she was doing God's work, both medically and emotionally, when she was called out on an emergency.

"Maddie," Spence said.

She ignored him, still steaming over his comment.

Ryan, her cop brother, raced into the cabin. "Maddie, you're okay." He hugged her and she welcomed the embrace.

"Did you find Red?" Nate asked Ryan.

Ryan broke the hug. "Sorry, sir. I'll go help check the property."

"I found him," a voice said through the chief's and Ryan's shoulder radios.

Maddie gripped the kitchen counter, bracing herself.

"How is he? Over." Nate said.

"Disoriented and confused from a knock to the head. And he's missing his gun."

As Spence cracked open his eyes the next morning, he focused on remembering where he was and how he'd ended up here. Wrestling with a disturbing, groundless feeling, he took a few deep breaths to help him recall what had happened.

That's right, Nate made him pack a bag last night and they'd moved Spence to a one-bedroom guest cabin on Echo Mountain Resort property. Spence's own cabin was no longer safe due to broken windows and the fact the attacker could return.

Spence swung his legs off the bed, planted his feet on

the floor and glanced around the rustic room with wood-paneled walls. Rubbing his temples, he remembered how things slipped out of his mouth last night past his internal censor—a side effect of his concussion no doubt—so he decided to stop talking. He'd answer direct questions when asked, but otherwise he kept his thoughts to himself.

He remembered the look on Maddie's face when he'd referred to her as *just a paramedic*. That comment certainly didn't come out the way he'd intended. What he'd meant was she wasn't a trained bodyguard and shouldn't have been put in the position of protecting Spence physically against a man twice her size.

Then again, perhaps her misinterpretation of his comment would make her angry enough to keep her distance, because ordering her to leave hadn't worked.

He stood slowly, breathing through the pain of a headache, and slipped into a sweatshirt and jeans. Opening the door, he wandered toward the kitchenette and flipped on an electric hot water kettle. As he glanced out the window over the sink, he remembered the broken windows at the cabin.

"Need to call someone to fix the windows," he muttered to himself.

"Already made the call."

Startled, he spun around and spotted Maddie sitting cross-legged in a thick-cushioned chair with a book open in her lap in the living room. The gas fireplace glowed next to her. She'd gone to battle for him last night and could have been seriously hurt.

"What are you doing here?" The words escaped his lips before they passed through his internal filter. He sounded irritated even to himself, although a part of him was relieved to see her.

She offered a pleasant smile. "Good morning to you, too, grouchy Gus."

He rubbed his forehead. "Sorry. I... I wasn't expecting to see you today."

"The chief asked if I could meet him here to discuss what happened last night. My brother spent the night at my place because I saw the guy's face and he was worried about me. Your protective detail is parked outside. Aiden let me in to wait for the chief. I hope that's okay."

It was more than okay. Not good.

"Is Nate on his way?" He needed her to give her statement and leave as quickly as possible.

He wanted her to stay.

"Nate should be here in about twenty minutes."

"How's Officer Carrington?"

"Concussion, but otherwise okay."

Another person assaulted because of Spence.

"That's not your fault, either," she said.

He turned his back to her, frustrated that she knew what he was thinking. He'd been an expert at masking his feelings and thoughts with a bright smile and friendly demeanor. It was important to keep the mask firmly in place because the confidence in his eyes eased his patients' fears.

Masking his feelings also gave him a sense of control, which right now he desperately needed.

He reached for a mug on the rack and noticed his hand was trembling. Clenching his jaw, he grabbed the mug and placed it on the counter. He wrapped his fingers around the cool ceramic, hoping to stop the trembling. What was the matter with him?

"Tea's up on the left," Maddie said.

He opened a cupboard.

"Your other left," she teased.

He frowned at his own mistake. He knew his left from his right, but felt like he was under a microscope with her watching his every move. A moment later she stepped up beside him.

"I could use a fresh cup of coffee." She pulled a single-serve cup off a carousel and plopped it into the coffeemaker. "These cabins have all the comforts of home."

When she pressed Brew, he noted such delicate fingers on the woman who'd defended him with a hiking stick. He'd never noticed that before, nor had he noticed the faint freckles dotting her nose.

She cocked her head and focused her curious green eyes at him.

"What's that look?" she said.

What could he say? That he was noticing things about her he shouldn't? That he felt vulnerable and appreciated her presence more than she could know?

"I'm hungry." It's all he could come up with.

"Okay." She half-chuckled as if she knew that was not what he was thinking. She opened a drawer and pulled out a paper menu. "I'll order room service."

Spreading the menu out on the countertop, she nibbled at the corner of her lip as she ran her forefinger down the list of breakfast options. "They've got lighter fare like fruit or muffins, or heartier items like oatmeal, or egg scramblers with your choice of meat, veggies and cheese. Oh, and check out the Monster Mash skillet—potatoes, meat, veggies, the works." She cast him a sideways glance. "I'm thinking you're a Monster Mash kinda guy."

"Sounds good." He turned to go sit at the table and she touched his shirtsleeve. Warmth trickled up his arm to his chest. He wished she wouldn't do that.

"You're not done," she said. "You have to pick ham, sausage or bacon, then cheddar, Swiss, or Colby jack cheese, and there's a list of seven veggies to choose from."

"Too hard. Toast is fine."

He went to the table and sat down, releasing a sigh of tension. Making all those decisions first thing in the morning was stressing him out. It shouldn't, should it? He pressed his fingertips to his temples.

A few seconds later, her grounding hand touched his shoulder. He glanced up. She actually smiled at him. "Do you trust me?"

Trust a woman? What a joke. Yet this wasn't Andrea, it was Maddie McBride, closet ninja, dedicated paramedic and…

Amazing woman.

"You shouldn't have to think that hard, Doc." She frowned.

"I… Sure, you've saved my life. So, yes, I trust you."

"Good, I'll order for you."

He nodded and closed his eyes. She didn't take her hand off his shoulder as she made the call. "This is Maddie McBride in the Juniper Cabin. I'd like to place an order. One Monster Mash with ham, cheddar, spinach and mushrooms, and a bowl of oatmeal with brown sugar and walnuts. Oh, and a side of toast with jam. Great, thanks." She squeezed his shoulder. "It'll be here in thirty to forty minutes."

"Thanks."

"I'll get your tea."

"You shouldn't be waiting on me. You shouldn't even be here." That was uncalled for and so unlike him. She was only trying to help.

He needed to keep his mouth shut.

She slipped her hand off his shoulder and went to get their drinks.

"I'm sorry," he said. "I'm not usually this irritable."

"You're suffering from a head injury, lack of sleep and assorted other aches and pains. You're doing a lot better than I would be under the circumstances."

She returned to the table and placed the mug of tea in front of him. "I hope green lavender is okay."

"It's fine."

She carried her coffee to the chair in the corner. He wished she would sit at the table with him, yet he'd been a jerk again, told her she shouldn't be here. In truth, he'd snapped at her because he hated being damaged in any way, shape or form, and letting her wait on him only drove home how fragile he must seem to everyone.

"What's the book?" he asked, hoping to engage her in conversation.

"Something I found on the shelves." She motioned behind her to a built-in bookcase. "It's a mystery about a woman who buys a bed-and-breakfast, finds a will in the basement and when she investigates, someone tries to kill her."

"Right, because you don't have enough of that in real life," he said.

"Hey, your sense of humor is coming back. Bravo."

"I guess."

"But?"

He shook his head and glanced down. She continued to study him.

A few awkward moments passed as anxiety circled around in his gut.

"Spence?"

When she spoke his name he could hardly ignore her.

"What if...?" he started, fingering the rim of his mug. *Don't say it.*

"What if, what?" she prompted.

"What if I can no longer practice medicine?"

"Because of your head injury?"

He nodded, a ball forming in his throat.

"Hey, the MRI showed a mild concussion, that's all. The swelling will go down and you'll be back to normal soon."

"You and I both know head injuries aren't that simple."

"Maybe not, but you have to think positive. The MRI could have looked a lot worse."

"You don't understand."

"Right, because I'm just a paramedic."

He snapped his attention to her. "That came out wrong last night."

"Then what am I not smart enough to understand?"

"It's not about being smart, which we both know you are. It's about…me."

"A little more, please?"

He sighed. "Without medicine I'm…nothing." Spence's voice cracked.

She stood and crossed the room. He had to look away, didn't want to see the pity in her eyes.

"Look at me," she said, placing a gentle hand against his cheek.

Glancing into her sparkling green eyes, he found himself holding his breath.

"Don't talk that way," she said. "First, you're going to be fine, and second, you're worth a lot more than your job."

He couldn't rip his gaze from her sincere, determined expression. How had he never noticed this woman before, never noticed her natural radiance and positive energy?

Because you weren't in the market for love. Not then, not ever.

"A lot more," she said, her voice taking on a husky edge.

Was she feeling it, too, this arc of emotional connection sparking between them?

Pounding on the cabin door shattered the moment. Maddie snapped her hand away from his face as if she'd nearly gotten it caught in a trap.

"Dr. Spencer!" a woman called.

He started to get up, but Maddie stopped him with a firm hand against his chest.

"I'll get it." She went to the door. "Who's there?"

"Nia Sharpe. It's an emergency!"

Maddie opened the door to the resort's concierge. The patrolman assigned to protect Dr. Spencer hovered beside her.

Nia, who was also Aiden's girlfriend, motioned to Spence. "You've got to do something. It's Aiden. He can't breathe!"

FIVE

Spence's hesitation worried Maddie. It was like his brain was slow to kick into gear.

Maddie snapped into action. "Nia, did you call 9-1-1?"

"Yes."

"What happened?" Spence asked. He motioned for Nia to lead them to Aiden.

"I found him in the barn," Nia said, heading across the property. "He fell or was pushed." She touched Maddie's arm. "Do you think it has something to do with—"

"Let's focus on one thing at a time," Maddie said. "Did you see him fall?"

"No, I was late. I was supposed to help him reorganize the loft, but when I got there he was on the ground, gasping for air and looking at me like...like..."

"Like what?" Spence pressed.

Nia glanced at Spence, tears welling in her eyes. "Like he was scared."

Aiden, scared? Maddie had grown up in her cousin Aiden's house and had never, ever known him to be afraid. Of anything.

Then again, when people were injured and felt vulnerable, they were often overcome with fear, like the fear that had taken hold of Dr. Spencer repeatedly over the past eighteen hours. Fear that his head injury was more serious than it looked; fear that he'd never practice medicine again. Maddie's heart ached for the man.

When they reached the barn, Maddie rushed to Aiden's side. "Aiden, can you hear me?"

He gasped for breath, his blue eyes widening with panic. Dr. Spencer knelt on the other side of him. The police officer assigned to Spence stayed close.

"What do you think, Doctor?" Nia asked.

When he didn't respond right away, Maddie said, "Let's rule out the obvious."

Spence glanced at Maddie.

"Diaphragm spasm," she said.

"Of course," he agreed.

"What does that mean?" Nia said.

"Simply put, he got the wind knocked out of him," Maddie said.

She and Spence pulled Aiden's knees up to his abdomen. Maddie watched her cousin's reaction.

"What are you doing?" Nia said.

"Trying to relax his abdominal muscles," Maddie explained. "Aiden, can you breathe slowly in through the nose and out through your mouth?"

He did as ordered and she found herself pretending he wasn't her cousin because the look of panic on his face was making her stomach twist into knots. She could definitely understand why Nia, who'd fallen deeply in love with Aiden, was so upset.

"You think that's all it is?" Nia said, directing the question to Dr. Spencer.

"We can't be sure until he's checked out at the hospital and they take some X-rays," he said.

Good, a professional, doctor-like answer. Maybe Spence was coming around and remembering everything that he could do.

"I'll check his pulse." Dr. Spencer pressed his fingers

to Aiden's wrist and glanced at his own watch, another sign that the fog was lifting.

"Aiden?" Maddie said. "Breathe in slowly, buddy, that's it. And then out…" she coached.

The sound of a wailing siren cut through the tension.

"Nia, go get the paramedics," Maddie said.

Nia raced out of the barn.

"It's 110," Spence said.

It could be high due to anxiety. Spence must have thought the same thing.

"Aiden, you're doing great, buddy," Spence said. "We think you've had the wind knocked out of you. Keep breathing with Maddie."

Aiden looked at Maddie.

"You heard it from the doc," Maddie said. "Breathe and relax."

"Hey, what are you doing here?" Rocky said, rushing into the barn with the cute paramedic named Vivian pushing the back end of the stretcher. Rocky's smile faded when he saw Dr. Spencer.

Rocky knelt beside Maddie. "Pulse?"

"A hundred and ten," the doctor answered.

"We got this," Rocky said in dismissal.

Dr. Spencer stood slowly with an odd expression on his face. Was he offended that Rocky was taking over? Or relieved? Sometimes he was hard to read.

Nate rushed into the barn. "What happened?"

"We don't know," Nia said. "He fell or was pushed—"

"Pushed?"

"He's the most coordinated person I know," Nia said. "He wouldn't have fallen off the loft."

They glanced up at the fifteen-foot drop.

"I got here as soon as I could." Scott Beckett, the resort's security manager and Bree's boyfriend, joined the group. "How is he?"

Rocky glared at Maddie. "Really?" he said, irritated by all the people hovering over him.

"Let's give them some space." Maddie herded the group toward the exit. She realized she was missing one. Glancing over her shoulder, she noticed Spence still standing by the paramedics.

"Spence?" she said.

"But…" He hesitated, watching Rocky and Vivian tend to Aiden. "I'm a doctor."

Rocky shook his head, offended by the comment.

"You're off duty," Maddie said. "Come on, let them do their job."

Spence didn't move for a second. A cold chill skittered across Maddie's shoulders. She didn't want to think it, but couldn't help herself—the doc's brain injury was, in fact, more serious than anyone suspected. What else would make him seem so lost?

No, she wouldn't go there. Once the swelling went down, patients with brain injuries could spring right back to normal, no problem. They didn't necessarily suffer long-lasting effects and were able to reenter their lives without missing a beat.

As Dr. Spencer stepped away from Aiden, Maddie touched his arm. "Good thing we were here."

"Yeah." Was that sarcasm lacing his voice? If so, that meant he had the presence of mind to know he wasn't functioning at one hundred percent.

Chief Walsh, who was questioning Nia outside, waved them over. "Did he give you any indication he thought someone was around, that he felt threatened?"

"By the time I got to him he couldn't speak," Nia said.

"Hey, he's tough. He'll be okay," Scott encouraged. Nia nodded, but didn't look convinced.

The paramedics rolled Aiden out of the barn on the stretcher and Nia rushed to his side, walking with him to the ambulance. Maddie suspected Aiden's injuries weren't serious, yet Nia's reaction tore at her insides.

As they headed back to the cabin, Maddie wondered if she'd ever experience that kind of profound love, that kind of connection with a man. She'd thought she'd had it with Waylan. As teenagers he'd helped her through some of the darkest days of her life after Dad left, Mom withdrew emotionally, and then even she moved away. Waylan's love had been the beacon of light that sparked hope for Maddie each and every day.

Then Waylan had abandoned her for a more exciting life in the city.

"What is it?"

She snapped her attention to Dr. Spencer. "What?"

"Your expression—it's rather sad."

"I'm fine."

She sensed he knew she wasn't fine at all.

They returned to the small cabin and Nate shut the door. "The officer will remain posted outside."

Maddie wandered to the kitchen table and grabbed her mug of coffee. She'd slept poorly last night in her apartment, the violence of the day invading her dreams. At two in the morning she'd finally given up, knelt beside her bed and prayed. Prayer always calmed her runaway thoughts.

As Nate poured himself a cup of coffee, Spence leaned against the counter. "Anything on the bearded man from last night?"

"Why don't you take a seat?" Nate motioned to the kitchen table.

Maddie and Spence joined him. Nate cleared his voice as if hesitating to share bad news.

"I don't like the sound of that," Spence said.

"And I don't like anything about this case. Gwen gave me her statement. She never sent you the text message asking for help."

"Wait, but the message came from her phone," Spence said.

"She lost her phone a few days ago. She used a find-your-phone app, which led her into the mountains. She struggled with the assailant and fell."

"So a guy I don't know gets ahold of Gwen's phone and sends me a text to lure me into the mountains to what? Kill me?"

"It's looking that way." Nate leaned forward. "You need to seriously consider making a list of potential enemies."

Spence shook his head in frustration.

"The sooner you figure out who's after you the quicker your life can get back to normal," Maddie offered.

"Work on that list, Spence," Nate said.

"I wouldn't know where to start."

"Right, because Dr. Dreamboat has no enemies," Maddie said.

"None that are angry enough to want me dead."

"You may not realize how angry they are," Nate said. "What about dissatisfied patients or family members who disagreed with your course of treatment? Someone from your past?"

"I'll help him get started," Maddie said.

"Good, thanks," Nate said, and then redirected his attention to Spence. "I need you to remember if the guy said anything last night that could help us figure out who he is."

Spence glanced at Maddie, then back at Nate.

She sensed he didn't want to say something in front of her. Well, tough beans. She wasn't leaving.

"I remembered something this morning," Spence said. "The man said 'you'll pay for your sins.'"

Nate frowned. "What sins?"

Spence stared into his coffee. Shame twisted his features, but shame about what?

"What is it?" Maddie pressed.

Spence snapped his attention to her. "Nothing."

"Spence?" Nate said.

"What do you want me to say?" He stood suddenly and gripped his head. "I need to lie down." He marched into the bedroom and shut the door.

Nate shared a concerned look with Maddie. "I'm worried about him."

"He'll be okay. He's sore and frustrated that he isn't working, ya know, saving lives."

Nate eyed the bedroom door. "He doesn't seem like himself. What do you think's going on?"

"Sorry, but I don't know him that well."

"You see him all the time at the hospital."

"I hand off patients and leave. The doc and I have rarely spoken for any length of time, well, until yesterday."

"But you know how positive he usually is, how upbeat and happy. This guy…" He shook his head. "I'm not sure I know this guy."

"It's still Dr. Spencer. You've never seen him wounded and worried. He's really worried."

"That's good. That means he's taking the threat against his life seriously."

That wasn't what Maddie had meant. Spence was terrified that his life was over because he'd be benched from practicing medicine.

"I wasn't done discussing the case," Nate said.

"He should rest if he feels he needs it. I can text you when he awakens."

"Are you staying all day?"

"Maybe, if you think it's a good idea."

"Definitely. Having a medical professional close by gives me peace of mind. I'm not sure about Spence's judgment right now."

Spence was hiding. There was no other way to describe it. As he lay in bed staring at the ceiling, he realized he was hiding from everything: regrets from the past, Nate's probing questions, the possibility he might have made enemies angry enough to want him dead, and the unnerving feeling that he was never safe.

Except when Maddie was close.

He sat up. It was unfair to put her danger, and he wasn't a coward by nature, yet the few hours of rest had eased his headache and made him feel almost normal, like his old self.

His typically charming self would be quick to forge ahead with his life. Figuring out who was after him was the first step. His usual self would also be quick to apologize to Maddie for his sharp tone. She knew he was struggling and yet she'd covered for him in the barn when they'd assessed and treated Aiden. She was Spence's closest confidant at this point. He should appreciate her efforts, not take her for granted.

Or push her away.

His phone vibrated with a call from Dr. Carver. He cleared his throat, needing to sound strong, confident.

"Hi, Ruth, how are you?" he said in the most charming voice he could manage.

"You sound better."

"I am better, thanks. What's the word on Aiden McBride?"

"Bruised tailbone and mild concussion. Apparently he was reaching for something and lost his balance. I heard you were there when it happened?"

"Yes, Nate put me up in a cabin at the resort because of the break-in at my place last night."

"Oh, Spence. How frightening."

"I'm okay. Safe at the resort under police protection."

"Which cabin are you staying in? I'll send the assistant over to the resort."

"Actually, let's not involve anyone else at this point.

Chief Walsh thinks it could be personal, that someone might be after me, so the fewer people in my orbit the better."

"Spence, I'm sorry."

"Thanks."

"Do you have any idea who it could be?"

"None. A disgruntled patient perhaps, or someone who thinks I've wronged him?"

"But everyone loves you here."

"I'm sure not everyone."

"Well, let me know if there's anything I can do to help. In the meantime, get well and I'll take you off the schedule until further notice."

He didn't like the sound of that.

"I'd still like to work once I'm up to it."

Silence answered him.

"Ruth?"

"Spence, you just told me someone is after you. Do you think it wise to bring that kind of danger to the hospital?"

"No, but—"

"I'm surprised you made the suggestion."

He heard the message behind her words: any logical-thinking person, not suffering from brain trauma, would have better sense than to talk about coming back to work and bringing trouble with him.

"Just didn't want you to forget about me," he joked. "How's Gwen?"

"Vitals are good. She's out of the woods. You did excellent work out there, Dr. Spencer."

"Tell her I said hi."

"I will. And don't worry about your patients or staffing. Take as much time off as necessary, months if you need it. You've earned it."

"Thanks."

He ended the call and stared at the phone in his hand. Months off work? He'd lose his mind.

The stress of being cooped up in a one-bedroom cabin and not doing his life's work sparked another headache. He couldn't stand feeling useless.

Helpless.

He glanced out the window at the rain falling from the gray sky. The darkness matched his mood. He had to stop denying the possibility that someone was targeting him, and figure out the identity of his tormentor.

If he couldn't convince Maddie to distance herself he might as well join forces with her to investigate who was after him. She was a bright woman with a calming nature who didn't seem interested in a romantic entanglement like the other ladies in town.

He opened the bedroom door and glanced across the cabin at the chair where she had been sitting earlier. It was empty.

He was alone.

Disappointment fell heavy across his shoulders. He hadn't realized how much he appreciated her presence until just now.

Going to the kitchen area, he opened the refrigerator and was greeted by a dozen or so casserole dishes, plastic containers and fresh juices. He spotted a white container and cracked it open. It looked like the breakfast Maddie had ordered him.

The cabin door opened. "Hey, you're awake." Carrying two large bags in her arms, Maddie toed the door shut behind her.

"Let me help," he offered.

"Actually, I'm perfectly balanced." Her lips curled into a pleasant smile. The tension eased across his shoulders. She slid the bags onto the counter and cracked open the refrigerator. "I was afraid of that."

"Where did it all come from?"

She raised an eyebrow. "Like you don't know."

"I don't, honest."

"All your lady admirers." She began rearranging the food and adding to it from her grocery bags. "The whole town knows about last night's break-in and that you're temporarily homeless."

"Wait, I'm not sure it's a good idea for people to know I'm here."

"They don't know you're in the Juniper Cabin, only that you're at the resort. Saving Aiden this morning got everyone talking."

"You did more of the saving than I did."

She pinned him with those incredible green eyes. "Yeah, what was that about?"

He crossed his arms over his chest. "I froze. That's never happened to me before."

"You're still recovering," she said, as if that was an acceptable answer. "In the mood for lunch? I brought brain food so we could focus on the EP."

"Extended play?" he questioned.

"Enemy project."

"Ah, right. I'll eat my Monster Mash as long as it's here."

She shut the refrigerator door and looked at him. "I want you to know, nothing you say to me leaves this cabin. You can trust me, Doctor—" She caught herself. "Spence."

They spent the afternoon making a list of potential enemies, although not the entire afternoon. Maddie encouraged Spence to lie down a few times because she sensed the strain was irritating his headache. How did she do that? How did she know what he was thinking? How he was feeling?

They also took a break to meet with a forensic artist.

Spence and Maddie came up with a pretty good likeness of the bearded man who broke into the cabin last night.

Maddie had set up a whiteboard on the kitchen counter where they listed five potential enemies. He shared the odd, threatening emails he'd been receiving, and when she glanced at each one she crinkled her nose in concentration. The expression would be adorable if it wasn't her way of focusing on the threat against Spence's life.

"This one is awfully cryptic. 'Your mistake has become my destiny.' What's that mean?"

"Haven't a clue."

Maddie pointed to the whiteboard. "Any of these people could consider your behavior a mistake. For instance, Roger Grimes holds a grudge because you reported suspected abuse of his fourteen-year-old daughter, Megan. Was reporting him a mistake?"

"Last I heard, Children's Services was still investigating."

"And Anthony Price is upset with you because…?"

"His fiancée, Theresa, and I had coffee in the cafeteria a few times."

"And Anthony thinks it was more than just coffee?"

"I've heard Theresa has a crush on me. I can't control that."

"No, of course not," she teased.

"Why are you needling me?"

"Sorry, it's that whole, 'you've gotta laugh about it so you don't cry about it' thing. Humor is an awesome coping mechanism."

"What have you used it to cope with?"

"Family stuff. Let's focus." She pointed to a name. "Why is Lucas Winfield on the list?"

"He's a seventeen-year-old kid that was brought in with hallucinations. He ingested an overdose of edible cannabis. I know it's legal in Washington, but not until you're twenty-one. I reported it to Nate."

"Lucas isn't going to try to hurt you over that, is he?"

"His parents were so upset they sent him to military school. He ran away. I hear he's still missing."

"Whoa, I didn't know about that."

"The parents are keeping the running away part quiet. I guess they felt responsible on some level."

"The burdens we carry," she sighed.

"What burdens do you carry, Maddie McBride?"

She turned to him from the whiteboard. "Nothing I can't handle with prayer and humor."

He wanted to question her more, but suspected she would deflect again, wanting to finish his list.

"Who's the Tomlin family?" she asked.

"Oliver Tomlin died in my ER back in Portland from medication complications. No one told us he was on a certain medication that interacted with the nitroglycerin we gave him for chest pain. His blood pressure dropped so low he died of a heart attack." Spence shook his head. "So frustrating. Either his wife, Tina, didn't know he was on the drug, or she chose not to tell us for some reason."

"That's sad."

"I heard that family fell apart after Oliver's death."

"You heard?"

"I left my position in Portland a few months after he died, but an associate of mine keeps me posted, as does the hospital administrator. The Tomlins sued the hospital for wrongful death. The courts dismissed the suit."

"Okay." She stepped back. "That's a pretty solid list, but haven't you left someone out?" She quirked an eyebrow at him.

"I don't think so."

"What about Dr. Danner?"

"William? He's harmless. A lot of bark, but no bite. Kind of like a Yorkie."

Maddie burst out laughing and pride swelled in his chest. He'd done that. In the midst of all this darkness, he'd made her laugh. Spence wanted to do it again, tomorrow, the next day and the day after that.

She composed herself and sat with him at the kitchen table, still eyeing the whiteboard. He might feel proud that he'd made her laugh, but he couldn't afford to get used to having her around all the time.

Even though he wanted her around. All the time.

It was nearly dinnertime and he considered asking her to stay for a meal. He had plenty of food.

"Aunt Margaret is in a knitting club with Anthony's grandmother, so perhaps she can get the scoop on his state of mind, and I think cousin Bree is friends with Lucas's aunt, Beth. Maybe she can find out what's going on with Lucas. You focus on the Tomlins."

"I think we should give the list to Nate."

"We will, but not everyone likes talking to the police. Nate can check the status of the abuse charge against Roger, and it would be nice to know where Dr. Danner was when Gwen went looking for her phone. I don't trust the guy. Ruling out Dr. Nasty should be our first step."

"Dr. Nasty, huh? Do we all have nicknames?"

"Pretty much. So, we're good?"

He'd be better if she'd stay for dinner.

She glanced at him.

"Yes, we're good," he said.

Do you want to have dinner with me? The words got caught in his throat. What was the matter with him? He wasn't fifteen asking a girl on a first date.

Which was exactly the point. He shouldn't be inviting Maddie to dinner given their current situation. Wasn't he the one who'd wanted her to keep her distance?

Her phone beeped with a text and she glanced at it. "I'd better go."

"Yes, that's a good idea."

She glanced at him. "Sick of me already, huh?"

"Not exactly, but it's time you leave."

She didn't move to get up. Studying him intently, she said, "You're trying to get rid of me. What's wrong? Is it your head? Do your ribs hurt? What do you need?"

Way too much to ask of her.

"I'm fine."

"I've stopped hearing you when you use those words. Try again."

"There's no reason for you to stay." He figured being so direct would drive her away.

She shot him a side glance. "What are you up to?"

"Excuse me?"

"You seem intent on me leaving. What did you do, text one of your lady friends to come over for dinner?" she teased.

Of course he didn't, but he couldn't tell Maddie the truth, that he was developing feelings for her.

"Ooohhh, you really did." She stood and grabbed her purse. "I hope you cleared that with Nate."

"Maddie—"

"I get it, I do." She cut him off. "You deserve more stimulating social interaction beyond me grilling you about your enemies."

"Did you want something to eat before you go?" he said, feeling incredibly awkward. "I've got plenty."

"Nah, your lady admirers made that food for you." Maddie headed toward the door. "Enjoy it with your date. I'm staying at Bree's cottage across the way if you need anything."

"She lives here?"

"She's the grounds manager for the resort, so they set her up in a cottage on the property. You've got my cell number."

"I appreciate it. I don't know how I'd manage without you."

She turned to him. "What did you say?"

"I appreciate it."

"The other part."

"I don't know how I'd manage without you?"

"Wow, a compliment. I'm not sure what to do with that," she teased. "My brother's got protective duty right outside, so you're safe, okay?"

He nodded. Wanted to say something. Couldn't.

"Have a good night." She closed the door behind her.

Spence rushed across the cabin, stopping mere inches from the door. What was he doing? She was gone. He wanted her to leave, to get some time off from babysitting him.

A part of him wanted to call out, to thank her again for saving his life.

He couldn't possibly thank her enough.

She deserved to hear his sincere thanks, but he'd been so careful not to cross the line, not to give her any signals that he was interested in her other than as a partner in crime prevention.

As he stood there, staring at the door, he wondered what made him think she had any inclination in that direction. For all he knew the rumors could be true about her and Rocky, that they were secretly in love but they couldn't make it public or one of them would have to resign from work.

Regardless of her dating situation, Spence owed her a debt of gratitude, and letting her assume a woman was joining him for dinner seemed to bother her just now. He could read it in her eyes. He'd moved past trying to constantly push her away and felt like he owed her an apology.

He flung the door open. "Maddie?"

Spence peered into the dark night, but she was gone. He strained to see her. How was that possible? She'd left only moments ago.

"Maddie!" he called out, louder this time.

Silence echoed back at him. He glanced toward her sister's cottage, but didn't see Maddie's silhouette crossing the property.

"What are you doing?" Maddie's voice echoed.

He snapped his head left.

"Let go!" she said.

Spence took off toward the sound without a jacket or hat. He didn't feel the cold, not when panic was lighting him from the inside.

A car engine roared to life.

Spence caught sight of taillights speeding away.

"Maddie!" he called after the vehicle, but it was too far away.

From his peripheral vision he saw a second car speeding toward him. Closer, closer...

SIX

A black SUV screeched to a stop, blocking Spence. Officer Ryan McBride, Maddie's brother, jumped out. "What are you doing, Dr. Spencer?"

"Your sister," he said, trying to catch his breath. "Someone took her." Spence pointed, but the car had turned the corner.

Ryan glanced at Resort Drive, then back at Spence. "Are you sure?"

Still breathing heavily, Spence nodded, the exertion threatening to spike another headache.

"I think you're confused. Maddie went to Bree's. Come on, I'll show you."

"No, someone took her!" Spence shouted.

Ryan put out his hand in a calming gesture. "Doc, relax, she texted me. She's okay."

Spence frowned. Could he be mistaken? Or was he completely losing it?

"I heard her voice," he said. "Demanding someone let her go."

"Come on." Officer McBride motioned Spence to his truck.

Spence climbed into the passenger seat and they drove the short distance to the cottage in silence. The police officer probably thought Spence had gone completely nuts, or at the very least he wondered why Spence was so worried about Maddie.

They knocked on the cottage door and Bree answered, holding back her golden retriever.

"Oh, hi. I thought you were Maddie," she said.

"You mean she's not here?" Ryan said.

"She's on her way."

Ryan looked at Spence. "Make and model of the car."

"It was too far away, but I think it was a small pickup."

"What's going on?" Bree said, her eyes rounding.

"Someone took Maddie," Spence explained.

"We don't know that for sure," Ryan said. "She could have gone off with a friend."

"It didn't sound like a friendly interaction," Spence said.

Ryan ripped his phone off his belt.

"Come on in." Bree motioned to them.

Spence and Ryan joined her inside. Ryan paced the front hallway as he called Maddie. "Answer the phone," he muttered.

"Text her," Spence said.

"She could be helping a friend." Bree glanced at Spence. "She's always there when they need her."

Didn't he know it.

Ryan stared at his phone, waiting. A moment later he glanced up. "She's not responding to my text."

"Let me try." Bree slipped her phone out of her pocket and sent a message. "An SOS will get her attention." She sent her message and glanced at Ryan, offering a supportive smile.

But seconds stretched into minutes, and there was still no response from Maddie.

Ryan reached for his shoulder radio. "I'm calling the chief."

"Rocky, give me my phone," Maddie demanded, adjusting herself in the front seat of his truck.

"Come on, can't you live without it for two minutes?"

"You make it sound like I have a problem."

He shot her a side glance as he pulled onto the highway.

"I don't have a problem," she protested.

"Yeah, right."

"You're enjoying this, being in control."

He handed her the phone. "That's not what it's about."

"What then?"

"It's about you looking out for yourself for a change."

"Uh, I've been taking care of myself for ten years, since Mom moved away."

"Try again."

"You're not making any sense."

"You put everyone else first, your brother, friends, and now that arrogant doctor."

"Why do you dislike him so much?"

"He was never your favorite person in the world, either."

"True, but I appreciate him for helping save my cousin last year."

"And by luring the bad guys away from Cassie, Dr. Dreamboat increases his hero status," he muttered.

"I don't think he was doing it for hero status."

"You sound like you know the guy. No one knows him, not really. His smile hides something dark and tragic. You were the one who said that."

"Since the assault in the mountains I've seen another side of him."

"Wonderful," Rocky said, sarcastic.

She glanced out the window. "Where are we going?"

"Healthy Eats. I'm buying you dinner."

"I'd better text Bree."

He shot her a look.

"It's rude not to let her know I won't be home for dinner. Although, I could bring her something."

"Home? The cottage isn't your home, Maddie. Why are you staying there anyway?"

"It's convenient."

"You mean it's close to Dr. Dreamboat."

"You are really busting my chops tonight."

"Because I worry about you."

Maddie sighed. This was probably why folks thought she and Rocky were a couple. He always seemed so solicitous and caring. Then a thought struck her: Could he truly be in love with her? No, she couldn't go there right now.

She glanced at her phone and noticed a missed call and text from her overprotective brother, and a text from Bree.

Worried about you.

She texted a response to both of them.

I'm fine.

She pocketed her phone and turned to Rocky. "I thought you had a date tonight."

"Blew me off."

They pulled into the crowded parking lot of the town's most popular restaurant. Once inside Healthy Eats, Nate's sister Catherine, the owner, greeted them.

"Hi, guys," she said. "I've got a booth in the corner or a few spots at the counter."

A booth sounded romantic and Maddie didn't want to give Rocky the wrong idea. Maybe it was time they had *that* discussion.

"What do you think?" he said.

"Counter's fine."

He motioned her ahead and they found seats. Catherine was quick to serve their drinks. Coffee for Rocky and hot chocolate for Maddie.

"I'll see what Bree wants for dinner." She pulled out her phone and texted her cousin.

"You could order it while we're eating, then it'll be hot when you get back to her place."

"Good plan. It will probably take her a few minutes to look at the menu online anyway." She pocketed her phone and gazed into a mirror behind the counter. She spotted a few local residents eyeing Rocky and Maddie sitting together. The rumors were certainly going to fly by morning.

She turned to him. "Can I talk to you about something?"

"What's up?" he said, blowing on his hot coffee.

"We're friends, right?"

He glanced at her with furrowed brows. "Is that a trick question?"

"Be honest."

"Haven't I always been?"

In that moment, as she studied the curious expression on his handsome face, she realized he would make a wonderful husband someday. Just not for her.

"Dr. Carver made a comment about you and me being, ya know, a couple," she said.

"And how did you respond to that one?"

"I didn't know how to respond. I was shocked."

He stared into his mug of coffee. "Right."

So it was true. He cared about her as more than a friend.

"Oh," she said. "I'm sorry."

He shrugged. "I get it. I know how much Waylan hurt you when he left." Then he looked straight into her eyes. "I would never hurt you, Maddie, ever."

"I know you wouldn't. You're my very best friend."

A sad smile eased across his lips. "Ouch."

She wanted to say more. She wanted to apologize that she didn't have romantic feelings for him. Had Waylan emotionally damaged her so badly that she was incapable of falling in love with a kind man?

No, she wasn't broken or damaged. She just wasn't attracted to Rocky like that.

Like she was attracted to Dr. Spencer.

She stirred her hot chocolate, frustrated. Would she always be destined to fall for the wrong guy? Either ambitious men who put their careers before love, like Waylan, or enigmas like Spence?

Although Rocky was acting a little bossy tonight, he was generally kind and funny. The doctor, on the other hand, had been challenging and moody since the assault, and before that he'd always seemed aloof bordering on arrogant.

The absolute wrong kind of guy with whom to build a life. Maddie wanted stability, not chaos.

She glanced at Rocky. If only…

But she didn't feel that way about him. Now that the question was out in the open she hoped it wouldn't ruin their friendship.

"You are very special to me," she said.

"Apparently not special enough."

"Rocky, you're a great guy but—"

"Let's leave it at 'Rocky, you're a great guy.'" He cracked a half smile. "It's okay." He redirected his attention into his coffee. "But a piece of unsolicited advice? At some point you have to move on."

"You mean past the heartbreak?"

He nodded. "Maybe even start a life somewhere outside Echo Mountain."

"Why? I like it here."

"As long as you're here because you want to be here, not because you're afraid to leave." He glanced at her. "Or because you're waiting for them to come back."

"Them?"

"Waylan." He paused. "And your parents."

She stirred her hot chocolate, thoughtful. Was it true? Was she afraid to leave, to move on with her life? Did a part of her cling to her extended family and friends in Echo

Mountain because she was secretly hoping the people she loved would return?

"I'm sorry if I offended you," he said.

"You didn't."

Sirens drew her attention outside. Two police cars pulled into the lot, lights flashing.

A few seconds later, the front doors opened and her brother stormed into the restaurant followed by the police chief and Dr. Spencer. Her heart skipped a beat.

Ryan's cheeks flared bright red as he approached her. The doc's expression was unreadable. She shifted off her stool, panicked. "What happened?"

Ryan opened his mouth and shut it again, as if he struggled to form words.

"Ryan, tell me," she demanded.

"Let's take this outside." Nate motioned for her and Rocky to join them.

Privacy was a good idea considering the diners filling the restaurant. As they marched to the door, her heart hammered against her chest. Was it Aunt Margaret? Bree? Was Aiden's condition worse than they thought?

Nate motioned them toward his patrol car. Ryan suddenly turned and shot dagger eyes at Rocky, and then glared at Maddie. "What's going on here?"

That judgmental, accusatory tone set her teeth on edge. "We were eating dinner," she said as if it was the most obvious answer in the world.

"You disappeared and didn't answer my call," Ryan snapped.

"I texted that I was fine."

"You took her against her will," Dr. Spencer directed at Rocky.

"I think your head injury is messing with your judgment, Doc."

"Rocky," Maddie admonished.

"What? He's accusing me of kidnapping you. That's crazy."

"I heard Maddie say, 'Let go of me,'" Spence said. "She obviously didn't want to go with you."

"And then you ignored me and didn't respond immediately to Bree's text," Ryan added. "With everything that's going on? Really, Maddie?"

"Let's all take a breath," Nate said. "Maddie, what happened after you left Dr. Spencer tonight?"

"I was walking to Bree's cottage and Rocky pulled up." She glanced at the doctor. "Rocky grabbed the strap of my bag and pulled me into his truck, which is why I said 'let go.'"

"So you did not go willingly?" Spence said.

"He was being playful. Not forceful. You must have misunderstood."

"At least you're okay," Ryan shook his head and turned toward his cruiser. "Come on, Doc."

Spence didn't move. It was like he was waiting for Maddie, that he wasn't going anywhere unless she was with him. She surely didn't want to ride in the patrol car with her brother and suffer through an angry lecture.

"Chief, I'm really sorry about this," Maddie said. "I had no idea going to dinner with Rocky would cause such a misunderstanding. I was about to order food to take to Bree. Can I still do that? Rocky can drive me to Bree's cottage."

"I'll wait and give you an escort," Nate said. "Spence, go on back with Officer McBride."

"I'd rather wait for Maddie," Spence said.

With a frustrated sigh, Rocky marched back into the restaurant.

"Officer McBride," Nate said. "Head back to the resort. I'll bring Dr. Spencer and Maddie."

"Yes, sir," he said, getting into his cruiser.

"Ryan, I'm sorry," Maddie called out.

Her brother slammed the door shut.

"Go ahead and order the food," Nate said to Maddie. "We'll wait for you out here."

With a nod, Maddie turned toward the restaurant, frustrated that Rocky's good intentions had caused such tension between her and her brother.

"Maddie?" Spence said.

She glanced over her shoulder at him.

"I'm glad you're okay," he said.

Maddie had barely spoken to Spence on the ride back to the resort. He assumed she was upset that he'd overreacted about her disappearance. He'd apologized to her in the squad car, but Nate said Spence did the right thing.

"It's always better to be vigilant than to ignore your gut," Nate said.

Maddie stared out the window.

In this case, Spence's gut had been wrong. Maddie hadn't been in danger. She'd been out with her work partner. It bothered Spence that she'd refused to have dinner with him, yet went off with Rocky.

When Spence asked her why she'd ignored her brother's call, she explained that she'd been in a heated discussion with Rocky and figured responding to her brother and cousin via text would suffice. She said that Rocky had been trying to make a point: Maddie always put everyone else first, but never herself.

The car went silent after that comment as if she was ashamed, that caring so much about others was a personality flaw.

It wasn't a flaw. It was a gift. Hadn't she put Spence's welfare above her own ever since they'd found Gwen on the trail?

Nate dropped Maddie off at her cousin's cottage and

took Spence to the cabin where Ryan waited. Spence apologized to Maddie's brother for overreacting, but the officer said it wasn't necessary, that his irresponsible sister should have answered his call and texted more than a simple "I'm fine."

Spence wanted to argue the "irresponsible" remark, but thought better of it. As he and Ryan ate dinner, Spence learned that Ryan felt very protective of Maddie, which drove her crazy because she considered herself an independent woman.

He and Ryan watched TV for an hour and Spence turned in early.

Even now, well past midnight, he was unable to sleep. Perhaps another symptom of his concussion, or he could be wired from tonight's excitement. So worried about Maddie being kidnapped, he'd caught himself praying for her safety.

Hang on, praying?

Spence shook his head and rolled onto his back, staring at the ceiling. The lights were off in his room, but the full moon glowed through the sheer curtains.

He felt incredibly alone, detached from everyone. The brain trauma was messing with him again, making him moody and sullen. He wasn't alone; he had plenty of friends.

Then again real friends would know the truth about the patient he'd lost in Portland, about Spence's brother who'd died at only eight years old. True friends would know about his fiancée's betrayal that cut him so deeply he'd become an expert at keeping people at a distance with his effusive charm and practiced smile.

Well, he'd kept everyone at a distance except Maddie. She'd somehow seen right through his facade.

He started to drift, recalling how Maddie talked him down from his precarious ledge after the attack in the hospital; remembering the lovely image of her curled up on the chair in the cabin. It helped to visualize that image, a content and peaceful Maddie reading a book close by.

Then the images turned violent, images of his enemy coming for him.

Coming for Maddie.

He jackknifed in bed, his heart pounding. Needing to distract himself, he slipped on a sweatshirt and opened his bedroom door. Officer McBride was sitting at the kitchen table looking at his phone.

"Shouldn't you be asleep?" he asked.

"Not happening anytime soon." Spence wandered to the kitchen counter and made some tea. He motioned to the table. "Mind if I…?"

"Sure, have a seat. I was reading a book on my phone."

"About your 'irresponsible sister' comment earlier…" Spence started.

"That was harsh. I was upset," Ryan said, putting his phone in his pocket. "She's so frustrating sometimes, but I love her."

"Frustrating how?"

"Stubborn, opinionated. I think it's a defense mechanism."

Spence glanced at Ryan in question.

"She's dealt with her share of pain," Ryan continued. "Dad left us when she was fourteen and I was seventeen. Mom fell apart and Maddie tried so hard to make it better, to make Mom better. But you can't fix other people, ya know?"

Spence nodded that he understood. He remembered how he'd wanted to help his own parents deal with their grief after Bobby had died, but at thirteen, Spence had no clue what to do.

"Anyway, when Maddie was fifteen Mom moved away to be with a cousin in Florida. Didn't exactly invite her teenage daughter along," Ryan continued. "So Maddie moved in with Aunt Margaret. Maddie loves our aunt and cousins, but it's not the same. I think she felt like it was her fault somehow that my folks left."

"That's tough on a teenager."

"Yeah, and then there was the idiot boyfriend." Ryan shook his head.

"A jerk?"

"Actually he was really good for her. Brought her out of her funk."

Jealousy tweaked in Spence's chest. "Then why is he an idiot?"

"He moved away for school and basically dropped out of her life. It was traumatic." Ryan glanced at Spence. "I think that's what makes her Maddie, the bullheaded woman who will never leave Echo Mountain."

"She won't leave because…?"

"She'll never run away like my parents and Waylan."

"You can move away and not be running from something."

"Yeah, try telling her that."

Spence considered Ryan's words.

"Anyway, I know I overreacted when she disappeared with Rocky, but it's that big brother thing, which is unnecessary because she is one strong woman." A proud smile eased across his lips.

He had every right to be proud of his sister. Spence was not only proud, but also incredibly grateful.

The peaceful moment was shattered by a shrill alarm coming from the resort.

Ryan pushed back his chair and went to the front window.

"What's going on?" Spence said.

"Not sure. Dispatch," he said into his radio. "You get a call for an alarm at Echo Mountain Resort?"

"Affirmative. Engine 52 and ambulance are on the way."

"A fire?" Ryan asked.

"Affirmative."

Someone pounded on the cabin door.

"It's Nia!" a muffled voice cried.

Ryan opened the door to the hotel's concierge wearing a frantic expression.

"Fire truck and ambulance are on the way," Ryan said.

"We can't wait. There's a fire in the kitchen. They think a little girl is inside. We need your help."

"Let's go." Spence approached the door.

Ryan blocked him. "No, we've got orders."

"It'll take emergency five to seven minutes to get here," Spence said. "We can't wait."

Ryan considered for a second. "I'll call the chief."

"Call him on the way." Spence grabbed a jacket and marched out of the cabin. "Where's Aiden?" he asked Nia.

"I paged him. He might be wiped out from the fall today. Went to bed early? I don't know."

As Spence, Nia and Ryan jogged across the property, Ryan radioed that they were assisting with rescue efforts. By the time they reached the south entrance, guests had evacuated the resort and smoke was seeping out of the kitchen windows.

Ryan approached a small group of employees who were hovering by the entrance. "Everyone okay?"

They all nodded that they were.

"I'm Edith, head cook," a middle-aged woman introduced.

"Didn't the sprinklers go off?" Ryan asked.

"Strangely, no," Edith said.

Scott stumbled out of the building assisting a young woman.

"My daughter? Did you see my daughter?" a man in his thirties asked Scott.

"No, not yet." Scott helped the woman to a nearby bench.

"I've gotta go find her."

Ryan blocked the young father. "Sir, you need to stay back."

Spence put a calming hand on the man's shoulder. "What's your name?"

"Rich."

"Rich, fire crews will be here any minute," Spence said.

"I'll go back in." Scott burst into a round of coughing.

"You've inhaled enough smoke," Spence said. "Do we even know she's inside?"

"Edith," Ryan said. "Was a little girl in there?"

"Yes, she came to watch us bake pastries for tomorrow's breakfast buffet. I thought someone grabbed her on the way out." She glanced at coworkers who all shook their heads that they hadn't.

Spence kept a firm grip on the father's shoulder to prevent him from rushing into a burning building.

"Where did you last see her?" Ryan asked Edith.

"Near the dishwasher. The smoke was coming from the storage closet, where we keep the linens. I don't get it. There's nothing flammable in there."

"You stay here," Ryan said to Spence and the father.

Ryan covered his mouth with his jacket sleeve and rushed into the building.

Spence scanned the group outside. Guests clung to their loved ones as they watched and waited for news about the fire.

"I didn't see any flames," a thirtysomething redheaded man said.

"I hope it wasn't Tina smoking a cigarette in the closet," a teenager said.

"I thought she quit," the redheaded man said.

"Who's Tina?" Spence asked.

"Our new assistant baker. Single mother of three," Edith offered. "Has anyone seen her?"

They all shook their heads that she didn't exit the building with them.

Spence eyed the smoke-filled hallway. Ryan was looking for a little girl near the dishwasher, but didn't know about the single mother who'd possibly been smoking in the closet.

Sirens echoed from the highway. They were still too far away. If Tina had accidentally set the fire…

Spence gripped the dad's shoulders and looked him in the eyes. "Rich, I'm putting you in charge. Make sure everyone stays clear of the building. That includes you. And assist the fire department when they arrive."

The father nodded. "Okay."

Spence turned and raced into the building.

He thought he heard someone shout his name from behind, but didn't let it distract him. He had to get inside; he had to help.

Shoving his jacket sleeve against his mouth, he slogged his way through the dense smoke. He stumbled down the hallway, wondering why the sprinklers hadn't gone off. He flung open the kitchen door.

"Ryan, it's Spence! Where are you?"

"I've got the girl!" Ryan said.

"There's another woman in here!"

"I've got her, too! Get outta here!"

Something snapped around his neck and yanked him back. Spence dug his fingers between his neck and what felt like braided rope.

The pressure cut off his airway. Someone shoved a cloth over his mouth, making it even harder to breathe.

"Don't fight it."

The rope loosened and he gasped for air, inhaling whatever was in the cloth.

The alarm grew distorted, sounding like the wail of an animal caught in a trap.

"Relax. It's almost over," the voice whispered.

SEVEN

"Spence!" Maddie called, pacing outside the door to the resort.

She couldn't believe he raced into a smoke-filled hallway. What was he thinking? He wasn't wearing equipment to protect him against fire. Was he that desperate to save lives?

Or was this bad judgment due to the brain injury?

And where was Ryan? He was supposed to be watching Spence, keeping him from doing anything foolish like rushing into a burning building.

Unless Ryan was also inside.

It took every ounce of self-control not to sprint into the resort after Spence, and possibly her brother, but common sense dictated she hang back.

Emergency vehicles finally pulled up. Vivian and her partner, Karl, pushed a stretcher toward the resort. Maddie spotted Sam Treadwell climb off Engine 52.

"Sam!" she called as he approached in full gear. "I saw Dr. Spencer run inside, and my brother might be in there, as well."

"Without gear?" he said, frustrated.

"Find them, please find them."

Sam motioned to his team. As they started for the door,

it swung open and Ryan came out, holding a little girl in his arms. A young woman clung to Ryan's shoulder.

"Ryan!" Maddie cried rushing to her brother. He handed the little girl to paramedics, and Maddie threw her arms around him.

"Anyone else inside?" Sam asked.

"I don't think so."

Maddie broke the hug. "Spence, where's Spence?"

"I told him to get out." Ryan scanned the area. "I thought he was ahead of me."

"We got this," Sam said. He and his team entered the resort.

"Are you okay?" Maddie asked her brother.

"Yeah."

She hugged him again and he said, "Hey, it's okay. Now you know how I felt when you didn't answer my call earlier." It wasn't a shaming comment, it was a caring one.

"I'm sorry about that," she said.

"I know, I know."

She broke the hug. "I'm worried about Spence."

"He called out to me. He was fine."

"He's still in there?" As Maddie glanced toward the resort, she realized the terrified, thirtysomething woman with brown hair clung to Ryan's shoulder.

Maddie nodded at her brother. "Have the medics examine her."

Ryan turned to the woman. "Ma'am, let's get you checked out."

She didn't respond, just stared at her hand that gripped his jacket.

"Come on, you're okay," he said, leading her to the ambulance.

Maddie took a few steps closer to the door, hoping to get a better look, hoping to see the guys from Engine 52 escorting Spence out of the building.

The alarm suddenly clicked off, blanketing the grounds in an eerie silence. She felt someone touch her shoulder. She glanced into her cousin Bree's eyes.

"Spence is still inside," Maddie said.

"The firemen will get him out."

Maddie nodded. A second ambulance pulled up to the side entrance. They were obviously prepared for multiple injuries.

Her cousin Aiden rushed toward them.

"You okay?" Nia asked.

"Of course I'm not okay. My resort's on fire." He glanced at Nia. "Sorry, hon." He kissed the top of her head. "How did this start?"

"We're not sure," Nia said. "Smoke suddenly filled the hallways from the kitchen area."

"Dr. Spencer is in there," Maddie said.

"Spence? Why?" Aiden asked, worried about his friend.

Maddie stared at the building. "I guess he needed to help."

"I should've gotten here sooner," Aiden said. He took a step toward the resort.

Nia blocked him. "Don't even think about it."

"Here comes Sam," Maddie said. The firefighter and his team came out of the building assisting two more people, but not Spence.

Maddie's heart sank. Before she could ask the firefighter about Spence, he spoke to the group.

"Everyone, you can go back to your rooms. It wasn't a fire, just a lotta smoke contained in the kitchen." Sam approached Aiden. "You've got a prankster on your hands. Someone set off a smoke bomb."

"Did you see Dr. Spencer?" Maddie asked.

"I saw county paramedics wheeling him away from the side exit," Sam said.

Maddie nodded. She didn't like that county had taken

Spence because she didn't know those paramedics and couldn't push them for information about his condition.

As everyone started talking around her—Aiden barking orders, Sam speculating on the damage and the kitchen staff asking if they should go back inside and finish the baking—Maddie glanced beyond Aiden and spotted two men wheeling Spence toward an ambulance. The hair on the back of her neck pricked.

"Maddie?" Bree asked.

"How's Tina?" Aiden asked Ryan.

"She's okay. Relieved she didn't start the fire."

"Sam says it was some kind of smoke bomb," Aiden added.

"Kids?" Ryan said.

"Maddie, what is it?" Bree gripped Maddie's arm.

Maddie couldn't take her eyes off Spence being loaded into the ambulance.

Something felt off, but she wasn't sure what. Maybe she just needed to see for herself that he was okay. Or maybe it was something else…

"Maddie!" Ryan called out.

That's when she realized she was running toward the ambulance.

Follow your gut.

Bree had driven that message home over and over again to everyone in the McBride clan. As Maddie tore across the property, the ambulance sped off through a fog of smoke.

And there, on the ground, was a body.

"Spence," she gasped.

"Maddie!" Ryan caught up to her. "What are you—?"

He must have seen the body, as well.

She redirected her attention from the vanishing ambulance to the body, trying to calm her frantic heartbeat. Maybe it was someone from the fire who'd wandered out and collapsed.

Maybe it wasn't Spence.

She dropped to the ground and realized it wasn't Spence, but a paramedic. A gasp-choke escaped her lips.

The young paramedic sat up, rubbing his head.

"What happened?" Ryan said.

"We found an unconscious male by the south exit. Secured him in the back of the ambulance but when I opened the driver's door someone clobbered me."

Maddie snapped her attention into the fog, where the ambulance had vanished. "They took him, Ryan. They took Spence."

Spence opened his eyes, cataloging his surroundings. How had he ended up in an ambulance? He didn't think he'd inhaled that much smoke, but must have because he felt nauseous and disoriented. With the oxygen mask firmly over his face, Spence struggled to communicate with the male paramedic.

"Just relax," the young man said. "I'm Tyler, and my partner Eddie is driving."

Spence didn't know Tyler, which didn't help ease the tension in his chest. If only Maddie had been on duty and called to the scene.

Maddie. The sound of her shouting his name echoed in his mind. She *had* been there.

The ambulance jerked left and Tyler flew out of sight.

"Eddie, slow down!" Tyler shouted. He shifted back to the bench beside Spence and knocked on the window between them and the driver. "What's wrong with you?" Tyler shook his head and glanced at Spence. "Sorry about that. Eddie just broke up with his girlfriend."

Spence knew the pain of heartbreak; the memory of finding Andrea in the arms of another man still cut him to the quick. He surely must have inhaled too much smoke to be thinking about that disaster. He'd put that painful memory behind him, buried it deep where it could no longer hurt him.

The siren clicked on and the ambulance sped up.

"Eddie! It's mild smoke inhalation!" Tyler shook his head. "He's a good driver, don't worry." Tyler took Spence's blood pressure.

Spence removed his mask. "I don't know you."

"I'm Tyler, remember?"

"I've never seen you at the hospital. I'm...a doctor."

"I usually work in Skagit County, but they called us in on the resort fire." He adjusted the oxygen mask over Spence's mouth. "Please keep this on."

"Ambulance 112, this is base. Over." A voice said through Tyler's shoulder radio.

"This is Ambulance 112. Over," he responded.

"What's your twenty? Over."

Tyler knocked on the divider. "Eddie! They want our twenty!"

No response.

He knocked again. "Eddie!"

The ambulance swerved. Tyler jerked back, slamming into a cabinet. Gripping his head, he shouted, "That's enough! I'm driving!"

He pounded on the divider with his fist.

In Spence's eyes it seemed like everything was moving in slow motion. Had he inhaled more smoke than he thought?

Breathe, he coached himself. *Keep breathing*.

The ambulance pulled over.

"Hang tight," Tyler said, and disappeared from view.

Spence wasn't sure how long Tyler was gone. In his condition he didn't have a clear sense of time.

"Kyle," a voice said. "Your brother needs you."

His brother?

"Bobby?" Spence croaked.

"Yes, Bobby needs you. Let's go." A man's face came into view, but he wore a surgical mask and thick, tinted glasses.

"Bobby's here?" Spence said as the doctor led him out of the ambulance.

"Yes. I tried to help, but he's asking for you."

"Bobby," Spence hushed.

The ground tilted beneath his feet, but the doctor with the tinted glasses kept him upright, guiding him into the woods.

"What happened?" Spence said.

"He fell, remember?"

Spence nodded. Yes, he remembered. They were playing superheroes and Spence dared Bobby to jump across a ravine like Batman.

The doctor led Spence up a trail, his legs weak and unsteady.

"You're the only one who can help him."

Spence forced himself to be strong, to make it to his brother.

To save him this time.

They approached an overlook. The doctor let go of Spence's arm and retreated into the forest.

"Where is he?" Spence said.

"Down there. Can't you see him?"

Spence peered down into the mass of nothingness. "I can't..."

"Kyle," a voice echoed. "Kyle, help me."

Spence squinted to see below, to see his brother, but was blinded by darkness.

"Bobby?" Spence called back.

"Don't let me die!"

"I'm coming, Bobby!" Spence dropped to his stomach to lower himself to the ledge where his brother lay injured.

This time would be different. He'd help Bobby.

He'd save him.

"I'm coming, Bobby!"

"Spence!" a woman shouted.

Was Maddie down there with his brother? Together, Spence and Maddie would save Bobby for sure.

He grabbed on to a tree root and let his feet dangle, just like before, only he knew what to do this time. He was a doctor.

He was about to let go when firm hands gripped his wrists.

"Pull!" a man ordered.

In a swift movement, Spence was up on the trail lying on his back. "No, I have to get to Bobby."

He struggled to get up, but someone restrained him.

"Shh, it's okay." A pair of brilliant green eyes looked down at him.

Maddie.

"Take it easy, Spence," she said.

"Bobby, Bobby needs me."

She shone a bright light in his eyes. "He's been drugged," she said to someone.

Spence realized Nate was holding him down. "You're okay, buddy. Just relax," Nate said.

"Not okay. Bobby's hurt."

"Who's Bobby?" Maddie asked Nate. He shook his head.

"My little brother," Spence said, fighting the restraint of strong hands pressed against his shoulders.

"We've gotta get him to the hospital," Maddie said.

And he was up, being led away from the ledge, away from his brother.

"No, Bobby, no!" The pain and grief of his brother's death rushed though him. "It's my fault. He's dead because of me."

Maddie and Nate didn't want the Echo Mountain Hospital staff to witness Spence in such a disoriented state, so they took him to Cedar River, a hospital one county over. Nate had a friend there and made a call, asking if they could treat Spence quietly, without drawing unnecessary attention.

They loaded Spence into the county ambulance. Maddie stayed in the back with him and Ryan drove the ambulance to the hospital. The other paramedic, Tyler, had sustained a head injury and rode in front.

"It's my fault. Bobby... I killed my little brother," Spence whispered.

"No, you didn't kill anyone," Maddie said.

His eyes popped open. "Didn't you hear him? He was calling my name."

"Shh," Maddie said, stroking his soft, ash-blond hair. "Spence, look at me."

He blinked and looked into her eyes. "My brother..."

"It's okay. Everything's going to be okay." She didn't know what else to say.

"Bobby..." Spence closed his eyes.

This situation was growing worse instead of better. The perpetrator had assaulted not one, but two paramedics, kidnapped the doctor and tried to make him climb down a mountain. And how had he done that? By messing with Spence's mind. Which meant the attacker knew details about Spence's life. It was time Maddie knew the same details.

They pulled up to the hospital and Maddie opened the ambulance doors.

"Maddie," Spence said.

"I'm here."

Nate walked up to her. "They're letting us come in through the side entrance."

"Thanks. It would help if we knew what happened to Spence's brother."

"Detective Vaughn is working on it."

An ER doctor and nurse came out of the building. "I'm Dr. Reece. We'll take it from here."

"I need to stay with him," Maddie said. "He's disoriented and argumentative. My presence will keep him calm."

"This way."

Maddie and Nate followed them into the hospital, Maddie even more determined than ever to stay close to Spence.

A few hours later Maddie sat beside Spence's bed in the ER, waiting for results from a drug test. He'd been drugged, no question in her mind. Otherwise he wouldn't have been so out of it, and he surely wouldn't have tried to rappel down a mountainside at night with no equipment.

To get to Bobby, his little brother, who wasn't even there.

Her phone rang and she recognized her aunt's number. "Hey, Aunt Margaret."

"I heard about the fire at the resort. Is Dr. Spencer okay?"

"He will be."

"I had tea with Iris Price and she told me Anthony and Theresa are doing just fine. Set a wedding date for September."

"That's good news."

"Tell Dr. Spencer I'm making two more casseroles and a fruit plate for him."

"I'm sure he'll appreciate it."

"How about you? Are you okay?"

"Yes, ma'am. I'm good."

"Keep in touch, okay? Even if it's an email, but not text, I haven't figured out the texting thing yet."

"Sounds good. Love you."

The curtain pulled back and Nate motioned her to join him, away from Spence.

"I can't leave him," she said.

"I've got you covered." Nate motioned to a man standing a few feet away. "This is bodyguard Adam Swift. He owns a personal security firm and is going to keep an eye on Spence for us."

"Ma'am," Adam said in greeting.

In his thirties, he had short brown hair, a square jaw and wore a serious expression.

"How do we know we can trust him, Nate?" she asked. "No offense, Adam, but we've had a couple of crazy days."

"We served in the military together," Nate said. "He's solid and his is one of the top-rated agencies in the Seattle area."

With a nod, she followed Nate out of the ER into the lobby, leaving Adam to keep watch over Spence.

Nate led her to a secluded corner. "Spence had a brother named Robert who passed away at eight years old. Spence was thirteen. The report indicates that Spence and his brother were playing in a forest and Bobby fell. He sustained life-threatening injuries and died."

She glanced toward the ER examining area. "That's horrible."

"It sounds like Spence blames himself."

"But he was just a kid."

"You don't have to convince me. All that guilt must have come rushing back tonight."

"Because the kidnapper who assaulted the paramedics and drugged Spence shoved his failures in his face."

"Which means the kidnapper knows about his past."

"Yes, I figured that out, too." She crossed her arms over her chest. "Why is all this happening now? What triggered the attempts on his life?"

"Perhaps the answer is in your list of suspects."

"You got my email, right?"

"I did."

"Did you check out Dr. Danner's whereabouts during the time Gwen went searching for her phone?"

"Still working on that. Hard to believe professional jealousy could be behind this."

"You don't know Danner," she said wryly.

He glanced across the lobby. "I thought I knew Spence."

"Grief isn't something easily shared, especially when guilt is attached."

"True. Do you need a lift back to Echo Mountain Resort or will you be staying here?"

"I'm staying."

"Adam is a good man. He can protect him."

"Yes, but Adam a stranger. Spence needs to see a familiar face when he wakes up."

"Sounds good. I'd better get back. Adam can drive you and Spence to the resort when he's released. Keep me posted on his condition."

"Of course."

As Maddie headed to the ER examining area, she decided to find someone to cover her shift starting tomorrow at three. She didn't want to be away from Spence for a full twenty-four hours.

She called Vivian, but it went into voice mail so she left a message. "Hey, Vivian, it's Maddie. I'm in a pinch and need to get my shift covered, or at least part of it. It starts at three tomorrow afternoon. Let me know either way, okay? Thanks."

Maddie considered calling Wiggy Wunderman but knew Rocky would not be happy with her if he got stuck with the guy's nonstop chatter for a twenty-four-hour shift.

Suddenly a code blue echoed across the hospital PA system. Dr. Reece and a nurse rushed past Maddie into the ER exam area.

Where she'd left Spence.

Her heart slammed against her chest as she raced to the door and pushed it open.

"What's going on?" she said.

Adam blocked her.

"Get me the crash cart!" Dr. Reece shouted.

The words sent a chill down Maddie's spine.

EIGHT

The room seemed to close in. They needed a crash cart for Spence?

"Come on," Adam said, escorting Maddie out of the examining area.

Once in the lobby, she turned to him. "But I need to… you need to…someone needs to stay with him in case… in case…"

"Let the doctors do their job."

She snapped her attention to him. "I'm worried about someone coming after him again. Guard the door, don't let anyone in without an ID badge."

"You'll stay here?"

She nodded but couldn't speak, a knot of fear tangling her vocal cords. Adam crossed the lobby and stood guard beside the door.

Nate rushed up to Maddie. "I was almost outside and heard the code. It isn't—"

"Spence." She glanced at him, but didn't really focus.

Nate led her to the waiting area. "I don't understand."

"It must be the drugs." She glanced at Nate. "The only way this could happen is if the attacker gave him a drug that slowed down his heart or affected his breathing." She fisted her hands to stop the trembling. "Which means the perp has medical knowledge."

"That narrows things down," Nate said.

Silence vibrated around them like a low-frequency hum of an air-conditioning unit. Her gaze drifted to the door to the examining area. She'd treated her share of trauma patients with heart issues, but Spence was a healthy, active man in his thirties. What drug had he been given that affected his breathing or made his blood pressure drop dangerously low? "We brought him here thinking he'd be safe, yet he's in there fighting for his life," Maddie said. "This has got to end, Chief."

She stood and paced the waiting area. Nervous energy, frustration and even rage were tearing her up inside.

"Detective Vaughn is investigating the names you sent over. So far, no word on Lucas Winfield's whereabouts, and Roger Grimes is still under investigation about the abuse allegations. Detective Vaughn contacted a detective friend in Portland to look into the Tomlin family."

"Well, apparently Anthony Price and Theresa are back together, so we can scratch him off the list of revenge seekers. It mystifies me that Spence would have an enemy angry enough to want him dead."

"Or punished for a perceived wrong." Nate glanced at his phone. "I've got to take this." Nate went outside.

Maddie willed the ER examining area doors to open, wanting the doctor to come out and tell her Spence was okay.

Spence had to be okay because she would not accept any other outcome. She took a deep breath and said a silent prayer.

Nate returned wearing a frown. How could this night get any worse?

"What?" she said.

"Dr. Danner didn't show up for his shift today."

Spence squinted against the bright sun shining through the window. He realized he was in a hospital, but it wasn't

Echo Mountain Hospital. Panic gripped his chest. Had the brain injury caused him to pass out?

"There you are," Maddie said, approaching his bed.

"Where am I?"

"Cedar River Hospital."

He nodded, but didn't ask the next question burning in his mind. *How did I get here?*

"What's the last thing you remember?" Maddie said.

"A kitchen fire at the resort. I went inside to find a young woman and then, then I was in an ambulance. Why was I in an ambulance?"

"Some creep-O knocked out the driver and drove off with you in the back. He drugged you, assaulted the other paramedic and tried convincing you to throw yourself off the mountainside. Do you remember that last part?"

Spence closed his eyes. Bobby's voice, he'd heard Bobby's voice.

"My brother," was all he could say.

"Your kidnapper was messing with your head, big-time. We think the drug caused hallucinations and worse, your BP dropped so low they almost lost you last night."

He nodded. Took a deep breath. And felt her hand touch his shoulder.

"I'm sorry," she said. "About your brother."

She knew the truth. He let Bobby die.

"Did they find the man who kidnapped me?" he said, not able to make eye contact.

"Spence, look at me."

He glanced into her eyes.

"Your brother's death was not your fault."

"You don't know anything about it," he snapped. "You weren't there."

"No, I wasn't. But I know a thirteen-year-old boy shouldn't be held responsible for an accident. Is that why you went into medicine?"

He nodded.

"It's a blessing you did. Think of all the people you've helped as a doctor."

"It'll never be enough," he said. "I didn't help the one who mattered most."

"If Bobby were here right now, do you think he'd want you be punishing yourself like this?"

He glared at her. "He's not here. That's the point. And what are you, my counselor?"

An expression he'd never seen before flashed in her green eyes. His words had hurt her, deeply. Probably a good thing. He had wanted to drive her away, and perhaps this would finally do it.

She slipped her hand off his shoulder and went to the window. He suddenly wanted to apologize. He wasn't a cruel man and the thought of intentionally hurting her flooded him with guilt.

Worse, she knew his biggest shame, the one thing that drove his every thought: he was a failure who let down the people he loved most. What else would explain Andrea falling for another man? Because Spence hadn't been loving enough, caring enough.

Good enough.

His failures started long before that. After his brother's death he'd never been able to recapture his parents' love. No matter what he did or how hard he tried, he continually let them down.

Maddie's phone vibrated and she pulled it out of her pocket. "I'll be right back," she said, walking past him without looking up.

She disappeared into the hallway leaving him alone with his thoughts and despair. It always seemed less painful when she was nearby talking to him, forgiving him.

But she deserved a better man than a damaged doctor with emotionally paralyzing scars of shame.

Being in the hospital wasn't helping the situation, especially since Dr. Carver would eventually hear he'd been admitted again, delaying his return to the schedule. She had questioned his decision to return to work the other day. What would she think when she heard he'd hallucinated his brother's accident?

The longer he stayed here the worse it was for his career, his life.

He shifted out of bed, letting his bare feet touch the cool vinyl floor. He seemed steady enough. Taking a few steps, his head grew light, but he forged on.

"Whoa, whoa," Maddie said, coming into the room and gripping his arm for support. "What are you trying to do?"

"I'm leaving."

"You sure that's a good idea? You coded last night."

"Because of a drug reaction. I suppose you think I should spend another night in the hospital?"

She crossed her arms over her chest, but didn't answer.

"I get it, now you're not talking to me," he said.

"Why should I? I only seem to make you angry with your snappy comments and insults. And ya know, I don't deserve that. All I've done is try to help you stay alive. So you're welcome and goodbye." She turned to leave.

Spence gently grabbed her wrist. "Wait."

She turned to him with fire in her eyes.

"You know what they say about people being the hardest on those closest to them?" he said.

Clenching her jaw, she nodded.

"In the past few days I've become closer and more comfortable with you than anyone else in my circle of friends," he said. "What I'm trying to say is, I'm lashing out because, on some level, I know that you'll forgive me. But that's not the only reason."

The clench of her jaw softened.

"Maddie, the thought of something happening to you

because of my problems..." He hesitated before continuing, "Well, it makes me crazy, and I lash out. It's no excuse for my behavior and I am sorry. To be blunt, I don't have much experience with this type of relationship."

Spence released her wrist. He said his piece and figured she'd leave. Instead, she narrowed her eyes as if assessing his confession.

Finally she said, "Nate hired you a bodyguard. His name is Adam and he'll take us back to the resort."

That's it? Spence thought. He'd bared his soul to her, admitted that he felt closer to her than anyone else in his life, and all she could say was a bodyguard would take them back to Echo Mountain?

His heart sank. The damage was done. He'd successfully driven her away and should be happy.

"Do you need help getting dressed? I can get a nurse," she said.

"No, I'll manage."

With a nod, she left the hospital room.

As the bodyguard drove them back to the resort in his SUV, Spence's words taunted Maddie.

I'm lashing out because, on some level, I know that you'll forgive me.

Had that been her problem all along? That her ability to forgive was actually a weakness that made people take advantage of her?

No, she wouldn't believe that. Her faith had taught her the importance of forgiveness and love, two things that always opened the door to grace.

Sure, she'd suffered painful relationships, but that shouldn't affect her desire to forgive others. She was strong in her faith, so something else was niggling at her thoughts on the drive back to Echo Mountain.

I don't have much experience with this type of relationship.

What kind of relationship? She wasn't sure. It was indefinable in the traditional sense. She knew private things about Spence that he'd worked so hard to keep hidden, like how his brain injury had affected his abilities after the attack, and how he blamed himself for his brother's death. He wanted to keep these things a secret, yet needed to lean on someone, trust someone.

Maddie had shown up at the right moment in the forest, and had the necessary skills to both save his life and become a confidant.

What would happen when the mystery was solved and the perpetrator was charged and locked up? Would there be a relationship between her and Spence then?

Probably not. Her goal in life was to stay grounded and fight, not run from challenges. She wondered if Spence ran from his Portland position because of his patient's death. Starting a new life with a clean slate was great in theory, but it seemed to Maddie that you brought all of your emotional baggage with you, so who's to say you wouldn't recreate the same situation in a new town?

No, Maddie wasn't running away like her parents or Waylan. She enjoyed helping people through her work as a paramedic, and volunteering at church and the homeless shelter.

Spence, on the other hand, was a professional who could land a job anywhere, and would probably head back to a big city where he belonged.

You'd better guard your heart before it gets broken, she warned herself.

"Do you want me to drop you off somewhere?" Adam the bodyguard asked, eyeing her through the rearview mirror.

"No, I'll go back to the resort with Dr. Spencer." She

glanced at Spence, whose eyes were closed. "Unless you'd rather I not come back with you?"

He didn't answer.

"Spence?"

He glanced at her. "Sorry, what?"

"I'm going to the resort with you, unless you'd rather I not."

"I—" he stuttered, "I wouldn't mind the company, if you can work it into your schedule."

She shot him a look. Wouldn't mind the company?

"I guess that sounded less than enthusiastic," he said. "I feel guilty about taking you away from your life."

She glanced at Adam. "I'll go to the resort. Can we swing by my apartment first?"

"Sure."

She gave him the address and turned back to Spence. He'd closed his eyes again.

She touched his arm. "You okay?"

"Still tired from whatever drug they gave me yesterday."

"Rest is probably the best thing."

They'd stopped by her place, she'd packed a bag and they headed for the resort. Aiden greeted them with a key to a new cabin. Nate suggested they relocate in case the assailant had seen which cabin Spence had come from last night. The general assumption was that the assailant set off the smoke device in order to draw Spence out of hiding.

Maddie and Adam were helping Spence settle into the new cabin when she finally got a callback about shift coverage. She'd made a lot of calls that morning, trying to find a sub.

"Hey, Vivian," Maddie answered. "Thanks for calling back."

"Yeah, so I'd love to take your shift, but I'm in the city and won't get back until eight. I could cover you from around nine tonight through the end of your shift tomorrow, or is that too weird?"

"No, that would be great." Maddie was pleased that she found the partial shift coverage. "Text me when you're ready to take over and we'll swing by your place to pick you up."

"Sounds good. Is Rocky on tonight?"

Maddie suspected Vivian had a crush on Maddie's friend. "He is."

"Cool. Okay, then talk to you later."

Maddie smiled. Maybe there was hope for Rocky's love life after all. She joined Spence in the living area where he was leaning back in a thick-cushioned chair, his brows furrowed.

"What's bothering you?" she said.

"They still haven't found Dr. Danner."

"Yeah, that's weird. I mean, how is he involved in all this?"

Spence shook his head.

"Where's your bodyguard?" she asked.

"Adam is outside checking the grounds for—" he made quotes with his fingers "—vulnerabilities."

"He seems professional. Well, I was able to get most of my shift covered."

"I don't think that's a good idea."

"What, taking time off?"

"Going out in public. You're safer here, with me and Adam, or at Bree's or even your Aunt Margaret's farm."

"Whoa, slow down. I'm not the one they're after, remember?"

"You're a part of this now, Maddie."

"I'll be safe at the firehouse. Chances are we won't even be called out during the first six hours of the shift. Besides, the cops in town have the sketch of the bearded guy so they'll be on the lookout."

"I think you should call Nate."

"I'm sure he has more important things on his plate." She could tell Spence was worried. "Okay, I'll let him know I'll be on shift from three to nine."

"Good." He stood and walked to the kitchen counter. "I've decided it's time for me to stop being so passive."

"Passive? You've been injured multiple times. That's not being passive."

"Regardless, I'm done being terrorized. And now they've got Dr. Danner?"

"We don't know that for sure."

"I need to put a stop to this, protect myself, and you."

"You're still recovering. Maybe you should take it easy."

"I'm done taking it easy." He pointed to the whiteboard. "I'm going to check people off the list one by one. I'll contact Theresa—"

"Not necessary. My aunt told me Anthony and Theresa have set a wedding date."

"Good, how about—?"

"Nate's on it. He told me at the hospital that Roger Grimes is still under investigation and there's no word about Lucas's whereabouts. Hey, I've got an idea."

"Skip work?"

"I'll be fine. So Roger Grimes is an insurance salesman, right?" she said.

"How do you know that?"

"He stopped by the firehouse to see if any of us needed life insurance. I could call him and act like I'm interested, then get him talking to get a sense of his state of mind."

"No, it's too dangerous."

"We could meet at a coffee shop. I'll have my brother sitting in the corner keeping watch."

"I feel like we'd do better by starting at the beginning, with Gwen."

"You mean visit her in the hospital?" Maddie asked.

"Yes."

"What's she going to tell you that she hasn't told Nate?"

"She trusts me." He turned to her, his blue eyes reflecting a kind of raw emotion she'd never seen before. "Like I've grown to trust you."

She wasn't sure what to say.

I don't have much experience with this type of relationship.

She was about to ask him to define their relationship so she could be on the same page, when he said, "I'm sorry if that was too forward. I haven't felt this kind of close connection to someone in a very long time."

She struggled to process her own feelings, wanting desperately to keep things professional. "I'm glad I could be there for you."

Maddie started her shift at three and by seven o'clock it looked like it was going to be a quiet evening, as she'd predicted. Sitting in the lounge at the fire station, she was reading the local paper when she came across a story about a burglary at the Winfield home.

She sat up straight. The house had been trashed, and nothing expensive had been taken, mostly food, supplies and flashlights. Stories like these sparked fear in local residents, fear that a homeless person had become desperate enough to commit a crime.

There was a homeless encampment north of town, close to a bus stop that allowed the residents to commute to work either in Echo Mountain or surrounding communities. The homeless residents Maddie had met while volunteering were good people that had fallen on hard times and needed temporary help.

As she studied the newspaper, she had another thought: Lucas could have come home and taken what he needed to survive on his own.

She pulled out her phone to share her observation with Spence. Rocky flopped down next to her.

"Thanks," he said.

"For what?" She pocketed her phone.

"Not sticking me with Wiggy."

"You're welcome. I thought you were out getting dinner."

"Let's take a drive and pick up some burgers."

She considered, wanting to keep her word to Spence about staying at the firehouse if not on a call.

"What? You want Chinese instead?" Rocky said.

"No, burgers are fine."

They got into the ambulance and headed out. Any emergency calls would be patched through to their vehicle.

"Did you hear Dr. Danner didn't show up for his shift today?" Rocky said.

"I did hear that."

"Being that you're so close to Dr. Perfect you probably know more scoop than any of us."

"We're not that close."

"Uh-huh. So what do you think happened to Danner? Went fishing and got eaten by a salmon? Got lost on a nature walk?"

"Very funny. Actually I'm wondering if he's behind the attacks on Spence and has fled the state."

"Spence?" Rocky shot her a side glance. "I thought you weren't that close."

"He wants me to call him Spence. What's the big deal?"

Rocky shook his head. "You can be so naive sometimes."

"Ambulance 64, please respond to an injured party at 890 Industrial Drive. Over."

Maddie grabbed the radio. "Ten-four, base."

Rocky flipped on the siren and they sped off. A few minutes later they pulled up to an office building under construction. It had only partial outer walls, and looked downright creepy at night.

"I didn't know these crews worked past five," she said.

"Probably kids messing around and someone got hurt."

They grabbed the equipment and headed to the stairs. "Dispatch, did they give a floor number? Over." Rocky asked.

"Fifth floor. Over."

"Service elevator?" she asked Rocky.

"I need my exercise." Rocky winked, heading for the stairs.

Maddie appreciated Rocky's lighthearted nature at times like this. It was important to balance the stress with humor when heading into a tense situation. They made it to the fifth floor.

"Echo Mountain Emergency!" Rocky called out.

A crack whistled through the air.

NINE

Maddie instinctively grabbed Rocky and pulled him to the floor.

Another crack rang out, and only then did she accept what was happening. She called in on her radio. "Dispatch, someone's shooting at us. Send help! Over!"

"Officer Carrington is on the way. Over."

"Fifth floor, tell him we're on the fifth floor. Over," Maddie said. "Red's on the way," she said to her partner.

When Rocky didn't answer she glanced at him. A bloodstain spread across his jacket.

"No, no, no," she muttered, grabbing gauze out of her bag.

"My partner's been hit," she said into her radio.

Rocky groaned and opened his eyes. "What's happening?"

"Someone's shooting at us."

"Get out of here. Go!" he ordered.

Another shot pierced the night air. Heart pounding, she knew there was no way she could leave her friend.

She also knew she might die tonight.

Without having spoken her truth to Spence.

She should have told him she'd felt it, too, an unusually close connection that scared the wits out of her because in her experience that kind of emotion was usually followed by pain.

"Man, that stings," Rocky said.

She put more pressure on his shoulder wound to stop the bleeding. "You'll be okay."

"I'll be better once you're safe."

"I'm waiting for the police." She glanced nervously over her shoulder.

"Why is he using us as target practice if we're here to help him?"

"Unless it was a trap."

"A trap?" Rocky sat up and winced.

"It might have something to do with Dr. Spencer."

He snapped his attention to her. "What are you talking about?"

"Spence didn't want me to go on shift tonight. He thought it might be dangerous, but I said I'd most likely be at the station and ignored his concern…and now, now you've been shot, because of me."

"Knock it off. None of this is your fault."

She couldn't make eye contact, ashamed that she'd put his life in danger because she hadn't taken Spence's warning seriously.

"Hey, look at me."

She slowly turned to her friend.

"Did you shoot me in the shoulder?"

"No, but—"

"No. This isn't your fault."

"Maddie McBride!" a man called out.

Rocky touched her arm. "Don't."

"What do you want?" she shouted back.

"Tell me where Dr. Spencer is and I won't hurt you."

"Are you kidding me? You shot my partner! Police are on the way!"

"They won't get here in time." His voice seemed closer.

Her pulse raced. They had to get out of here. She

gripped Rocky's uninjured arm and whispered, "Let's move."

With a nod, Rocky stood. She shouldered the medical supplies bag and they stayed low.

"It's a simple question!" the assailant yelled.

And if she gave the answer, Spence would be assaulted again, plus the shooter would have no reason to keep her and Rocky alive.

"Ambulance 64," dispatch called over the radio. She turned down the volume so it wouldn't make them easy targets. Then she realized the shooter probably figured they would head for the service elevator.

"Stairs," she whispered to Rocky. She hoped he could manage the stairs in his condition.

With his uninjured arm around her shoulder, they passed the elevator and turned a corner.

Another shot rang out.

Maddie pulled Rocky down again.

She heard the stairwell door swing open a few feet away.

Two more shots were fired.

She held her breath. Prayed.

"Are you hurt?" It was her brother's voice.

She snapped her eyes open and saw him standing over her, his gaze focused beyond them.

"I'm okay," she said.

Officer Carrington burst through the stairwell door, gun drawn.

"That way." Ryan motioned and crouched beside Maddie.

Red took off in pursuit of the shooter.

"Ryan? I… I…" Her voice caught in her throat.

"You did good, sis." Ryan kept his hand on his firearm and his gaze focused in the direction of the shooter.

"Did you hit him?" she asked.

"Not sure. How's Rocky?"

"A little bloody, but I'll live," Rocky said. "You guys got here fast."

"Dr. Spencer called the chief, worried about Maddie being on shift tonight, so I've been monitoring your calls. Got here as soon as I could."

"Stop! Police!" Red's voice echoed.

More shots rang out and she automatically ducked. A few seconds later, her brother squeezed her shoulder. She glanced up as Red approached them. "I think you hit him," Red said to Ryan. "He was limping to his car down below. He took off in a small SUV. I'll call in the description." Red spoke into his radio.

Maddie suddenly realized her brother was not in uniform. "Wait, you're off duty."

He smiled. "Never off duty for family."

A sense of dread awakened Spence. He shouldn't have napped after dinner, but his sleep schedule was off because of the drug working its way through his system.

Well, that and the constant worry that Maddie was in trouble.

He went into the living room and was greeted by Adam, who sat at the kitchen table. "Good nap?"

"Sure, I guess." Spence eyed the microwave clock. It was nearly nine, which meant Maddie's sub would already be there to relieve her. Spence hoped Maddie would return to his cabin, at least to let him know she was okay. A text or phone call would satisfy some people, but he always felt better when he saw her in person.

A firm knock echoed across the cabin.

Adam went to answer it. "Stay out of sight, Doc."

Spence went into the kitchen where he couldn't be seen from the door.

"Yes?" Adam asked.

"It's Nate."

Adam let him inside and Spence stepped out of hiding. "I didn't expect you to see you tonight unless... What happened?"

"Adam, can you give us a few minutes?"

"Sure." With a nod, Adam left, shutting the door with a click.

"What is it?" Spence pressed.

"Let's sit down."

"Tell me she's okay."

"She's okay."

Relieved, Spence went to the sofa and collapsed. Nate sat in a chair on the other side of the coffee table.

"They got a false call and someone was waiting," Nate said.

"The guy from the mountains?"

"We don't know for sure."

"What happened? Did he hurt her?" Spence fisted his hand.

"He fired at them—"

"But she's okay?"

"Yes."

"That's why I told her not to go to work. I was afraid something like this would happen because of this mess I'm in. And I'm ending it. I'm going down the checklist one by one and scratching off these so-called enemies before she gets seriously hurt."

"This is why I came by to talk to you, because I knew it would make you crazy."

"Of course I am. Wouldn't you be crazy if it was Cassie?" Nate narrowed his eyes at Spence.

"You're sure she's not hurt?" Spence redirected.

"Not physically, but tonight will be hard to forget. Her partner, Rocky, was shot."

"Why? Why shoot at either of them?"

Nate glanced at the Echo Mountain PD hat he clutched between his fingers.

"Nate?"

"He wanted your location."

"Great, just great. Tell me you caught the guy."

"He got away, but was shot. I alerted the hospitals. It's just a matter of time before he shows up needing medical attention."

Spence leaned back against the sofa. "So, it's almost over."

"I'd like to think that, too, but…"

"But what?"

"You didn't recognize him when he broke into your cabin, right?"

"I'd never seen him before."

"I doubt a complete stranger would try to kill you multiple times, and shoot at two paramedics to get your location without a good motivation."

"Meaning what?"

"He was hired by someone."

"You're saying he's a hit man?"

"Yes, but not a very good one. I think he's an amateur, or small-time criminal, which means we'll catch him."

"Maddie and I will help expedite the process."

"No, I want you to take it easy."

"I can't. Not until I know Maddie is completely out of danger."

"Maddie? What about you?"

"If something happens to me, it happens. But if anything were to happen to Maddie…" His voice trailed off.

"Spence, this thing between you and Maddie—"

"I like her, Nate. A lot."

A knock was followed by Adam cracking open the door. "Someone wants to see you, Dr. Spencer."

Adam stepped aside and Maddie entered the cabin.

Spence couldn't control the rush of relief at seeing her beautiful face. In three steps he crossed the room and held her in his arms. It felt so natural, like he'd been hugging her for most of his life.

Then he worried that the embrace was making her uncomfortable.

Breaking the hug, he looked into her eyes. "You're okay," is all he could say.

She nodded, and hugged him again.

The next morning Spence awoke with a sense of peace and his headache was finally gone. Maddie had spent an hour with him last night, relaxing in front of the fire. He encouraged her to talk about what had happened—the fear and the adrenaline rush of being shot at—to help her process the traumatic experience.

Then her brother showed up and escorted her across the resort compound to her cousin Bree's cottage. The cottage had a state-of-the-art alarm system and her brother would stay on the premises to keep watch, as well.

Although the assailant had been shot, they didn't know how seriously he'd been injured and feared he might continue his quest to come after Spence and Maddie.

Frustrated, Spence knew what he had to do: stop being a victim and take more aggressive action. He got dressed and opened his bedroom door, half-hoping he'd find Maddie sitting at the kitchen table. Instead, he was alone.

He spotted a note on the refrigerator from Adam explaining he was outside on the porch getting some air if Spence needed him.

What Spence needed was to feel better and put an end to this deadly drama.

He also needed Maddie.

He *needed* her? How had that happened?

Spence brewed tea and glanced out the kitchen window.

The sun shone in such contrast to the murky dread hovering at the recesses of his brain.

Dread, frustration, helplessness.

Maybe he should have another MRI to see if the swelling had increased because these weren't typical feelings for Spence. He was generally content, as long as he was working.

Work withdrawal could be causing him to feel anxious, well that and the thought he'd almost lost Maddie. He clenched his jaw. She was an innocent in all this, responding to a SAR call in the mountains and saving his life. He couldn't thank her enough.

He wondered if he was so drawn to her because she took care of him without judgment or criticism, and graciously put up with his mood swings.

He remembered the look on his parents' faces after Bobby's death, their expression of disappointment and disgust. It followed him throughout his life.

The cabin door opened and he turned with a smile, hoping to see Maddie. Adam poked his head inside. "Bree wanted to drop off some food."

"Great, thanks, Adam," Spence said.

"I'm staying out here for a little while longer," Adam said.

Spence couldn't blame him. Being inside all the time was starting to drive Spence crazy.

Maddie's cousin Bree entered the cabin carrying a large bag.

"Thanks for the food, Bree," Spence said.

She slid it onto the counter. "Of course."

"How's Maddie?"

"You mean, where's Maddie?" She raised an eyebrow, opened the refrigerator and started loading it with food. "She's still asleep. Ryan will keep watch until I get back.

I suspect she'll want to come over and share some of this food. Mom made most of it."

"I'm very grateful to your entire family."

She shut the refrigerator door. "Then how about doing something for us?"

"Sure, anything."

She folded her paper bag with delicate precision. "It's about Maddie."

"What about her?"

"This is going to sound corny but—" she sighed "—be careful with her. She seems tough but she's been hurt, a lot. And before you say anything about me misreading things—"

"I wasn't going to say that."

"So you admit there's something going on between you two?"

He glanced at the sofa where Maddie had leaned against his chest last night as they watched the fire.

"Yes, there's something," he said.

"I don't want this to sound disrespectful, I mean my brother thinks highly of you, as does the chief…"

"But?"

"I always got the feeling this was a temporary stop for you, that after a few years you'd move back to the city and a more prestigious medical practice. What I'm saying is, if you don't think you'll take this thing with Maddie to the end, then stop right now. Don't let her come over and take care of you. She's got such a big heart and she's been hurt by people who supposedly loved her."

"I would never intentionally hurt her."

"I'm sure you wouldn't, but I know my cousin. She'd do anything for someone she cared deeply about, even at her own expense."

Bree slipped the bag under her arm and started for the

door. "Sorry if this conversation made you uncomfortable, but I'm protective of my cousin."

"I know the feeling."

"But was I right? About you wanting to move on after Echo Mountain?"

"It's a possibility, yes."

She turned to him. "That's too bad. I just don't see Maddie going anywhere. She loves her family and community too much to leave."

As she opened the door, Maddie and Ryan stepped onto the porch.

"What are you doing here?" Maddie said with a curious expression.

"Delivering food from Mom," Bree said. "I'd better get to work."

Maddie and Ryan came inside and joined Spence at the kitchen table.

"Any word on the guy who was shot last night?" Spence asked Ryan.

"He hasn't shown up in any area ERs yet, but we found the vehicle abandoned in a shopping center parking lot. It's registered to someone named Alex Moors. You know him?"

"The name is not familiar."

"Maybe he was a patient, either here or in Portland?" Maddie suggested.

"I'll look into it," Ryan said.

"Actually, let me," Spence offered. "I can make some calls to my former employer and determine if he was one of my patients."

"That'd be great." Ryan glanced at his sister. "Don't go anywhere alone. It's easier for us if you two stay together, under Adam's protection."

"Sounds good," Maddie said.

"Text if you need anything."

"I will. Thanks, Ryan." She hugged her brother and he left. She smiled at Spence, "So, you ready to get to work?"

"Oh yeah."

"What's first?"

"First, you tell me you slept okay."

"I'm famished." She went to the refrigerator.

"I'm sorry," he said, assuming she'd evaded the question because he wouldn't like the answer. "Did you sleep at all?"

"Here and there, and in between I'd pray."

"Pray?"

"I'd say prayers of gratitude that I wasn't hurt, that Rocky wasn't seriously hurt, that my brother wasn't shot by the creep, all that stuff."

She shut the refrigerator, holding a plastic container in her hand. "You ever have eggs baked in ham cups? They're yummy."

Bree's words taunted him. *If you don't think you'll take this thing with Maddie to the end, then stop right now.*

He should shut down the relationship brewing between them because he didn't know where his career would take him. He was a drifter, a nomad who didn't feel connected to any specific place, whereas Maddie belonged in Echo Mountain with her family.

"I've made a decision," he said.

Maddie slowly placed the container on the table. "That sounds serious."

"It's about us."

Maddie's eyes widened and she gripped the back of a chair as if bracing herself.

He struggled to form the words. It would start with an apology for all the violence he'd brought into her life. He opened his mouth, but nothing came out.

"Well, you're not down on one knee so you're not about

to propose," she teased. "Let's see what else could it be?" She eyed the plastic container. "You hate ham cups?"

"I don't want you to get hurt."

"That makes two of us. Let's have breakfast."

"I should be telling you to leave."

"What, and miss my aunt's cooking?"

"You're teasing but I'm trying to be serious."

"I know, it's just…" She sighed. "There's so much serious stuff going on right now. Can't we just take it easy and enjoy a nice meal together?"

He sighed. "Sure."

After a hearty breakfast, Spence contacted the Portland hospital but there was no record of an Alex Moors having been treated there.

He decided to visit Gwen at the hospital and while he was there, inquire about Alex Moors. Perhaps if Ruth saw Spence fully functional, it would give her confidence that his condition was improving.

Maddie would go with him, and they'd keep Nate and her brother in the loop.

Spence was impressed by bodyguard Adam's ability to catalog each and every person in their immediate surroundings to assess danger. They made it to the hospital shortly after lunch. Maddie bought a colorful plant from the hospital gift shop for Gwen.

Since Spence had a relationship, make that a friendship, with Theresa in Billing, he decided to check with her to see if there was a patient record for Alex Moors.

Maddie waited outside the office. Spence wondered if she was uncomfortable because he'd told her that Theresa might have a crush on him. Or could Maddie be jealous?

"Hey, Theresa," Spence said, entering her office.

She glanced up from her computer screen with pleasant

surprise. "Dr. Spencer." She stood to greet him. "I heard what happened. We were all so worried."

"I'm doing better thanks. I was wondering if you could do me a favor."

"Sure, anything."

"Can you check to see if there's ever been a patient at Echo Mountain Hospital named Alex Moors?"

"Of course. Who is he?" She tapped on her keyboard.

"We're not sure, possibly the man who's been threatening me."

Her fingers froze on the keyboard. She glanced up with concerned brown eyes. "I'm so sorry you're dealing with all this."

"Thanks. The sooner we figure out who's orchestrating the attacks, the sooner I can put it behind me."

She redirected her attention to the screen. "Let's see, Montlake… Muir. No Moors." She glanced up. "Sorry."

"Ah well, it was a long shot."

She came around to the front of her desk. "Be careful." She gave him a hug and he politely returned the gesture.

"Excuse me," a male voice said.

Theresa released Spence. A furious-looking Anthony stood inside the office clenching reddened fists by his sides. The man looked ready to explode.

"I'd appreciate it if you'd keep your hands off my fiancée," Anthony said.

"Cool it, Anthony," Theresa said, sitting behind her desk. "Dr. Spencer's been through a lot."

Spence nodded at Anthony. "Congratulations on your engagement. I heard you set a date."

The thirtysomething man glared at Spence.

"Ready, Dr. Spencer?" Maddie said from the doorway.

With a nod, Spence joined Maddie. Anthony shut the door behind them.

"Yikes, that was awkward," Maddie said.

"He's possessive."

"A control freak like that would drive me batty."

"At any rate, there's no record of an Alex Moors," Spence said.

"Huh, so he wasn't a patient," Maddie said.

"Doesn't look like it."

They approached Gwen's hospital room and Maddie touched his jacket sleeve. "You sure I should go in with you? Maybe she'd feel better talking to you alone."

"You helped save her life. I think she'd find comfort in seeing you." Spence motioned Maddie into the room. "Knock, knock."

Gwen's mother, Allison, helped her daughter sit up in bed.

"Dr. Spencer, hi," Gwen said.

Spence noted that her color looked much better than when he'd found her.

Maddie offered Gwen the colorful plant. "This is for you."

Gwen cast a wary glance at Maddie.

"Not sure if you remember Maddie McBride, but she helped me save your life up in the mountains," Spence said.

Her mom took the plant. "Gwen, what do you say?"

"Thanks."

Gwen's mom placed the plant on the window ledge next to half a dozen other arrangements. She turned back to Maddie and Spence. "I can't thank you enough for what you've done for Gwen."

"Of course," Maddie said.

"Do you think Gwen will be released soon, Doctor?" Allison asked.

"Actually, I'm off the rotation for a while," Spence said.

"Why?" Gwen asked, hugging her midsection.

"Recovering from brain trauma," he said, not wanting to share the other reason. "I'm sure Dr. Carver will release you as soon as she thinks it's appropriate. I was wondering if you'd be up to discussing what happened the other day in the mountains."

Gwen shrugged. "Sure, I guess."

"Is it okay with your mom?" Spence asked.

Allison nodded. "Of course."

"I heard you lost your phone and went looking for it by using an app," Spence started.

"Borrowed Mom's phone."

"Without my permission," Allison added.

"I said I was sorry."

"You're right, you did."

Gwen pouted for a second, then continued. "I hiked into the mountains, thinking I'd left it up there."

"So you've been to that location before?" Spence said.

"Me and my friends go up there sometimes to hang out."

"And smoke pot," her mom offered.

"Mom!" Gwen said.

Allison sighed. "I'm going to get a cup of coffee."

"I'll go with you," Maddie said.

The women left Gwen's room and she sighed. "Nothing I do makes her happy."

"She loves you. She's worried about you."

"Whatever."

Spence pulled up a chair. "So, you went looking for your phone," he prompted.

"The app said I found it, but all I saw was this guy lying on the ground. At first I thought he was hurt or something. I said, 'Hey, you okay?' He stood up and was wearing this creepy ski mask. I totally freaked and ran, but he caught me and threw me down. That's all I remember."

"That must have been terrifying. I'm sorry."

"I'm glad you were there. Why were you there, anyway?"

"I got a text from your phone asking for help."

"But I didn't have my phone."

"We'll let the police figure that part out."

She nodded, thoughtful. "I wonder if this has something to do with Wicker."

"Who?"

"A guy who hangs out with us, that's his nickname. He's older, in his twenties. He gets us pills sometimes."

"Did you give his name to Police Chief Walsh?"

She shook her head.

"Why not?"

"I don't want to get anyone in trouble."

"It's Wicker's choice to sell drugs to minors, not yours. If he's older he should know better, right?"

"I guess."

"Dr. Spencer?" a man said.

Spence turned to see Vince Brunson, board president, standing in the doorway. "Hi, Mr. Brunson."

"I thought you were on leave."

"I am, just checking on my favorite patient."

"I was under the impression you're in no condition to be treating patients."

"I'm not here in an official capacity."

Ruth brushed past Brunson and entered the room. "Spence," she said with surprise in her voice. "I didn't expect to see you."

"Dr. Carver, I'm not sure it's a good idea for a staff member with a brain injury—"

"As I said, this isn't an official visit," Spence interrupted.

Brunson sighed, shook his head and left.

"What's his problem?" Spence muttered.

"You want the full list?" Ruth winked, then turned to Gwen. "How are you doing today?"

"Better. Throat's sore."

"From the tube. A good thing it wasn't a serious injury, and you could breathe on your own," Ruth said.

"When can I go home?" Gwen asked.

Ruth consulted her tablet. "Don't you like the food here?" she teased.

"Orange Jell-O has never been my favorite."

"What then, red or purple?" Ruth asked. "We don't want to discharge you too soon."

Gwen released a deep sigh.

"And after you're released I hope we don't see you back here anytime soon." Ruth winked.

"I think this experience has scared Gwen enough to stay out of trouble until she goes to college next fall," Spence said.

"If I get into college," she muttered.

"I can help with that," Spence said. "I aced my SATs."

"Yeah, but you're a doctor. You're brilliant."

"I work at it." He winked.

He glanced at Ruth, who suddenly seemed distracted. "Ruth?" he questioned.

"Where's your mother?" Ruth asked Gwen.

"Getting coffee with Maddie."

"Can you have her find me when she returns?"

"Why? Is something wrong?" Gwen's eyes widened.

"No, everything's fine. I'd like to go over your care instructions for when you go home."

"See, she's talking discharge." Spence patted Gwen's shoulder. "I need to speak with Dr. Carver for a minute."

Spence motioned Ruth out of the room. Once in the hallway and out of earshot, Spence turned to his friend. "What is it? Are her injuries more serious than you've let on?"

"No, that's not it." Ruth sighed, hugging her tablet to her chest. "The ER is swamped. I'm down two doctors and we're barely able to keep up. If there's a big emergency we'll have to send patients to Cedar River, which could potentially affect our reputation and maybe even our rating."

"It's about serving the people we can serve."

"I know, but the board is on my back to keep our numbers competitive."

"You can't control what's happened to me, or Dr. Danner's mysterious absence."

"I don't feel like I can control anything lately. Ah well, thanks for the shoulder."

"I'm feeling better. Do you want to reconsider me for the rotation?"

"Have you resolved who's after you?"

"No, but —"

"Oh, Spence." She placed a hand on his arm. "You're a dear, but the last thing I need is for your trouble to follow you here and put patients at risk. If you were thinking clearly you wouldn't have asked, can't you see that?"

"I was just trying to help."

"I know, and I appreciate it. But it would be best to keep your distance from the hospital until this settles down."

He nodded and she offered a kind smile. "Are you still staying at the resort?"

"Yes."

"Good, be safe."

Maddie and Allison approached them.

"Mrs. Taylor, I'd like to talk to you about how to care for your daughter once she's released." Ruth led Allison back into Gwen's room.

"How'd your talk go with Gwen?" Maddie asked.

"Good."

"You're not convincing me."

"Something she said is bothering me."

"What?"

"Why would the guy feel the need to hurt Gwen if his face was covered by the mask?"

"Where are you going with this?"

"Maybe she knew him, but isn't able to identify him. Perhaps one of her criminal friends who's dealing drugs. But why kill me?"

"He was afraid Gwen would break down and reveal his identity to you?"

"Scary thought. I should let Nate know she might not be safe." Spence pulled out his phone and spotted a text message from Danner.

Meet me @ Crescent Falls. Alone. Or people will die.

TEN

Maddie didn't like any of this—the mysterious text from the arrogant doctor, Spence's decision to meet him, or the police department's strategy to stick close and listen through the small radio device Spence kept in his pocket.

Spence was hopeful this would help the investigation, that Danner had critical information about the case.

"You're sure you're up to this?" Nate asked Spence.

"Yes."

Nate eyed Maddie in the rearview mirror for confirmation. She shrugged.

"Guys, it's not like we have much of a choice here, right?" Spence said.

"I could send Ryan up there dressed in your coat and hat."

"I appreciate your concern, Nate, but we need information in order to move this case along, and I doubt Danner is going to share it with the police, especially if he's into something criminal. I'm not sure you guys following me up there is a good idea, either."

"As opposed to you going out there on your own?" Nate snapped. "No, this is the best plan. You were right to contact us for backup."

Actually, it had been Maddie who demanded Spence get support from the police, even though he resisted. Danner wanted Spence to come alone, but Maddie wouldn't allow it. She didn't trust Danner, nor was she sure Spence was in the best mental or physical condition to handle this on his own.

"Officer McBride and I will position ourselves to watch the interaction," Nate said. "If something feels off, we'll jump in to help."

"What could go wrong?" Spence said. "He wants to talk to me, that's all."

Ryan glanced over the front seat. "Then why did he mysteriously disappear without an explanation?"

"He's right, Spence," Maddie said. "We don't know what's really going on, or how Danner is involved."

Spence glanced across Maddie at the bodyguard on the other side of her. "Adam, keep her safe."

"I will, sir."

Spence didn't look convinced, concern creasing his features. She placed her hand over his, interlacing their fingers. He looked into her eyes.

"I'll be fine," she said. "Especially if I know you're focused, you're being careful and you're not taking any chances, okay?"

"Yes, ma'am."

They pulled up to the trailhead and the men grabbed their gear.

"It won't be dark for another three hours," Nate said. "Let's wrap this up before nightfall." He and Ryan started for the trail, but Spence turned to Maddie.

His expression of determination mixed with regret tore at her insides. She wrapped her arms around him and gave him a hug for encouragement. When she released him, he tipped her chin to look into his eyes.

"I… You…" she said, wanting to admit to Spence, as he had to her yesterday, that she felt a close connection to him, as well.

"I'll be fine," he said.

He brushed a quick kiss against her lips, turned and marched toward the trail. When Ryan raised an eyebrow, Maddie crossed her arms over her chest. "Don't let anything happen to him," she said to her big brother.

Ryan offered a mock salute. He and Nate followed Spence, the three men disappearing from view.

Lord, please protect him.

She hadn't been able to confess her true feelings, and he was gone again, heading into a potentially dangerous situation.

"Let's get in the car," Adam said.

She climbed into the backseat and shut the door. What was the matter with her? What kind of coward would keep such blessed feelings to herself?

Someone who knew once you spoke the words, you couldn't take them back. You couldn't edit or revise them once they were out in the open. Yet deep down she worried that these feelings were born from this tumultuous situation, that perhaps this wasn't true love, this wasn't...

Oh, stop lying to yourself.

These feelings were real, and she feared the pain that would follow if she opened her heart completely to this complicated man.

Adam joined her in the car and shut the door. "They'll be okay."

She nodded, once again using the power of prayer to calm her fears.

Spence hadn't been completely honest with Nate, Ryan or Maddie, or he would have told them he wasn't functioning at his usual 120 percent. Today his energy level was more like 70 percent. Not good. Yet he'd just offered to get back on the rotation. Maybe Ruth was right about him not thinking clearly.

About a quarter of a mile from the falls, Nate and Ryan veered off and took another trail that would place them above the rendezvous point.

Spence's head had started aching a few minutes ago, and his breathing felt more labored than usual. He reminded himself he couldn't be expected to hike at his peak performance, not after everything that had happened over the past few days, starting with the knock to his head that left him struggling with intermittent anxiety and confusion.

Yet he wasn't confused about his feelings for Maddie. Or was that part of the brain trauma? He knew such injuries could cause a patient's personality to change, that his way of thinking could have shifted, opening up his heart to the possibility of love and a life partner. If that was the case, could it shift back? Could he wake up one day and decide love was too dangerous to take a chance on?

Spence snapped his attention to the present. Maddie had asked him to stay focused and not take any chances. Well, he'd failed on the first count, as runaway thoughts about Maddie distracted him from the goal: find Danner and get information that could help put an end to the threat on his life, and her life.

As he approached the last switchback before he'd reach Crescent Falls, Spence sensed someone was watching him. He scanned the surrounding area, and his gaze landed briefly on Nate, who offered a thumbs-up from above. Spence ripped his gaze from his friend and continued on. Almost there.

The air was fresh and damp, the intensity of the falls pounding on rocks around the corner. He made the turn.

His breath caught at the sight of the powerful falls. He allowed himself to be enamored with the beauty of nature for a few seconds as he continued to the rocky shore that led to the massive body of water at the bottom of the falls.

He redirected his attention to his surroundings, doing a three-sixty scan of the area, looking for his colleague. He stopped himself from glancing at Nate in case Danner was watching from a hidden spot.

"Danner!" Spence called out, his voice echoing back at him.

As he gazed across the water, he noticed a splash of red on the rocks up ahead.

A body.

Instinct kicked in and Spence broke into a sprint. The spray from the falls showered him as he got closer to the victim. Someone—maybe Danner—was hurt and Spence could help. He reached the body and slowly turned it over.

Bill Danner.

Spence felt for a pulse. Rapid and shallow. Spence squinted in the direction of his police backup, and motioned for help.

Then he heard a click.

He turned back to Danner, who was pointing a gun at Spence's chest. "Who came with you?"

Spence raised his hands. "It's okay, they're here to help. I'm here to help. What's going on?"

Danner got to his feet and winced, clutching his side. His face went white.

"You're hurt. What happened?" Spence said.

"Like you don't know?"

Blood stained Danner's jacket.

"Bill, come on, let me help you."

Danner flicked the gun sideways.

"Put the gun down," Spence said.

"Move!" Danner threatened.

He was seriously injured and acting irrationally. Spence did as ordered, hoping to talk the guy into surrendering the gun.

Danner motioned Spence up a trail that led to a plateau beneath the falls. If not for the dangerous situation it would be a breathtaking spot, so close to the powerful falls as water cascaded from above to hit the small lake below.

Danner shoved at Spence from behind, and he almost went over, but fell to the ground instead.

"Why did you set me up?" Danner said.

Spence got to his feet. "What are you talking about?"

"Don't play innocent, Dr. Perfect. It had to be you."

"Bill, calm down, let's talk about this."

"Like you talked to the feds?"

"William Danner! Drop your weapon!" Nate called. He and Ryan were following them up the trail.

Danner didn't take his eyes off Spence. Heart pounding, Spence thought this was it, the guy was out of his mind and was going to shoot him in cold blood, in front of authorities.

"I'm not going to jail for something I didn't do!" Danner shouted, his voice competing with the pounding of the falls.

"Put down the gun and we'll figure this out," Spence pleaded.

"Last warning!" Nate called.

As Danner cast a nervous glance over his shoulder at Nate, Spence lunged for the gun.

They struggled, Danner weakened by whatever injury he'd sustained. Spence ripped the gun out of Danner's hand and he stumbled backward, falling into the water below.

Spence dropped the gun and ripped off his jacket, ready to jump in after him.

"No!" Nate suddenly blocked him. "Officer McBride, go!"

Ryan ripped off his backpack and jacket, shucked his boots and dived into the water.

"I didn't mean for him to fall," Spence said.

"I know." Nate called into his radio for a search-and-rescue team.

Ryan's head bobbed up above the waterline, then disappeared again as he searched for Bill Danner.

"He was injured before he went in," Spence said. "He's not going to be able to pull himself up."

"Calm down, buddy," Nate said. "Ryan's done rescue work like this before. Why was Danner threatening you with a gun?"

Spence shook his head. "He accused me of setting him up, said I talked to the feds. About what? What was he into?"

Ryan popped his head up above the surface. He had his arm around Danner's chest and was pulling him toward the shore. Nate and Spence rushed down the trail and helped lift him out of the water.

"Let's start resuscitation," Spence said.

They took turns giving Danner mouth-to-mouth and doing chest compressions. Spence finally found a consistent pulse. "Got it," he said. "How long until SAR gets here?"

"Twenty to thirty minutes," Ryan said.

"Let's keep him warm and monitor his pulse," Spence said.

He wasn't going to let him die. He couldn't let him die.

"Spence," Nate said.

Spence glanced at him.

"Good work."

"But—"

"I saw what happened. It wasn't your fault."

Maddie had hoped for quick and easy resolution to whatever drama Dr. Danner was involved in. But when SAR team members starting showing up at the trailhead her hopes were destroyed.

She flung open the car door.

"Maddie, wait—"

She shut the door on Adam's protest and rushed to the first SAR member she knew, fireman Sam Treadwell. "What's going on?"

"Got a call for an injured male by the falls."

"Who is it?"

"I don't know. Gotta go."

"Really?" she said to herself. "I'm going to slug my brother."

"Why are you upset with your brother?" Adam asked, now standing beside her.

"He should tell us who needs rescuing."

"Come back to the car and I'll find out."

She nodded and went back to the SUV. Adam stayed outside, speaking into his radio.

Anger seemed like the better option right now because if she believed it was Spence who'd been injured, that might ignite a ball of grief in her chest that would consume her.

Ryan obviously knew how she felt about Spence after the very public kiss they shared. Why hadn't he notified Adam who'd been hurt? Unless it was Spence?

That was it. Spence had been seriously hurt and Ryan needed to tell her in person.

Adam opened the car door and handed her the radio. "He wants to talk to you."

She snatched the radio. "Ryan, I'm going to—"

"Maddie, it's Spence."

Emotion clogged her throat.

"Maddie?" he said.

"I'm here. Tell me you're okay."

"I'm okay."

But there was something odd in his voice. "Why did you call SAR?" Then panic struck her. "Is Ryan…?"

"Your brother's okay, too. The SAR call was for Dr. Danner. We'll be down as soon as we can."

"Thanks. I'm—"

"Maddie, put Adam on," Nate ordered.

Handing the radio to her bodyguard, she closed her eyes and let relief wash over her. She hadn't realized how tense she was, how close to completely falling apart.

A fleeting thought touched her consciousness—if this raw fear was what it felt like when potentially losing the man you loved, could she embrace love again?

Although Nate tried to get Spence and Maddie to go back to the cabin on resort property, Spence refused. He said he was done hiding from his troubles, and he was going to wait at Cedar River Hospital for news on Dr. Danner's condition.

Maddie chose to stay with him for emotional support. She could tell something intense happened at the falls, even if he wasn't ready to share the details.

Nate arranged for Maddie and Spence to wait in the doctors' lounge, a less conspicuous spot. As Spence paced from the soda machine to the refrigerator across the room, Maddie tried to come up with the right words to calm him down.

She struggled to figure out what was causing the anxiety: guilt or frustration? Or a little of both? Whatever it was, it could affect his recovery and she could no longer sit by and watch him stress out.

Relying on humor, she stood and bumped into him as he paced across the room.

"Excuse me," she said.

He tried stepping around her, but she blocked him again, and again.

"Excuse me, excuse me," she said.

"Maddie."

"Spence?"

"Why are you pestering me?"

"Because you need to chill out, Doc. You're giving me whiplash. Now sit down and talk to me." She took his hand, surprised he didn't pull away, and led him to a small sofa. They sat, but she didn't release him. "Dr. Danner will be okay, right?"

"I'm not sure."

"You and Nate resuscitated him?"

"Yes, but he was hurt before he went in the water."

"Hurt, how?"

"He seemed to be in extreme pain, had a puncture wound and he was acting irrationally." He started to get up.

She squeezed his hand. "Please stay here with me."

He leaned back against the sofa. "I'm hoping something he said can help authorities figure this out."

"What did he say?"

"He accused me of setting him up. I have no idea what he was talking about."

The door opened and Nate joined them. "Anything on Danner?"

"Nothing yet," Spence said.

"We found Alex Moors. Someone stole his truck yesterday so he wasn't the one shooting at Maddie and Rocky."

"Has the shooter been treated for a gunshot wound at area hospitals?" Spence asked.

"Neither Cedar River nor Echo Mountain Hospital have treated a gunshot victim."

"So he's still out there," Spence said.

"Do you think he died of blood loss and is lying on the side of the road somewhere?" Maddie asked.

"That would be a relief," Spence muttered, then glanced at Maddie. "Sorry, that was inappropriate."

"You're frustrated. We get it," Maddie offered.

"Detective Vaughn is investigating Danner's bank records, phone records, the works. We need to figure out why he thinks you set him up. What happened tonight has given us another piece of the puzzle."

"And what's that?" Spence said.

"There's something going on, maybe criminal, and Danner thinks you're involved. That could be why someone wants you out of the way, because they also assume you're involved. I need you to think, Spence. Try to remember anything strange or out of the ordinary that happened to you in the last month or so."

Spence shook his head, obviously frustrated. "Just the threatening emails."

"Did you find out who sent them, Chief?" Maddie asked.

"Not yet. IP address was the coffee shop in town. I'd prefer you go back to the resort instead of hanging around the hospital."

"We will, after we get word about Danner," Spence said.

The door opened and a nurse poked her head inside the lounge. "Dr. Spencer? The patient is asking for you. He's…" She hesitated. "He may not make it. Internal injuries."

Spence went to the door and Maddie followed him. Nate and Adam stayed close as the nurse led them to the ER area where they were treating Dr. Danner. Maddie feared Spence would blame himself for Danner's death.

"I can't let all of you in," the nurse said.

"We'll be right outside," Nate said to Spence.

Maddie touched Spence's arm, wanting to offer support, but it was like he didn't even feel it, like he was numb.

The nurse opened the door. The doctor treating Dr. Danner looked up at Spence. "I'm sorry. He's gone."

Spence wasn't sure what frustrated him more, the death of a colleague or the possibility that the death was related to whoever was out to kill Spence.

The worst part was seeing people get seriously hurt or die as collateral damage. This was Spence's fault because of something he'd seen or heard or knew, and someone wanted him dead.

Someone who didn't care if others got in the way like Gwen, Rocky and now Bill Danner.

Everyone was quiet on the ride back to the resort, especially Maddie. He could only imagine what she was thinking, something along the lines of "how did I get myself into this mess?"

The situation was getting worse instead of better, and Spence felt even more helpless than when he'd first been attacked in the mountains.

"Do you think it has something to do with the hospital?" Maddie suddenly said.

"Why do you say that?" Spence asked.

"Dr. Danner accused you of setting him up, yet the only thing you have in common is your work, right?"

"True, we weren't exactly friends outside of the job."

"Then maybe that's where we need to start. Something that happened at work involving the two of you."

Nate glanced over his shoulder into the backseat. "Did a patient die or sue the hospital?"

"We haven't had a patient die in the ER since I've been here. As far as lawsuits, there haven't been any filed against me."

Nate nodded and turned back to look out the front window. Adam drove and continued to scan the mirrors.

"We'll figure it out," Maddie said, placing her hand over Spence's, which rested on his thigh.

"Am I dropping you off at your aunt's farm or the cottage?" Adam asked Maddie.

"Take me back to Spence's cottage. We've got work to do."

Nate glanced over his shoulder again. "Like what?"

"A little research, nothing dangerous."

"Research?" Spence said.

"I'd like to try a relaxation technique to help you remember things."

"I don't understand," Spence said.

"You've been under a lot of stress. When we're stressed out, we can't focus clearly on things that should have raised red flags but we've brushed them aside because of our stress."

"You're going to hypnotize him?" Nate said.

"No, nothing like that. Look, Spence has been in fight-or-flight mode for days. His body and mind can't drift into a relaxed state, so he's unable to access important memories because he's like a Ping-Pong ball, bouncing all over the place. If you can relax the body and quiet the mind, things come to you that you don't notice when your mind's active and anxious. Does that make sense?"

"It does, but I'm not sure anything could get me to relax right now," Spence said.

"It's worth a try. Worst-case scenario is you won't remember anything, but you'll feel safe and relaxed for a few minutes."

"That would be something different."

The thought of being conscious yet feeling relaxed for even a few minutes was a foreign, but welcome thought.

When they arrived at the resort cottage, Adam had them wait in the vehicle until he gave the all clear signal. A few minutes later, he waved them inside.

"I'm getting picked up at the resort," Nate said. "You two stay safe and I'll check in tomorrow."

"You got my message about Gwen possibly being in danger?" Spence said.

"Yes. Retired Chief Washburn has offered to keep watch, both at the hospital and when she's released."

"Good," Spence said.

As Maddie and Spence approached the cabin, he couldn't help but scan the surrounding area, looking for the next threat.

"You okay?" Maddie asked as they went inside and shut the door.

"Sure, just hungry I guess."

"I'll heat something up." Maddie pulled containers out of the fridge.

Once again, Spence had a quick flash of what a home must feel like, with a lovely woman humming her way through dinner preparation.

"Have them leave it at the front desk and I'll pick it up later." Adam's voice cut through his thoughts.

"More friends are dropping off food," Adam said. "I'm not sure how we're going to keep your specific location concealed unless we continue moving you."

"Like musical cabins," Maddie joked.

How did she do that? How was she able to joke and tease when so much tension surrounded them? That's right, she derived strength from God. He wondered if her God would forgive another sinner and embrace Spence.

Spence went to the kitchen to help Maddie.

"I've got this," she said. "Why don't you relax?"

He went into the living room and checked his phone for emails. "Here's something. The Tomlin family has relocated to Florida."

"The whole family?" Maddie said.

"Apparently. The oldest son got into college down there so the mother and daughter decided to move with him."

"Florida, the other end of the country. I think we can scratch them off the list."

"Which leaves Lucas and Roger."

"That's if we stick with the original list. I'm wondering if all this is directly connected to Dr. Danner somehow, that we should focus on him. Besides, I have a hard time seeing a kid like Lucas coming after you. He always seemed like a gentle boy to me."

"People aren't always what they seem."

Maddie pulled plates out of a cabinet and slid them onto the table. "You mean, like you?"

He eyed her. "What are you implying?"

"It's just that Dr. Dreamboat's smooth charm and good mood seemed like a cover for something else."

He shot her a crooked smile. "You see right through me, don't you, Maddie McBride?"

The cabin suddenly went dark.

"What—?" Spence said.

Something crashed through the window.

ELEVEN

Spence heard a pop followed by a hiss.

"It's a smoke bomb!" Adam said.

"We need to get out of here," Spence said.

"No, that's what he wants. Lock yourself in the bedroom with Maddie! I'll get that thing outta here and neutralize the assailant."

"Maddie?" Spence said.

She held up her smartphone that lit the way. Spence wrapped his arm around her and they went into the bedroom as ordered. If Adam wasn't able to neutralize the attacker, this could go bad very quickly.

And Spence would not allow anything to happen to Maddie.

That's when he realized she was trembling. The violence of the past few days must have finally caught up to her.

"Let's hide you in the bathroom," he said.

"But—"

He stopped her protest with a soft kiss. "I'm going to protect you this time, okay?"

"But I can help."

"You're helping by giving me piece of mind. Stay in the bathroom and lock the door. Call 9-1-1." He encouraged her inside and pulled the door closed.

Hand on the bed, he felt his way back to the desk and grabbed the sturdy chair. A solid crack to the assailant's head should do it. Hopefully Maddie had called for help and the police were on the way.

After a few minutes he feared that Adam had been assaulted outside, but Spence couldn't both protect Maddie and help Adam.

The silence inside and outside of the cabin made him edgy. What he wouldn't give for a peaceful evening alone with Maddie.

Instead, he hid in the bedroom. Waiting. He decided to use his intellect to outwit his attacker. Spence went to the window and scanned the property.

Someone kicked the bedroom door once, twice.

Spence opened the bedroom window.

The intruder kicked the door again.

Spence rushed across the room, standing beside the door. He gripped the chair, ready to strike.

Another slam.

The door flung open. Spence whacked the chair against the intruder's shoulders. The guy stumbled a few feet.

Spence hit him across the back of the head. The guy went down, giving Spence the opportunity to draw him away from Maddie.

Spence climbed out the window and took off toward the resort, then redirected himself, not wanting to bring trouble to innocent guests. Floodlights shone from the storage barn ahead, where SAR held their meetings. Spence aimed for the barn, knowing there'd be enough places to use as cover inside until help arrived.

He cast a quick glance over his shoulder and spotted a man stumbling after him. Good. Protect Maddie. That was all Spence cared about. Draw the danger away from her.

Spence reached the barn door, relieved that as a SAR

team leader he knew the code to unlock it. He darted inside, left the lights off and found a hiding spot up on the loft.

With a calming breath, Spence texted Nate his location. Surely Nate had returned to the scene. The wail of sirens outside confirmed his hope.

Spence stood flush against a storage locker, clutching a two-by-four in his hands. Deep breathing, he coached himself. He had to slow the adrenaline rush or it could make him clumsy.

The creek of wooden stairs echoed through the barn.

The attacker was closing in.

Bright lights suddenly flooded the barn.

"What are you doing in here?"

It sounded like Scott the security manager's voice. Spence peeked out and saw the masked attacker dive off the stairs and land on top of Scott. The men tumbled, fists flying. Spence climbed down the stairs and tried pulling the attacker off Scott. The attacker slammed Spence's back against a post and elbowed him in the ribs. Spence coughed and doubled over.

"This isn't over," the guy growled in Spence's ear and scrambled away.

"Scott?" Spence went to assess the security manager's injuries. "Hey, buddy, you okay?"

Scott cracked his eyes open. "Yeah. Who was that guy?"

"Same masked creep who came after me in the mountains." Spence examined Scott's face.

The barn door swung open. "Police!" Nate shouted.

Spence pointed. "That way!"

Nate and Red took off in search of the assailant.

"You should get ice on it as soon as possible," Spence said.

As he helped Scott sit up, a terrible thought struck him. What if the guy went back for Maddie?

"Nate? Maddie's still in the cabin!" he called out.

No one responded. Spence started to get up, but Scott stopped him. "Hang on."

Scott spotted his radio a few feet away and winced as he reached for it. "Aiden, it's Scott. Maddie's still in the cabin. What's your twenty?"

They waited. No one responded.

Spence grew more anxious.

"I'm at the cabin," Aiden answered.

"Maddie is in the bathroom," Spence said.

Scott repeated her whereabouts into the radio.

"Roger that," Aiden said. "I found the bodyguard outside. He's injured but okay."

Spence sighed with relief.

Nate and Red rejoined them. "There's another door in back. He's gone but—" Nate interrupted himself, "Spence, you're bleeding."

Spence glanced at his hands, and then looked at Nate. "It's not my blood."

"Not mine, either," Scott said.

"How is this guy still functioning with an untreated bullet wound bleeding all over the place?" Nate said. "Come on, we need to get back to the cabin."

"Maddie!" someone called from the bedroom.

Maddie recognized Aiden's voice. She unlocked the bathroom door and glanced past him. "Where's Spence?"

"At the barn. He's okay. They're on their way back."

As Maddie went to the kitchen table, she noticed the windows had been opened to clear the cabin of residual smoke.

"You okay?" Aiden asked.

She sat down. "Sure, fantastic."

"I guess that was a dumb question." Aiden shifted onto the arm of the sofa.

"I don't mean to be snappy," she said. "But I don't know

how much more of this I can take. Every time we think we're safe, something blows up in our faces, literally. Speaking of which, what happened to the smoke bomb?"

"The bodyguard took it outside and was clobbered by the assailant."

"Is he okay?"

"Yeah, but he'll probably have a headache. He's outside talking to Nate."

The front door opened and Nate entered with Spence, Red and Adam. Spence reached for her and she went into his arms. The automatic hug whenever Maddie and Spence were reunited felt so natural. Someday she hoped the hug would be motivated by happiness, not relief.

"Where did you go?" she asked him.

"Outside to draw the guy away from you."

"You get points for protecting Maddie," Nate said. "But I'm afraid this means we need to move you again."

Adam rubbed the back of his head.

"You need a trip to the ER?" Nate offered.

"Nah, just ice." He went to the freezer.

"Do you want me to talk to Quinn about using his fortress apartment?" Aiden offered.

"Who's Quinn?" Adam said.

"He owns the resort."

"No," Spence said. "I'd rather you stash me someplace where no one else will be in danger if he finds me again."

"What about the farmhouse?" Maddie asked Aiden. She hadn't let go of Spence's hand, and he didn't pull away.

"What, so I can put your aunt in danger?" Spence said. "No, that's not an option."

"But it gives me an idea," Nate said. He pulled out his phone and made a call.

As Nate conferred with someone on the phone, Maddie led Spence to sit with her at the kitchen table.

"Thank you," she said.

"For what?"

"Protecting me."

"Protecting you? I'm the reason you're in danger in the first place."

"Stop it. I was out for a walk in the mountains. You didn't ask me to join you, although that would be something to look forward to." She forced a smile. "You and me out for a pleasant walk, enjoying the crisp air and the stellar views of the Cascade Mountains. What do you think, interested?"

"How can you bounce back so quickly after having your life threatened?"

Maddie squeezed his hand. "It's this little thing I call faith. Besides, the image of us walking in the mountains gives me something to look forward to when this is over."

"I… I'd like that, too," Spence said softly.

"We're all set," Nate said, joining them. He glanced from Maddie to Spence. "Everyone okay?"

"That's one word for it," Aiden smirked.

He obviously heard them discuss their future romantic stroll.

"So, what's the plan, Chief?" Aiden asked.

"We'll use an Echo Mountain Rentals cabin as a safe house instead of keeping you here at the resort. It's off-season so the company has plenty of available properties. Since Cassie works there I'll have her make the arrangements. We'll play a little guessing game with the cars to make sure you're not followed to the safe house."

"I'm sorry about all this, Nate," Spence said.

"Not your fault, buddy."

"That's what I've been trying to tell him," Maddie said.

The next morning Maddie awakened fully clothed on a bed in the rental cabin. Someone had tucked a soft fleece blanket around her body.

Spence.

Maddie felt blessed that Echo Mountain Rentals had a three-bedroom cabin available to use as a safe house. Adam took turns with her brother keeping watch and sleeping, while she and Spence relaxed in separate rooms.

Not that Maddie slept much.

Events of the past few days filled her mind with anxiety as she relived the attacks. Only now did she fully appreciate how Spence must have been feeling since that first attack in the mountains: constantly on edge, afraid, nervous.

Somehow she'd been able to compartmentalize those feelings, at least until last night when she'd lost it and launched into an uncontrollable trembling fit after the smoke bomb crashed through the window. Her breakdown seemed so out of character considering she wasn't the type to fall apart. As a paramedic she'd seen gruesome things and had never lost her nerve.

Perhaps she was physically spent and emotionally exhausted from the accumulation of attacks since that first assault in the mountains.

She decided to pray for strength, a coping mechanism she'd perfected since childhood. She'd been so resentful when her parents left, but prayer had eased that pain, and eventually she'd learned to accept that which she could not change.

Finally, and only recently, her prayers had focused on forgiveness, in her mind the most direct way to grace. And thanks to finding grace, she'd grown to embrace all the feelings involved with learning to forgive. She suspected Spence could use some of that forgiveness, especially for himself.

"Lord, why do we have such trouble forgiving ourselves?" she whispered. She sat quietly with the question for a few moments, and then she got up to start her day.

The men had offered her the bedroom with the private

bath, which she appreciated. Splashing water on her face, she wondered how Rocky was doing. She dried her face and gave him a call but it went into voice mail.

"Hey, it's Maddie checking in. Hope you're feeling better. Wish I could do more, but I've been pulled down a rabbit hole. You don't want to know. And I don't want another lecture. Anyway, text me and let me know you're okay, okay? Bye."

She glanced at her clothes. They weren't particularly dirty, but she didn't relish wearing the same clothes two days in a row. Oh well, she'd have to think about that later.

She opened her bedroom door.

Spence looked up from a laptop on the kitchen table. "Good morning."

"Hi." She ambled toward him.

"Your cousin is picking up some fresh clothes and will drop them off at the police station for Nate to bring over."

She was impressed that he knew what she'd been thinking.

Ryan came out of the guest bathroom. "How are you doing, sis?"

"Hungry."

"We've got bagels and cream cheese in the fridge."

"And fresh fruit," Spence offered.

"Where's Adam?" she said.

"Getting some sleep." Ryan nodded toward a bedroom. "Coffee's on the warmer."

"Thanks." She went and poured herself a cup, then shifted onto a chair at the table. "What are you up to?" she asked Spence.

"Going through emails and reports, trying to figure out what Danner and I had in common."

"How's that going?"

"Nothing so far. Might help if I could get into his email accounts."

"We'll put somebody on it," Ryan said.

"You guys have got a lot on your plate," Spence said. "Trying to keep me safe, while investigating whatever is really going on, plus Danner's death. I'd like to do my part."

"Let's keep looking into your files," Maddie suggested. She made herself a bowl of fresh fruit and pulled a chair close to Spence so she could also see the screen.

Spence froze.

"Wait, is there sensitive information I shouldn't see?" she asked.

"No, it's just, you smell good."

She glanced at Ryan, but he hadn't heard the comment.

"Sorry," Spence said. "Another case of words slipping past the filter?"

"Actually, I thought it was nice."

The way he looked at her, she almost thought he wanted to kiss her. Probably not a good idea in front of her over-protective brother.

"So, back to your emails," she prompted.

Spence refocused on the screen.

As he scrolled through the emails, she spotted one titled Discrepancy?

"What's this?" she asked.

He opened it. "I ran into Heather Finnegan at the grocery store and she asked about a billing error. We don't get involved with billing so I forwarded it to Ruth, who sent it to Theresa." They both studied the screen. "Ruth got an answer from Theresa, who cc'd me on the result."

"What about this email from Danner?" Maddie pointed. "He sent this to all the doctors on staff." She read the email, in which he complained about medical supplies being shortchanged, while profits soared. "Did you agree with him?"

"I never had a problem. I tended to delete a lot of emails

I felt had been resolved or were a waste of time. Bill liked to stir things up so I may have deleted anything else with that subject line that came into my email box."

"Hmm. It would be helpful to see those deleted emails."

"But they're gone."

"Actually, my old boyfriend taught me a trick." She glanced at Ryan, who narrowed his eyes at her. "It's legal. I'm trying to access Spence's trash, not anyone else's."

"Be careful," Ryan said. "If you find something, we want to be able to use it in court." He redirected his gaze out the front window, looking for signs of trouble.

"We'll go into your settings to see if we can dig out the deleted emails," Maddie said.

"Old boyfriend?" Spence said.

"Old jerk boyfriend," Ryan clarified from across the room.

"Hey, you didn't always think he was a jerk," Maddie said, searching Spence's settings.

"How old?" Spence said.

"My age." She smiled.

"I meant how long ago did you break up?"

"About a year and a half ago. We dated for five years. I thought we'd get married." She wasn't sure why she said it, but for the first time it felt okay. Her chest didn't ache, not even a little.

"That serious, huh?" Spence said.

"Very serious. Waylan helped me through some rough times. He was a computer genius and got into a prestigious school in California, center of the tech world. After a few months he stopped returning my calls, my texts. He had an exciting new life with no room for the old small-town girlfriend."

"Idiot," Ryan muttered.

Maddie smiled at her brother's protectiveness.

"It's challenging when your career takes you in a different direction than the person you love," Spence said.

"Is that what happened with you?" she asked, not taking her eyes off the screen.

"What do you mean?"

"There was a rumor going around that you were married back in Portland."

"Never married, but I had a fiancée."

"And your career split you up?"

"Not exactly. It was shortly after Oliver Tomlin died in my ER and I felt that I needed a change."

She looked at him, incredulous. Life got tough and people ran away, including her father, her mother and Waylan. She couldn't believe Spence was one of them. "You abandoned your fiancée because of a work crisis?"

"It's more complicated than that."

"Sure it is," she said in a sarcastic tone.

Oh well, she couldn't expect his armor not to have a ding or two in it, could she? Better to know now, before she fell too hard and too deeply in love with him.

"I caught her with another man," he said.

Maddie's fingers froze on the keyboard. "Oh."

"It was probably my fault. I was so dedicated to my work I didn't have enough time to devote to my relationship."

Maddie looked straight at him. "Do you blame yourself for everything that happens?"

He shrugged.

"Well, stop. Bad things happen, and they often teach us new coping skills. So instead of blaming yourself for your fiancée's choices, feel the hurt of grief and move on."

"That's good advice."

"Just remember, your problems will always follow you, and God will always forgive you."

She went back to accessing his deleted emails. "I can

only access trashed emails within the past thirty days, but since the first attack was this week, I'm thinking we should find something in here."

He placed a gentle hand on her shoulder. "Thank you."

"It's not that hard. I could teach you—"

"That's not what I meant."

She glanced at him. A slight smile tugged at the corner of his lips.

"All this shame I carry around, here," he whispered, closing his fist and pressing it against his heart. "Yet somehow you made it hurt less."

She couldn't breathe, couldn't think for a second, then snapped back to reality.

"It shouldn't hurt at all," she said. "You should let it go and surrender it to God. Let Him do the heavy lifting."

Spending time with Maddie made Spence realize what he'd been missing. They shared a kind of closeness he could honestly say he'd never experienced with another person. He'd loved Andrea, but she'd never understood his work, what made him so dedicated to helping patients. After their breakup, he suspected she'd been more enamored with the title of Doctor's Wife than with Spence himself.

Maddie McBride had never seemed impressed by Spence or anyone else, for that matter. She was a grounded, down-to-earth woman with a strong sense of spirituality. And being around her, feeling her trust in God, made him want to give it a try.

They spent the morning going through his files, ate lunch and then Maddie rested. Ryan and Adam took turns keeping watch, although Nate felt confident their location was secure. He said as much when he'd dropped off Maddie's clothes while she was napping.

Later that afternoon the bedroom door opened and

Maddie marched out. She approached Spence, who was checking work email, trying to keep up with activity at the hospital.

"Something's bothering me." She sat down at the table and motioned to the laptop. He shifted it in front of her. "The financial discrepancy you forwarded to Ruth. What was the problem?"

"Heather said she was double-billed, both from Urgent Care and the hospital ER for the same treatments. Ruth said it was a computer glitch, that Theresa resolved the issue."

Maddie opened another email. "You didn't see this one because it went right into spam. This patient is emailing you with a question about drug charges."

Ryan wandered up behind them as Spence read the email.

"I remember," Spence said. "The patient was admitted complaining of chest pains. We ran tests and determined he was having an anxiety attack. Stress can cause those symptoms."

"His wife is asking about two medications that showed up on her bill. Did you order these?"

"I don't remember." Spence glanced at Maddie. "I'm not sure I like where this is going."

"Well, there's either a glitch in the billing system at Echo Mountain Hospital, or—"

"Someone's committing fraud," Ryan offered.

Spence's phone vibrated and he glanced at it. "It's Dr. Carver."

Maddie nodded that he should take the call.

"Hi, Ruth, what's—?"

"Spence, I'm so sorry," she said.

He sat straight. "What's wrong?"

"It's the board—I tried talking them out of it but they're letting you go."

TWELVE

"I don't understand," he said, as the room seemed to tip sideways.

"They feel that considering your condition—"

"My condition?"

"Spence—"

"I was attacked. I deserve time to recover."

"They've lost confidence. Someone sent the board president a list of your odd behaviors recently, like running into a burning building at the resort, and trying to scale down a mountain screaming your brother's name."

"How could anyone know—"

"It doesn't matter. They won't risk keeping you on staff and using bad judgment, like you did with Gwen the other day."

"With Gwen? What are you talking about?"

"You were off rotation, Spence. You had no business prescribing a pain medication."

"Wait, I didn't—"

"You initialed the order. She had a reaction and her blood pressure dropped dangerously low."

"Ruth, you've got to believe me, I gave no such order."

"I have to go. The meeting is still in session. They've agreed to buy out your contract, but you're no longer welcome at Echo Mountain Hospital or Urgent Care. I am so sorry."

The call ended. As did his career, his life. His odd behavior these past few days, thanks to his head injury, could mean he'd never practice medicine again.

Never make things right.

"Spence?" Maddie said, touching his arm.

"The hospital is releasing me."

"That's insane," Ryan said. "They can't fire you for being injured."

Spence stood and went to the window, gazing across the vast expanse of green.

"Ryan's right," Maddie said. "They can't let you go."

"They just did."

Sudden clarity struck him head-on. He turned to Maddie. "It makes sense."

"Spence, no."

"What better way to shut me down than to question my mental state and ban me from the hospital?" he interrupted her. "They've repeatedly failed to kill me, so they dream up another way to destroy me. No one will believe anything I say if my mental ability is questioned. Ruth said I prescribed a pain medication for Gwen, but I didn't. So obviously I'm being set up."

"But you're a brilliant and kind doctor. And you're back to your old self," Maddie said with a lift of her chin.

The confidence and defiance reflecting in her eyes gave him strength in the midst of chaos. "You're right. I'm putting an end to this."

"Doc?" Ryan said.

"I'm going to the hospital to speak with the board."

"You're not supposed to leave this cabin," Ryan said.

"I've been hiding long enough, being shuffled around and putting people I care about in danger," he said glancing at Maddie. "I need to speak with Nate. I've got an idea that could turn this whole thing around and draw them out in the open."

"I'll call the chief." Ryan pulled out his phone.

Spence went to Maddie and searched her eyes. "Your belief in me has given me the strength to do what is necessary. It will be over soon, but this," he said as he took her hand, "will not."

She smiled and he pulled her against his chest.

"It's the chief," Ryan said, handing Spence the phone.

Maddie stepped back and studied Spence's expression.

"Hey, Nate," Spence said.

"Ryan just told me. I can't believe they're letting you go."

"It's a strategic move on their part. Maddie and I have a theory that someone at the hospital might be committing fraud, but that's not why I had Ryan call. I'm going to the hospital to appeal my termination."

"Spence, I'm sorry about the job, but I'm not sure that's wise. I mean, do you really think you can persuade them to reinstate you?"

"That's not the goal."

"Wait, you don't want your job back?"

"Right now I want to be free from this violence and feel safe again. I'll interrupt the board meeting, make an impassioned appeal, draw attention to myself and probably get kicked out of the building. Actually, Officer McBride shouldn't accompany me because I don't want to put him in an uncomfortable position."

"Your goal is to get arrested?"

"No, to draw out my enemy. While I'm shouting about being unjustly fired, I'll threaten the hospital. I'll make it clear that I've got evidence that could shut them down. I'll fire my bodyguard, flag a taxi and very publicly tell him to drive me to my cabin. You will be waiting, ready to arrest whoever comes after me for the supposed evidence. We'll get ahead of him, Nate. We'll finally put an end to this thing."

"You sure you want to do this? People tend to gossip and if word gets out you had a full-blown meltdown at the hospital it could ruin your reputation."

"Can't worry about that. This is our chance to outmaneuver these guys. Board meetings usually last four hours. It's already in session, so I've gotta act now."

"Okay, I'm in. It's three o'clock. Let's say you get to the hospital by four, speak to the board and then get a cab. That puts you at the cabin between five and five thirty. Detective Vaughn and I will be waiting inside. I've still got your spare key."

"Sounds good."

"I'll have Officer McBride take Maddie someplace safe."

"Actually, it would lend credibility to the situation if she's there to witness the fallout. We've been inseparable for days so it would look suspicious if I showed up without her."

"If this whole doctor thing doesn't work out, you could be a detective," he joked.

"I'll keep that in mind, thanks."

"Put Officer McBride back on the phone."

Spence handed the phone to Ryan, who received instructions from Nate.

"You thought all that up in the last five minutes?" Maddie said. "I'm impressed."

"Thanks. Do you want to go with me or would you prefer to sit this part out? It might get tense."

"Oh right, because things haven't been tense these past few days." She smiled.

"You've got a comeback for everything, don't you?"

"Well, make sure you come back to me after you lure that creep to your cabin."

"I promise." He brushed a soft kiss against her lips.

Spence stood before the hospital board and pleaded his case in the most intelligent and calm way possible. He truly was fighting for his job, but on a deeper level he was fighting for something even more important: the safety of those he cared about.

His friends, his Echo Mountain family and, most important, Maddie.

If pretending to lose his temper meant he'd seal the deal on his termination and be ostracized from the community, he'd accept the outcome.

He'd learned he was more than just a doctor.

Spence was a man who'd fallen in love with a remarkable woman, a man who'd grown curious about her faith, and considered the possibility of embracing the Lord.

But for the moment, he wasn't done speaking his truth to the board.

"I've grown to appreciate the tight-knit community here in Echo Mountain and would never do anything to jeopardize any of these fine people," he said.

"We understand your intentions are good," Barbara Tune said. "But you have to see it from our point of view. You're suffering from a head injury that has caused lapses in judgment personally, and professionally you prescribed a medication that harmed a patient."

"I challenge the fact that I prescribed that medication," he said.

"It has your initials," Barbara said.

"Someone must have forged them."

"Dr. Spencer," Vince Brunson, board president started, "Crying conspiracy does not help your case. If you're not of sound mind, you wouldn't know you're putting patients at risk. You'll have to trust us to do our job and weigh the facts."

"I'd like to know who brought you that information, personal information, about what's been going on the past few days."

"Do you deny these events happened?" Vince said.

"I do not. But there were extenuating circumstances."

"We know you were attacked and almost killed in the mountains, and we're truly sorry," Anna Estes said. "This isn't personal."

"Yet you're using personal experiences, traumatic experiences, as just cause to release me. I've been under a lot of pressure these past few days. I've been assaulted multiple times—"

"Yet you requested to get back on the rotation," Vince said.

"I didn't want to abandon the hospital."

"So you'd chance your enemies following you into the hospital, thereby putting patients at risk?" Vince leaned back in his chair. "What are you into, Dr. Spencer? I'm curious what you do in your off hours that led to this violence."

Heat rushed to Spence's cheeks. No, none of this was his fault and thanks to Maddie he finally felt that truth in his heart.

"Sir, I was lured into the mountains where I was assaulted. I've been threatened ever since, and I have no idea who's after me or why."

"Which is exactly why you should stay away from Echo Mountain Hospital."

"But to be fired? Is that really necessary?"

"The decision's been made," Vince said. "Dr. Carver shouldn't have let you in here. You're dismissed."

"I'm not done."

Vince glanced at Spence, and then motioned to Ruth. "Call security."

This was it. The drama was about to unfold.

"Sir," Spence said.

A few board members glanced down at their papers in uncomfortable silence. Board president Brunson narrowed his eyes at Spence and muttered, "Shoulda known you were too good to be true."

The door opened and a security officer entered the room.

"Escort Dr. Spencer out of the hospital," Vince said.

Ruth shot a helpless glance in Spence's direction.

The officer reached for Spence's arm.

"I know the way." Spence went to the door, stopped, and turned to the board. "You're making a mistake."

With a grip of Spence's arm, the officer pulled him out of the boardroom.

"This is ludicrous," Spence said as the guard escorted him to the exit. He spotted Maddie and Adam at the end of the hall near the doors.

"They have no right to dismiss me!" Spence shouted. "This isn't over!"

"Spence, calm down," Maddie said.

The guard marched him outside where people passed by glancing his way with interest. Spence yanked his arm free. "Enough!"

His friends stepped up beside him. The security guard waited near the door to make sure Spence didn't reenter the hospital.

"Hey, it'll be okay," Maddie said.

"Stay away from me. Everyone stay away."

"I'll get the car, sir," Adam said.

"Don't bother. I'm done with all of you, this hospital, this ridiculous town."

"Don't talk like that," Maddie said.

"They think they've got stuff on me to justify my release?" Spence said. "I've got even more on them." He motioned to a nearby cab, hired by Nate in advance.

"Dr. Spencer, let us help you," Adam said.

"What, you think I'm crazy, too? You won't after you see what I've got on these brainless bobbleheads." He yanked open the cab door and clearly gave his address to the driver before climbing into the backseat.

As the cab pulled away, Spence glanced back only once, in time to see Maddie's genuine frown.

Well played, he thought.

Now he hoped it was worth it and the attacker followed him home.

Adam dropped Maddie off at the Echo Mountain rental house where Ryan was waiting. Since Spence was under Nate's protection, and Maddie under her brother's, the bodyguard was released from duty for the remainder of the afternoon and evening.

Maddie ached to go home to her apartment for a little alone time, maybe to soak in a hot bath or read book as a distraction from what was going on at Spence's cabin.

He put himself in the line of fire to finally end the threat against his life. Some might think it crazy, but Maddie felt Spence made a good call, an offensive decision to throw the perpetrator off his game and draw him out for a change.

Spence was taking control and it felt right.

So much had happened this week. The attack on Gwen, multiple attacks on Spence, and… Rocky. She decided to check in and sent him a text. Instead of responding to her text, he called her.

"Hey, I didn't mean to bother you, but I wanted to see how you're doing," she said.

"I'm good, ya know, healing."

"I'd like to bring something over like—"

"Aren't you on the run with Dr. Dreamboat?"

"I meant when this was over. I'm hoping it will be sooner than later."

"How can you be so sure?"

"Got a hunch," she said.

"Well, I appreciate the offer, but I'm good. Vivian stopped by on her break and brought soup and a casserole, and some kind of crazy tea."

"It's healing tea from Healthy Eats!" Vivian called from the background.

Thank You, Lord, Maddie said to herself. She was grateful that Rocky's heart hadn't been so broken by Maddie's rejection that he wouldn't find comfort in another woman's arms.

"I'm glad Vivian's there," Maddie said.

"She's bossy," Rocky said.

"You like bossy."

"Yeah, I guess. So I heard the doc was fired."

"How did you hear about that already?"

"Someone at the hospital told Vivian there was a big blowout. The doc had a complete meltdown."

"Hey, I called to talk about you, not Spence."

"I'm good. I've got everything I need, plus the boss has approved paid time off for my recovery since it happened on duty."

"That's great."

"Yeah."

Silence stretched between them. It was as if Rocky had something more to say, but couldn't with Vivian in the room.

"I'm sorry you got hurt by all this," Maddie said.

"Make sure you don't get hurt," he warned.

"I won't."

"Really? Even when he leaves town? Because we both know you're not going anywhere."

That stung, not only because Rocky brought up the possibility of abandonment, but also because it felt like he was judging her again for needing to stay in Echo Mountain. Had he been right? Was she still in town out of some warped hope that her loved ones would return?

"Maddie?"

"I'm glad you're okay, Rocky. Take care."

"I didn't mean to—"

"Talk to you later." She ended the call rather abruptly, but couldn't stop herself.

His comment stirred up all kinds of fear and pain she'd kept safely tucked away. Sure, he'd commented on her motivation for staying in town before, but hearing it again made her wonder if she'd been fooling herself all these years. She thought she'd moved on, that she'd processed the grief of abandonment, but perhaps it was still driving her every decision.

"How's Rocky?" Ryan asked.

"Better."

"Then why do you look serious?"

"It was something he said."

"What?"

She glanced at her brother. "You think we do what we do because Mom and Dad left?"

"Can you be more specific?"

"Like you becoming a cop to protect people, like you always tried to protect me because our parents weren't around?"

"Yeah, tried and failed."

"I can't help it if I'm a self-reliant woman."

"In answer to your question, yes, things like that have to affect you on some level. Although I probably became a cop to boss people around because my little sister never listened to me." He winked.

"So, our past experiences drive our decisions?"

"Sure, that's how life works I guess."

Her phone vibrated with a text from Spence.

Checking in. How r u?

She answered that she was okay and praying for his safety.

When this is over and we are safe, will you take me to church?

She smiled as warmth filled her chest.

Of course.

Gotta go. <3

She held the phone to her heart and said another prayer.

"You'd better watch it or you're going to break that thing," Ryan said.

"What, the phone?"

"Your heart."

"Very funny." She got up and went to the laptop. "I still can't believe they fired him."

"He's been acting kind of funky since the knock to the head," he said, glancing out the window.

"He's fine now."

"If you say so, Doc."

"I do say so, and I'd like to give Dr. Carver and the hospital board a piece of my mind on the subject."

Her phone vibrated with a call and she hoped it was Spence, but instead, an unrecognizable number popped up. "Huh."

"Huh, what?"

"I don't know who this is."

"Let me answer."

She handed the phone to her brother. "Hello...? Sure." He held the phone against this chest. "It's Dr. Carver. Be nice."

Maddie snatched the phone. "Dr. Carver?"

"Maddie, I'm worried about Spence. He's not answering his phone. It seems like you two are friends so I thought I'd call you."

"I'm sure he's okay."

"He was so agitated this afternoon. I've never seen him lose his temper like that."

"He felt he was being wrongly dismissed. And I agree. I've been with him since the first assault in the mountains and his condition has improved significantly. In another week or two he'll be one hundred percent."

"I know, I know. It wasn't up to me. I did my best to persuade the board to give him time to recover before they made their decision. But they had concerns, like prescribing inappropriate drugs."

"He never prescribed that drug for Gwen and he'll prove it, along with other things."

Ryan got in her face and shook his head, indicating she shouldn't allude to the fraud case.

"What other things?" Ruth said.

"False accusations," Maddie recovered.

"Well, I hope he does. He's a fine doctor and a good man. That's why I'm so worried about him. If only he'd respond to my messages."

"I'm sure he will when he can."

"I feel responsible, like I've let him down. Oh, Maddie, if he does anything foolish like hurt himself."

"Dr. Carver, really, don't worry about anything like that. He's fine. I promise."

"Okay, well if you do speak with him..." her voice trailed off.

"Dr. Carver?"
"Who's there...? No!" A crash echoed through the line.
"Dr. Carver!"

THIRTEEN

Maddie jumped to her feet. "Ryan, call for help."

"What's wrong?"

"It sounded like someone broke into Dr. Carver's house."

"Dispatch, this is Officer McBride," he spoke into his radio. "I've got a suspected breaking and entering at…" He trailed off as he glanced at Maddie. "Where does she live?"

Maddie gave him the address. She'd been called to the doctor's house when her husband fell off a ladder and needed transport to the hospital.

"There was an accident on Highway 2. It might take twenty minutes to get a unit there," Dispatch said.

"That's too long. We can make it in ten," Maddie said.

"What's this 'we' stuff?"

"Let's go." Maddie grabbed her brother's arm and pulled him toward the door.

"Chief ordered us to stay in the cabin."

"Someone's got to help her, Ryan."

"I'll call Adam to relieve me."

"There's no time for that. Come on, Ry. I'll stay in the car until you secure the scene." Maddie rushed outside.

Communicating via text messages with Maddie had given Spence a great sense of calm. But it was time to focus and get ready for the perpetrator he hoped was on the way. Spence should have thought of this plan sooner, luring the guy out of hiding so Spence and the police could be in control for a change. It could have saved his reputation for sure. But more importantly, it would have kept a lot of people out of danger, especially Maddie.

When the violence was over and the case solved, what would happen to Maddie and him then? Maddie was a lovely, smart and positive woman, someone he could see himself traveling with, spending a week hiking in the Canadian Rockies. Her grounded nature pulled him away from the edge of panic, but there was more to it than that. She had faith in him, which felt…good.

Nate gave Spence a signal and put his finger to his lips. He must have heard something outside. Spence and Detective Vaughn shared a glance, readying themselves.

They'd shared their plan with Spence when he got to the cabin. Spence would pretend to be having a temper flare-up, going through files and looking for supposed evidence against hospital board members and staff.

Nate and the detective would hide out and wait for the assailant to break in. Spence hoped his performance had been convincing and word had spread that about him wanting revenge on the hospital. Drawing the perpetrator into their trap was a solid plan, but if he didn't get the message, Spence might have torched his reputation for nothing.

Detective Vaughn motioned to the bedroom. As they intensely focused on sounds coming from that part of the cabin, the tension threatened to trigger a headache.

No, he would not be thrown off because of that first assault in the mountains and subsequent concussion. Nate stood on one side of the bedroom door and Detective Vaughn on the other side. Nate motioned for Spence to continue going through files and shouting words of frustration against his enemies.

"They'll never get away with his!" he shouted. "Firing me? What right did they have to fire me?" Spence threw a mug across the room, shattering it to pieces. "They won't ruin my career with their accusations!"

A squeak from the other room indicated the guy had opened the newly-installed bedroom window.

"They're all going down, starting with the ego-driven Vince Brunson, then Barbara and—"

"Nobody's going down, Doc."

Spence glanced up. At first he didn't recognize the man because he'd shaved his beard, and his hair was blond instead of dark brown. He must have altered his appearance to elude authorities, but there was no doubt in Spence's mind: this was the man who broke into his cabin.

"What are you doing here?" Spence said.

"Finishing what I started." He stood just inside the bedroom as if skittish to join Spence in the main living area. He couldn't know there were two police officers flanking the bedroom door, could he?

"Why are you trying to kill me?" Spence said.

"You're bad for business."

"What business?"

Nate stepped into the doorway and aimed his gun at the perp. "Drop the weapon."

The guy didn't move at first, then let the gun slip from his fingertips. It hit the ground with a clunk.

"Turn around, hands behind your head," Nate ordered.

Detective Vaughn stepped closer, gun drawn.

Spence didn't move, wasn't sure what to do. It was over, well not completely, but at least the direct physical threat had been neutralized.

"I said turn around," Nate repeated.

The guy slowly turned, putting his hands behind his head. Nate grabbed his wrists and secured them behind his back with cuffs.

"Get in here and sit down." Nate shoved him into a living room chair.

"Hey, Chief," Detective Vaughn said, holding the perp's gun in her hand. "It's Officer Carrington's gun."

"So you're the guy who assaulted my officer the other night? You're just racking up the charges. What's your name?"

"Tom Wick."

"Tom Wick, you're under arrest," Nate said, and read him his rights.

Spence stepped around the kitchen island and approached the man, who was in his twenties. "Wait, Wick as in Wicker?"

Tom snapped his gaze to Spence.

"What's a wicker?" Nate said.

"Wicker is the name of the guy who deals pills to kids like Gwen."

"Is that right, Wicker?" Nate said.

Clenching his jaw, the guy glanced beyond Nate at the door.

"So this was about drugs?" Spence asked Tom.

"Sure," he said, sarcastic.

"Let's lock him up, Chief," Vaughn said.

"Ya know, Mr. Wick, once we shut the cell door, it's over," Nate said. "But if you cooperate, tell us who else is involved, we could advocate for you."

Tom shot him a look of disbelief, and went back to staring at the door.

Spence stepped into Tom's sight line. "Why me?"

Tom looked away.

"What do you think, Detective Vaughn?" Nate said.

"He doesn't deserve any mercy, that's for sure," she said.

Yet Spence had learned from Maddie that everyone, even criminals, deserved mercy.

"I don't know. I think he wants to talk to us, don't you, Tom?" Nate pushed.

Tom glared at Nate. "Lawyer."

Nate held his gaze, probably trying to intimidate him into changing his mind. Instead, Tom snapped his attention toward the windows and his eyes rounded with fear.

"No!" Tom jumped to his feet.

Nate shoved him back in the chair. "Where do you think you're going?"

"Fire!" Tom shouted.

Spence, Nate and the detective were so focused on Tom they didn't see the bright orange flames crawling up the windows.

"Bedroom!" Nate shouted.

He grabbed Tom by the arm and pulled him to his feet. They ran into the bedroom, but flames sprang up across those windows, as well.

"Grab blankets," Spence ordered. "We'll soak them with water and make a run for it."

"We're gonna burn!" Tom shouted.

Spence pulled blankets off his bed, and Detective Vaughn grabbed one from the sofa. Spence flipped on the kitchen sink and quickly soaked each blanket. He worked best in a crisis, which was what made him a good ER doc.

After he and Detective Vaughn doused the blankets, they each took one.

"It'll help get us out without being burned," Spence said, grabbing the fire extinguisher.

"When you get outside, hit the ground and roll," Spence said. "I'll be waiting with the fire extinguisher. Keep your eyes closed when I blast you with the CO2."

Nate and Spence shared a knowing look.

"See you out there," Spence said.

Gripping the knob with the edge of the wet blanket, Spence whipped open the door and sprinted through the flames. Once free and clear of the fire, he dropped the fire extinguisher, hit the ground and rolled, smothering any residual embers on his clothes.

He jumped up, grabbed the fire extinguisher and turned to assist the others. With a guttural cry, Detective Vaughn sprinted out of the cabin, tossed the blanket and hit the ground.

"Close your eyes!" Spence shouted, and got her with a few short bursts of CO_2.

"I'm okay, I'm okay," she said, and jumped to her feet.

The sound of a car speeding away drew his attention. "Look!"

"I'll try and get a plate number!" She took off in foot pursuit.

Spence refocused on the cabin, anxious for Nate and Tom to get out of there. What was taking them so long? They should have been right behind Detective Vaughn.

Spence got as close as possible. "Nate!"

Did they find another way out? Then a horrible thought struck Spence: What if Tom assaulted Nate and the perp went out another way?

"Go, go, go!" Nate shouted.

The two men burst from the burning cabin, Nate shoving Tom from behind. They both hit the ground and Spence shot them with the CO_2.

"I'm good," Nate said, standing.

Spence examined Tom. "You okay? Were you burned?"

Tom gasped for breath, eyes wide.

"He was having some kind of attack," Nate said. "I had a hard time getting him out of there."

Spence noted Tom's labored breathing. "Asthma?" Spence asked.

Tom nodded.

Spence searched Tom's pockets and found his inhaler,

held it to his mouth and administered the medicine. "Try to relax. You're safe now."

Detective Vaughn raced up to them. "I called in a description of the assailant's car. Units will be on the lookout. Emergency fire and paramedics are on the way."

"They'll send the engine from Wallace County," Spence said. "It's closer."

Nate glanced at the fire consuming the cabin, then back at Spence. "Man, I'm sorry."

"Yeah," Spence said.

Grief settled across Spence's shoulders. He'd helped build the cabin with a local contractor. Even though he hadn't planned to stay in Echo Mountain forever, it was his home, a place where he felt safe, and at peace. The locals had embraced him in a way no one else ever had.

A flash of memory drifted across his thoughts: Maddie in the kitchen singing her heart out. He would have enjoyed cooking a meal for her in his cabin.

"Good thing you cleared out the trees around the cabin or this thing could've gotten outta hand," Nate said.

"Which is why I did it. Plus the humidity and moist ground will discourage the fire from jumping."

"So now the question is, who set the fire? You?" Nate said, hovering over Tom.

Tom shook his head, his breathing strained. "No, no fire. Only—" he gasped "—give the doc an overdose. Make it look like suicide."

"Why?" Spence said.

Tom shook his head.

"Don't shake your head," Nate said. "Answer him."

"He paid me...five thousand."

"You were going to kill a man for five thousand dollars," Nate said, his tone flat.

"And stay out of jail...for dealing drugs," Tom admitted.

"The guy who hired you to kill Dr. Spencer is linked to the drug activity?" Nate said.

Tom focused on his breathing and stared straight ahead, the flames reflecting in his eyes.

"Let's go." Nate pulled him to his feet.

"The paramedics should check him out, Nate," Spence said.

"He's fine." Nate tossed Vaughn the keys and she went to get the car, which they'd hidden from view.

"Nate," Spence said. "I can't let you take him in until he's officially checked out."

"This guy tried to kill you, what, five times, and you're worried about his condition?"

"Five times?" Tom said.

"Unless you can't count," Nate snapped.

"I stole the girl's phone and passed it to someone. I broke into his cabin twice. That's it."

Nate got in Tom's face. "You used her phone to lure Spence into the mountains, where you tried to kill him. That's how this all started."

Tom vehemently shook his head.

"And you attacked me in the hospital, hijacked the ambulance with me in back and tossed a smoke bomb into my cabin," Spence said.

"No, not me. I stole the phone and broke into your cabin twice—the first time to kidnap you, and tonight to drug you."

"Who hired you?" Spence said.

"I don't know."

Nate narrowed his eyes.

"I don't!" Tom protested. "Got instructions from text messages."

Sirens wailed as emergency vehicles motored down the main road to the cabin.

"We'll figure this out at the station," Nate said.

* * *

Maddie and Ryan pulled up outside Dr. Carver's house, set back on secluded property. Ryan turned off the engine and looked at her. "I mean it, Maddie. Stay in the car. Do not get out, do not come looking for me. And lock the doors."

"Okay, okay."

Ryan got out of the SUV and pointed through the window. She hit the lock button and mouthed "thank you."

She watched him climb the front porch to Dr. Carver's house and hesitate. That's when she realized the door was ajar. He withdrew his firearm, eased the door open and disappeared inside.

Maddie waited for what seemed like forever. She checked her watch. Only a few minutes had passed. Oh, how she wished the paramedics and police would arrive.

She grew anxious. What if Dr. Carver was injured and needed medical help? No, Ryan would surely text her.

Her anxiety made sense considering the call from Ruth, plus Spence's plan to set himself up as bait to draw out the bad guy. Maddie knew they had probably turned off their phones, but she felt the need to make a connection with him all the same. She called him but it went into voice mail.

"Hey, Spence. So I'm sitting outside Dr. Carver's house, kind of freaking out here because we think someone broke in, and I wanted to say, I'll be glad when all this is over. I know that challenging times help us appreciate the good times and all that, but, well, I wanted to say I'm looking forward to grabbing pizza with you, or going to Healthy Eats, if that's your thing. Anyway, I hope everything went well tonight."

A flash of movement caught her eye. It was Dr. Carver stumbling on the fringe of her property.

"Oh no." Maddie pocketed her phone and jumped out of the car.

As she jogged toward the doctor, she considered how upset Ryan would be with her right now. But she couldn't sit here and watch the woman wander off into the surrounding forest.

"Dr. Carver?" she called out.

She kept walking, heading toward the trees, wavering from side to side. As Dr. Carver passed by a shed, she stumbled and collapsed. Maddie rushed to her side.

"Dr. Carver? Ruth?"

Maddie took her pulse. It was solid at eighty beats per minute. She pulled her penlight off her keychain and checked her pupils. They were dilated. Had someone drugged her, as well? Maddie pulled out her phone to text Ryan.

A firm hand shoved a cloth over her mouth. She punched and kicked, but couldn't stop what she suspected was chloroform from shutting down her brain.

Her arms weakened and her legs lost their fight. Darkness consumed her as someone dragged her into the forest.

After Tom was treated at the scene, Nate, Detective Vaughn and Spence headed to the police station. Spence struggled to fill in the blanks as he watched Tom say something to Nate through the one-way glass. Probably asking for his lawyer again.

The door opened and Nate motioned to Spence. "He says he wants to talk to you."

Joining Nate and Detective Vaughn in the interrogation room, Spence sat across the table from Tom.

Tom finally looked up. "Thanks, ya know, for the inhaler."

"Of course."

"You didn't have to do that." Tapping nervous fingers

on the table, Tom finally said, "It wasn't personal, Doc. All the stuff that happened to you."

"I need to know why it's happening," Spence said.

Tom shrugged.

"Tom," Spence started, "I appreciate that you don't want to incriminate yourself, but I need answers. Without them my life and the lives of people I care about continue to be in danger. Will you help me? Give Nate something we can use to figure out who's behind all this?"

Tom considered. "I guess I'll be busted for the drugs anyway."

"And attempted homicide of two police officers and Dr. Spencer," Nate added.

"I didn't know cops would be there. Like I said before, I was hired to make the doc overdose." He glanced at Spence. "Sorry. I was desperate for the money."

"And I'm desperate to get my life back. I've lost my job, which means I can't treat people who need my help, like you when you had your asthma attack," Spence said. "Please, tell us something."

Tom studied his hands and nodded.

"You've asked for a lawyer," Nate said. "Are you now waiving that right?"

"Yeah."

"Then let's start at the beginning," Nate said. "When were you first contacted about kidnapping Dr. Spencer?"

"I got an anonymous text last week. Said they knew about my business, but wouldn't go to the police if I did a few things, like kidnap Dr. Spencer."

"Kidnap him and do what with him?" Nate pressed.

"Leave him at Wallace Falls."

"What were you going to do, hike up there with an unconscious man over your shoulder?"

"I was supposed to leave him behind the public bathrooms at the trailhead."

"You have no idea who wanted him and for what purpose?" Nate pressed.

"No."

"And tonight's assault?"

"They promised me five grand to make him overdose."

"On what?"

"I don't know. They gave me the drugs."

"You're telling me you've never seen who's behind this?" Nate said.

"No, we had a drop-off spot. Same place I got my drugs."

"Back up. The supplier of your prescription drugs is also the person who wants Spence dead?" Nate asked.

"I don't know for sure. I leave money in a locker at the bus station and pick up a bag with the pills. Yesterday they texted me and said to pick up drugs at the locker, not my usual stuff. Something in the blue bottle would make the doc go to sleep."

"And then you'd torch the house?"

Tom shook his head. "No one said anything about setting a fire."

"Where's your phone?" Nate said.

Tom nodded at his pocket. Nate dug it out and scrolled through the text messages. "Vaughn," he handed her the phone. "See if you can trace this one."

"Yes, sir." She took the phone and left the interrogation room.

"How long have you been dealing to kids?" Spence said.

"Not long. It started with adults."

"You know what the sentence is for dealing prescription drugs in Washington State?" Nate said. "Add that to the assault and attempted murder charges and—"

"It got away from me, I guess."

"Then get it back," Spence said. "Do something to help yourself here."

"If I can tell the feds you helped us solve the local crimes, that would go a long way to helping your cause," Nate added.

"It wouldn't surprise me if he worked at the hospital," Tom said.

"Why do you say that?" Spence asked.

"Because when my supplier sold me the drugs, I'd also get a list of names of patients who'd been released with prescriptions for painkillers. My supplier must have assumed they'd make good customers."

The door burst open and Detective Vaughn motioned Spence and Nate out of the interrogation room. Once in the hallway, Vaughn said, "There was a break-in. Ruth Carver was assaulted, and..." She trailed off and glanced at Spence before finishing. "Maddie McBride is missing."

FOURTEEN

Spence couldn't think past the knot twisting in his chest. Maddie was missing? How was that possible? She'd been safely stashed in the Echo Mountain Rentals cabin with her brother, and Spence knew Ryan wouldn't let her out of his sight.

After locking Tom in a cell, Nate drove Spence and Detective Vaughn to the Carvers' house.

"What were they doing there?" Spence asked.

"Apparently Ruth was on the phone with Maddie when someone broke into the house," Nate said.

"They should have called 9-1-1."

"They did, but a car accident on Highway 2 slowed response teams."

"And so Maddie and Ryan decided to help her," Spence said. "Which still doesn't explain how Maddie went missing."

"We'll know more after we talk to Officer McBride," Nate said.

"He shouldn't have left her alone," Spence said.

The car grew quiet. Of course casting blame didn't help matters, but desperation drove his words. He was desperate that nothing should happen to Maddie.

Because he cared about her. A lot.

When they pulled into Ruth's driveway, he spotted an

ambulance. Spence jumped out of the car almost before it came to a stop.

"Spence!" Nate called after him.

As Spence rushed toward the house, someone called his name. He turned toward the source and saw Ruth being tended to by a paramedic on a front lawn bench.

"Ruth, are you okay?" Spence said, approaching her.

"Hi, Dr. Spencer," the paramedic they fondly called Wiggy greeted him. "She won't let us take her to the hospital."

"I'm not seriously injured," Ruth said. "Just foggy."

Wiggy packed up his gear and went back to the ambulance.

"What happened?" Spence asked Ruth.

"I was on the phone and someone broke in." She glanced at him. "I called Maddie because I was so worried about you after the blowup with the board."

"Why call Maddie?"

"You weren't answering your phone. Then I heard someone in my house. I was terrified, and ran out the back door. But I must have tripped and hit my head because the next thing I know I'm on the ground with the paramedic standing over me. But before that, I thought I heard Maddie's voice."

"She was with you?" Spence said.

"She was checking my pulse, I think. Where is she?"

"Ruth! Ruth!" Cal shouted, frantically stumbling up to them. He reached out and pulled his wife into his arms.

"Oh, Cal. I was so scared."

"I know. It's okay." Cal glared at Spence. "This is your fault. Now they're after us, too."

"Cal, don't," Ruth said, breaking the hug. "I'm fine. But the house is a crime scene so we'd better get a room at the resort." She nodded at Spence. "When you see Maddie, thank her for calling 9-1-1."

Spence couldn't respond, fear constricting his vocal cords. He assumed no one had informed Ruth that Maddie had gone missing, and he didn't want to upset her further. Cal led Ruth away without saying another word to Spence.

As Spence climbed the porch steps, he heard voices arguing inside the house. Nate blocked him at the door. "This is a crime scene."

"Meaning what?"

"We need to keep it intact."

"I understand. Where's Ryan?"

"Easy, Spence. He took a nasty hit to the head. If you can keep your cool I'll let you in, but stay in the front hallway."

Spence nodded and Nate let him pass. As Spence entered the house, he saw Ryan sitting on the stairs being checked out by the other paramedic, Vivian.

"No lacerations, and your pupils look normal," Vivian said, analyzing the back of Ryan's scalp. "We could transport you to the hospital just to be sure."

"No thanks," Ryan said.

Vivian stood. "Keep the ice pack on your head. And if your symptoms get worse—vomiting, passing out, memory loss—get to the ER ASAP."

"Will do."

Vivian left and silence filled the hallway. Ryan finally looked at Nate. "I told her to stay in the car. Why didn't she stay in the car?" he said, his voice cracking.

"We'll find her," Nate said. "I've got Red checking with neighbors about any suspicious vehicles in the area. Detective Vaughn, after we're done here I want you to go assist."

"Yes, sir."

"Tell me what happened when you arrived at the house," Nate redirected to Ryan.

"I searched the entire first floor but couldn't find Dr. Carver. I went upstairs and somebody clobbered me."

"They found Ruth out by the shed, unconscious."

"What was she doing out there?" Ryan asked.

"She was trying to get away from the intruder, tripped and hit her head," Nate said.

"But she remembers Maddie taking her pulse," Spence offered.

"And now Maddie's missing because she was trying to help," Ryan said. "Why? Why would they take her?"

"To get at me," Spence said.

"Maybe to make an exchange." Nate glanced at Spence. "You for Maddie."

"But if she can identify her kidnapper, they'll never let her go," Ryan said.

"He's probably wearing a mask, like he did before in the mountains," Nate suggested.

"Don't you have that guy in custody?" Ryan said.

"He claims he wasn't the masked man, which means there are more perps involved in this," Nate said. "Keep your phone handy in case he calls you directly, Spence."

"That's the best-case scenario," Vaughn muttered.

Nate narrowed his eyes at her.

"Sorry, Chief," she said.

"So what now?" Spence said. "I can't wait around for the next horrible thing to happen. I need to do something to find Maddie, do more digging to figure out who is involved."

"The feds have been called to investigate the suspected fraud," Nate confirmed. "But if you want to help, do your research at the station. I need to stay here and process the scene."

"I'll take him back." Ryan stood and motioned Spence outside.

As they silently walked toward Ryan's dark SUV, Spence couldn't chastise the man. Spence suspected Ryan was doing plenty of that himself.

As they got inside the vehicle, Ryan released a deep sigh, leaned against the headrest and closed his eyes.

"Do you need me to drive?" Spence offered.

"It's not my head injury." He looked at Spence with bloodshot green eyes. "I never should have brought her with me."

Spence knew that feeling, the feeling of intense guilt that grabbed hold of you and squeezed until you thought you couldn't breathe. He'd felt that same guilt after his brother had died.

Yet Maddie had shown Spence how to let go.

"If you hadn't brought her with you, she would have been alone and vulnerable in the cabin," Spence offered.

"If anything happens to her…"

"We'll pray that it doesn't."

With a nod, Ryan started the vehicle.

Spence glanced out the passenger window surprised that even though he was being sucked into a maelstrom of utter panic about Maddie's safety, the word *pray* felt natural rolling off his tongue.

The woman had truly affected him in the deepest way, a way he'd never expected. She'd shown him what true forgiveness looked like and opened his heart to faith.

Dear Lord, please keep my Maddie safe.

He hoped it didn't seem selfish to pray for her safe return. He had no idea how to appropriately pray for anything or anyone. Then he remembered Maddie's words: *You don't have to think about prayer. You just do it.*

So he did. All the way to the police station.

The pounding in Maddie's head felt like someone was tapping at her skull with a blunt instrument. And it was starting to drive her nuts.

She opened her eyes and struggled to focus. Where was she again?

A soft glow pulsed from a gas lantern on a table across the room. The room was empty except for the table and lantern. She sat up, leaning against a wood wall. She was on the floor of a rustic cabin.

Darkness reflected back at her through the multipaned window. It was nighttime.

How did she end up here? The last thing she remembered was checking on Dr. Carver.

Something was shoved against her mouth.

She lost the ability to fight.

Then nothing.

Standing, she pressed her fingertips to her temples in the hopes of relieving the pain. But why was she here? What did the kidnapper want from her?

As she went to the window, she realized she wasn't wearing shoes, only socks. She felt for her phone but her jacket was missing, as well. Glancing across the cabin, she noted a blanket on the floor where she'd regained consciousness.

Awfully considerate for a killer.

She wondered how long she'd been here. Hours? Days? No, the drug wouldn't have incapacitated her for that long.

The light from the gas lamp flickered. From the looks of the wick, it would probably burn for only another few hours. Then complete and utter darkness would fill the cabin.

Flurries fell from the sky as the full moon illuminated the white ground and snow-covered trees. If only she could escape the sparse one-room cabin. Thanks to the moonlight she could see well enough to find a path and hike to safety, even though she didn't know where she was exactly. She figured getting out of the cabin and fighting the elements had to be a better choice than staying here and waiting for her captor to return.

A soft vibrating sound drifted across the cabin. She

snapped her head around, trying to make sense of where it was coming from.

The blanket—it was coming from the blanket.

She scrambled across the room, thinking it was her phone, that somehow she'd managed to keep it.

Tossing the blanket aside, she spotted a phone but it wasn't hers. She picked it up and read a text.

You are safe. There is food under the table.

Could this get any stranger? She reached below the table and pulled out a soft-sided cooler. She unzipped the flap and peered inside: fresh fruit, cheese and raw vegetables.

So she'd been kidnapped by a health nut?

Hang on, if he'd texted her that meant…

She called 9-1-1.

"9-1-1 Emergency."

"This is Maddie McBride. I've been kidnapped. I need help."

"I'm sorry, ma'am, what did you say your name was?"

"Maddie McBride."

"Please stay on the line while I contact our chief."

"Okay."

"Can you tell us where you are?" the dispatcher asked.

"I have no idea." She scanned the surrounding area. "Somewhere in the Cascade Mountains. All I see are lots of trees."

"Maddie, it's Nate. Are you okay?"

"I've been better."

"He hasn't hurt you?"

"No, and he left me dinner. This whole thing is seriously creepy."

"Describe your surroundings."

"It's a one-room log cabin with multipaned windows overlooking the forest. There's a wood stove, but no wood."

"Stay on the line. We're going to trace your phone signal."

"Okay, sure." She grabbed the blanket off the floor and cloaked it around her shoulders.

"Maddie?" Spence said.

Her fingers tightened around the phone. "Spence, it's good to hear your voice."

"What happened? How were you kidnapped?"

"I was checking on Ruth and someone grabbed me from behind. Then I woke up in this strange cabin with a massive headache."

"He didn't take your phone?"

"He did, but he left me a different one. It's weird, like he's trying to take care of me, like he doesn't want to hurt me. But Spence," she confessed, "I'm kind of freaking out here."

"You're a ninja, remember? And the toughest person I know."

She half chuckled. "Yeah. But if something happens—"

"Don't, don't say it."

She squinted to see better out the window. "But Spence?"

"Yes, Maddie."

"Oh, this is stupid."

"Talk to me."

"I was going to say, well, even with all the threats and craziness this past week, I've enjoyed the time we've spent together. That's twisted, isn't it?"

He didn't answer right away.

"It's okay," she said. "You don't have to agree in order to make me feel better."

"Maddie, I would give anything to be able to switch places with you right now because," he admitted, "I love you."

She closed her eyes, and felt a tear warm her cheek. "I thought I was crazy, ya know, because I feel this way."

"Then we're both crazy," he said. "Hang on… Nate is trying to tell me something."

A few long seconds passed.

"What's going on?" Maddie said.

Spence didn't respond.

"Spence?"

"Nate can't track the phone."

"Then how can I tell you where I am?" she said, gazing out the window.

"Have faith, Maddie. You taught me that," Spence said.

A man in snow gear, including face mask, came out of the forest and was heading toward the cabin with a definite limp.

"It's him. He's back." She stepped away from the window.

"How do you know it's—?"

"He's limping. It's the guy Ryan shot. Okay, okay," she said, considering her next move. "He's wounded. This could be my chance to get away."

"Maddie—"

"I've got to focus." She shoved the phone into her pocket and her fingers touched metal keys. Her house and car keys. She slid the keys between her fingers and curled up with the blanket around her shoulders, pretending to be asleep.

A thumping sound echoed from the other side of the door. He was tapping snow off his boots.

The dead bolt clicked.

The door squeaked open.

"Still asleep?" a man said.

She didn't move, didn't breathe. A surge of determination gave her a new kind of strength thanks to Spence's words.

I love you.

"Time to eat something," the man said.

She didn't answer. If only he'd come close enough, she'd nail him with the keys.

Adrenaline pulsed through her body all the way to her fingertips.

"Maddie?" he whispered.

She remained still, curled up. Floorboards creaked as he approached.

Through cracked eyelids she saw him kneel by her side.

She swung her arm and nailed him in the face with the keys. Stunned, he stumbled back and she jumped to her feet, delivering a kick to his gut. He doubled over and she raced past him out of the cabin.

Pulling the phone out of her pocket, she said, "I don't see a car, or other cabins, or anything. We're in the middle of nowhere!"

She ignored the wet ground chilling her stocking feet and the panic spiking her blood pressure. She sprinted toward the forest where she'd find cover.

"What else do you see?" It was Nate's voice. "Lights below? A clearing, anything?"

"Nothing distinguishable. There's no obvious road, either."

"Where's the perpetrator?"

She cast a quick glance over her shoulder, but he wasn't behind her. "He must still be in the cabin."

"Run, Maddie, run!" It was her brother's voice.

She practically dived into the forest but couldn't find a clearly marked trail. Without the moonlight, her vision was limited.

"It's dark and I don't have shoes or a coat." She kept moving.

Finally out of breath, she dodged behind a boulder and collapsed. "What now?"

"Keep the line open," Nate said. "We're still working on tracking your location."

She started shivering, her body's natural response to the cold, and she struggled to focus on something else, something other than the chill in her bones. Not easy when the moisture from the snow was soaking through to her skin.

"Hang in there, Maddie," her brother said.

"I think we've got something," Nate offered.

As she focused on her breathing, reality permeated her thoughts. They'd never get to her in time. They didn't even know where she was. And if they didn't find her soon, she could succumb to hypothermia.

Nate, Ryan and Spence kept talking to her, but after a while their voices seemed to fade.

She felt herself drift, then felt nauseous, dizzy.

"Have faith," she whispered, repeating Spence's words. "Have faith," she repeated over and over again.

"That's right, have faith," a man said.

Spence?

She glanced up and saw his broad form standing over her.

"Spence."

He extended his hand and she took it.

FIFTEEN

"Maddie!" Spence shouted at the speakerphone.

There was no response. He glanced at Nate and Ryan, who stood close by in the conference room.

"What happened? Where did she go?" Spence said.

"He found her." Ryan slammed his fist against the table and paced to the opposite side of the room. He spun around. "Why couldn't we track the phone?"

"He disabled the GPS," Nate said.

"Then why let her call us at all?" Ryan said.

"To show us he's in charge," Nate offered.

Spence couldn't take his eyes off the speakerphone. Waiting, *praying*, to hear Maddie's voice.

"That's right," a gravelly male voice whispered through the room. "Watch your step."

Spence jumped to his feet. "Let her go!"

Nate placed a hand on his shoulder. "He's messing with your head."

"Almost there," the man said.

"His voice," Nate said. "It sounds like he's trying to mask it by talking from back of his throat."

Ryan stood in the corner, eyes widening with fury. "Come on, give us something," he ground out.

"I've got dry socks in the cabin," the man whispered.

"S-s-s-ocks," she said.

Spence's legs gave way and he collapsed in a chair.

"And we'll have dinner."

"D-d-d-dinner."

"Yes, you and me."

Nausea rolled through Spence's gut. He'd never felt such helplessness or desperation in his life. At this point he'd do anything to ensure Maddie's safe release.

"That's it," the man said. "Let's get you comfortable."

Spence's eyes were glued to the speaker, yet a part of him feared what might happen next.

Seconds stretched into minutes.

Nothing.

Nate glanced at his phone. "9-1-1 just confirmed the call ended."

Ryan shoved a chair aside and stormed out of the room. Nate spoke to someone on the phone in low tones, and Spence glared at the speaker with such intensity he thought it might melt.

"I don't care if he's in a meeting, we need assistance ASAP. A witness has been kidnapped." Nate headed for the door. "Hang on. Spence, I'll be in my office working on getting help from the feds."

Spence nodded, but couldn't speak. He had no words.

Nate left the room and the utter silence started to erode Spence's hope.

His fault. It was his fault.

Spence had involved Maddie in this by accepting her help from the beginning. Why hadn't he tried harder to drive her away? Instead, he'd leaned on her, relied on her and now she was being terrorized by Spence's enemy.

"God, I'll do anything," he whispered, assuming God understood his meaning.

And he would. He'd sacrifice his own life if it meant saving hers.

Because he knew he could not live in a world without Maddie McBride.

His phone vibrated with a call—a blocked number.

"Hello," he answered.

"I don't want to hurt her," a throaty voice whispered.

Spence's heart dropped. "Then let her go."

He stood to get Nate.

"If you involve the police, I will kill her."

"What do you want?" Spence sat back down.

"You."

"I'll do whatever you ask."

"I know you will."

An hour later the energy in the police station was stifling. Spence had finally received instructions on where to meet the kidnapper and when—three hours in the mountains beyond Deception Pass. But Spence had no vehicle or hiking gear.

He had a bigger problem: he had to leave the station without creating suspicion. He didn't like keeping Nate out of the loop, but he wouldn't risk Maddie's life if the kidnapper figured out Spence had backup.

For all he knew, the kidnapper had a partner in the police station. At this point they weren't ruling anything out, and Spence didn't trust anyone to save Maddie's life.

But he had the power to do so. And he would.

Reaching out to Ruth seemed like the best strategy. She and Cal were at the resort taking it easy. He asked if he could stop by, hoping to borrow one of their cars.

Spence approached Nate's office doorway and waited for him to finish his call.

"Good, keep me posted." Nate hung up and glanced at Spence. "How are you holding up?"

"I need to distract myself. Thought I'd check on Ruth

at the resort. Who knows, maybe she remembered something else that can help us."

"I'll have Adam take you. I assume you want to be kept in the loop about Maddie?"

"You know it."

Nate called Adam and asked him to return to the station. As Spence went to the exit, he passed Ryan, who didn't even look up. Of course not, Maddie's brother probably blamed Spence for her being kidnapped.

Spence surely did.

He went outside and pulled his jacket closed in front. Glancing up at the mountain range in the distance he shook his head. If it was this cold down here...

Fighting the image of Maddie suffering from hypothermia and being tended to by a killer, Spence tried thinking of something else, anything else. But her bright smile and emerald green eyes filled his thoughts. Gentle, caring green eyes.

"Please, God," he whispered.

A few minutes later Adam pulled up and motioned for him to get in.

Ruth looked exhausted, Spence thought as he entered her resort room. She motioned him to the dining table and he sat down.

"Is Cal here?" Spence said.

"Went to get me something from the snack bar."

"Probably just as well."

"He shouldn't have said that before, about it being your fault. He was upset."

"I know the feeling." He glanced at his friend. "I need a favor."

"Sure."

"I need to borrow a car."

She leaned back in her chair. "What's going on?"

"I'd rather not involve you further."

"Please, tell me what's happened."

"Someone kidnapped Maddie."

"Oh, Spence."

"The kidnapper wants to meet, alone. I haven't told police."

"You can't go by yourself. It's too dangerous."

"I have no choice. I have to save her, Ruth. I have to…" His voice trailed off.

"You love her," Ruth said.

Spence nodded.

Ruth grabbed her purse. "Cal drove us over in my car."

"Will he be upset with you for letting me use it?"

"I'll handle Cal." She pulled keys out of her purse.

When Spence reached for them she hesitated before letting go. "Please be careful."

"I will."

Since Adam was posted in the hallway, Spence slipped out of Ruth's room through the patio door and left the resort without being detected. He didn't feel all that great about leaving his bodyguard in the dark, but felt he had no choice.

Spence decided to stop at a store outside of town to pick up clothes and a warm jacket since his things were destroyed in the fire. He also purchased blankets, boots and fresh clothes for Maddie, along with a thermal blanket to treat exposure.

Second thoughts about excluding Nate taunted him, but he couldn't risk involving the police.

An hour later he made it to the trailhead and after a short hike, he spotted the small cabin in a clearing. Heart pounding, he crossed the property and stepped onto the stoop.

What if she was gone? What if the kidnapper had moved her, or worse, killed her?

Please, God.

With a deep breath, he opened the door and went inside. The first thing he saw was Maddie on the floor. He quickly scanned the room, but she was alone.

If the kidnapper left her alone without locking the door that meant...

"No, no, no," he muttered, rushing to her side. "Maddie, can you hear me?"

He checked her pulse—sixty beats per minute.

Thank God.

Pulling off his pack, he dug out the warming blanket. Her clothes weren't as wet as he'd expected, which was good. He wrapped her snugly in the blanket and kissed her forehead.

"She'll be okay."

Spence whipped around and saw Ruth's husband leaning against the doorframe.

"Cal?"

"You know I'd never hurt her," he said in his normal voice. "She's a lovely girl and that family has been through enough." Cal stepped inside and locked the cabin door. He clutched a gun in his hand.

"I don't understand," Spence said.

"It's simple. You're too perfect."

"Excuse me?" Spence held Maddie close, stroking her hair.

"We had to do something to destroy your reputation before you opened a Pandora's box."

"You? That was you in the mountains with the mask?"

"No, that was Anthony. Mr. Wick procured her phone and passed it to Anthony. He was supposed to ensure you had a fatal accident."

"But why?"

"Stop pretending. You'd discovered our side business. You kept asking Ruth about billing discrepancies."

Spence shook his head. "No, Cal—"

"You were building a fraud case against us. You insinuated as much at the hospital board meeting. Anthony failed to kill you in the mountains, but then you suffered brain trauma and we decided to capitalize on that instead of killing you. Almost convinced you to kill yourself trying to save your brother."

"You were the ambulance driver, the doctor who led me into the mountains?"

"The one plan that worked in our favor. I had to draw you out of whatever resort cabin you were hiding in and knew you couldn't resist saving people from a fire. Anthony drugged you in the kitchen and dumped you outside. Once paramedics got you into the ambulance I knocked out the driver and drove off. If only you would have ended your life then and there."

"But why kill Dr. Danner?"

"He was going to mysteriously leave town and we couldn't have that. An investigation of his disappearance would have exposed our operation."

"Danner was a part of this?"

"He discovered what we were doing so we paid him off. But he grew a conscience, the fool. Then your girl went poking around in hospital files and found potentially damaging information. We set up Danner to take the fall. Anthony was supposed to deal with him. He beat Danner up pretty good, but Danner got away. You'd think I would have learned to do things myself." Cal shook his head.

"So this was about money?"

"Money, and the fact I wouldn't enjoy prison food."

Spence continued to stroke Maddie's soft hair. "And Ruth?"

"Ah, my beloved wife. She came up with the idea."

Spence couldn't believe what he was hearing. "Cal…"

"What?" he shouted. "Don't use that condescending tone on me, Dr. Perfect Spencer."

Silence stretched between them. Cal had the power, the control. Spence glanced at Maddie, unconscious in his arms. There was no way he'd trust Cal with Maddie in this defenseless condition.

"So what now?" Spence said.

"You take this." Cal placed a medication bottle on the floor and toed it with his boot. The bottle rolled to Spence. "It's an easy way to go. You were so despondent about Maddie that you killed yourself."

Spence glared at Cal. "You're going to kill her?"

"No, but she was missing and presumed dead so you lost all hope," Cal shrugged.

Spence stood. "Take her to the hospital and I'll do whatever you want, after I get proof that she's been admitted."

"Who do you think you are?" He aimed the gun at Spence's chest.

"Those are my terms," Spence said. He loved Maddie and had to fight for her…to the end.

Suddenly Maddie started seizing.

Spence turned and dropped to her side. "What did you give her?" he shouted at Cal.

"A mild sedative, hours ago."

Spence thought he saw Maddie wink.

Cal stepped closer.

Spence spun around and tackled Cal.

The low rumble of men's voices awakened Maddie, but something told her not to open her eyes. She shoved back her anxiety and listened intently.

She heard Spence's voice, and then another familiar voice.

Cal Carver.

"Who do you think you are?"

"Those are my terms," Spence said.

She'd heard enough to know Cal was the kidnapper, and he was threatening their lives. She had to do something to distract Cal so Spence could get the upper hand.

Pretending to have a seizure seemed like the best option.

Spence knelt beside her. She hoped he saw her wink, then...

He spun around and charged Cal.

A gunshot rang out.

There was nowhere to go, no place to hide in the one-room cabin. The men crashed to the floor beside her.

Another shot rang out. She pinched her eyes shut.

Pounding vibrated through the cabin. "Police! Open the door!"

"He's got a gun!" she shouted.

The police pounded again.

Cal and Spence continued to roll and punch.

The gun slid across the cabin floor. Scrambling for the weapon, she grabbed it and jumped to her feet, wavering.

"Stop!" she shouted, but the men kept fighting.

Due to the effects of hypothermia and the quick movements of the men, she couldn't get a clear shot off.

Nate, Ryan and Red burst into the cabin. Her gun was still aimed at the two men swinging at each other.

Ryan and Red pulled them apart.

"Red, cuff Cal and get him outta here," Nate said.

"Yes, sir."

"Maddie," Nate said. "You can put the gun down."

She glanced at him through watery eyes.

Ryan nodded that it was okay. She lowered the weapon and Nate eased it out of her hand.

"Spence?" Nate said. "Whoa."

Maddie snapped her attention to Spence. Blood oozed down his jacket sleeve.

"No!" She stumbled across the cabin and collapsed beside him.

"You're okay," he said, blinking those soft blue eyes at her. "That's all that matters."

Then, with a slight smile on his face, he closed his eyes.

SIXTEEN

Someone was humming.

Spence didn't know the song, but it didn't matter. He recognized her voice, even when she hummed.

"Maddie," he said, his voice raw.

"Hello there, Dr. Sleepy."

He turned toward the sound of her voice.

She smiled, a full-blown, uninhibited smile that warmed his heart.

"You're okay," he said.

"I am. And you'll be okay, too."

"What... Was I shot?"

"In the shoulder. The bullet went right through you."

"The police...how did they find us?"

Nate stepped up beside her. "I had Red keep an eye on you after Adam took you to the resort. Red saw you leave and kept you under surveillance."

"I wanted to tell you."

"It's all good. I'm glad we got there in time."

"What took you so long?" Maddie asked.

"We found Ruth's car in the parking lot, but weren't sure which trail to follow. Your brother figured out how to track Spence."

"What about Ruth?" Spence said.

"Arrested, along with Cal, Anthony and even Theresa,"

Nate said. "Apparently her flirtatious demeanor was meant to determine what you knew about the fraud scheme."

"So this wasn't about a personal enemy out to get me?" Spence said.

"No, sir," Nate said. "You happened to ask the wrong questions and they thought you were figuring it out."

"Tell him about Lucas," Maddie said.

"Right, the local teen who ran away from military school has been back in town for weeks," Nate said. "Broke into his parents' house and stole money and food. He was picked up at Camp Lakemont hanging out with friends."

"I'm glad he's okay," Spence said.

"Needless to say, his parents aren't pressing charges," Nate said.

"Nor are they sending him away again," Maddie offered. "I heard they're going to try counseling instead."

"That's good news. How's Gwen?"

"Back home with her mom," Maddie said.

"I didn't order that drug," Spence defended.

"No, but someone made it look like you did," she said.

"My guess would be Ruth," Nate said. "She also treated Cal's gunshot wound, which is why he didn't show up at a hospital."

"I still can't believe she was involved. And I had no clue," Spence said.

"You were focused on more important things, like saving lives." Maddie squeezed his hand.

That's when he realized they'd been holding hands. The warmth of her skin drifted all the way up his arm and uncoiled the tension in his chest.

"The feds are building the fraud case," Nate said. "Still hard to believe how it all played out. We're glad you're okay." He nodded at Spence.

"I'm glad you put a tail on me."

"I guess I know you better than I thought. Let me know when you're up to giving an official statement."

"I can do it now." He shifted in bed.

Spence wanted Maddie to leave. He needed time to process what should happen next, and come up with a logical reason that they should end their relationship.

"The painkillers might impede your memory," Nate said.

"I'd like to give it a try."

He slipped his hand from Maddie's. Her eyes widened for a second, then she smiled. "I guess that's my cue to leave. I'll check in later." She leaned forward and kissed his forehead. "Love you," she whispered.

She left the room and he released a heavy sigh.

"When did you figure out it was Cal?" Nate said, pulling up a chair.

"Not until he showed up at the cabin. I got instructions where and when to meet him. I found Maddie unconscious and tended to her the best I could. Then Cal shows up spouting nonsense about me uncovering the fraud, about Danner finding out and them paying for his silence. I was stupefied. I mean, Ruth?"

"She'd do anything to keep the hospital in the black. Not that it excuses her behavior, but she put some of the money back into the hospital."

"She had to know she'd get caught."

"I guess she thought she was smarter than the rest of us. What was Cal's plan for you and Maddie?"

"I'd kill myself because I was so despondent about Maddie being kidnapped. But she pretended to have a seizure to distract him."

"That Maddie, she is certainly special," Nate said. "The way she cares about people."

"Yeah, she almost died because she cares about me."

"That's not your fault and you know it." Nate stood. "Get some rest. I'll check in tomorrow."

Spence nodded and closed his eyes.

No matter what anyone said, a familiar pit grew in Spence's stomach: guilt, shame and remorse. It *was* his fault that Maddie had been drugged and kidnapped.

Love you.

When she'd spoken the words, his heart cracked a little bit more because he knew he shouldn't act on his feelings for her. He couldn't rip her away from her Echo Mountain family. She belonged here, but Spence…?

With all of his possessions destroyed, his home burned to the ground and his job gone, he didn't feel like he belonged anywhere. And he certainly didn't have much to offer Maddie.

No, he had depended on her enough, and he'd even fallen in love with her. But if he truly loved her, he'd accept that she deserved someone better than him, someone without all the baggage he carried around like a fifty-pound weight.

He'd stay in town long enough to help with any loose ends of the case, and then he'd quietly leave without fanfare or attention. After being checked out by a doctor, he'd get cleared to practice medicine again and start someplace new, someplace where they didn't know about his tumultuous history.

Your problems will always follow you and God will always forgive you.

She was probably right, but he couldn't think about that now. He needed to do what was best for Maddie.

Maddie needs you, a voice whispered.

He disregarded the voice, because if he listened he didn't stand a chance of getting out of town with his heart intact.

* * *

The next day he convinced Nate to let him speak with Ruth, who was sitting in lockup. Spence needed closure, an explanation, something. How could such a remarkable woman get sucked down such a dark path?

"You sure?" Nate said, gripping the door to the city's two cells.

"Yes. Is Cal with her?"

"He's in the conference room being questioned by the feds."

"Good." Some part of him wanted to believe it had been Cal's idea, and his wife went along with the plan because she loved her husband.

Nate opened the door and Spence entered the lockup area. Ruth glanced up from her position sitting on the cot. She shook her head and buried her face in folded arms across her knees.

"Two minutes," Nate said, and left them alone.

"Ruth?" Spence said.

She glanced up with desperation in her eyes, yet oddly not remorse.

"Why?" he said.

"There's a lot of pressure running a hospital, Spence. You have no idea. The board expects financial results and patients expect quality care and…" She paused. "Things just happened."

"And hiring me?"

She cracked a sad smile. "That felt like the one good thing I did. I hired a doctor who cared more about patients than the bottom line. Then you discovered what was going on, and our perfect doctor became a liability."

"But I didn't."

"It seemed like you had with all your emails and questions about billing. Anyway, it doesn't matter. It's over." She sighed. "And ya know? I'm relieved."

"I had no idea you were under so much pressure. I wish you would have—"

"What? Asked you for help? Really? Get out of here, Spence. You're making it worse with your platitudes and compassion."

He struggled to process how this could have happened, how he had no clue his friend was cheating the system.

"Go on," she said. "Go be perfect somewhere else."

Spence left the cell area and spotted Maddie's brother, Ryan, waiting in the hallway.

"Chief wants me to take you to the farm," he said.

"Okay, thanks."

With no place to live since his cabin had been destroyed, Spence asked to stay at the resort, but the McBride clan had a better idea; they invited him to stay at Margaret's farmhouse.

Ryan took Spence to the superstore on the way so Spence could buy clothes and toiletries. Spence was starting all over again. He'd done it before, but it felt different this time. He felt…melancholy.

"You sure I'm not putting your aunt out?" he asked Ryan.

"Nah, she lives to serve. Kind of like Maddie." Ryan shot Spence a side-glance. "So…?"

"So, what?"

"You and Maddie? You're going to dump her, aren't you?"

"That's a little harsh."

"Then you're staying around to date her?" Ryan asked, hopeful.

"I'm going to let her get on with her life without me."

"Sorry, Doc, but that's a lame excuse."

A few seconds of silence passed between them.

"Look," Ryan started. "I know my sister can be stubborn and bossy but she's a great person."

"You don't have to convince me of that."

"Then what's the problem? She really cares about you, and I sense you feel the same way."

Spence glanced out the window. "She belongs here, in Echo Mountain with her family. I don't."

"Since when?"

"Since the fraud, the kidnapping, the random assaults. My reputation has been destroyed and I can't expect the people of Echo Mountain to get past that."

"Come on, you know how forgiving these folks are."

Spence closed his eyes, withdrawing into his thoughts. Was Ryan right? Was Spence making excuses because he was afraid of being hurt again?

When they arrived at the farmhouse, Spence actually thought Maddie might be waiting with her bright smile and wry sense of humor.

Instead, the house was quiet. Margaret led Spence to an upstairs bedroom and encouraged him to relax. She said sweets and coffee would be available whenever he came down.

He stretched out on the bed, careful not to jar his arm. The splint reminded him not to exert himself in order for the gunshot wound to heal.

He finally felt safe, although emptiness consumed him.

Hours later he awakened to the sound of muffled voices drifting through the floor. He washed up in the private bathroom and cracked open the door to the hallway. It sounded like a party was going on downstairs. He shut the door and pressed his forehead against it. How could he face people after everything that had happened, after he'd been manipulated by someone he trusted? They all probably lumped him into the mix with the Carvers and Dr. Danner.

As a criminal.

Glancing at his suitcase, he was tempted to escape down the back stairs. Instead, he opted to greet the visitors. When he reached the front entryway, he could hardly believe his eyes. The living room was packed with local residents enjoying refreshments and laughter.

"There's Dr. Spencer," Margaret said, clapping.

The group broke into applause. Spence froze, unsure what to do.

Margaret approached him. "They randomly started showing up. But if you're too tired to visit…?"

"No, it's okay." He strained to see if Maddie was among them.

Her auburn hair didn't stand out in the crowd.

"Dr. Spencer, good to see you on your feet." Board president, Vince Brunson, approached him and extended his hand.

"Mr. Brunson." They shook. "I need to apologize—"

"No," he interrupted Spence. "I'm the one who needs to apologize. I jumped to the wrong conclusion. Chief Walsh told me what was really going on. I'm sorry the board took our frustrations out on you. To that point, we had an emergency meeting this morning and would like to offer you your job back."

"What? Wait, but my head injury, my erratic behavior…"

"Some of which was orchestrated by Dr. Carver. Besides, I'd like to think I'd be brave enough to run into a burning building to save innocent people." He smiled. "When your shoulder heals and you feel ready to return to the rotation, get cleared by an MD and your job will be waiting."

"Hey, buddy," Nate said, joining them. He nodded at Vince as the board president went to greet SAR member Sam Treadwell.

"This feels like a dream," Spence said.

"I wasn't sure if you'd be up for company, but when folks in town get an idea in their heads, well, it's hard to talk them out of it."

That's when Spence noticed a Congratulations sign hanging across a window.

"What's that for?" he asked.

"They're congratulating you for exposing the fraud scheme and surviving the week of being stalked."

"I… I'm not sure what to say."

"Hopefully they won't demand a speech."

Adam the bodyguard approached them and Spence reached out to shake his hand. "Thanks for everything. I'm sorry I skipped out on you at the resort."

"Apology accepted but I wish you would have let me help."

"At the time I felt like I couldn't risk it. So, what's next for you?"

"Heading back to Seattle tomorrow. New client."

"Hopefully lower maintenance than Spence," Nate said with a chuckle.

The men chatted briefly about the case, and then Spence spent the next hour visiting with each and every person in the room. He was stunned by their overwhelming support. They were curious about the week's events, genuinely concerned about his injuries, and supportive of his future in town.

Filled with conflicting emotions, he turned to go upstairs for a break and found himself face-to-face with Roger Grimes.

The man whose daughter Spence suspected had been abused reached out to shake Spence's hand. Spence hesitated.

"Please, Doc," Roger said.

They shook hands.

"I know I was angry with you, said some harsh words

and I'm sorry about that," Roger said. "Thanks to your suspicions we found out Megan's boyfriend has been hitting her."

"That's terrible, Roger. I'm so sorry."

Nate joined them.

"That kid is some kind of bully," Roger said.

"Turns out he was the one sending you the hate email, Spence," Nate offered.

"You were paying attention when I wasn't, Doc," Roger said. "I can't thank you enough."

"You're very welcome."

"Speech, speech, speech!" the group chanted.

As Spence glanced at the guests, he spotted Maddie step out from behind a few SAR members. She offered her sparkling smile as if encouraging him to speak from his heart.

The guests quieted and Spence cleared his throat. "Thanks for coming to see me today. It's been quite an interesting week."

They chuckled.

"All of this, your well wishes and congratulations, means more to me than you can possibly imagine. I want you to know, whatever happens next, that I will hold this memory close to my heart, always."

He noticed Maddie's smile fade.

Spence held up his cup of coffee. "To the amazing people of Echo Mountain."

They raised their cups and cheered. Ripping his gaze from Maddie's, he placed his cup on the front table and headed for the stairs, needing to decompress for a few minutes. The heady emotions from the past hour were tearing him up inside.

"Spence?" Nate said from the bottom of the stairs. "You okay?"

"Yeah, sure. I'll be back down in a few minutes."

And he would, after he finished packing.

* * *

Maddie could tell Spence was overwhelmed. She suspected he didn't have much experience with such a supportive network of people. She wondered if he purposely isolated himself from others in order to protect them from his perceived failures. She'd put it together earlier today that he'd been running ever since his brother died. His fiancée's betrayal confirmed his failure at love, and then his patient dying in the Portland ER probably chipped away at his confidence as a doctor. Although he acted as if he hadn't been affected, Maddie could tell it cut him to the core.

She stood at the bottom of the stairs, wanting to go up and talk to him. But what would she say? How could she convince him to open his heart and trust love again? Trust himself, and God?

If there was one thing she'd learned from being abandoned by loved ones, it was that she couldn't control anyone else's decisions. All she could control was her own.

She'd never forgive herself if she walked away without fighting for something she cared about deeply. Maybe she could help Spence believe it was okay to forgive himself and take a chance, plant some roots in town and accept support from people who cared about him.

As she climbed the stairs, her pulse sped up. *God, please help me find the right words.*

Once she reached his room, she placed her open palm on the closed door. Took a deep breath, and knocked. "Spence?"

"Come in."

Opening the door, she sucked in a quick breath. He was packing a suitcase. She knew a part of him didn't want to go, didn't want to run away again. Humor and faith had always helped her in the past, and that gave her an idea.

Quirking her mouth into a teasing smile she said, "Hoping to make a clean getaway, huh?"

"Just getting ready."

"For the great escape?"

He shrugged. "I guess we should talk."

"About what—world events, church news, or maybe the latest gossip in Cassie's blog? Come on, I'll help you pack." She grabbed a pair of socks and rolled them up.

Handing him the socks she said, "Don't forget your resentment."

He narrowed his eyes at her and took the socks.

She handed him another pair. "Or your shame," she said with a smile.

She tossed a pair of jeans at him. "Oh, and guilt, you wouldn't want to leave guilt behind. You simply couldn't survive without all that guilt."

"Okay, I get it."

A slight smile teased the corner of his lips.

"Look, I've learned I can't change anyone's mind, nor should I. I don't know what your journey is or what God has in store for you, but what I do know is that you've been your own worst enemy for a very long time, always beating yourself up. I think people get used to beating themselves up and it becomes routine. That's what happened to me when my parents left, and then the boyfriend left. So, Dr. Kyle Spencer, I will not try to force you to stay in Echo Mountain, but I will continue to pray that someday you'll be able to let go of all that pain so you can experience true joy because that is my wish for the people I love." With a ball of emotion rising in her throat, Maddie wrapped her arms around his waist. This hug would have to last her a lifetime.

She released him and went to the door.

"Wait," he said.

Her breath caught as she fought back tears.

"Vince Brunson offered me my job back," he said.

She slowly turned. "No kidding. Then why are you packing?"

"Habit?"

Hope flitted in her chest. "How about trying a new habit," she said, closing the distance between them.

"Like what?"

She slid her arms around his waist again. "Like…love."

"Sounds intriguing."

"And surrender."

"Uh…not sure—"

"Surrender all that guilt, shame and pain to God. Let Him carry your burden."

"Maddie McBride, you are—"

"What? Bossy? My cousin Cassie always tells me that."

"I was going to say amazing."

"Oh, I definitely like that better than bossy."

He tossed the jeans on the bed, missing the suitcase completely, and framed her face with his hands. "Maddie, I love you, but I may not stay in Echo Mountain forever. I will go where I'm most needed."

She smiled, realizing the comfort of home could be found anywhere with the man she loved.

"Hmm, a life of service," she said. "I like the sound of that."

And she kissed him.

* * * * *

Christy Barritt's books have won a Daphne du Maurier Award for Excellence in Suspense and Mystery and have been twice nominated for an RT Reviewers' Choice Best Book Award. She's married to her Prince Charming, a man who thinks she's hilarious—but only when she's not trying to be. Christy's a self-proclaimed klutz, an avid music lover and a road-trip aficionado. For more information, visit her website at christybarritt.com.

Books by Christy Barritt

Love Inspired Suspense

Visit the Author Profile page at Harlequin.com.

MOUNTAIN HIDEAWAY

Christy Barritt

Truly I tell you, if you have faith as small as a mustard seed, you can say to this mountain, "Move from here to there," and it will move. Nothing will be impossible for you.
—*Matthew* 17:20

To all the children my husband and I work with every Sunday at Kempsville Christian—your faith inspires me. Thank you for being a part of my life.

ONE

Tessa Jones flung herself across the couch toward the lamp and pulled the switch so hard the ceramic base nearly toppled onto the wooden floor below. With quick breaths, she darted toward the wall.

She pulled her sweater closer around her neck and forced air into her lungs. Anxiety pressed down on her and adrenaline surged, the mix making her head spin.

Slowly, she edged toward the window. She had to look. She had no choice.

With all the lights extinguished in her home, anyone lurking outside shouldn't see her. Still, she had to be careful. She had no idea who or what was on the other side of that glass. Here in the middle of nowhere, there were no neighbors to hear her scream, to rush to her rescue. If something happened to her, she might not be found for days.

That had worked to her advantage...until today.

At this moment, she craved having someone nearby to help her, to be a second set of eyes. But she'd been mentally preparing for months to be self-reliant if a situation like this ever occurred. She'd only hoped it would never come to this.

As she turned toward the window, her eyes adjusted to

the darkness. She stared hard yet cautiously into the abyss of thick woods surrounding the property.

Certainly, the speck of light bobbing on the horizon had just been her imagination. There was no one out there among the trees and the steep landscape of the mountain terrain. There couldn't be. No one even knew this place was here.

Blackness stared back, and her heart slowed.

It had been her imagination. Just her imagination. Maybe her paranoia. It didn't matter, as long as what she'd seen hadn't been real.

Just then something flickered in the distance.

She blinked, her momentary relief instantly vanishing. She clutched her chest as her heart thumped out of control. Despite the cold, sweat spread across her forehead.

The light was small, like a flashlight, and it continued to bob through the woods.

Someone was walking. Toward the cabin. Toward her.

Leo's men had found her, she realized.

Fear paralyzed her.

It didn't matter that she'd run through this potential scenario a million times. That she'd rehearsed what she would do. That she'd planned the best course of escape.

Right now, all of those thoughts disappeared.

She'd been here eight months. She'd thought she was safe. She'd prayed she was.

But God had stopped answering her prayers a long time ago.

The beam grew larger as it neared the property. Whoever was holding the light had probably seen the lamp on. Knew that Tessa was here. Hiding, at this point, would be fruitless.

No, she had to run.

She shook her head, thoughts colliding inside.

If she ran, the mountains would kill her, even if whoever was after her didn't. It was too dark. There were too many cliffs. Too many unknowns.

Either way, she had to move, and now!

She grabbed a backpack from her closet. She'd put it together just in case something like this ever happened. It had a flashlight, some cash, some water and a small blanket. After she slung the bag over her shoulders, she crept to the back door. She had to be decisive, to stop hesitating. If she wasn't, the person out there would reach the cabin and might hear her leave. Might sneak around to the back and catch her.

It took every ounce of her determination to pull the door open. A brisk wind blew inside. Though it was late autumn, the air felt brutally cold here in the middle of the mountains, especially at night.

She was going to miss this cabin. Miss this life.

The thought of starting over again made Tessa's head pound, made her feel as though a rock had been placed on her chest.

But she'd have time to worry about that later. Right now, she had to concentrate on surviving.

She quietly closed the door behind her. On her tiptoes, she started toward the woodshed in the distance. She'd hide out there and see what unfolded. She didn't have much choice. If the intruder came too close, she could dart into the woods. She'd take her chances there before she'd take them at the hands of the ruthless men who Leo had probably sent after her.

Ducking behind the rough wood of the shed, she crouched, desperate to stay concealed. As the wind blew, the leaves swept across the ground. The sound, normally comforting, made her nerves tighten.

She held her breath, listening for any indications of the intruder.

She heard nothing.

That was when her mind began running through scenarios and she remembered—

Her car!

Of course, anyone after her would see her car. They'd know she was here. They'd tear everything apart until they found her. And once they found her… She shuddered to think of what would happen then.

If she somehow happened to escape, they could easily trace her license plate. They'd put one and one together. She felt hunted and as if there was no safe place for her to hide. Her cubbyhole away from the world had been compromised.

She'd have to start over again with a new identity, a new home, a new everything.

How could she go on like this for the rest of her life? Living with this kind of fear wasn't living at all. It was surviving.

Just as she closed her eyes, on the verge of praying for mercy, she heard a bang. She clutched her chest. As she peered around the corner, the back door flung open.

The wind! Tessa realized.

The door had never latched easily. In her haste to get out of the house, she must not have pulled hard enough.

Now there was no hiding the fact that she was nearby. It was a matter of evading the intruder more than it was about hiding.

Despair bit deep. Maybe it would just be easier to give up.

No, Tessa reminded herself. No matter how tempting the thought might be at times, she knew she couldn't surrender. Leo didn't deserve to win, and she wouldn't go down without a fight.

Leo McAllister, her ex-fiancé, had already turned her life upside down when she'd caught him in the middle of smuggling blueprints for dangerous weapons to terrorists overseas. She'd tried to gather evidence to nail him, but she'd failed. That was when she'd known she had no choice but to run.

He'd sent men after her and they'd soon found her at the first place she'd sought refuge—an old house she'd rented with cash and a fake name. She'd discovered the cottage off a lonely country road in the rolling hills of Virginia and had thought she'd found the perfect hideaway. She'd been wrong. While coming home from buying groceries, she'd seen the men inside her temporary home and had fled.

Tessa had barely gotten away. She wouldn't have escaped if it hadn't been for a drawbridge that she'd crossed just in time.

Now Tessa waited, holding her breath, to see what would happen next. In theory, she'd been living like this ever since that life-changing day when she'd discovered Leo's true colors.

The light appeared again.

The intruder was inside her cabin now, she was certain.

A voice drifted out, but she couldn't make out the words.

As the wind brushed her again, her nose tingled. It wouldn't be too long before her ears, her cheeks and her fingers all went numb. So many things could go wrong right now.

She squinted as someone stepped out the back door. The flashlight nearly caught her, but she tucked herself back behind the shed in time. As she saw the beam fade to the other side of the property, she stole another glance.

The man on her deck was tall and broad. He wore a black coat—leather, maybe—and low-slung jeans. He didn't look familiar but, then again, it was dark. Besides, the McAllisters had enough money to hire people to do their dirty work. Leo would never do this kind of job himself.

The man stepped off the deck and walked around the

side of the house. Her heart pounded in her ears as she waited for what seemed like hours. He circled the house twice. Shone his light into her car. Surveyed the area around the cabin.

Then he started toward the woods near the shed.

Tessa held her breath. *No! Not back here.*

His footsteps stopped.

Slowly, the sound faded, almost as if he was…retreating?

She counted to ten before peering around the corner again. In the distance, she saw the light disappear into the woods. He was leaving.

He was *leaving*!

But why? Maybe he wasn't one of the men after her. Maybe he was just a passerby whose car had broken down or a hunter checking out the area. Maybe he'd gotten lost on the winding road and had come looking for directions.

None of those things sounded quite true, even in her own mind, but she couldn't think too long.

Once the light disappeared well out of sight, she hurried to the house.

She'd forgotten her car keys. She had to grab them and get out of here. There was no time to waste.

She shuddered as she scrambled over the crispy leaves across her backyard. She sprinted up the steps, mentally reviewing where she'd left them. She couldn't risk turning the lights on. Relying on her memory, she rushed toward the kitchen table. Her purse was there.

Had the man seen it? Had he looked inside and seen her license?

Her hands trembled now. She snatched the bag, her gaze frantically searching the countertop for the keys. Thankfully they were right beside the coffeepot where she'd left them.

She lunged toward them and felt the metal against her fingers.

Now she just had to get out of here.

Just as she turned, she sensed someone behind her. Before she could scream, a hand covered her mouth.

And, for the first time in years, she prayed.

Trent McCabe hated to scare the woman—to scare any woman. But if he didn't grab her now, she'd run. Then he'd never have any answers to the heavy questions hanging over his head.

He couldn't let her get away. There were too many reasons why it would be a bad idea.

He kept one hand firmly over her mouth and his other arm locked her elbows against her body. He lifted her off her feet, and she kicked, flailing. But she wasn't going anywhere. Trent would give her a few minutes and, once she was worn out from struggling, he'd try to talk to her. She'd left him with very few options.

She fought against him, each jerk full of fight. He had to admire her for that. But he'd fought enough battles and had enough muscles and brawn to easily overtake her. She would wear out much sooner than he would. He just had to be patient.

She paused and her chest heaved as if she was gulping in breaths. His heart lurched as he realized just how terrified the woman was. He'd never meant for things to play out like this. He'd just been so desperate to find her.

"I'm not going to hurt you. I just have a few questions," he murmured in his most calming, apologetic voice. "Quiet down."

His words had the opposite effect and seemed to propel her back into action. She began thrashing again, trying desperately to get out of his grip. This woman wasn't going to give up, was she? She had more fight than he'd guessed.

Trent stood there, waiting patiently. But he gave her credit for her efforts. She was giving it all she had.

"Listen, your mom sent me," he finally said.

She slowed for a moment. Without even seeing her face, he knew the wheels in her brain were turning, were processing the information. That was a good sign.

"I'm going to move my hand from your mouth so we can talk. Okay?" he soothed as a tremble began shaking her muscles.

She remained where she was, her breathing too shallow for her own good.

"Okay?" he repeated.

Finally, she nodded her head.

One of his hands slipped back down to his side. She remained eerily still, not saying a word but unable to run. He waited for her to speak.

They said good things came to those who waited, and the saying had proved to be true more than once in his life. Though it had also proved deadly. He hoped that wouldn't be the case now.

"My mom's dead," she finally said, her voice just above a whisper.

"No, she's not. You and I both know that."

"Let me go. Let's talk like two humans." Her voice shook with emotion, yet based on the tight cadence of her words, she was trying to control her fear.

Guilt flashed through him. He hated for this to be his only means of talking to her. His mom had raised him better than this. But what else was he supposed to do? Drastic situations called for drastic actions.

He had his doubts, but he realized that acting as if she was his captive wouldn't get him very far. Hesitantly, he released his clamp across her arms. "Fine. Let's talk."

As soon as she was out of his grasp, she darted to the kitchen counter and grabbed a knife from the butcher block. She held it in front of her. Even in the dark, Trent could see the desperate gleam in her gaze. "Step back."

He raised his hands. "I'm not going to hurt you."

"You break into my home, practically take me hostage and then tell me your intentions are golden? I don't think so."

"Don't forget that I also let you go," he reminded her, willfully trying to gain her trust. He knew he could easily work that knife from her hands, but he'd scared the woman enough already. "I didn't want you to run away. That's the only reason I grabbed you like that."

"Justify it however you want. You need to get out of my house. Now." She pointed toward the door with her knife.

"I just want to talk. Besides, this isn't your house, is it?"

She held the knife higher, her chin rising in stubborn determination. "I thought I made myself clear. Get out. Now."

Trent took another step back, hoping the woman would realize he didn't want to hurt her. He couldn't blame her for doubting that. "Your mom has been searching for you."

The dark concealed her face, but he sensed her shoulders slumping. "Like I said, my mom is dead."

"You and I both know you're lying, Theresa." He watched her face as he used her name. He only wished there was more light so he could see. Any of the small hints she might offer to prove he was telling the truth were erased by the darkness.

"That's not my name." Her voice shook even harder. "I'm Tessa Jones."

"Your name is Theresa Davidson." She was thinner now. Her hair was long and light brown when it used to be shoulder length, curly and blond. But he'd been searching for six months, and he felt certain this was the woman he was looking for. "I'm Trent McCabe, by the way."

"I'm going to call the police." Her words didn't sound remotely convincing.

"Go right ahead. I'll wait here while you do it." Their conversation felt a bit like a game. He'd made his move, she'd made hers and they continued to go back and forth. Trent knew good and well that she wouldn't call the police. She had too much at stake. People who wanted to disappear did not call the police.

"Why are you doing this?" Her voice cracked with desperation. "I'm giving you the chance to leave. Please. Just go."

"You have a lot of people who are concerned about you." Seeing the worry in her loved ones' eyes had been enough to compel him to stick with this case long after the time and funds had run out. He'd seen something in her family that he'd seen in himself all those years ago: pain and hurt. If possible, he wanted to spare them any more heartache.

"You have the wrong person." She said each word slowly, forcefully. It was almost as if she was trying to convince herself of the truth.

But Trent heard the emotion there. The doubt. The fear. The moment of hesitation. There was no question this was the right woman.

But she wasn't going to give this whole act up now. He didn't know what had driven her to come here, to hide for all these months. But it must be a strong reason.

Whatever it was, she wasn't budging. He had to think of a different approach because this one certainly wasn't working. She wasn't in the right emotional state to change her mind.

"Okay, okay. Look, I'm sorry to have scared you." He took a step backward. "I'll leave."

He kept backing up until he reached the front door. A moment of hesitation hit him, and he started to try to persuade her again, but thought better of it. The woman was spooked. The fear that he'd seen in those big blue eyes of hers would make sure that any pleas for logic would go unheard.

He couldn't actually see the blue, but he remembered

it from the photos of Theresa. Her eyes had been one of her most striking features. He recalled the earnest, sincere look—it was one that couldn't be faked.

He'd guess that this woman hadn't lost that sincerity, either. The warmth in her eyes was something that was a part of her. The ability to show her character with one look, expressing deep emotions, communicating without a word.

Kind of like Laurel. His heart ached at the memory.

He gripped the doorknob, took one last look at the shadowy woman who still stood on guard and stepped outside.

Just as he did, a bullet pierced the air.

TWO

Tessa froze at the sound. Someone was shooting! There was more than one person who'd shown up here. She should have known better.

Before she could react, the man—the intruder—dived back into the house and slammed the door. "Get down!"

She must not have been moving fast enough, because he threw himself over her. The knife flew from her hand and clattered to the corner.

"We've got to get out of here!" he grumbled.

She stiffened with alarm at the very suggestion. "I'm not going anywhere with you."

"I'm not the one firing at you." His breath was hot on her cheek, and his closeness caused heat to shoot through her. She'd been so isolated that human touch seemed foreign, surreal. In order to survive, she'd been forced to keep her distance from people.

"This could all be an elaborate scheme on your part," she said through clenched teeth. "*Elaborate* being the key word."

"I promise you that I'm on your side. I don't want to die, either, and if we stay here, that's what's going to happen." He looked at her a moment. "Can you trust me?"

"I don't even know you! Of course I can't."

"You're going to have to decide who you trust more, then—me or the men shooting outside your house."

"Neither!" Her answer came fast and left no room for uncertainty.

As a bullet shattered the front window, his gaze caught hers. "Please, Ther—Tessa. I don't want you to get hurt. Your family would be devastated if you were. These men must have followed me here."

Something in the man's voice seemed sincere, and the mention of her family softened her heart. What if they *had* hired someone to find her? She could see them going to those measures.

She'd known when she disappeared they would worry. But what else could she have done? Leo would kill them, too, if they knew too much. Leaving without giving them a reason had been the hardest thing she'd ever done.

Tessa snapped back to the present and realized that she had little choice at this point but to go along with this Trent guy. Hesitantly, she nodded. "Fine, I'll trust you for now."

"Good. Now we're getting somewhere. We've got to get out here and make it to my Jeep. I'm sure those men outside have got their eyes on the doors. Are there any other exits?"

"The basement. We can escape from the storm cellar. The door opens at the other side of the hot tub. The exit is hard to see, especially with the leaves covering the ground at this time of year."

"Perfect. Show me how to get there."

With trepidation, Tessa crawled across the floor. As she passed the iron poker by the fireplace, she briefly entertained the idea of grabbing it and knocking out the man beside her. Maybe she could get away on her own and take her chances. But Trent had proved himself to be quick and able. Besides, that would only cost them more time.

She reached the basement door and nudged it open. Blackness stared at her on the other side, so dark and thick that her throat went dry. The basement was the last place she wanted to go. But what choice did she have?

She half expected Trent to push her down the stairs, lock her in the damp space and later gloat that she'd fallen for his ruse. Ever since Leo, Tessa had a hard time trusting people. The situation at the moment felt overwhelming with all of its uncertainties.

"You'll be okay." She heard the whispered assurance from behind her.

He seemed to sense her fear. She nodded again and forced herself to continue. When she reached the first step, she stood, still hunched over and trying to make herself invisible.

Another window shattered upstairs. Someone was definitely desperate to kill her. She only hoped she hadn't trusted the wrong person.

Just as she reached the basement floor, her foot caught. She started to lunge forward when a strong hand caught her shoulder and righted her. "You okay?"

"I'm fine," she whispered, still shaky.

When her feet found solid ground, she expected to feel relief. Instead, her quivers intensified. She couldn't see anything down here. Someone could be hiding, just waiting to attack.

Trent gripped her arm. "Can you tell me where the stairway that leads outside is?"

"To the right."

He propelled her forward, not waiting for her to gather herself. Before she realized what was happening, he led her up another set of steps, through some cobwebs, and then stopped.

"Stay right here," he whispered.

With measured motions, he slid the latch to the side and cracked the exterior door open. Moonlight slithered inside, along with a cool burst of air.

As she listened, her heart pounded in her chest with enough force that she felt certain anyone within a mile could hear it. This could be it. She could die.

Leo and his minions had finally found her. She'd known it was only a matter of time before her ex located her and ensured she remained silent about his prestigious family's dealings with terrorists.

What she wasn't sure about was this man with her now and his role in all of this. She knew this: there were people out there prowling around and searching for victims, for people to take advantage of. She'd never be that person again, not if she could help it.

The man was closer now, too close. Near enough that she could feel his body heat, that she could smell his leathery aftershave. Unfortunately, he was also close enough that she could catch a glance of his breathtaking, although shadowed, features. Even in the dark, she spotted his chiseled face, his perceptive eyes, his thick and curly hair.

"How fast can you run?" he whispered.

"I was a sprinter in high school." As soon as the words left her mouth, she clamped her lips shut. Why had she said that? Why had she given any indication of who'd she'd been in her past life, her life before hiding out here in the mountains of Gideon's Hollow, West Virginia?

"You're going to need to utilize some of those skills now," he muttered. "On the count of three, we need to make a run for it. Jump in my Jeep and go. No hesitating. No looking back. Can you do that?"

She nodded before finally choking out, "Yes, yes, I can do that."

"Take my hand." A wisp of moonlight slithered through the crack and illuminated his outstretched fingers.

She swallowed back her fears and slipped her hand into his. She'd act now and think later. She had no other choice.

"One. Two. Three!" With that, he burst out of the basement and flew like a bullet toward the woods.

She hardly had time to think, to breathe. All she could do was try to remain on her feet as trees and underbrush and boulders blurred by. Somehow she avoided falling or tripping or tumbling forward. It had something to do with the strength that emanated from the man in front of her. He seemed so in control, even in such a precarious situation.

A shout sounded in the distance. She thought she heard more scurrying, but everything moved too fast for her to put it together. Another gunshot rang out.

Something straight ahead glinted in the moonlight. The next moment Trent pushed her inside a dark vehicle that had been concealed by the nighttime and the thick woods. Before she could catch her breath, he hopped in the driver's seat and they squealed onto the road.

Her heart pounded out of control as she tried to absorb what had just happened.

She'd just survived one attempt on her life. Now she braced herself for what this man might do with her next.

"Put your seat belt on!" Trent yelled, snapping his own in place.

Thankfully, Tessa listened, though she could barely carry out the request. Her hands trembled too badly. Finally the mechanism clicked in place.

He hit the accelerator and the tires turned against the steep, winding mountain road. This road was tricky enough in the daytime, but right now, with no overhead streetlights and dull, no longer reflective guardrails, it would be a particularly treacherous drive.

But he had to get out of here fast. Whoever was shooting at them wasn't playing around. They were shooting to kill.

Who were those men? How had they found him? And the bigger question, why did they want Tessa dead?

Trent knew he'd been careful. But something must have triggered someone with less than honorable intentions to the fact that he'd tracked down Tessa.

He'd assumed she had run away because of her broken engagement. Further digging into her past had shown she was in massive credit card debt, had lost her job and had been seeing a psychologist.

Some feared she'd lost it. There had been no signs of foul play in her disappearance. Just a note: "I have to go. Don't try to find me."

Her family didn't believe any of that, though. They feared she was in trouble. Maybe she'd seen a crime and fled. Maybe someone had forced her to write that note. Had forced the massive purchases on her credit cards.

They claimed she'd never seen a psychologist, that she was happy and one of the most stable people one could meet.

Trent had been trying to discover what was reality and what was fiction.

Had the men who were after them—whoever they were—talked to Bill Andrews after Trent?

Bill owned the cabin where Tessa was staying. Trent had questioned him about her disappearance and, as they discussed Tessa, the man had mentioned his fond memories of the times when she had come with his family to an old hunting cabin he owned in West Virginia. Bill hadn't been back in years.

On a whim, Trent had decided to check the place out. No one was supposed to be staying there. But when Trent had seen the light in the window, he'd suspected that his hunch was correct. Tessa had known about the cabin and was using it to hide out.

The vehicle outside the residence hadn't been her car. She must have gotten a new one, along with taking a new name. The woman had to be intelligent to make it as far as she had without being detected.

Maybe Bill had told those men about his cabin, just as he'd told Trent. More than likely, though, the men who were shooting at them had followed Trent here. That meant that he'd led these men right to Tessa. He should have been more careful. Maybe there was more to her story than he'd assumed.

He'd have time to think about that later. He'd promised Tessa's mom that he'd do everything in his power to bring her daughter home safely, and that was exactly what he planned on doing. He would have to formulate his moves carefully in order to make that happen.

He watched the speedometer climb, knowing these speeds weren't safe on the winding road. Beside him, Tessa was deathly quiet. He stole a glance at her and saw how pale she'd gone, saw how her knuckles were white as she gripped the seat. The woman was terrified.

His gaze flickered to the rearview mirror. Just as he feared, headlights swerved onto the road behind him. A car closed the space between them by the second.

"Hold on!" Trent gripped the steering wheel as he pressed the accelerator even harder.

"Are you trying to get us killed?" Tessa's voice sounded thin and fraught with tension.

"The exact opposite, actually." He saw the car behind them gaining speed, nearly close enough to rear-end them. One bump could send his Jeep into the massive rock wall beside them. One nudge could propel them to their death. He'd seen fatal car accidents plenty of times before, from back when he'd worked patrol.

He couldn't let that happen now. There weren't many options for what he could do out here, but thankfully his training in the military and as a detective had taught him a thing or two. The road didn't have many intersections and the nearest one was probably three miles away, at least. That meant he had three miles of trying to drive faster and with more control than the guys behind him. It was the only way he'd outwit them.

He continued to gun it, careful to stay in control. Tessa let out a soft moan beside him. "I can't watch."

"Probably a good idea."

"Do you have a gun?"

He resisted the urge to glance her way and try to read her expression. He couldn't afford to take his eyes off the road. But what in the world was she getting at? "I do."

"Where is it?"

"In my jacket."

Before he realized what was happening, Tessa reached into his coat and pulled out his Glock.

"What are you doing?" Alarm captured his voice.

"Trying to stay alive," she muttered. She rolled down the window, and gusts of frigid air whipped inside the Jeep. With more guts than he'd realized the woman had, she leaned outside and fired the first shot.

The car behind him swerved.

"Where did you learn to shoot like that?" he shouted over the wind.

"I've been taking lessons."

The car behind them quickly righted and charged even closer. Tessa fired again, and the sound of rubber skidding across the road filled the air. The car kept coming. Just then, the back glass of the Jeep shattered.

The men were shooting back. If they managed to pierce a tire, Trent and Tessa would be goners.

A bend in the road appeared. The area was even narrower with a cliff on one side and a rock wall on the other. This was their only chance.

Trent braced himself. "Hold on!"

He grabbed Tessa and pulled her inside before she got herself killed.

Ahead, the trees disappeared and the nighttime sky was all that was visible. Tessa sucked in a deep breath beside him.

This was a twenty-five-miles-per-hour curve. He remembered it well. It was sharp, merciless and adorned with several danger-ahead signs.

He had to think quickly.

Instead of slowing down, he gunned it. They charged toward the open sky ahead. One wrong move and they'd free-fall off the mountain. It was a chance he had to take, especially since the other option meant certain death.

God, be with us!

"You're going to kill us!" Tessa screamed.

At the last minute, he jerked the wheel to the right. The Jeep skidded, nearly going into a spin.

His heart pounded out of control as the edge of the cliff neared. The car fishtailed, started to right itself, but suddenly spun.

Trent held his breath, lifting up more prayers.

Lord, please help us stop in time. Our lives depend on it.

THREE

Tessa opened her mouth but the scream stuck in her throat. As the Jeep veered closer and closer to the edge of the mountain, her life flashed before her eyes. Her regrets. Her time apart from her loved ones. Everything she'd been through over the past year.

She didn't want things to end this way.

God, please! It was the second time today she'd found herself praying, something she hadn't done in months. Maybe it was time to change that.

Suddenly, the Jeep righted itself. Before three seconds had even passed, she felt Trent press the gas again. They accelerated down the road, her heart pounding radically out of control with each second of forward motion.

She looked over her shoulder just in time to see the car behind them swerve. The tires screeched before the horrible sound of metal hitting metal filled the air.

Her eyes squeezed shut as the vehicle charged over the edge of the cliff.

Tessa felt the color drain from her face as a sick feeling gurgled in her stomach.

"You okay?" Trent stole a glance her way.

She nodded, still shaky and queasy. "I guess."

"At least they're not following us anymore."

"That's one positive." She couldn't think of many. She'd

been plucked from her obscure life and into a nightmare. Now she was hanging on for dear life on a thrill ride she'd never wanted to be a part of.

Someone was clearly trying to send a message.

She'd been discovered, and now she was in a Jeep with a stranger who might or might not be trying to kill her. For all she knew, this man was a part of this elaborate scheme. Maybe his plan involved earning her trust just so he could stab her in the back. Some people got their kicks that way.

Just then Trent pulled off the main road and onto a smaller one. They snaked through the mountains, turning a couple more times before they reached a driveway similar to the steep, narrow one that had led to her own cabin.

She didn't ask questions, though her mind raced as she tried to process everything. She needed a plan, just in case things turned ugly. She'd have to take her chances and run if this man turned out to be a thug. The woods were more survivable during the day when she could see what was coming. She'd even risk plunging herself into the wilderness at nighttime if she had to. It wasn't ideal. But she'd do that before she surrendered.

The man stopped in front of three cabins, cut the engine and turned to stare at her.

When he didn't say anything, she cleared her throat. "Where are we?"

He nodded toward the closest cabin. "This is where I'm staying while I'm in town. I rented all three."

"All three? Why did you do that?" Was it because he'd brought others with him? Because he wasn't a one-man operation, as he'd claimed? She felt as if the wool had been pulled over her eyes again.

"I just saved your life. Maybe you can stop thinking the worst of me," Trent said.

Her throat tightened at his easy assessment of her. "Why would you say that?"

"Your feelings are written all over your face. And to answer your questions, I rented all three cabins to lessen the chance that anyone would find me or ask questions. I paid in cash. The only person who should know I'm here lives in Texas. He keeps these for friends to use during hunting season."

Despite his explanation, Tessa rubbed her arms, realizing just how isolated she was out here. Trent could kill her, dispose of her body and no one would find her for weeks. "I see."

"Let's go inside and talk." Trent's voice left no room for argument.

He started to get out, but Tessa froze where she was, fight or flight kicking in. Once she left the safe confines of the car, there was no going back. Was this really a good idea?

"Tessa?" He paused and stared at her, peering into the open door.

"What about those men who followed us?" She replayed the bullets, the chase, the car going over the cliff.

"They're dead. We have some time."

"Who are they?" she whispered, realizing the timing in all of this. It couldn't be coincidental that Trent had showed up on the very day she'd been discovered by Leo's men.

"I was hoping you could tell me."

"All of this trouble didn't start until you arrived."

"Please, come inside so we can talk." His voice softened, almost as if she was exhausting him.

She shook her head, still needing more reassurance. "I could be walking into a trap."

"I'd love to tell you more. But we're safer inside."

Finally, she nodded. She was only biding her time right now. Trent could easily overpower her if he wanted to. He was simply being polite at the moment.

Nausea rose in her gut as he led her to a cabin. Was

she out of her mind doing this? What other choice did she have? If she hadn't willingly come, no doubt Trent would have found a way to drag her here against her will.

Still, a small part of her wanted to hear what he had to say.

After all, he'd mentioned her mom. He'd had opportunity to kill her already and he hadn't done it.

Lord, if You're there and if You're listening, please be with me. Give me wisdom.

Even though she knew her words probably fell on deaf ears, hope pricked her heart. Right now she wanted to believe again, and that was more than she'd felt in a long time. Funny the things desperation could do to a person. She'd been desperate for a long time, but the word had taken on a new meaning today.

Tessa stepped inside the old cabin. It was small, with only a tiny kitchen, a cozy living room and an upstairs loft, which was probably the bedroom. The walls were made of wood planks, and everything had a rustic feel to it, from the hunter green accessories to the brown leather couch.

"I'm not going to waste time with formalities or by offering you something to drink," Trent started. "Have a seat and let's get down to business."

Tessa nodded as he led her to the couch. He sat a respectable distance away, his gaze intense as he observed her. He reminded her a bit of a soldier, only without the uniform. He looked tough and strong and like someone she didn't want to mess with.

"Tessa, your family hired me to find you. They're very concerned about you."

She wanted to deny she had a family, but instead she listened.

"I've been searching for you for six months and my investigation finally led here. Aside from being a PI, I'm a former detective from Richmond, Virginia. Before that,

I was an army ranger. I've had more than my fair share of experience when it comes to tracking down people, whether they're terrorists or runaways."

She wanted to ask a million questions. How had he found her? She'd been so careful. There was no trail.

But obviously someone else besides Trent had discovered her, as well. Was there anywhere she'd be safe? Ever?

"I have no idea what's going on, but I'm hoping you can fill in some of the blanks," Trent finished.

She opened her mouth, almost desperate to pour out the truth to someone. It had been so long since she'd had a listening ear, and it was so hard not having anyone to speak with about the things that burdened her heart.

Feeling Trent's watchful gaze and realizing he was waiting for her response, she shook her head. "I don't know what you're talking about. I wish I could help. I do. But you have the wrong person."

His gaze remained fixated on her. Agitation stirred there. "Why are you playing these games?"

He wasn't going to easily take no for an answer, was he? If she'd thought Trent was just a pushover who'd accept her explanation and leave her alone, she was wrong. Despite that realization, she repeated, "As I said, you have the wrong person."

"Tessa, you and I both know that's not true."

Her chin trembled as she tried to subdue her emotions. She'd always been a terrible liar, even after rehearsing this speech for nearly a year. "This is a horrible misunderstanding. I'm sorry you've gone through so much trouble. As soon as I can get my car, I'll be out of your hair—"

He leaned closer. "If this is a misunderstanding, why were those men trying to kill you?"

She swallowed deeply, trying to compose herself. Otherwise, her words would come out jumbled and high-pitched and give away the fact that she knew more than she admitted. "Says the man who broke into my home. Now I'm alone in a cabin with him and no one else knows I'm here. That's enough to scare any woman. Let's face it— you're just as much of a threat as those men were."

He didn't move, didn't flinch. He just continued to stare, intense and focused. "You're right. I'm not the only person you should be scared of," he reminded her, his eyes cloudy, almost angry, yet very controlled at the same time. "You're saying you have no idea who those men were?"

Tessa shook her head, trying to protect herself and buy time until she could figure out another plan. "None. Maybe they had the wrong person, just like you."

It was true. She'd never seen those men before. But her gut told her they were Leo's friends. They'd finally found her, despite her best efforts.

When she'd gone on the run, she'd remembered her best friend's family had a cabin out here that they never used anymore. She'd even remembered where they left the key. Using the place had been a no-brainer. Tessa had simply had the power turned back on and asked to have the bills sent to the West Virginia address.

She'd found a job at a travel agency in the small town, and was able to earn just enough to pay her electrical bill, buy groceries and tend to a few other necessities. Her plan had seemed perfect.

Trent stood and began pacing in front of her. "We're not going to get very far if you don't tell me the truth, Tessa."

She rubbed her hands, now sweaty, against her jeans. "I'm sorry you've gone through all of this trouble. I don't know what else to say. I didn't ask you to get involved. You're going to have to tell your client that you were unsuccessful, even after six months."

Her poor mom. To pay for all of Trent's work, she'd probably had to drain her savings account. It would be just one more hardship her family had to endure. How much could they take? Tessa certainly didn't wish any of this on them.

But she had to think of the bigger picture. She'd rather her mom be poor and worried than dead and buried.

Finally, Trent stopped pacing. His hands went to his hips as he assessed her again. "Fine. You're free to go, then."

Tessa stood, trying to gather her courage.

There was a part of her that wanted to trust Trent, that wanted someone to help her out of this situation. Yet she knew it was better to face hardship by herself, to make her own way.

"Great." Her voice trembled as she rose. She stepped toward the door, a million possibilities racing through her head. All of them seemed to end in disaster.

"You know it's ten miles until you reach town."

She nodded, her throat dry. "I know."

"It's dark."

She nodded again, her anxiety growing into a bigger hollowness by the moment. "I realize that."

She took another step when he grabbed her arm.

"You're one stubborn woman. You're still going to set out on your own? Even after everything that's happened?"

She only stared at him.

Finally, he dropped his hand. "Look, we didn't get started on the right foot. I don't think you should go. It's not safe. Stay in one of the cabins here, okay? No strings attached. I just don't want to see anything happen to you. Understand?"

She stared at him, trying to measure his sincerity. Her emotions clouded her judgment at the moment, though, and she didn't know what to say. She really had no other options, and certainly he knew that.

"Whether you claim to be Theresa or not, your family won't survive me coming back to them with the news that you're dead. So do this for their sakes, not mine."

His words got to her. Images of her family flashed through her mind, and finally she nodded. "Okay, but not because of this family you keep on talking about. I'll do it because I hate the dark."

Her gut twisted as she said the words. Her family was the most important thing in her life. Everything she'd done, she'd done for them.

She hoped they'd forgive her for all the hurt she'd caused.

Trent stared at the woman in front of him, wishing she would come to her senses. Why was she being so stubborn? Even while dealing with her fear, he'd noticed how she continually lifted her chin, as if she was just humoring him.

There was no denying that the woman had gumption—or that she was easy on the eyes, even with her new look. He actually liked her hair the darker shade. He'd always appreciated the more natural look. The other pictures he'd seen, she'd been dressed in business suits, with expensive-looking haircuts and perfectly coordinated accessories.

The woman before him now was absent of makeup. She wore jeans, layers of a T-shirt, a henley and a flannel shirt. Her boots were small enough to look feminine, but also well worn. The change in her was remarkable. She'd more than changed her physical appearance. Her desperation and need for survival had changed her from someone who was pampered into someone practical.

Despite how frustrating she was, Trent couldn't stand the thought of her striking out on her own again. He was certain the woman was in danger, and he didn't know why yet. Her fiancé—former fiancé—had told Tessa's family that she'd had a mental break. According to Leo McAllister, one minute they'd been talking about the wedding and the next she'd gone crazy. She'd begun throwing things, accusing him of things. Leo had tried to stop her, but she'd taken off. No one had seen her since then.

Trent had known going into this that he might be confronting someone who'd flown off their rocker. But when he looked at Tessa, that wasn't the impression he had.

Was he so drawn to this case because of Laurel? It was the only thing that made sense. Guilt had been eating at him for years. He'd thought he had the emotion under control. But something about Tessa's big blue eyes made him travel back in time. Flashes of that horrible day continued to assault him and try to take him away.

He couldn't afford to immerse himself in the guilt and grief right now.

And he didn't want anyone else to go through it.

"I'll show you to your cabin, then." He put his hand on Tessa's back and led her to the door. He figured she would object, that she'd flinch until his hand slipped away. But she didn't.

Her eyes had gone from fearful to dull. He'd seen that look before, the one that came when emotions were overwhelming, when they'd hammered a person so much that they began to feel like a shell of who they'd once been. He'd been there before.

He unlocked the cabin door and pushed it open. Even though he'd been keeping an eye on the place and felt certain no one knew he was here, he still instructed Tessa to stay where she was. Then he checked out every potential hiding place before deeming the cabin clear.

"Will this be suitable?" he asked her.

She nodded, her arms crossed protectively over her chest. "Yes."

"Tessa, I'm sorry."

"For what?" she questioned.

He shook his head, trying to find the right words. "For whatever you went through."

She opened her mouth as if to object but then closed her lips again.

He took a step toward the door when he heard her speak again.

"What do I do now? Just wait here? Indefinitely? Until those men find me again?"

He turned, praying he'd know what to say. "That's up to you, Tessa. You can let me help or you can keep denying who you are. Things will move a lot faster if you just tell me the truth."

She stared at him. A moment of complacency flashed in her eyes. Then stubborn determination reappeared. "If I had something to tell you, I would."

He stepped closer, wishing she would stop playing these games. "You know more than you're letting on."

They stared at each other in a silent battle of wills.

Finally Trent nodded. She would tell him in her own time, and that was that. Until then, he'd do his best to keep her safe.

"Have it your way, then," Trent said.

Her face softened with...surprise? "I'm going to bed."

He stepped toward the hallway, feeling crankier than he should. He'd sacrificed a lot to come here—time, his own money, in some ways his reputation. He hoped it wasn't all for naught. "Maybe some sleep will give you a fresh perspective."

Even better, maybe some sleep would give him perspective, because a lot of the conclusions he'd drawn before coming here were proving to be dangerously incorrect.

An hour later, Tessa still stared at the space around her, feeling a mix of both uneasiness and relief—uneasiness at being here and the circumstances that had led to it and relief that she was away from Trent.

Had her mom really hired him to find her? Tessa had known her family wouldn't give up easily. But she'd hoped to hide away so well that there was no hope of that ever happening.

She paced the room, knowing she wouldn't get any sleep tonight. Not after everything that had happened. It wasn't even a slight possibility.

In the light of the cabin she'd gotten a better look at Trent. He was tall, broad and appeared to be made of solid muscle. His hair was blond with a tint of red, curly and cropped close. When his lip had started to twist up, she'd thought she'd seen a dimple on the left cheek of his very defined face.

Sure, he was handsome. Very handsome.

But sometimes a wolf looked like a sheep…or, in this case, like a ruggedly handsome Ken doll. That made him even more dangerous.

Pushing aside those thoughts, she realized that she needed to learn the lay of the house. That way, if she needed to run or hide, she at least had an idea of what her possibilities were.

The living room was simple and outfitted like most rental properties would be. There was a well-used leather couch, several magazines on the outdated coffee table and a small dinette nestled against the wall in the kitchen.

She headed toward the bedroom, determined to check that all of the windows were locked. She had to remain on guard and careful. But as soon as she stepped into the room, she stopped.

The painting on the wall.

It was by Alejandro Gaurs.

His paintings were exclusive to the world-renowned McAllister Gallery.

The art gallery that Leo's family owned.

Her breath caught.

Had she been tricked? Did Leo own this cabin? Whoever did had obviously bought the artwork at his gallery.

What if Trent had tricked her? What if he really was working for Leo?

That had to be it, she realized. Trent had convinced her that her mom had sent him, but that was all a lie. He was working for the enemy. He'd led her right into the lion's den.

Panic rose in her.

She couldn't take this risk.

She had to get out of here. Now.

FOUR

Tessa grabbed her backpack and slipped out the back door, trying to remain in the shadows. She looked toward Trent's cabin then toward the woods, but saw no one.

Moving quietly, she headed for the trees. As soon as she took her first step into the depths of the forest, she realized what a precarious place she was in. These woods could kill her.

But it was a chance she had to take.

Everything inside her told her to run fast, but she knew she had to take it slow. She couldn't be careless. One wrong step and she could break a bone. Even worse, she could fall to her death from one of the many cliffs in the area.

Slow and steady won the race. That was the saying, at least.

As Tessa left every bit—however small—of security behind, her trembles deepened. How was she going to get out of this situation? How would she last out in the wilderness? She'd read books on surviving out in nature, but everything she'd learned seemed to leave her thoughts. She only hoped the information would return as instinct kicked in.

That same intuition had kicked in when she'd grabbed Trent's gun in the car. All of those days at the shooting range had paid off. She'd been unable to buy her own gun—she'd never get past the background check, especially not with her fake name. But at least she'd picked up a few valuable skills in the process.

Tessa manipulated herself between the massive oak trees, over boulders and down steep declines. This area was so vast, so wild, so beautiful. But it could also be deadly, especially in the pitch-black. A hunter had died only a few months ago when he'd gotten lost out here. His body had been found downstream a week later.

Her mind churned as she continued her trek. When she started to maintain a steady pace, her thoughts went from survival to Trent McCabe and that painting she'd found in the cabin. It linked him to the McAllisters.

Leo was a powerful man. He was capable of extraordinary farces that could fool the wisest of people. He had to have some connection with that cabin. It was too much of a coincidence otherwise.

How had she been fooled again? The kindness in Trent's voice was deceitful. He'd sounded so trustworthy. He'd even used a story about her mother. He probably knew how to manipulate. Those were the worst kind of criminals, the ones who gained a person's trust only to stab them in the back. Sometimes literally.

She squeezed her eyes shut at the memories.

Just then, something snapped behind her.

She froze. What was that? A nighttime creature? A mountain lion? A bear?

Her pulse spiked again.

She looked for the reflection of eyes—either human or animal predator—but saw no one. Was something stalking her out there, just waiting for the right moment to pounce?

Tessa picked up her pace. Slow and steady only worked if a person wasn't being chased.

She had a phone in her backpack. But who would she call? Who could she trust to help her?

No one, she realized. Except her family, and she couldn't pull them into this.

As she glanced around, every direction looked the same. Which route led away from her cabin? Which path would keep her safe from the deadly bluffs that dropped hundreds of feet to the river below? One moment of distraction and now she was turned around. She'd lost her sense of direction.

Panic began to rise in her.

Another twig snapped in the distance.

She was definitely being followed.

By Leo's men? By Trent—who was also one of Leo's men, apparently? By an animal?

None of the options were comforting.

Despite her earlier mantra of remaining slow, she burst into a run. She had to move, and fast. Every second she lingered could cost her life.

Branches slapped her in the face, gnarled tree roots reached out to trip her and rocks tried to twist her ankle. She pushed forward, her breathing too shallow for her own good.

She could feel a presence behind her now, sense that her pursuer was closing in.

Just then, her foot caught on another root. She started to lunge forward but caught herself on the rough bark of a pine tree.

She gasped as the prickly wood cut into her skin, as her ankle throbbed.

Tears tried to push from her eyes—from even deeper than that. They tried to push up from the deepest part of her heart, which felt too battered and bruised for words. She was so tired of living in fear, of constantly looking over her shoulder.

"Tessa!" someone said.

She knew that voice.

Trent.

Of course he'd been watching her. He'd probably just been waiting for her to run. But why was he drawing this out? Why didn't he just kill her while he had the chance?

Unless there were other motivations at play.

Did he plan to torture her? Find out how much she knew? Whom she might have told? Where she might have hidden any documents she'd kept as proof of what Leo's family had been doing?

The thought caused a new surge of panic in her.

She pushed herself from the tree and hobbled forward. Kept moving. What other choice did she have?

She tried to keep her eyes on the ground, to watch her steps. But it was so dark out here. There were so many trees and so much underbrush.

"I won't let you out of my sight, you know," the man called.

She looked behind her again and spotted Trent. He walked toward her, his actions measured and controlled. He wasn't even panting with exertion as he took long strides her way. Meanwhile, her legs kept pumping as she tried to keep pace.

Fabulous.

"Just leave me alone!" she mumbled.

"I don't want to hurt you, Tessa."

"You can't prove that." She stopped trying to run. Even though she'd been jogging every day and trying to build up both her strength and endurance, the upward climb on the mountain was doing a number on her legs and lungs. Her ankles throbbed. Her lungs refused to get enough oxygen to fill them.

She'd done a lot of things in preparation for a moment just like this—shooting lessons, working out, reading survival guides and forming emergency procedures. All of her planning seemed to disappear into a haze, though.

Fear and exhaustion did terrible things to people; the emotion robbed them of any security. It didn't seem as if that long ago she'd been confident and self-reliant and living her dream life. Today she was always looking over her shoulder, questioning every move and second-guessing every decision.

How had an ordinary girl living an ordinary life somehow turned into this? This wasn't supposed to happen. She should still be at home with her family. Still working in the art museum. Back then, life had seemed so safe and comfortable. What she wouldn't give to go back and return to the way it used to be.

That wasn't an option, though. She had to keep fighting. She couldn't let her enemies win.

Speaking of enemies, Trent was getting closer—close enough to grab her.

Suddenly, some kind of survival instinct took over. Adrenaline surged in her, giving her a strength she didn't know she had. She sprinted through the darkness.

Don't let him catch you.

"Being out here isn't safe, Tessa," Trent continued. "Let's talk this out."

She rounded a bend of trees and, before she knew what was happening, the ground crumbled beneath her.

She desperately grabbed the air, trying to find anything possible to grip on to as she slid downward. Failure meant she'd slip to her death, hundreds of feet to the river below.

It was too late: her life flashed before her eyes.

"Tessa!" Trent saw Tessa disappear, and panic engulfed him. He charged toward her, no longer fearful of jolting her into doing something stupid. She'd already done that.

He rushed toward the decline and peered down, expecting the worst. His heart slowed, but only temporarily.

There she was, hanging on to a tree root, her eyes wide with despair.

"I'm going to get you up, Tessa. Just hold tight." He dropped to his stomach, trying to secure himself so he could grab her.

She moaned, her eyes squeezing shut. "Why don't you just kill me now? Why are you drawing this out and pretending to be a good guy?"

He grabbed her wrist. "I *am* a good guy."

"You've fooled me once. Not again." She refused to let go of the root she held on to.

What was she talking about? This wasn't really the time to argue. This was the time to get her to safety. "Let me help you. Then you can ask me whatever it is you want."

"You work for Leo McAllister."

His muscles tightened from the strain of trying to grab her, of trying to make sure her grip didn't slip and send her plunging to her death. "Leo has been worried about you. He put up a monetary reward for your return. But I'm not working for him."

"What?" Her voice sounded breathless.

Her wrist slipped. He needed a better grip and a little cooperation from her or they'd both end up tumbling down the mountainside. "I'd be happy to chat more in a minute. Right now, I need to make sure you don't die."

"Stop playing games—"

Before she could argue anymore, he grabbed her arm with both of his hands and heaved her onto the ledge. She landed beside him, and they both sprawled backward onto the hard rock beneath them. Silence fell between them as they each sucked in air.

That had been close. Too close.

Trent willed his heart to slow, but his adrenaline was still pumping at the close call. With one more deep breath, he propped himself up on one elbow and turned toward Tessa. "Why would you think I'm working for Leo?"

She cringed as if in pain but still managed to scowl. She pushed herself up also, rubbing her wrist as if it was sore. "One of the paintings from his gallery is hanging in that cabin."

"If I understand correctly, the paintings from his galleries are sold all over the world. *Prints* of them are sold all over the world. I do know that much."

"It's too big of a coincidence."

"There is such thing in life as a coincidence, darling. That's what this is. I'm not working for Leo or his family. I take it that would be a bad thing if I were?"

She stared into the distance, resting her arms on her knees. "I've already said too much."

"What's it going to take for you to trust me?" He peered at her, trying to get a better look at her face in the deep blackness of the forest.

"The only person I can rely on is myself."

"Your mom is Florence. She loves lilacs, makes the world's best chicken Parmesan and she has your eyes. Your sister looks more like your dad, who died of cancer five years ago. He was a good man. Quiet, a hard worker and he could build anything out of wood."

Tears glistened in her eyes. Finally, some of her walls were coming down. He was able to see beyond her facade, and the woman lurking there was broken, scared and alone.

A fierce surge of protectiveness rose in him.

He had to keep pushing. The mention of Leo had caused a reaction in her; it was his best lead. "Your family trusts Leo."

Suddenly, she straightened. "What do you mean?"

"I mean that Leo has been working with your mom to find you. He seems very concerned."

She let out a moan and ran a hand over her face. "But Leo didn't hire you? That's what you're saying?"

He shook his head. "No. Your family hired me."

"Does Leo know where you are?" Fear crackled in her voice.

"No one knows where I am. I update your mom weekly. Last she heard, I was in the DC area. Coming here was a last-minute hunch. I wanted to be certain before I gave her any hope." If Leo really was the bad guy here, just as Tessa seemed to be claiming, had he used his supposed concern for Tessa as a ruse for following Trent here and locating her himself? It was a possibility he had to consider.

Tessa's head dropped into her hands, and for the first time since he'd met her, she looked defeated, ready to give up. At least, ready to cry.

He needed to do something to relinquish her defeat. Sitting here wouldn't help, and he didn't know her well enough to give her a hug.

Finally, he stood. They couldn't sit here all night. It wasn't safe. "Let's go back to the cabin. Please. We can talk there, make sure you're okay and figure out what happens next."

With hesitation, she put her hands into his. It wasn't a romantic gesture, though she was certainly beautiful enough that the idea could be entertaining. No, it was a matter of survival, of the two of them sticking together in the middle of this bleak wilderness.

He glanced her over, looking for a sign of broken bones, of deep cuts. "Are you hurt?"

She shook her head, her expression still listless. "Only my ego."

"Stay close to me. Understand? Next time you might not be so lucky."

She nodded. Without saying anything else, he led her up the mountain, taking it slow this time. His thoughts turned over what she'd said. Whether she'd meant to or not, she'd given him insight into her past. She'd all but admitted that she really was Theresa Davidson. She did know Leo. Yet, all of that noted, she seemed terrified.

He needed to get to the bottom of her story, but now wasn't the time to do so. He needed to take her somewhere safe. He hated to see a woman look this frightened, to see someone this shaken. If there'd been a different way to do things, he would have changed his plan of action. If he'd known earlier what he knew now, his approach would have been different. But what was done was done.

As they neared his cabin, he pulled Tessa behind a tree, his muscles tightening as instinct kicked in. That instinct told him that something indiscernible was wrong.

"What it is?" Her eyes were as wide as the full moon overhead.

He put a finger over his lips and nodded toward the distance. "Listen."

Silence stretched—the only sounds were that of dry leaves clicking together and rustling in the breeze. Occasionally, an owl hooted or a squirrel scampered past.

Then he heard it again. A crackle. He exchanged a glance with Tessa. She'd heard it, also.

A roar sounded. A burst. An explosion.

"What is that?" Tessa whispered.

"That was my cabin. It just went up in flames."

FIVE

A shudder rippled through Tessa.

They were here. Those men had found them. Again.

She looked over her shoulder. Their pursuers could be anywhere. They could be within reaching distance. Their guns could be pointed at Tessa and Trent now.

Trent's hand on her shoulder brought her back to reality.

"What are we going to do?" Her voice sounded as raw as her throat felt.

She'd said *we*, she realized. Somewhere in the process she'd decided she was in it with Trent. She had little choice in the matter, it seemed. Not if she wanted to stay alive.

"We need to lie low until we know the coast is clear." He took her arm. "Come on. Let's start moving."

She wanted to argue, wanted to give a million reasons why venturing back into the woods was a bad idea. But she didn't. Almost on autopilot, or perhaps it was the shock—whatever it was kept her moving silently through the woods. She was too scared to stop, too charged with adrenaline to grow weary, too on edge to feel safe. Even the autumn chill didn't bother her as much as it normally would.

They moved briskly through the woods, putting distance between themselves and the flames. Where would they go? They couldn't go back to Trent's Jeep. Besides, the tires were probably melted from the heat of the blazing inferno that used to be Trent's cabin.

But Trent and Tessa couldn't meander through these woods all night, either. Trent might be built like a soldier—a very handsome soldier—but he was still human. She couldn't expect him to work wonders.

"Salem," she muttered. The older gentleman's kind eyes fluttered through her memory, solidifying her idea.

Trent looked back at her. "What?"

"We're going to need help. I bet Salem would let us borrow one of his cars."

"Who's Salem?"

"He owns the hardware store in town. He only lives a mile away from my cabin."

"You sure you can trust him?"

She nodded, not a single doubt in her mind. "Yes, I'm sure. Believe me, people go through a rigorous criteria with me before I'm able to put any faith in them. Experience has taught me it's better that way."

Trent nodded. "Okay. We need to figure out how to get to his place."

"It was west of my cabin, just a little farther down the road."

Of course, a mile in this terrain was different than a mile of highway. Especially at night. So many things could go wrong.

He froze and put a finger over his lips. Prickles danced across Tessa's skin and she held her breath. What did he hear?

She scooted closer to him. That was when she heard it, too. A twig snapped in the distance.

Trent grabbed her hand and tugged her closer. Quietly, they moved toward a grove of trees. Trent pulled her between a huge boulder and a fortress of foliage, then squeezed in beside her. They both remained motionless.

Tessa could hardly breathe as she waited to see what would unfold. Maybe it was just a wild animal they'd heard and not one of the men desperate to kill them.

Just as the thought entered her mind, she heard another movement. The sound was so subtle that she thought she'd imagined it. But then she heard the rustling again. And again.

Someone was walking. Close. The footsteps seemed to barely hit the ground, but the crunch of dry leaves gave them away.

Tessa felt Trent squeeze in beside her. He was near enough that she could feel his heart beating at a steady rhythm against her arm. She could feel the heat coming from him.

"We lost them," a deep voice muttered in the distance.

Silence passed and Tessa could sense the man following them was within arm's reach.

"I don't know how they got away, but I've been searching this mountain for an hour," the man continued. "They must have had a car hiding somewhere, because they're gone."

Another moment passed. The man was talking on the phone to someone, Tessa realized. Leo, maybe?

"Somehow they got out of the cabins before the bomb went off. This guy who's helping her is good. He's making our job harder."

Tessa's heart stuttered, suddenly grateful that this stranger beside her had shown up when he had. She'd be dead without him.

"I know, I know. This woman has taken up too much of our time and energy. We need to put this behind us, and there's only one way to do that," the man said. "Don't worry, I'm not giving up. You can count on me."

At that, the footsteps retreated.

But neither Tessa nor Trent budged. Because one wrong move and they could both die.

Trent waited at least fifteen minutes. He figured that was a safe passage of time to ensure the man chasing them was gone and this wasn't some elaborate trap. This whole situation ran a lot deeper than he'd realized. The danger that had been chasing them was far greater than he'd guessed.

At least Tessa seemed to trust him—however reluctantly—a little more. She hadn't scowled at him in the past hour. She hadn't argued when he instructed her to hide in the woods. That was a start, he supposed.

It had brought him unexpected delight when her gaze had softened, and he'd seen something shift inside her. But it scared him that his joy went deeper than the satisfaction over gaining her trust. Something about the woman intrigued him.

When the coast seemed to be clear, he crawled out of the hiding spot. Thank goodness the little nook had been there. Finding it had been a blessing of God. Without it, they would have certainly been discovered.

Trent surveyed the area once more before motioning for Tessa to follow. "We're not going to last very long out here in these woods. I hate to say it, but I think we need to go to your friend's house tonight. By tomorrow morning it might be too late."

"Too late? What do you mean, too late?"

"I'm saying that if you were close to this Salem man, then anyone after us is likely to discover that information. They'll tear apart every area of your life here. They may go after him next, trying to get some information from him about you."

She gasped. "No, not Salem. I can't let anyone else get hurt because of me. I just can't."

"Let's go there now and warn him."

She nodded, looking numb still. Anyone whose life had been turned upside down like this would feel the same way. Before she could think too much, Trent led her back in the direction of her cabin. Traversing these mountains and woods would make the journey take longer, but they couldn't risk walking alongside the road.

Tessa was a trouper. Though the night was cold, she kept moving, kept pushing ahead. Sometimes the walk was treacherous, but she didn't let that deter her. The woman was stronger than he'd given her credit for, and he could admire that.

"We're getting closer to your cabin," he said. "You said Salem lives a mile away, correct?"

She nodded. "I'm turned around, though. I feel as if every direction I look is the same."

"I can get you there." He glanced at the compass on his watch. "The road is about a half a mile south of us and we've been walking parallel to it. If we keep going in this direction, we should hit his property soon."

"I'm glad you know what you're doing. How do you know what you're doing?"

"I was a ranger. Survival is one of the top priorities."

"You saved my life tonight."

"Actually, if you hadn't run from that cabin when you did, we could both be dead. They were going to kill you and then me to ensure I didn't talk."

"They're ruthless like that."

"Who are 'they,' exactly?"

He saw the veil go up around her again. He had a feeling that would happen every time he brought up the past.

"Leo hired them to kill me."

Her answer made him blanch. She actually had opened up and, boy, had it been a doozy. "Say that again?"

"My ex-fiancé, Leo McAllister, hired men to kill me. That's why I've been on the run."

Of all the things he'd thought she might say, that wasn't one of them. "Why in the world would he do that?"

"I walked in on his family as they were planning to do an arms deal."

"What?" Certainly he hadn't heard her correctly.

She nodded. "The family doesn't care about art. Beneath their paintings are blueprints of various weapons—nuclear, biological, chemical."

"No…"

She nodded again. "They have a friend who works for a defense contractor who develops these plans. He's been getting the information, and they've been working together to sell it to terrorists overseas."

"You found out what they were doing and then ran before they realized it?"

She frowned. "Not exactly. I discovered what they were doing, but the family didn't know that initially. I snuck back into the office. I actually had a double major in college—art history and computer science—so I was able to hack into their server and copy all the information on where the shipments were going. I changed the address in their system so those blueprints wouldn't get into the wrong hands."

"What happened to that information detailing their contacts?"

Her frown deepened. "I was going to give it to the FBI. However, Leo came into my office in the middle of the transfer. The jump drive flew out of my hand and into an AC vent. I had to attend a business meeting with him. While there, he got a phone call informing him that he'd been hacked. I knew he'd soon discover that I was behind it and, when he did, he'd kill me. So I left right after that meeting. I ran and I knew I couldn't look back."

"That's not Leo's story, you know."

"I can only imagine the lies he came up with."

"He said you'd gotten into a fight. That you'd been off balance and you flew off the handle. He even had a psychologist come forward and say she'd been treating you."

"They paid her to say that. I've never even been to see a counselor. That's not saying I don't need to—especially after this whole ordeal. But I've never done it."

"Tessa, did you ever go to the FBI with the information you knew?"

"I sent an anonymous tip, but apparently nothing came of it. The family is charming like that. They can talk their way out of and into almost anything. My only comfort was in knowing that I stopped one deal, at least."

Her story was so unexpected that it was a lot to comprehend, almost too much. It was going to take a while for that information to even begin to make sense. "You didn't even tell your family about any of this?"

"It all happened so fast. Besides, I knew if I was totally off the grid that Leo wouldn't even be able to threaten my family. I had to lose all contact with them, for their own safety. It was the hardest thing I've ever had to do."

Trent's heart pounded. He could imagine the choices she'd had to make. Knowing what he did only deepened his attraction to the woman. She was more than a pretty face. She also had character. "So you've been here in Gideon's Hollow?"

She nodded, her breathing more shallow than he'd like it to be. But the hike was strenuous and the cold biting. What did he expect? "I tried to isolate myself. I thought I'd done a good job...until today when you showed up."

The way her words trailed out wistfully made him wonder. But just then a light appeared in the distance. He'd save any more questions for later.

* * *

Tessa ducked behind a tree and watched carefully. Those were headlights. Was this Salem's house? His driveway?

"That's him!" she whispered. She recognized the headlights of his vintage Ford truck. That vehicle was his pride and joy.

"He's out late," Trent muttered.

"He plays bridge every Tuesday night with his friends. His wife said he doesn't usually get home until midnight. It's his splurge."

"Let's stay here a couple more minutes, just to be certain it's him. We can't be too trusting."

Tessa watched as the truck pulled to a stop in front of the brick ranch Salem called home. A moment later, she saw him climb out and smiled. He was like a granddad to her.

The man was tall and thin and slightly hunched. He had a fringe of gray hair and a reassuring smile. Getting to know him, though she often felt as if it was a mistake, was one of the only pleasures she'd allowed herself since coming to West Virginia.

Her grin quickly vanished when she realized Salem could be in danger because of her. Whether Tessa approached him tonight or not, he could still be in a situation she'd never intended to put him in.

She'd befriended the man while working at the travel agency next door to his hardware shop. Though she'd initially tried to avoid him, it eventually had become impossible. He was always asking her how she was settling in, inviting her over for dinner, and his wife always baked cookies for her.

Just once Tessa had agreed to go eat with them, and she'd had a delightful time. It had been one of the only times since she'd moved here when she'd felt she was really a part of a community.

That realization had scared her. She'd instantly retreated back to her planned, organized and secluded life. It was for reasons just like this that she'd retreated. The people she cared for were in danger because of her.

"I don't see anyone else. I think we should go now and move quickly," Trent said.

"I hate to put him in this position," Tessa muttered, suddenly having second thoughts.

"He's already at risk, and it's not your fault. Tessa, we have little choice here, not if we want to survive. Do you understand that?"

Slowly, she nodded.

"Let's go, then." Trent took her hand again and began pulling her forward. At least his hand was warm and strong and gave her a dose of courage.

She sucked in a deep breath as they emerged from the cover of darkness. Part of her expected to feel the sting of bullets, to hear the sound of gunfire. But it was peaceful and quiet as they skirted around the gravel lane leading to the warm house in the distance.

Staying near the edge of the foliage, they rushed toward the house. By the time Tessa reached the front door, she was panting.

She glanced at Trent and got an approving nod from him before knocking. It only took a minute for the door to open.

And, to her shock, Salem stood there with a gun pointed right at them.

SIX

Trent raised his hands, fearing the worst. After everything that had happened tonight, nothing would surprise him. There was practically an all-out war being waged on Tessa.

Before he could say anything, Tessa jumped in. "I know it's late, Salem," she started. "I'm sorry if we scared you, but I had nowhere else to go."

The older man's gaze left Trent and he glanced suspiciously at Tessa. "Who's he?"

"He's…a friend," she said. "You can trust him."

"You sure?" he asked protectively.

She nodded. "Positive."

Slowly, Salem lowered his hunting rifle. He glanced behind them, scanned the background and then stepped aside. "Come on in."

A plump woman shuffled into the room, pulling her royal blue housecoat around her more closely. A heavy wrinkle formed between her eyes when she spotted everyone at the door.

"Salem? What's going on?" The woman paused when she saw Tessa. "Tessa! What in the world are you doing here at this hour?"

"I'm sorry, Wilma." Tessa frowned, suddenly looking as though she was carrying the weight of the world on her shoulders. "I'm afraid I've put you both in a horrible situation."

"What do you mean?" Salem asked, his hands going to his hips and his perceptive eyes absorbing every motion, movement or twitch Tessa displayed—which were a lot right now. Despite the fact she was probably trying to conceal her panic, it was obvious she was a nervous wreck.

"Some men are after me. They came to my house. We got away but they found us again. I've got to get out of town. I hate to ask this, but could I borrow one of your cars?"

"Men are after you?" Salem repeated.

Tessa nodded. "It's a long story. The less you know, the better."

"Shouldn't you call the police?"

"Right now, I'm better off running."

Salem started at her another moment. "You're sure?"

She nodded again. "Unfortunately."

"Oh, Tessa." Wilma pulled her into a hug. "Why is this happening to someone as sweet as you?"

Trent knew this was an emotional moment, but time was of the essence right now. The longer they stayed here, the more likely it was they'd be discovered. But not only that, it increased the chance that someone innocent would get hurt.

Trent paced to the windows and pulled down the shades. Then he urged everyone to move toward the center of the room, just in case any bullets started flying. He had to take every precaution possible.

Tessa pulled away from Wilma's hug and glanced at Trent. "Let's just say someone very powerful wants to get revenge on me. Anyone I've had contact with is in danger." She shook her head. "I'm so sorry. I tried to keep my distance. But you both were so sweet that it was hard."

"Oh, darling," Wilma said. "You know we'd do anything for you. Of course you can use one of our cars."

Salem nodded solemnly. "I'll get the keys."

"Thank you for your help," Trent said. He switched one of the lamps off and surveyed everything outside from his position at the window. "We appreciate it."

"And who are you, exactly?" Wilma asked. Gone was her compassion and instead her shoulders rose, her eyes taking on a sharp, protective expression.

"Right now I'm her bodyguard."

Tessa's cheeks reddened. "He's someone my family trusts."

Salem returned with the keys and an envelope. "Here you go. There's some cash to hold you over."

"I couldn't possibly—" Tessa started.

"I insist."

He thrust the envelope into her hands. She looked down at it. She opened her mouth, but then closed it again as if she was speechless. "Thank you," she finally said.

"Where will you go?" Wilma asked, wringing her hands together.

Tessa glanced at Trent before shaking her head. "I have no idea."

Trent put a hand on her elbow, hating to break up the moment. He had little choice, though. "We need to move."

"We do," Tessa said, shoving the money into her pocket.

"There's one other thing," Trent started, his voice softening with compassion toward this couple who'd shown them so much kindness. "Is there anywhere the two of you could go for a few days? I fear you're in the line of fire because of your association with us."

"I couldn't stand the thought of anything happening to you," Tessa said, reaching for the older woman in front of her. The two of them stared at each other, something unspoken passing there. Compassion, understanding, concern for each other.

"We can go to stay with my sister," Wilma said. "She lives in Kentucky, and she'd be tickled to see us."

"What about the store?" Tessa asked.

"We'll put Dale in charge. You remember him? We've left him running the place before. He used to work for us full time, and he still fills in on occasion. He'll be fine while we're gone." Wilma glanced at her husband. "What do you say? It would be good to get away, right?"

Salem nodded. "It would."

"I think you should go now," Trent said. "We'll wait for you to grab a few belongings. But please hurry. There's not much time."

Trent's empathy for the couple warmed Tessa's heart. Maybe he wasn't the person she'd assumed he was when they first met. Of course, still believing he was an enemy seemed much safer than the alternative. The alternative meant her heart might feel free to explore her gut-level attraction toward the man. That possibility was crazy. The last thing she wanted was to entertain the idea of romance and love and happy-ever-after—they were all out of the reach of reality as far as she was concerned.

Salem nodded again. "Let's go grab a few things, just enough to hold us over. I'll call Dale on the road and tell him I'm taking Wilma somewhere as a surprise."

"Good idea," Trent said, glancing out the window again. "The fewer people who know, the better."

The couple disappeared for a moment. The jitters in Tessa's stomach intensified as the impending feeling of doom continued to close in. This could get uglier before it got better—if it even got better.

Trent squeezed her shoulder and pulled her from her

morbid thoughts. Electricity rushed through her with such intensity that she startled.

"You okay?" he asked.

She nodded, almost robotically. "Yeah, I guess so. As well as anyone would be in this situation."

"You're hanging in like a trouper."

"It's not even me that I'm that worried about it. It's Salem and Wilma. It's my family. There are so many other people who could be hurt because of my actions. And nothing you tell me is going to change my mind about that, so you can save your breath."

"I was going to say that I know this must be stressful for you." His gaze lingered on her, more insightful and perceptive than she would like.

Her cheeks heated. It had been a long time since her feelings were that transparent to someone. It bothered her and comforted her at the same time.

Just then, Salem and Wilma appeared with bags in hand. Tessa saw the fear in Wilma's eyes, and her guilt grew. She pulled the woman into another hug.

"Please be careful," Tessa whispered.

"I'm a tough old broad." She shrugged. "I've always wanted to say that, at least. I'll be fine. You just take care of yourself."

She gave Tessa a good motherly pat on the arm, matronly concern written across her expression.

After Tessa hugged Salem, they all went outside. Tessa made sure the couple was safely in their car before climbing in their loaner car herself. They'd been able to borrow a ten-year-old sedan. Salem liked to fix up cars in his free time, so he always seemed to have a couple of extras around.

Against her logic, she lifted up a prayer for the couple as they pulled away. *Lord, please give them safety. Cover*

*the eyes of my attackers. Help them not to see my friends
leave. Protect them.*

She opened her eyes and felt better immediately. She'd
forgotten how much comfort could be found in lifting her
worries up to her Creator.

Trent was staring at her as he cranked the engine. "Praying?"

She nodded reluctantly. "Desperate times call for desperate measures."

"Desperate times can teach us to depend on a higher
power, even when there's no storm raging around us. That's
the key we have to remember." He put the car into Drive
and took off down the road.

The night was dark and Tessa kept expecting to see another car pull out behind them and another chase to begin.
Thankfully, the road remained clear. She wondered how
long that would be true. She wasn't naive enough to believe her troubles were over.

Trent glanced over at Tessa and saw that ever-present
worry in her gaze. She was right to be so. This situation
was strenuous and taxing, even for the most levelheaded
person. Her concern for others—for Salem and Wilma
specifically—had touched him.

All of those theories people had about her, he couldn't
imagine them to be true. Obviously, she'd fled out of fear.
And she was still scared. Terrified, really.

Trent had been through war zones, and this situation
still felt especially intense and dangerous, much more so
than he'd anticipated.

"Where are we going?" Tessa asked, wrapping her arms
over her chest. Clearly, it was her way of putting up a wall,
of guarding herself and protecting the little security she
had left.

"I don't know yet," he answered honestly. None of this

had been planned. He'd thought he'd track Tessa down, convince her to go home to her family and that would be the end of it. He'd had no idea how intricate this web of danger would be.

She remained silent a moment, her eyes fluttering back and forth in thought. "My boss has a rental house about twenty minutes away from here. I think it we could camp out there for a day or so."

"And your boss?" Trent asked. "Where will she be?"

"She's been away at a spa for the past two weeks. But she said I could use the house whenever I wanted to. Even told me what the code is to get into the lockbox where the key is located."

"Let's try that. But we'll only stay for as long as absolutely necessary—maybe one night. The longer we remain in one place, the more likely we'll be found."

"Understood."

They drove silently, except when Tessa would throw out a direction. Thankfully the road behind them remained clear, without any warnings signs of danger to come. Just where had that man gone? What was he planning next? And what had he meant when he'd said, *This woman has taken up too much of our time and energy. We need to put this behind us, and there's only one way to do that*?

There were so many questions and so few answers. He didn't want to push Tessa too hard, not right now. They'd actually made some progress in trusting each other, and he didn't want to ruin it.

The tension didn't leave him. He knew at any moment, the seemingly peaceful drive could turn dangerous. Leo's goons obviously wouldn't stop until they got what they wanted—and what they wanted was Tessa dead.

"What do you think they'll do next?" she muttered, staring straight ahead. "How would you track someone down if you were on their side?"

That was a great question, but it was complicated. He let out a deep breath. "Considering the fact that I believe they followed me here, I think they're probably looking into your life in Gideon's Hollow now. I assume they left someone to keep watch over your house to see if you go back. They'll think of ways to talk to anyone you had contact with and look for any indications as to where you might run."

"What about my boss, Chris? Do you think they'll look for us at her place?"

"It's a risk we have to take right now. I'm hoping we're far enough ahead of them that they won't catch up yet."

"I see."

"If you left any emails on your computer, they'll examine those. They'll try to access your phone records."

"So how much time do we have?" She almost sounded resigned as she asked the question.

"Maybe a couple of days."

"It sounds as if we—I—need to go somewhere totally off the radar."

He stole a glance at her, trying to gauge her emotions. As the moonlight hit her profile, he sucked in a breath. Man, was she beautiful—take-his-breath-away beautiful. "You don't think I'm going to leave you alone, do you?"

"As far as I'm concerned, we're not in this together. You should go back and tell my family that you weren't successful. Maybe just tell them that I'm most likely dead. Whatever it takes to ease their pain. I'm assuming the not knowing is probably the hardest part for them."

"I led these men to you, Tessa. This is partly my fault. I can't abandon you." Leo must have been tracking his moves. Especially if it was like Tessa had said—the man had pretended to be a friend to her family when all along he was behind everything. The realization had solidified in his mind the longer he thought about it. That meant it was partly Trent's fault that Tessa was in her current situation.

"I don't want you to feel obligated. This is my problem, not yours. You should get out now while you can."

He couldn't imagine leaving her behind at a time like this. It wasn't even that he felt obligated—there was just some part of him that knew he couldn't abandon her now. The girl would be a sitting duck. Besides, no one should be terrified and alone.

He intended on sticking with her until this was resolved. He had a feeling her life depended on it. And, by default, so did his.

Tessa hated to admit it, but she felt grateful for Trent's steadfastness. Most people would have jumped ship at the first opportunity. But Trent was here and, even if she wanted to get rid of him, she wasn't sure she'd be able to. His presence comforted her, as did his size and skills. He'd proved himself to be more than capable.

But reality still haunted her. Leo's men had found her. If they went through her emails, they'd find correspondence with Chris, her boss at the travel agency. Thankfully, Salem didn't believe in email, so maybe those men wouldn't connect Tessa with the hardware-store owner and his wife.

Salem and Wilma were now out of town. Chris was also out of the area. Tessa could only pray they'd remain safe. They seemed to be the most at risk.

"Chris's cabin should be down this road," she said, her voice sounding more like a croak.

Trent turned down a narrow road. At the end of the street, a house appeared. Even in the dark, Tessa could see a gentle stream rippling behind the property. Trent pulled around behind the structure and cut the engine. "So we rest up and then we hit the road again in the morning. Sound good?"

Tessa nodded, overwhelmed by the task ahead of her. Was there anywhere she'd be safe? She typed in the code on the lockbox by the front door and found the spare key inside. They unlocked the door and stepped inside, hitting the light switch on the wall. A cozy cabin came into view.

Her throat tightened at the thought of staying here with Trent. It wasn't ideal. But what other choice did they have? At least the place was large enough that one of them could stay upstairs and the other downstairs. And she'd sleep with her door locked. She wouldn't take any chances, despite his dedication so far. One could never be too careful.

"We'll take off in the morning," Trent said, turning toward her.

As she glanced up at him and realized how close they were standing, heat rushed to her cheeks. She'd known he was handsome. But standing here in the light right now, there was no denying that the man was attractive.

She swallowed hard and took a step back, surprised at how appealing he seemed at the moment. "That sounds good. I'll stay upstairs."

He nodded, his eyes still on her as if he was trying to figure her out. He'd obviously noticed the change in her, seen the flash of embarrassment in her eyes. "Good night, then."

Before either of them could take a step away, a sound outside caught their ears.

Tessa saw Trent tense also, then he grabbed her arm, cut the lights and pulled her against the wall. Her senses came alive as adrenaline pumped through her.

No way had those men tracked her down already... had they?

Then they heard the sound again. It was clearly a car. Pulling down the lane. Coming toward the cabin.

SEVEN

Trent knew something wasn't right. No way would these guys pull up to a cabin in the middle of the night and practically announce their arrival. They were more cunning than that.

So who was here?

He peered out the window, saw a sedan pull up and the headlights go dark. Then a woman stepped out.

"Blonde, heavyset, midfifties."

Tessa visible relaxed beside him. "Chris. That must be Chris. But she wasn't supposed to be back for another week."

"Come on. We don't want to scare her." Trent pulled her away from the wall and opened the door just as Chris stepped onto the porch.

The woman gasped in surprise. "You scared the living daylights out of me!" Then her gaze fell on Tessa. "Tessa? What are you doing here?"

"I didn't mean to scare you. You said I could use the cabin whenever I wanted, and I thought you were at a spa."

Chris's eyes went to Trent, and she gave him a knowing look. "I see."

Tessa shook her head, her cheeks reddening. "No, it's not like that. It's actually a really long story. I just needed some place to go because of some problems at my own cabin. Like I said, I didn't expect you to be here."

"I decided to end my vacation a little early and have some downtime here at my mountain retreat." She held her flowered luggage up a little higher.

"We can leave," Tessa said, apology in her tone.

Trent wondered if Tessa realized exactly what she was saying, because they had nowhere else to go.

"No, no." Chris waved a hand in the air, suddenly acting as if this wasn't a big deal. "Please stay. Just let me get inside and put my stuff down."

"Of course." Tessa stepped aside, offering a fleeting glance toward Trent.

Trent could tell she felt awkward. Anyone would in her situation, and his heart twisted with a moment of compassion. Usually when he got focused on a task, he tried to clear away any emotions in favor of logic. Logic could help keep them alive.

But at the moment Tessa seemed so alone. There was something deeper inside Trent, something he couldn't exactly pinpoint, that kept him here. It wasn't an obligation. It wasn't duty.

It was purpose, he realized. It was no accident he was here to help. He believed God had ordained the timing.

Chris pushed past them and deposited everything inside the door before flipping on the lights. Once they were all inside and the door closed, she turned to them. "Anyone care to explain?"

Tessa cast another glance at Trent, and he could tell she was struggling to find the right words. He decided to step in. "Someone broke into Tessa's place, and she needed to go somewhere else for the night."

Chris eyed him suspiciously. "And you are?"

"I'm just a family friend who came to visit."

"I thought you didn't have any family," Chris said, turning back to Tessa.

Tessa laughed nervously. "I mean, everyone has family, even if there are some members you'd like to forget. Besides, he's a family *friend*."

"Well, I'm sorry to hear about your home," Chris said, accepting her answer. She walked into the kitchen and fixed a glass of water, taking a long sip before clanking the glass on the counter. "That must have been scary, and I'm glad I can be of help. You're welcome to stay here. There's one bedroom upstairs and I usually stay down here."

"I'll take the couch," Trent offered.

"Very well, then. I'm exhausted, so I'm going to turn in. I'll see you both in the morning."

She grabbed her things and shuffled off to the bedroom, shutting the door behind her. A moment later, the lock clicked in place.

"Thanks for covering for me," Tessa whispered, stepping closer and glancing toward Chris's closed door. "My mind went blank."

"It's not a problem."

She nodded upstairs and let out a deep sigh. "I'm going to turn in. I know we have a long day ahead. Good night."

His gaze lingered on her as she disappeared upstairs. She really was lovely. He'd known that even before he met her. But there was something about her that made it hard to pull his eyes away. Maybe it was the way her glossy hair swept over her shoulders. The way she nibbled on her lip when she got nervous. How her eyes told the story of what was going on in her head and heart.

When Tessa disappeared from sight, Trent pulled out his cell. Could they be tracking him through his phone? Was that how they'd found him here?

It was an idea he definitely needed to consider. But right

now he needed to call for help. When he finished this conversation, he'd ditch his phone, just to be on the safe side.

He dialed one of his old friends from the police academy, Zach Davis. The two had started on the force together in Richmond, Virginia. Later, Zach had moved up to Baltimore and then to a little island on the Chesapeake Bay. The bonds they'd forged through the academy had never faded, though. Trent knew Zach had a few weeks off before starting a new job as sheriff, so he would be the perfect person to help.

Zach answered before the second ring, his voice scratchy but alert. "Trent?"

"Sorry to wake you." Trent paced to the far side of the house and lowered his voice so no one would hear. The situation would be tricky because Leo McAllister was a man with connections. Plus, even though he'd chided Tessa for her trust issues, he had some himself.

The police had investigated Leo after Tessa had disappeared, but they'd found no evidence of wrongdoing. It didn't help either that no one, not even law enforcement, wanted to mess with the McAllister family. They were powerful, made big donations to charities, including the Fraternal Order of Police, and they had the ear of senators and other legislative leaders.

If Trent was wrong about Leo—if Tessa wasn't telling the truth, for some reason—then they'd be opening a can of worms that was best left untouched. That was why Trent knew there were only two people he could trust—Zach and their mutual friend Gabe Michaels.

For all he knew, the McAllisters could have men in the local police or even with the FBI. They were rich enough to buy anyone willing to sell themselves for a price.

"What time is it?" Zach asked, his voice groggy.

He glanced at clock in the distance. "Three thirty."

"I'm assuming this is important."

"Life or death. There's no one else I can trust. I need you to look into someone for me. His name is Leo McAllister."

"Okay…"

"He may have ties with terrorists."

"Sounds serious."

"I did mention life or death. However, this could go a lot deeper than just my life." Tessa entered his mind. But this was also greater than even her life. If what Tessa had told him was true—and he had no reason to believe it wasn't—then the lives of a lot of Americans could be at stake. A terrorist cell developing weapons was huge.

Trent filled Zach in on the other details about Leo that he knew.

"I'll see what I can find out and get back to you."

"There's no time to waste on this, Zach," Trent said. "You should be careful, too. If you try to breach their computer system, they'll be alerted. It's important to circumvent anything you do on the web."

"I'll start now," Zach said. "And I'll be cautious."

Trent only hoped he wasn't already too late.

Tessa couldn't relax. She'd forced herself to lie in bed, but she'd left all of her clothes on, even her shoes. Instead of crawling under the covers, she'd lain on top of them and pulled a spare blanket over her legs in order to stay warm. She felt better being dressed and ready to run if necessary.

Just one more rule of survival: always be prepared.

Her body was tired, but her adrenaline made it hard for her to sleep. She lay in bed, staring at the ceiling, replaying everything and fretting about what the future would hold.

What would it be like to believe that God was in control? That whatever happened, He could work it for good? Right now, she needed some hope and comfort. Relying on herself—even relying on Trent—just didn't seem like enough. It was going to take a force greater than the two of them in order to survive this.

She'd gone to church growing up, so she knew the scriptures. She just felt as if God had been silent in her life for the past year. Or was she the one who'd stopped talking?

When Tessa really thought about it, she realized her relationship with God had dwindled before all of this had happened with Leo. In college, she'd drifted away from her beliefs. She'd considered herself a Christian in name, but she hadn't lived like someone who followed Christ. No, she'd let worldly lures take hold in her life. She'd enjoyed the finer things—designer clothes, pampering herself, making her career her number one priority.

Leo had fit right in with that side of her. She'd loved the luxuries he'd provided; she'd even reveled in them. But looking back, she'd felt hollow inside during that time. All of those things hadn't brought her the satisfaction she'd hoped for. All it had done was to leave her wanting more and more.

When she'd gone on the run and everything had been stripped away, Tessa had to come to terms with who she was as a person, without the fancy clothes or perfect hair or admirable career.

She hadn't liked the image that stared back at her. Her changes had happened so slowly that she hadn't even realized they'd taken effect. Sin was like that: people could dip a toe in and before they knew it be fully immersed.

But those were things she'd think about later. Her thoughts turned to Trent. Despite her doubts, he'd been kind. He could have left her in the middle of the craziness, like most sensible people would have. But he'd stuck by her, even risking his life.

Her family trusted him. Maybe she could, too.

As she turned over in bed again, unable to sleep, her mind drifted from Trent to Chris. Why had her boss had such a strange reaction to her? Of course it was strange that Chris had found her here. Tessa couldn't deny that. But there was more to it.

Did Chris think that Tessa was up to no good? That almost seemed to match her reaction.

She and her boss had always had a peculiar relationship. Chris didn't really need to work or generate income. Her late husband had left her with a lot of money, enough to own three houses and take vacations whenever she wanted. But the woman liked traveling so much that she'd decided to open her own travel agency in town. They hardly ever had any clients. Tessa hadn't complained because the job helped her to pay the bills and the lackluster business kept her isolated.

Chris was in and out, though—more out than in. She basically trusted Tessa to run the business from the little storefront in downtown Gideon's Hollow. It was a nice, quiet job with very little interaction with those in town— ideal for Tessa.

Now she wondered if Chris had bought Trent's story. He'd told the truth. But Tessa knew that despite their best efforts, they'd been acting suspiciously. She'd never been a good liar. Even though Trent had sounded calm, one look at Tessa and Chris would have known that something was off.

She wished she could stop fretting about it, though.

As she started to drift off to sleep, she heard something downstairs. Just as she jolted upright in bed, her door flung open.

"Freeze! Put your hands up!" A police officer stood there, his gun drawn and aimed at her.

Trent kept his hands raised in the air, his gaze quickly surveying the men around him. Five men had burst into the house from both the front and back doors. They wore SWAT gear with helmets and carried military-grade weapons.

He'd taken one look and known he had no chance of taking them all down. So he'd risen from the couch and tried to keep his cool instead. But his thoughts clashed inside his head.

How had these men, whoever they were, found them here? He had his suspicions.

Chris had stepped out of her bedroom fifteen minutes ago, said she needed some air, and five minutes after she returned the men had invaded the house.

At the moment, Chris appeared unbothered. She stood by the front door with her arms crossed and a look of worry on her face. She'd been the one who led these men here. But why would she do something like this? What would her motive be?

A moment later, Trent saw one of the officers leading Tessa downstairs. Her arms were raised also, and terror stained her eyes. Anyone would be scared in this situation. Her gaze met his and he saw the questions there. He wished he had answers to give her.

A man—the one who appeared to be in charge—strutted up to Trent and got in his face. The man stared wordlessly, waiting for Trent to flinch, to break his gaze. Trent refused.

When he got no reaction from Trent, the man took a step back and glowered. "Arrest both of them."

"On what count?" Trent asked.

"Conspiring with terrorists, for starters."

"What evidence could possibly prove that?" None. There was no way they had any proof.

"Tessa has been on our watch list for quite a while. Unfortunately, you've proved to be her accomplice," the man continued. "We take threats like this very seriously."

This wasn't making any sense, not by any stretch of the imagination. "What agency are you with?"

"The West Virginia State Police. We're bringing you

in, but I'm sure the FBI will want a piece of you, also. You two have a lot of explaining to do."

Something still wasn't settling right in his gut. There were six men altogether and four had guns trained on Trent and Tessa. There was little he could do at his point.

One of the men pulled Trent's hands down and cuffed him. Another officer did the same for Tessa.

"You have the right to remain silent," the officer started.

Tessa struggled against the man. It was just the distraction he needed. As the man in front of him looked away, Trent reached back and grabbed an upholstery tack from the breakfast bar. Chris must have been re-covering one of her chairs. Working carefully, subtly, Trent pressed two tacks into his leather belt, praying no one would notice.

Just as he secured the second tack, his captor jerked his arms back and began leading him outside.

Tessa swung her head toward Chris as she passed.

"You did this, didn't you?" Hurt and betrayal were evident in her voice.

The woman shook her head, sorrow in her eyes. "I was already on my way home when they called me a few hours ago and told me what you'd been up to. I had to do my part to help. I always thought your background sounded kind of suspicious, Tessa. I just never imagined you were capable of this."

"I'm not. I'm not guilty of anything here," Tessa said, squirming as the office behind her shoved her forward. "Chris, you have no idea what you've done..."

The woman raised her chin. "I'm just being a patriot."

With another rough shove, the officer pushed Trent outside to a police cruiser. His eyes soaked in the unmarked car. It must have pulled up after the men got inside the house. Otherwise, Trent would have heard the car approach. After all, he hadn't gotten a wink of sleep. His mind was too busy turning over things.

He glanced around. Four men still had their guns in hand, ready to use. And Trent was handcuffed. This was no time to make a move or try to escape, especially if it meant that Tessa would be in the line of fire.

Right before he was escorted into the backseat of the cruiser, he let one of the tacks drop from his hands. With any luck, the tip would pierce the tire and maybe buy them some more time.

Thankfully, Tessa tumbled into the backseat beside him. He'd prayed they wouldn't be separated, because that would only make things more complicated.

The door slammed shut but no officers climbed in. They stayed outside in the lingering darkness, talking quietly among themselves. Chris stood on the porch, watching everything with her arms crossed and a look of both anxiety and pride across her face.

"I'm scared, Trent," Tessa whispered.

"You should be."

"Do you think they'll let us go if I tell them the whole story?" Her voice trembled.

He wanted to say, to do something to comfort her. But he had to tell her the truth. "Tessa, these men aren't the police."

Her eyes widened. "Then who are they?"

"My guess? They're men your ex-fiancé sent."

EIGHT

Tessa felt as though she might pass out. She'd thought she'd been anxious before, but what she experienced now was beyond any of her earlier apprehensions. She was downright panicky, to the point of fearing she might hyperventilate.

"What do you mean?" she whispered. "They had uniforms on."

"You can buy anything online. SWAT uniforms, fake badges. You name it."

A shiver raced through her and didn't cease. Her body continued to tremble and cold washed over her. "They're going to kill us."

"Listen, don't let on that you know anything. Okay? We'll figure a way out together. But we need to play it cool."

"So you have a plan?" She desperately hoped he did.

"Considering I have no idea what's going to happen, it's really hard to create a firm strategy of how to escape. So I'll do the next best thing."

"What's that?"

"I'll wait for the right opportunity."

"Here they come," she whispered.

Two men climbed into the front seat. The other four climbed into another cruiser. Tessa cast one more glance at Chris as they pulled away. How could her friend think that she was guilty? Didn't she know her any better?

Of course, Leo could be convincing. He could talk the most intelligent person into believing whatever lies he wanted to sell. Besides, if there really had been something suspicious, it *was* Chris's duty to report it. The woman had no idea the web of deceit that had been spun around her.

Okay, God, I'm listening. Maybe that's been the problem. It's not that You've been silent. It's that I haven't been ready to hear. I'm ready now. I'm sorry that it's taken this moment of absolute desperation to get me to this point.

The sun started to peek over the mountains as they headed east. Tessa assumed that meant it was probably approaching seven. The sun was coming up later now that it was getting cooler outside.

She tried to focus on the things she knew. The definites were more comforting than the uncertainties. That was why she watched the landscape out the window as they passed. That was why she concentrated on the sunrise. Why she listened to the men's voices in the front seat as they muttered quietly to each other. Glass separated them and she couldn't make out their words. But they definitely didn't have West Virginia accents. Trent was right.

She glanced at him then. She could see from the look in his eyes that he was mulling the situation over and running through possibilities. As strange as it might seem, she was glad he was here with her. Even though the situation felt practically hopeless, he was the reason she had a small grain of hope that they'd survive. Alone, she'd be dead by now.

He caught her looking at him and sent her a questioning look. "You okay?"

She shrugged. "Depends on how you define *okay*. I'm sure you're regretting taking this assignment, huh?"

"No, not at all."

"You could die because of it."

He leaned closer, close enough that she could feel his breath on her cheek. "Tessa, if what you've told me is true, this family needs to be exposed. I'm going to do everything I can to fight for justice."

Something welled in her—she wasn't sure what. Pride? Gratitude? He had the heart of a soldier, of a fighter, and she could appreciate that. The world needed people who weren't afraid to battle for what they believed in, to fight for the rights of others.

She wished she had some of that same resolve. Maybe she wouldn't be in this situation. Maybe she wouldn't have retreated in the first place.

Suddenly, the car lurched. It jerked to the right so hard that Tessa tumbled into Trent. Had one of the tires been shot out?

As the car pulled over to a stop on the side of the road, Tessa held her breath and waited to see what would happen next.

Was this the moment of opportunity Trent had mentioned?

"Stay here," the driver said gruffly.

Trent watched every move the bogus police officers made. It appeared the tack he'd thrown down had finally wedged itself into the tire and led to a blowout. Thankfully, the other car had gone ahead of them. That meant that it was just Trent, Tessa and the two men escorting them. However, Trent and Tessa were at a disadvantage because of their handcuffs. But hopefully that wouldn't be a problem for long. He'd been subtly trying to work the second tack he'd pressed into his belt into the lock mechanism of the handcuffs.

Finally, he heard a soft click. He'd done it.

Now he had to figure out how to reach Tessa without drawing any attention to the fact.

The driver jerked the door open. "You're going to have to get out while we change the tire."

He grabbed Tessa first and dragged her outside. Before the man could reach for Trent, he scooted from the car, making sure his handcuffs stayed in place for the time being.

"Guard them while I change this," the driver mumbled to his partner.

The other man—the slighter of the two—aimed his gun at Trent and Tessa. He appeared youngish—maybe in his midtwenties, and he was both scrawny and obviously outranked in this merry little group of bandits. The driver had called him Grath once.

"Stay over there," Grath said. "Don't make a move or you're dead."

"We're dead anyway, aren't we?" Trent said.

A gleam appeared in the man's eyes, and he nodded toward Tessa. "Not until the big man sees her. He wants to handle this personally."

That must be Leo. He wanted to make sure Tessa suffered. Trent didn't like the sound of that.

Immediately, visions of Laurel appeared in his mind. He couldn't let that happen again. Laurel had been his whole world and made him feel like the luckiest man alive. Sure, they'd had their problems. But they'd been happy together.

Until one of his supposed friends had stabbed him in the back. He'd been tasked with guarding Laurel while Trent was testifying in court.

The gang he was trying put away had threatened Trent's life if he proceeded with his investigation. He'd known Laurel would be in danger, as well. That was why he'd taken the extra precautions to keep her safe. He didn't want to be bullied.

But then one of his own friends, Richard, had been bought off. Richard hadn't pulled the trigger on Laurel himself, but he'd taken money and given away her location to men who'd been bent on revenge toward Trent. Those men had shot Richard in the shoulder, an injury that looked more serious than it was. Then those thugs had killed Laurel.

His friend had denied his involvement for weeks—months. But Trent had begun to trail him. He'd caught him meeting with a gang member. A check of his bank account had proved Richard had been paid off. When he'd brought the evidence to his colleagues, they hadn't taken him seriously. They'd thought he was obsessed and desperate to find someone to take the blame.

That was when Trent had left the police department and struck out on his own. Eventually, he'd taken his evidence all the way to the top and gotten some results. He'd pressed charges and Richard had gone to jail. But the whole thing had left Trent disillusioned.

He wasn't going to let the same thing happen to Tessa that had happened to Laurel.

Moving quietly, wordlessly, Trent slipped the tack into Tessa's hands. She felt it for a moment before looking up at him with confusion.

Subtly, he motioned toward his handcuffs. Her eyes widened with understanding and she nodded.

As Grath looked away for a brief second, Trent swung his leg through the air. His foot connected with the man's gun and sent it toppling to the ground. In that moment, the driver reached for his own gun and aimed it at Trent.

In a flash, Trent grabbed Grath and pulled the man in front of him to use as a human shield. The driver discharged his gun, and Grath let out a groan as the bullet hit his shoulder.

Before the driver had a chance to realize what was happening, Trent shoved Grath on top of him. The action afforded Trent enough time to grab the driver's gun.

The two struggled with the weapon. In a battle of strength, the barrel of the gun volleyed back and forth from the driver to Trent.

Despite the chill in the air, sweat sprinkled across Trent's forehead. The man was tougher than he'd given him credit for. Their struggle continued in what felt like slow motion.

"Give it up," the driver mumbled, his face red with exertion.

"Never." Trent used all the strength in him to aim the gun back toward the driver.

Both men grunted, bared their teeth. Their lives were on the line. Whoever was the strongest would live.

That man had to be Trent.

Suddenly, a gunshot filled the air. The driver let out a howl of pain. Trent's eyes traveled to the man's shoulder. A spot of blood grew there.

Trent jerked his eyes behind him. Tessa stood there, gun in hand. She looked shell-shocked, but okay.

She might have just saved his life.

With half of her handcuffs still around her wrist, she tucked the gun into her waistband and hurried toward Trent. "Are you okay?"

He took a step back from the driver, who was still alive but moaning with pain. "Yeah, I'm fine. We need to go."

"I'll get the tire. You move these guys out of the way?"

Trent stared at her a moment, unsure he'd heard her correctly. But she was already at the tire, unscrewing the lug nuts. "Got it."

He grabbed the driver and pulled him off to the side of the road. The man would be okay. His partners would come back to check on these two when they realized they were no longer responding. Grath would also be okay. He'd been hit in the shoulder, but it wasn't life threatening.

That meant it was even more urgent that Trent and Tessa got out of there fast.

"They'll...find...you," the driver muttered, teeth bared.

"We're going to make that as hard as possible," Trent said, patting the man's cheek. He reached into his pocket and grabbed the man's phone. Then he snatched the extra gun and some cash. He and Tessa were going to need whatever they could get in order to survive this.

He got back to Tessa in time to help her slip the new tire on. "A girl who knows her way around a car. Impressive."

"My dad insisted I know how to take care of myself."

"It's really paying off now," Trent said, helping her finish. "Come on. Let's go."

She climbed into the passenger seat as he slammed the driver's door shut. He cranked the engine and started down the road, his heart pounding as he realized what'd just happened. That could have turned out so much differently.

Thank You, Lord.

"We don't have much time," Trent said.

"What do you mean? You think those other guys will find us?" Tessa glanced back, as if expecting to see the second car. Then she began fiddling with the handcuff still left on one wrist. She unlatched it and stuck the tack into her pocket.

"Unfortunately, I fear they'll find us sooner rather than later. This car probably has a GPS and they'll be able to track us down."

"So what do we do?"

"We hold tight for a little while. As soon as we're able to, we'll ditch this car and get a new one."

"That sounds easier said than done." She shivered and stared out the window a moment, a certain melancholy washing over her. "You think those guys will be okay?"

He nodded. "They'll be fine."

"That's the first time I've ever shot someone."

"You saved my life." He glanced over and saw the worry across her features. He reached across the seat and squeezed her hand. "You were brave. You did the right thing. Those guys were ruthless, Tessa. There's no telling what would have happened when we got to whatever destination they were taking us to."

She nodded uncertainly. "Mentally, I know that. Emotionally, I'm still spinning."

He squeezed again before pulling his hand back to his side. "I know it's tough."

She drew in a deep breath. "I have to stop thinking about that. I've got to start focusing on survival."

With that, she opened the glove compartment.

Tessa riffled through the papers that had been left in the car. Certainly there was some information here, even if it was fake.

"What are you doing?" Trent asked her.

"I'm seeing if I can find anything useful," Tessa told him. "Maybe there's some evidence of what they were planning. Whatever information we can arm ourselves with, the better."

"I agree."

Tessa thought she saw a touch of admiration in his eyes. She continued to browse the papers, but saw nothing helpful. The car was registered to someone named John Tracy. The name didn't ring any bells with Tessa. Some sales papers indicated it had been purchased in Alexandria, Virginia. It couldn't be a coincidence.

Tessa had worked in a gallery outside Washington, DC, just a few miles from Alexandria. That was where Leo had based all his operations. This only solidified everything in her mind. Leo had hired these men and sent them after her.

How many were out there, searching for them? Right

now, it almost seemed like an unending army. There'd been the men at her cabin who'd driven off the cliff. The ones at Trent's cabins who'd followed them through the woods. Then this group. How many would Tessa have to defeat before she'd won the battle?

Tessa knew that someone with Leo's power, money and influence could afford to hire as many people as he wanted. He'd made millions on his arms trade. She'd sneaked onto his computer and seen the numbers herself.

What she'd never been able to figure out was his motive. Was it just the money? Did he really hate this country that much? Maybe it was both. Maybe it was just to carry out his family's legacy. Until eight months ago when she'd made her discoveries, Tessa had never had any indication that he had ties to terrorists.

After that, she'd been able to put some of the facts into place. Leo did have a lot of hushed phone calls and out-of-town business trips. She'd always thought it was because he was trying to secure new art deals.

Suddenly, something landed in her lap. She looked down and saw a wallet. "What's this?"

"I took it from the man driving the car. See what's inside."

She opened the bifold and saw at least six one-hundred-dollar bills. The man's driver's license read Tom Tracy and he was from Wilmington Heights. His picture seemed to glare at her from the plastic identification card.

She continued to go through the wallet and found two credit cards, a slip of paper with an address on it and a season pass to a local amusement park.

Funny, even men like John Tracy had a life outside criminal activities.

"Anything?"

She held up the paper. "An address."

"What is it?"

"It's in Wilmington Heights, Virginia. 123 Arnold Drive."

He handed her a phone. "This also belongs to one of the men who were after us. Look up the address on the map. I'm guessing it's near DC. Within an hour, at least."

"You think it's where they were going to take us?"

"It's my best guess."

Before she could pull up the map, the phone beeped. An incoming call.

A name popped up on the screen.

Leo McAllister.

NINE

Trent stared at the phone a moment, contemplating his options and weighing the possible consequences. He didn't have much time to make up his mind.

"What should I do?" Tessa asked. "If no one answers, Leo will get suspicious."

Trent held out his hand, decision made. "Let me have the phone."

Her eyes widened even more. "Are you…?"

He nodded.

After a moment of hesitation, she slipped the device into his hands. He drew in a deep breath before putting it to his ear and answering. "Hello."

"Tom, what's the word?" a deep voice asked.

Trent kept his voice neutral, trying to sound indistinguishable. "So far, so good."

"You running on schedule still?"

"By all calculations, yes."

"How's the girl?"

"Scared."

"Good. Wait till she sees me." He let out a diabolical yet untethered laugh.

Trent forced himself to let out a deep chuckle, also. He had to sound as if he was on Leo's side, even if the mere thought of it made him feel sick to his stomach. "Yes, sir."

"All right. See you in a few hours, then."

Trent hung up and glanced at Tessa. Again, his heart welled with compassion and protectiveness. Leo was planning something extremely painful as a repercussion for her betraying him. Trent couldn't let that happen. Anger surged through him at the thought. How people could be that twisted, that selfish, that evil was hard to fathom. Yet he'd seen his fair share of evil. He'd fought terrorists before. He'd won. He was determined to do the same here with Tessa.

"Well?"

"He says he'll see us in a few hours. Wherever they were going, it wasn't terribly far away." DC was probably three hours from here, but the suburbs could be reached in two or less.

"So what do we do?"

"Call the number on the back of those credit cards. See if we can find out how much is left on the credit line. We're going to need a new vehicle." He glanced at the dashboard. "And gas."

With trembling hands, she began making the calls. "It looks as if there's about five thousand," she said several minutes later. "You think we can get away with using these?"

"If we find a small dealer and we go at dusk so we're less recognizable. Or if I put a hat on to disguise my face a little more. There are a lot of factors here." They'd all raced through his mind at once, causing a small throb to start forming at the back of his head. There was so much at stake. One wrong move could end with both of them dead.

Not on his watch.

"Okay. Whatever we have to do."

"It's not ideal," he said. "But there aren't a lot of choices."

"You're right. If we are where I think, there's a town about fifteen minutes from here. It's small, but large enough to have a variety of businesses. Maybe we can find something there."

"Even better—look up some online ads." Buying from a private dealer was the best option. He prayed that everything would fall into place.

Tessa got busy, her fingers flying across the phone's keyboard and her gaze concentrated on the screen. "This one looks promising."

"Call them."

Tessa did as he asked. When she hung up, she said, "The seller said we can go to his house now. He has one of those credit card readers, so he'll let us use our cards."

"Perfect. Tell me how to get there."

Ten minutes later, they pulled up to a small house in the mountains. A man named Jim with long hair pulled back into a ponytail met them outside and showed them a faded red sedan he was selling.

"If I'd had more time, I would have cleaned it up for you. It's a little junky inside. My apologies," Jim said in a West Virginia drawl.

Trent peered inside and saw some old soda cans in the backseat, along with some napkins and a few magazines. That wasn't what concerned him. He really needed to see under the hood.

Jim popped it open for him and Trent examined the hoses and belts, checked the fluids and looked for any corrosion. Afterward, he cranked the engine and listened to it run for a moment.

"You two from around here?" Jim asked, crossing his arms and looking as if he had all the time in the world.

"Not too far away," Trent said. "We've been looking for a new car for the family. We didn't want to let this one pass us by."

The man tapped his knuckles on the side of the vehicle. "She may not be beautiful, but she's solid. I fixed her up myself. It's what I do—find oysters and make them into pearls and then I sell them."

Trent didn't have enough time to make all of this small talk. He stepped from the driver's seat and held out his hand. "We'll take it."

A smile spread across the man's face and he closed the deal with a handshake. "Sounds great. Let me go get my phone and card reader."

As he hurried into his house, Tessa looked up at Trent. "You think this can get us out of town?"

"The car seems to run well, even if it is junky. And the price is right. Now we just have to hope this payment goes through."

Jim returned with his smartphone. Trent's fingers were steady as he handed the credit card to him.

Jim looked at the card for a moment and then back at Trent. "Since this is such a large transaction, could I see some ID, also?"

"Of course." He reached back into the wallet and emerged with the driver's license. He tugged at his hat as Jim studied the picture a moment. The man looked at the image there and then back at Trent.

Trent held his breath, waiting for Jim's conclusion. This could ruin everything for Trent and Tessa. He only prayed Jim didn't look too closely.

"These pictures really make us look horrible, don't they?" Jim finally said with a laugh.

A chuckled escaped from Trent as he let out the breath he held. "You're telling me. Or maybe it's the fact I need bifocals but keep resisting. I don't feel old enough for that yet."

"Let me get this done." He swiped the card, waited a moment and then looked up with a smile. "All set."

"Perfect."

Jim handed him his card back, along with the car keys and title. "Enjoy!"

Trent glanced at Tessa, and she nodded. She took the keys from him. "I'll be driving this. I'll see you later… honey."

"I'll see you at home," Trent said, just as they'd re-hearsed.

They'd discussed abandoning the fake police cruiser a little farther down the road, hopping into the sedan and taking off.

Trent had walked four steps toward the cruiser when Jim called his name. His fake name. Had Jim realized what they were up to? Trent prayed that wasn't the case.

Trent froze, his skin pricking. He turned around, plas-tering on a fake smile. "Yes?"

Jim held out a bag of apples. "Here, take these. I have several trees on my property, so I like to give them away to everyone I can. No way I can eat all of them."

Trent slowly let out his breath. "Thank you."

He took the apples and smiled as he turned away.

"The town is about five miles from here. We're going to need to stop for some gas," Tessa said.

Just then, her stomach let out a grumble.

Trent tossed her an apple. "See if this will hold you over. We'll need get something to eat soon, too. Our energy will run out before our adrenaline."

"I could use a quick bite."

"We'll get it to go. We're not far enough away to feel comfortable."

Tessa shrugged her shoulders back. "I just can't relax. It's as if I'm waiting for a deer to pop out in the middle of the road at any minute. Only it's not an innocent deer. It's worse. But then I think—how would these guys know where we are?"

"They're pretty smart, so I'm not putting anything past them. Soon they'll realize that the two henchmen we left on the side of the road aren't answering their phone. They'll check things out. The men will be found on the road, taken to a hospital and they'll check in with Leo. We're basically on borrowed time here."

She shuddered again. "It almost feels like a no-win situation."

"It's not. You've handled yourself well so far. Your work with the gun was impressive, to say the least."

"All those lessons are paying off, I guess."

"I'd say so."

A few minutes later, a little town came into view. It looked like a classic mountain community with one main street filled with old buildings that could use some renovation. Still, the storefronts served the purpose they were needed for. There was a post office, a convenience store, a hardware store, deli and gas station.

While Trent got gas, Tessa hurried inside and cleaned herself up in the bathroom. She eyed the deli right beside the gas station, her mouth watering at the thought of a nice warm sandwich. Instead, she opted to grab some of the premade ones at the gas station, along with some bottles of water, crackers and a prepaid cell phone. She feared Leo would trace the one they used earlier, so they'd left it in the abandoned car.

She paid using the cash Salem had given her. She'd had to leave her backpack at Chris's, but at least she had this money, as well as what Trent had taken from the man who'd abducted them. She'd also kept Grath's gun, just in case.

One day, she'd repay Salem for all of his kindness. She had a lot of people to repay, for that matter. At the top of her list was Trent.

As Tessa left the store, she froze in her tracks.

Emerging from the deli were the four other men who'd been at Chris's place. They'd ditched their fake police uniforms and had fountain drinks in hand, talking merrily as if they were just some friends out for a good time.

She had to get Trent and get out of here.

Now.

TEN

Seeing the alarm across Tessa's face, Trent followed her gaze and spotted the men from the other SUV. He instantly turned around before they recognized his face. Tessa dropped behind a gas pump and pretended to tie her shoe.

Their gazes connected and no words were needed. This was a very precarious situation, and one wrong move would throw their entire plan into upheaval.

From where Trent stood, he could hear a phone ring. One of the men answered.

"What do you mean he's not picking up?" the man barked. "They were right behind us."

Trent motioned for Tessa to hop in the car. Remaining low, she climbed into the front seat and sank down. Trent finished pumping gas and screwed the lid back on the tank. He moved at a normal pace, remaining casual but keeping his back toward the men near him.

"We'll go check it out and make sure nothing happened," the man continued. "We know how important this is to you. You want the girl. Alive. Or, at least, alive enough that you can deal with her yourself."

A glance from the corner of Trent's eye showed that the men were creeping closer, walking toward their vehicle, which must have been parked out of sight on the other side of the station.

One of them glanced his way as he passed. Trent tugged his hat down lower. He had to keep a cool head.

Something seemed to register in the man's gaze.

"Trent?" Tessa questioned.

"Put your seat belt on."

"Okay…"

Before any more time could pass, Trent cranked the engine and pulled down the street. He glanced in the rearview mirror just in time to see the men turn and stare.

They were on to them.

It would take Leo's men some time to get to their car, which meant that Trent had to move quickly and carefully.

The thugs would most likely assume Trent and Tessa would take the road out of town, in the opposite direction from which they'd come. That was why Trent decided to hang a left and head around the block. They'd go back in the direction they came, but take a different route, one away from Leo's henchmen.

"They're still following us," Tessa said, peering behind her.

Spontaneously, Trent turned left and swerved into a side street. He wasn't going to lose them as easily as he'd hoped. He had to make a split-second decision.

Seizing a window of opportunity, he pulled into an open garage bay at an auto shop. As soon as he threw the car into Park, he hopped out and lowered the garage door.

"What are you doing?" someone said behind him.

Trent ignored whoever was speaking for a moment and remained beside one of the windows, holding his breath as he waited.

"Sir?"

Trent raised a finger, begging for the man's silence. Two

minutes later, the car chasing them squealed past, not even glancing in their direction.

His heart slowed for a moment. Maybe they'd lost them. He had to be patient, though, and make sure they'd really lost them. His hope was that the men would assume Trent and Tessa had headed toward the interstate instead of hiding here.

"Now, would you care to explain what's going on?" the voice behind him asked.

Trent turned and spotted a kid—he was probably in his late teens—staring at him, a wrench in his hand. An old Camaro was on a lift beside the boy.

Trent pointed to the garage door he'd lowered. "Sorry about that. It's just cold outside. I was wondering if you'd mind checking my oil?"

The kid still stared at him. "You don't know how to check oil?"

"I'm a little out of practice." Trent shrugged and did his best to look sheepish. Of course he knew how to check the oil. That excuse had been the first thing that came to his mind, though.

"Look, I get it. You're trying to hide something," the kid said.

Trent glanced out the window again. Still no sign of the men pursuing them. But they were on borrowed time. "What do you mean?"

The boy pointed back and forth between Trent and Tessa. "Are you two sneaking around, like in some kind of forbidden love story?"

The kid didn't seem like the *Romeo and Juliet* type. Obviously, he watched too much TV.

"No, no forbidden love," Trent said. "But if you must know, we are playing a little game of hide-and-seek. You caught us."

"Please don't rat us out," Tessa said, sticking her head out of her window.

The boy smiled. "As long as you're not here when my boss gets back, I couldn't care less. It's kind of fun to see adults your age having fun."

Trent ignored his remark and continued watching out the window.

"Any sign of them?" the kid asked, obviously having no idea just how dangerous this game was.

If those men came back, Trent would have to get the teenager out of here and quick. "Not yet."

"I can open the door on the other side and you can sneak out that way. It leads to an alley that ends right on the edge of town."

Trent stared at the boy a moment, surprised at his willingness to help.

The teen shrugged. "I play a lot of video games where I pretend to be hiding from the law. I've thought this through a few times."

Trent glanced out the window again and saw no one. Maybe—just maybe—his plan had worked.

"Thank you," Trent said.

They climbed back into the car, snapped their seat belts in place and waited as the boy opened the other garage door. He rolled down his window and handed the kid a twenty-dollar bill.

"Good luck!" the boy called.

Trent pulled out slowly and scanned his surroundings. There was still no sign of the other car. He started the opposite way from which they'd come, on guard in case it appeared again.

"I'm glad the boy was the only one in the garage," Tessa said.

"Tell me about it."

"Do you think we lost them?" Tessa asked, still slunk low in her seat.

Trent glanced in the mirror again. "I hope so. But we're not out of the woods yet, so to speak. They'll canvass the area for us. We need to get somewhere we can disappear for a while."

"Leo has a lot of resources. He'll utilize whatever he needs."

Tessa looked so alone as she said the words. Betrayal could do that to a person—make them unwilling to ever trust again. He knew the feeling all too well.

"It sounds as if Leo really hurt you," Trent said, pulling out of town and remaining cautiously optimistic.

She snapped her head toward him. "What?"

"Leo. It sounds as if he really hurt you."

She pulled herself up in the seat and frowned. "We had one of those whirlwind romances. I thought he walked on water."

"So that made it even harder when his true self was revealed."

"Exactly." She crossed her arms. "I never in my wildest dreams thought that this would happen. I saw a wedding in my future, kids, the perfect house. I went from being in the art world and wearing business suits every day to this."

She waved her hand up and down, showcasing her worn jeans, flannel shirt and sloppy ponytail.

"I actually think that's a pretty nice look on you," Trent said. Then again, he'd always preferred women who looked comfortable in their own skin to women with bleached hair, overdone makeup and uncomfortable-looking clothes.

Even though Tessa's face turned a tinge of red, she continued as she if she didn't hear him. "The man I thought I loved is now trying to kill me. It's possibly the worst ending to any fairy-tale romance that I could ever conjure up in my mind."

"I can only imagine how hard that was on you." His and Laurel's story hadn't supposed to have ended the way it had, either. But sometimes life just didn't work out the way people planned, and all one could do was make the best of the circumstances given.

She nodded. "Eye-opening to say the least. Definitely made me realize that I'm better off alone than I am trusting other people."

"You mean, trusting the *wrong* people."

She shook her head. "No, people in general. These months on my own have been kind of nice. There's been no one to let me down."

"Come on, you can't tell me that being alone is better than being with your loved ones. I hardly know you, but I can tell that much about you."

"I miss my family. I trust them. But I can't ever see myself having faith in others. Not after Leo."

"That's a shame. You'll be missing out. Life is much better when you share it with other people." He'd told himself that so many times. He felt like a hypocrite saying it now, because he certainly hadn't lived it out. He still held people at arm's length.

"And whom exactly do you share your life with?"

He swallowed hard. That was a good question. "I have friends."

"But you're probably married to your career, right?"

He swallowed hard again. She'd nailed him. No doubt, there was truth in her words. He had pulled away since Laurel died. He'd tried to keep his mind occupied with anything other than his pain.

Tessa didn't push anymore, and he didn't say anything. He continued driving, trying not to let her words bother him. At one time, his life had been full, as well. He'd had his friends in the police academy, and their comradery was unmistakable. Then he'd become a detective and been engaged to Laurel. Her family had lived close and they'd spent endless weekends having barbecues and cookouts and watching football games on TV.

All of that had changed when she'd died. Her family still blamed Trent, and he couldn't argue against their feelings. If Laurel hadn't been associated with him, she'd still be alive now.

He'd given up his career as a detective, started this PI practice and in the process become somewhat of a loner himself.

No, he didn't have any room to talk.

As they traveled farther down the road with no sign of the men behind them, Trent finally allowed his foot to ease off the pedal some. The day was gray with thick clouds above them, and the temperature was dropping by the minute.

He could really use some coffee, but no way was he stopping for any. "Did you buy any water?"

Tessa pulled a bottle from the bag, twisted the top and handed it to him. "I also have some crackers, muffins and a sandwich. Anything tempt you?"

"I'll take the sandwich. You should eat something, too."

She peeled back the plastic on the ham and cheese and handed it to him. Then she fished out some peanut-butter crackers for herself.

"How's my family doing?" she asked, her voice cracking.

"Your mom has been having some heart problems, if you want to know the truth."

Tessa rubbed her chest. "Really? My poor mom... I wanted to spare her all of this."

"Leo spun a pretty convincing tale about you," he said. "I didn't go into all of the details earlier, but he said he broke up with you after he caught you stealing money from the gallery."

"What?" Her eyes widened with shock.

Trent nodded, knowing the story was only going to become harder to swallow. "He said you needed the money because of all of your credit card debt."

"I don't have any debt. I only had one credit card in case of an emergency!" She shook her head and leaned back into the seat. "He had it all worked out, didn't he?"

"He was convincing when he told your family he'd do anything in his power to help find you."

"Of course he did! He wants to find me so he can kill me. They didn't believe him, did they?"

Trent shrugged. "The truth is, Leo brought in paperwork—evidence—to support everything he told them."

"He manipulated people or paid them off in order to get them on his side. He has people on his payroll who can create false backgrounds and financial histories. I can't believe this, yet at the same time it's not surprising."

"I know this is tough to hear, but you asked and I thought you should know everything."

"Thank you."

Trent stared ahead at the windshield. "Is that snow?"

It had been gray and especially cold all morning. But snow? He'd hoped it would hold off.

Tessa nodded. "They were saying a snowstorm was headed this way."

"What did they predict?"

"A foot of snow in a five-hour time range. That was the last I heard."

His gut churned. That wasn't a good outlook. They were not in a car suitable for any kind of snowstorm or bad weather.

"It's only the beginning of November."

She nodded. "I know. The brutal weather is getting an early start this year."

They needed to make it as far away as possible before the storm arrived. Because there was no way they'd make it otherwise.

* * *

Tessa's stomach still didn't feel full, but at least she had some food to settle it. As she watched the snowflakes come down harder and faster, a ripple of anxiety shuddered through her. Driving these roads in the snow was hazardous, even for the most experienced driver. Trent had purposely stayed on back roads. By all appearances, they'd lost the men who'd been after them, but Tessa had a feeling this wasn't over yet. Leo would indeed do everything he could to find them.

Trent had a white-knuckled grip on the steering wheel. The roads were getting slippery, Tessa realized. And the steep drop-offs on one side of the stretch of asphalt made this all the more treacherous.

"Any idea where we are?" Trent asked.

She shrugged. "I think we're north of Gideon's Hollow."

"Any small towns up this way? I'd even take a big one."

"We're in mountain country. I didn't take much time to explore during my stay here, but you can go miles out here without running into much except cliffs, rivers and inclines."

He didn't say anything.

She studied his stoic expression a moment. "This isn't good, is it?"

He shook his head, his gaze remaining focused out the front windshield. "If the snow comes down any harder, I won't be able to see. It's practically a whiteout."

"Should we pull over?"

"We'll see."

The sinking feeling in her gut sank even lower. Why did this situation keep getting worse? As if it wasn't bad enough that Leo's men were after her. Now it had to snow.

Lord, please. Help.

Again, desperation was leading her back to exploring the possibility that God actually cared.

What if He doesn't answer your prayer? a quiet voice asked. *What if He doesn't answer it in the way you want? Will you still be open to the idea that God is a loving God?*

She tried to shut out the voice.

God doesn't work like a vending machine. You don't put twenty-five cents in and get the candy of your choice. Faith is about trusting Him whatever the outcome.

Where was this internal conversation coming from? Maybe all of those days of growing up in Sunday school were coming back to her. Answers that she'd thought were buried were coming to the surface.

Perhaps she'd stopped trusting God just like she'd stopped trusting people. Maybe that was her biggest mistake of all.

Before she could dwell on it any longer, the car lost traction. It slipped across the ice, gliding dangerously in the direction of the cliff. Each second seemed to pass in slow motion yet incredibly fast at the same time.

Tessa gasped and reached for the dash to steady herself.

The snow made it impossible to see how close they were to careening off the mountainside. But for the third or fourth time in twenty-four hours, her life began to pass before her eyes.

She wasn't ready to go yet. She had conversations to finish, family to see, a relationship with God she had to make right. Plus, she still needed to clear her name.

Her eyes flung toward Trent. Though his gaze was intense and his grip tight on the steering wheel, he remained in control. That thought brought Tessa immense comfort. If anyone could maneuver out of this tricky situation, it was Trent.

With dizzying, mind-perplexing movement, the car slowed, slid and flirted with deadly danger.

Finally, the vehicle stopped gliding and came to a slow halt.

Trent glanced over at her, visibly releasing his breath. "That was close."

"Too close."

He grimaced. "I think this is the end of the road for us. It's too dangerous to go any farther."

"So what are we going to do? Just sit in the car wait for the storm to pass?"

"That's not safe, either. There are too many unknown factors. Too much risk of another car coming this way and ramming us. That would send us off the edge of this cliff."

"What are you suggesting?" She thought she knew the answer, but she hoped wrong.

"We're going to have to go and find shelter. On foot."

ELEVEN

Trent didn't want to do it. He knew the risks involved in leaving the safe confines of the car. But he also knew the dangers of staying in one place. The snow was coming down so hard that he couldn't tell where the road started or ended. There was no way he could attempt to drive again, not after that tailspin they'd just experienced.

Tessa was tough. He'd seen the strength in her gaze. Sure, she might be scared, but fear made people's reactions sharper. It could work to her advantage right now.

Despite that knowledge, his heart sank with compassion when he saw the trepidation on her face. The task before them was huge and would overwhelm anyone. Go walking in a snowstorm on a mountain road? It wasn't ideal.

"If you say so," she finally said.

"I'll check and see if there's anything in the trunk. Meanwhile, zip up your coat and tuck the legs of your jeans into your boots. Also, take the food we have and see if you can store it in your jacket. We're going to need everything we can get."

She nodded and began preparing for their journey.

Trent opened the door and a gust of frigid air rushed into the vehicle, confirming what he already knew: this was going to be hard. Arduous. Grueling.

He put his foot down, expecting to feel the ground. Instead, he felt air.

He sucked in a breath as he realized what that meant.

"What?" Tessa asked.

"We were only about two inches from going over the mountain."

Her eyes widened. "Wow."

"I'm going to have to climb out of your side. Carefully."

She nodded stiffly. "We can do this, right?"

He reached out and squeezed her hand. "We can. We just have to stick together, okay?"

She nodded again. With one more deep breath, she opened her door. More cool air rushed inside, attacking any warmth left on their skin. Carefully, Tessa placed her foot on the ground, tested it to make sure the solid surface beneath her was real and then stepped out.

Wasting no more time, Trent climbed across the seat and stepped out behind her. He watched each step carefully, uncertain where the ground began and ended. He opened the trunk and was relieved to see there were a few supplies that had been left by the previous owner, including a blanket and a flashlight. He took the blanket and wrapped it around Tessa's shoulders. Her coat was heavy, but she'd need all the warmth she could get.

There were also a couple of pairs of old work gloves. They'd be sufficient to protect their hands against the elements.

"Let's go." He put his hand around her arm so they could stick together.

As snow battered their faces, they started down the road. The weather had turned brutal and he wasn't sure what was colder: the snow or the wind. Trent prayed Tessa would be okay.

Every once in a while, the downfall would ease slightly and he could make out the wall of rock on one side of them.

As the ground declined steeply down into a river gorge, he could see the treetops on the other side.

Trent hoped that once this section of road broke, maybe a house would appear. A driveway. Anything.

They couldn't stay out here in these conditions for too long. But if they'd remained in the car, they'd be sitting ducks, and those men could have come upon them. "You okay?" he asked Tessa.

She squinted against the snow but nodded.

Every few minutes, he glanced behind him. Usually, all he saw was white. But this time, something else caught his eye.

A light appeared.

Two lights.

Headlights.

Tessa followed Trent's gaze. "A car! We should flag them down. Maybe they can help."

Before she could say anything else, Trent pulled her against the rock wall beside them. He pressed himself into her. She wanted to complain, but the heat he brought with him made the words stick in her throat.

"What are you doing?" she whispered. She had the strange desire to bury her face in his chest. Just to keep warm, she told herself. Not because he was her knight in shining armor.

"We don't know who that is," he told her, his breath hot on her cheek.

Her heart thump-thumped out of control—from the adrenaline of the situation, not from Trent's closeness, she assured herself. How many times would she have to mutter that to herself before she was convinced?

"But—"

His gaze locked on hers. "We know Leo's men are out there looking for us. We can't take any chances."

His words sank in. He was right. But her cheeks were so cold. Her nose. Her fingers. Her feet.

The coolness had crept through her jeans, through her shoes. Soon it would probably sink through her coat. If she survived Leo's men, frostbite just might kill her.

"Will they see us?"

"Our coats are covered in snow. I think the chances are good that we'll blend in. Just don't make any sudden moves."

Only moving her eyes, she glanced in the direction she'd seen the headlights. They were upon them.

She held her breath, waiting to see how the situation would play out. She prayed they'd be invisible.

"What do you see?" Trent asked.

"They're getting closer."

At once, visions of the car sliding on ice and hitting them filled her mind. There were so many dangers in being out here right now. All she had to do was take her pick of various fear-inducing scenarios.

"They're slowing down," she whispered.

"Are you sure?"

She watched carefully. "I think they're stopping."

"If they see us, just follow my lead, okay?"

She nodded. That was fine, because she had no idea what else to do. Running through the snow didn't seem like an option. There were too many unknowns.

"They're backing up," she muttered.

"Really? Can you see anything else?"

"I think it's them, Trent. The car is brown. A sedan. I can't be sure, but…"

"Just keep a cool head. Let's see how this plays out."

She nodded, Trent's words helping to ground her. He was right. They couldn't let panic alert these men to their presence.

"They found the car," Trent muttered. He took her arm

again. "We're going to start moving—slowly and carefully, until we can't see them anymore. If those men realize that was our car, they're going to come after us. We need to put some space between us and them."

"I agree."

He tugged her forward, still remaining close to the wall. Thankfully, the mountain curved away from the car behind them and helped them to disappear out of sight for a moment.

A sign appeared in front of them.

"Snow Current," Trent read. "One mile ahead."

"That's the ski lodge!" Tessa said.

"Ski lodge?"

She frowned. "But it's closed. From what I heard, it was booming about ten years ago until the economy forced the place to shut down. It's been abandoned ever since. My boss, Chris, as well as a few of my clients at the travel agency, used to talk about the place, but I've never been there."

"It's shelter. We need to make it there. It's only another mile. Can you do it?"

She nodded, eyes squinted and head lowered as gusts of cold, frosty air assaulted them.

"I can." Even if the thought caused dread to fill her. She wanted out of this snow. Now.

The rock beside them disappeared, and Tessa sucked in a breath, feeling the unknown swirling around her. Maybe it was the cold. Maybe it was messing with her mind. But she felt as if she'd just stepped out into a white abyss. The ground under her felt like packed ice but gave no indication if there was asphalt there still or if they'd veered off the road.

Trust. This was all a matter of trust, she reminded herself. She was going to have to learn her lesson and make some decisions…fast.

* * *

Though the snow concealed them, Trent couldn't help but feel exposed. They were walking into the great unknown, uncertain of each of their steps.

His gut told him that the men had discovered their car. If Leo's men had found the car, Trent had no doubt they would search ardently for them.

They'd been dressed in SWAT gear last time Trent had seen them. Then, at the café, they'd worn long sleeves with khakis. With any luck, those men weren't dressed to be in this weather. He only hoped that would work to his and Tessa's advantage.

Whatever happened, they had to get somewhere warm. These conditions could cause serious damage to their health. They needed a fire, to eat, to get warm.

He glanced behind him. Headlights.

The men were attempting to come after them in their car.

This wasn't good.

He grabbed Tessa's arm. "We've got to move."

Her eyes widened, but she didn't ask any questions. Just then, the rock wall beside them bent, allowing for some extra room. This was probably a roadside pull-off, Trent realized, remembering some of the small areas he'd seen that sported a small parking area, picnic tables and scenic overlooks. This might be the perfect place for them to hide. He pulled Tessa into the cove and instructed her to stay low. A picnic table was there, covered in snow. They crawled beneath it.

Trent kept an eye on the headlights.

The car stopped.

Slowly, the vehicle seemed to disappear.

They were slipping, Trent realized.

The car had hit a patch of ice and they couldn't make it up the mountain road anymore.

"What's going on?" Tessa asked.

"The road is too slick for them to continue, especially with this incline."

"That's good, right?"

"As long as they don't set out on foot."

"Trent?" Tessa whispered.

"Yes?"

"If we don't make it out of this alive, I just want to say thank you."

"Don't talk like that," he told her, his heart twisting with emotions he hadn't felt in a long time.

"No, I need to say this. You've gone above and beyond. Any sane person would have left me on my own by now, set me up to fend for myself. You had no obligation to stick with me, but you did."

Did she really think that he would have abandoned her? He wasn't that type of person. He'd set out to do a task and he intended on completing it. "We're going to be okay, Tessa," he assured her.

"Thank you, Trent."

He'd had no idea when he'd agreed to this assignment that this was what it would turn into. The danger had been much greater than he'd thought, as this case went much deeper than a simple missing person investigation.

Tessa's life was on the line. By default, so was his. Not only that, but his heart was getting involved. He could deny it all he wanted, but his feelings for Tessa were already starting to move beyond that gut-level attraction he felt toward her. He wasn't ready for that.

Even more worrisome was the realization that the safety of many people in this country was at risk.

Several minutes passed and finally Trent felt it was safe to leave. The men must have turned around and headed back. Their search would probably resume when the weather broke.

Trent and Tessa started their upward climb again, battling the elements, the slick road and their waning energy. Tessa's steps were becoming slower. Her breathing was heavier. Her face was red.

His heart panged with regret. He wished there was something he could do to help her. But their only choice was to keep moving.

One mile. On an ordinary day, that distance wasn't unthinkable. But in this weather—and in the mountains—it would take much longer. He estimated they were halfway there. Once they reached the abandoned ski lodge, it could still be a hike to get to the first building.

Lord, give us strength. Show us Your way. Protect Tessa.

They marched forward, one step at a time, no clue as to what was around them. The snow beat down, creating a white shield in every direction they looked. The elements battered them, made it hard to communicate, caused friction as their bodies collided with the air and snow.

Just as his foot hit something—something that felt more hollow than the ground prior—Tessa slipped out of his grasp and disappeared into the white below.

TWELVE

Tessa felt the ground vanish from beneath her. The air rushed from her lungs, and she let out a gasp. Before she realized what was happening, gravity pulled her downward in a free fall.

Her arms flailed.

Her feet kicked.

A scream stuck in her throat.

Finally, instinct kicked in. Her hands connected with something. She clawed at the slippery surface just within reach.

A brief window of opportunity.

A small chance to save herself.

Her body jerked to a stop. Her arms ached at the impact, her joints immediately sore from the harsh jolt.

But it didn't matter. She wasn't falling. Not for the moment, at least.

Her fingers had somehow managed to grip a wooden beam. Immediately, her arms burned under the strain of holding her weight. Her gloved fingers felt uncertain, weaker than she'd like, as if this was only a temporary fix.

Against her better judgment, she looked down. A swirling white mass beckoned beneath her.

The river, she realized.

This was a bridge.

She'd stepped off a bridge.

It suddenly all made sense, and her fear intensified.

This was going to be a horrible way to die.

As if to confirm that, her hands began to slip.

She couldn't hold on much longer. She wasn't strong enough. Her gloves were too slick. She was too cold.

Mom, I love you. I'm sorry you had to endure all of this. I wish I could have seen you again. Tell everyone how much I missed them.

If only her mom could hear her final words.

Lord, I'm sorry for how I must have let You down. I'm sorry I realized too late how important You are in my life. Please forgive me. I want to do better. I want to do right.

Her hand slipped again. Her heart raced as she felt her last inch of security disappearing.

Suddenly, Trent's hands covered hers. His face came into view. "I've got you, Tessa."

With an unnatural amount of ease, Trent gripped her hands and pulled her from where she dangled. She landed in the snow behind him.

Her heart raced.

She was on solid ground.

Finally.

Thankfully.

Trent knelt beside her, his eyes full of concern, his chest rapidly rising and falling with adrenaline. "Are you okay?"

She nodded. "I think so."

"Let's get you on your feet, then."

He helped her up. As soon as she put weight on her leg, she yelped in pain. When she looked down, she saw that her jeans were torn and blood gushed out.

"You must have cut yourself on the way down."

"I'll… I'll be fine." As soon as she said the words, she tried to take a step and nearly fell. Her face squeezed with pain.

Before she could contemplate her options, Trent swept her up in his arms and began walking. Apparently they were wasting too much time and had to move.

"I can't…ask you…to do this," Tessa said, her face still scrunched with discomfort.

"You didn't ask. I just did it."

Trent had been trained to travel in these conditions. He'd fought in Afghanistan—in both the dry and arid deserts and in the frigid mountains. Tessa hadn't.

Her strength was fading, and fast. He had to hurry.

At the moment, she seemed to melt in his arms. Her head flopped against his shoulder. Her lips were pressed into a tight line.

"We're going to be just fine, Tessa," he murmured.

"I can't ask you to do this," she whispered.

"Like I said, you didn't. I once carried one of my comrades in arms five miles up a mountain toward help," he told her, trying to keep her talking. "He weighed twice as much as you."

"What happened?"

"Roadside bomb. He got hit. I didn't. Our vehicle was destroyed. If we were going to get out of that village, we had to walk."

"I guess you escaped?"

"We did. My friend is doing just fine today, you'll be glad to know. Just like you'll look back one day and realize how crazy all of this was. It will be in the past tense. You'll move on." As he said the words, his heart lurched. Why did it bother him to think about her moving on one day? He had to put those thoughts out of his head.

"I hope so," she whispered.

He pushed forward, breathing easier once he knew he'd crossed the bridge. The lodge should just be a little farther up this road. Once there, maybe Tessa could get warm. He'd look for a first-aid kit. Maybe start a fire.

When Trent had seen her go off that bridge, his heart had dropped. He couldn't let Tessa die. He'd sacrifice himself if he had to. He'd feared he wouldn't be able to pull her from where she dangled.

But when he'd seen the absolute fear in her eyes, he knew he had to do everything within his power to do so. Leveraging himself while trying to reach her had been a struggle, but by God's grace he'd done it.

He continued to push forward, step by step. Slowly, the lodge got closer.

He glanced down at Tessa and saw her eyes had closed.

"Tessa," he called.

There was no response.

He shook her slightly. "Tessa."

She moaned.

This wasn't good. Trent had to get her somewhere warm, somewhere he could properly bandage her wound. They'd made it this far—he couldn't give up now.

Just ahead, during a break between snow gusts, another sign appeared—Snow Current. The insignia didn't have a "distance ahead" designation. No, it was a welcome sign.

They were here! They were at the lodge. Now he just needed to find a building to give them shelter.

He had no time to waste.

The snowstorm eased. He wasn't sure how long the interruption would last, but he was grateful for it. Maybe it would give him just enough time to find shelter.

Ahead, he saw a large lodge-like building. That was where they would go. It wasn't the closest building, but it was the one most likely to have a fireplace. Even though the smoke would be a giveaway that they were here, it was a chance he had to take.

Because he was determined to keep Tessa alive.

* * *

Tessa had wafted from lucid to delusional as she rested in Trent's arms. She'd drifted off for a moment and, in that instant, she'd been back at home with her family. They'd been laughing. She'd felt safe.

Even stranger, in her quasi dream Trent had been by her side.

The image had left her feeling warm and cozy. Too happy. What she needed was to keep her distance from Trent. It was the only way she could protect her heart— by remaining solo, and not getting attached.

It had been so long since she'd felt safe and loved that the dream had just seemed to mock her, to show her what she was missing.

At once, she pulled her eyes open. She sucked in a deep breath at the unfamiliar place surrounding her.

A fire crackled beside her, a blanket—blankets, for that matter—were piled on top of her. The room around her was large, almost overwhelmingly so. It smelled dusty and looked neglected.

Finally, Trent's face came into view. Everything came back to her. The men hunting them. The snowstorm. Falling from the bridge.

In each of those instances, Trent had saved her. She'd be dead now without him.

Her heart filled with gratitude. And maybe something else. The thought made her throat tighten with both joy and fear.

"How are you feeling?" he asked, peering down at her with concern in his eyes.

Had he been sitting there beside her the whole time? Watching her? Making sure she was okay?

Her cheeks flushed at the thought.

She tried to sit up, but her leg jolted with pain. That was right—she was injured. She'd almost died, for that matter. How had she gotten here? Trent must have carried her the entire way.

"You have a pretty deep cut," Trent said, tucking the blanket around her. "I cleaned it and put a bandage on it. Right now, we need to concentrate on getting you warm."

"How about you? Are you—"

He shook his head, his gaze steady and almost somber. "Don't worry about me. I'll be fine."

At his words, a shiver raced through her and a deep ache seemed to reach down to her bones, despite the warm fire crackling beside her. "It's so...cold."

"You'll warm up soon." He reached under the heap of blankets and found one of her hands. He began rubbing it in his own.

His touch—however utilitarian it was—caused her cheeks to warm. He was only trying to save her from frostbite, yet his touch was too tender for that. His hands, though callused, felt gentle.

Her gaze wandered the area as she tried to focus her thoughts on something other than Trent. They were in a huge room with a ceiling that stretched at least three stories high. Bright windows lined one wall, displaying the blizzard-like conditions outside. Huge wooden beams strapped the edges of the room, and the fireplace was probably taller than Tessa and surrounded completely in what looked like river rock.

"You found it," she whispered. "The ski lodge."

And somehow he'd managed to get her here, start a fire and remain intact himself. Maybe he was a superhero.

His eyes followed her for a brief moment. "I did. I built a fire and found some blankets in a few of the old rooms. I haven't been able to explore much else."

"How long was I out?" As she said the words, she realized how dry her mouth was. It felt like sandpaper. Not to mention the fact that her lips were chapped and peeling.

She inwardly groaned at the thought.

She could only imagine what she must look like. Not that she cared. She wasn't trying to impress anyone. But she could have died out there. If Trent hadn't been quick in his thinking and reacting, she would have fallen to her death into the river below that bridge. Even more, if he hadn't gotten her here, she could have frozen. She knew she wasn't home free yet, but her odds were greatly improved, and not by anything she'd done herself.

"We've been here for about an hour." He continued to rub her hands.

"Any sign of Leo's men?" She didn't even want to ask; she hardly wanted to know. Couldn't she just deal with one emergency at a time? She wished she had that luxury.

Trent shook his head. "No, not yet."

She didn't miss the *yet*. But she pushed the thought aside for now. They'd deal with that later. Hopefully much later.

She looked at Trent for a moment. It was the first time she'd been able to study him without suspicion. His cheeks were red and his hair glinted, probably from the snow.

That was when she caught a glimpse of it—the kindness in his eyes. It was the real deal, not something that was fake or meant to impress. Trent McCabe was a good, decent man.

"Don't worry about me." He let go of her hand, and she immediately missed his touch. He scooted back and stood. "I'm going to see if there's anything I can use to heat up some water. Some fluids would do us both good. You stay here and get warm, okay?"

She nodded, already missing his presence even though he hadn't left yet. "Okay."

As he retreated, she turned toward the fire. The glorious heat emanating from it warmed her face and thawed her frozen extremities. In the middle of all of this craziness, being here in the lodge at the moment felt like a little oasis. Sure, the blankets smelled musty. The whole place appeared abandoned, maybe even a little haunted. Snow blanketed the outside and the floor beneath her was cold.

But for just a moment, she felt she could breathe. She'd take whatever comfort she could get and hang on to it for as long as she could.

At once, she imagined this place as it might have been at one time. She pictured visitors in ski suits standing around, sipping hot chocolate and talking about the slopes. She envisioned families together, friends chatting, strangers bonding over their love of adrenaline rushes.

Now it was desolate. Forgotten. Empty.

Don't let yourself become just like this ski lodge.

She blinked as the thought entered her mind. Where had that come from? Why were all of these esoteric ideas hitting her? It was almost as if a force greater than herself was calling her back.

As though God was speaking to her in a quiet, gentle voice.

"I found an old pot."

Trent's voice plucked her from her thoughts. She looked over and saw him walk into the room with a cast-iron skillet and two coffee mugs. "That's great."

"There's no water here, so I used some snow to wash it," Trent said. "Now we just need to warm this snow up and we'll be in business."

Against her will, she shivered again. The motion was immediately followed by her teeth chattering. The reaction was so sudden, so strong that it surprised her. "I guess I'm colder than I realize."

"That's a good thing," Trent said, already working at the fire. "Your body is reacting and trying to keep you warm. It's a survival mechanism."

She nodded but felt overcome by her reaction. It was as if every single thing in her life was out of control—her body, her emotions, her circumstances. *When everything was stripped away, you learned who you really were.* That was what her dad had always said.

She'd been on a crash course these past several months, then.

She actually liked some of the things she'd discovered about herself. She was capable. She could survive without a latte from the drive-through every morning. Fancy restaurants were overrated. Those were the surface items she'd realized.

On a deeper level, she'd found she enjoyed having some peace and quiet, that family was more important than any job and that sometimes less was more.

With a somewhat contented sigh, she watched as Trent put the pot over the fire and gently stoked the wood there.

The man really was tough. He had to be cold, but he had some kind of inner strength that pushed him to keep going. A silent sense of responsibly caused him to put her needs above her own.

That thought did something strange to her heart.

She was entering dangerous territory, she realized. And she needed to put a stop to it before she ended up getting hurt again. This man was just doing his job. That was it.

She couldn't allow her thoughts to go anywhere beyond that.

Trent kept an eye on Tessa, hoping she didn't take a turn for the worse. When they'd arrived here at the lodge, she'd been totally out, and he'd feared he wouldn't be able to wake her. Thankfully, he'd started the fire and some color was returning to her cheeks. Despite that, her hands were still cold.

The cut on her leg was deeper than he'd like. She really should get to a hospital, but since that wasn't an option right now, he'd cleaned the wound and wrapped it with some bandages he'd found in a cabinet in the old kitchen. The wrap was a little brittle with age, but it would work.

While she'd slept, he'd found an old radio and picked

up a signal. To his dismay, a news report had caught his ear. The police were searching for a man and a woman in connection with an explosion in Gideon's Hollow, West Virginia. The woman was identified as twenty-seven-year-old Theresa Davidson who might be going by the alias Tessa Jones. Anyone who'd seen her was asked to report information to the police.

Had Tessa been set up again? First by Leo after she'd fled, and now by Leo as she ran for her life? That was certainly how it appeared. He must have gone to the authorities and revealed her real name.

As he glanced down at Tessa, his heart lurched in ways it shouldn't. Even being half-frozen, she was still lovely, especially with the firelight dancing across her face. Warmth had returned to her eyes, which was a good start. That meant that she was warming from the inside, also.

He poured some water from the pot into a mug. Though he wished he had some coffee to go with this, he didn't. At least the water would be warm. Carefully, he brought it to Tessa and helped her to sit up. He feared she couldn't remain upright on her own, so he let her lean back on his chest. She fit a little too snugly there.

"See if you can take a sip of this. It will help you warm up," he urged, bringing the cup closer.

She didn't argue. Tentatively, she put the cup to her lips and took a sip. "That was a crazy storm. It started, what? Three hours ago? It already looks as if a foot has fallen."

"It came on fast and heavy, that's for sure. If we hadn't found this place, I'm not sure we would have made it. The good news is that because the storm came so fast, Leo's men shouldn't be able to follow our footprints. They're also not dressed for this weather. But while we're safe here for a time, we can't get too comfortable."

"I wouldn't put anything past them." She paused with

her water raised to her lips. "Please drink something yourself, Trent. You need to get warm, too."

He didn't want to admit it, but sitting here beside Tessa made some kind of internal warmth surge through him. But she was right. He'd be no good to her if he didn't take care of himself, also.

Reluctantly, he moved away from Tessa for long enough to pour himself some warm water. He wanted to move back beside her, but he'd lost the chance. She was sitting up fine on her own. Instead, he lowered himself in front of her, near the fire. The heat from the flames felt good and for the first time since they'd gotten here, he allowed himself to relax for a moment—if only ever so slightly.

They'd survived their last battle. Soon they'd have to prepare themselves for the next. Right now, he needed to recharge.

"I bet this place was a beauty at one time. Don't you think?" Tessa asked, her head falling back so she could see the ceiling.

"Definitely." The old building was fascinating. It looked almost as if the owners had left the place in a hurry—there were still pictures on the walls, a couple pots on the stove in the kitchen. Just what had happened here?

"Do you ski?" Tessa asked before taking another sip of her water.

He shrugged. "I've been a few times. I prefer being on the water to being on the snow."

She smiled softly. "Me, too. I only went skiing once, and it was with Leo's family. It was somewhere up in Pennsylvania, and there was no expense spared." Her smile slipped into a frown. "I didn't realize at that time that all of those luxuries were paid for with money exchanged for innocent human lives."

"You didn't know."

Her frown deepened. "I didn't even question it. I just assumed their wealth was from the art gallery."

"It was a natural assumption. Art can be a lucrative business."

"I just feel so naive about everything—about Leo, his family, his money, his friends. I never considered myself a pushover before, but my eyes were definitely opened to how much of an optimist I can be."

"There's nothing wrong with being an optimist. I'd take an optimistic any day to some who's jaded and skeptical about everything. The world needs people who aren't afraid to trust." He took a sip of his water, grateful for a hot drink.

She straightened. "Well, that's not me anymore. Now I'm suspicious of everyone. I fear I've gone to the opposite extreme."

He met her gaze. "You haven't. You only think you have."

A flush rushed over her cheeks and she looked away.

Something passed between them in that moment, and Trent knew he'd let the conversation get too personal. He needed to get his focus back here. There was a time for survival and a time for romance. Right now was a time for survival.

He scooted toward some items he'd laid out by the fire and picked up a sandwich. "Here you go. It's not frozen anymore."

She eyed the sandwich a moment before taking it.

He picked up the other half and began eating, also. The bread was soggier than he would have liked, but it was good. Nourishment could be the difference between surviving or not.

As he glanced out the window again at the falling snow, he realized staying alive involved more than a man-against-man struggle. They were also battling nature.

He prayed that the storm would only protect them, and not be their demise.

THIRTEEN

"Sit tight for one minute," Trent said after he finished his sandwich. "I need to make a quick phone call."

Tessa nodded, curiosity creeping into her gaze.

He wandered out of the main room, but remained close enough that he could keep an eye on her and the windows—not that he could see much with the wall of snow that cascaded from the sky. But he had to remain vigilant in keeping watch. Those men were resourceful, so he wouldn't put anything past them.

He took the prepaid phone from his pocket and glanced at the screen, fully expecting not to have a signal out here in the middle of nowhere. To his surprise, one bar registered.

He silently thanked God, as it had to be by His grace that he was even able to make this phone call.

He punched in Zach's number, thankful he had it memorized. A minute later, his friend answered.

"I tried to call you back a couple of hours ago, but your phone went straight to voice mail," Zach said.

"Yeah, my phone is…indisposed at the moment. I have a new one." Trent shoved his shoulder against the wall, his gaze continuously surveying the area around him.

"Sounds as if there's a story there, but save it for later. I looked into this Leo McAllister. I couldn't find anything on him."

"Nothing?" Surprise rippled through him. That couldn't be right.

"Nothing criminal," Zach said. "Now, his family is a different story. On paper, they're squeaky clean. But I started digging a little deeper. According to my contact at the CIA, they travel abroad quite a bit and have been seen socializing with associates of people on a terrorist watch list."

"Really?" Not that he'd doubted what Tessa told him, but it was good to get another perspective. Zach was objective and his opinion on this would be invaluable.

"It gets better. Apparently, the McAllister family has been under surveillance for quite some time now. There was some kind of anonymous tip to authorities a little less than a year ago. Law officials haven't been able to find any evidence against them, though."

"Interesting." That anonymous tip must have been from Tessa.

"Listen, Trent, I don't know what your involvement is with this family," Zach continued. "But my friend said that the people they're suspected to have ties with are no joke. Apparently, there are two people associated with the family who've been found murdered. Again, there's no evidence tying the McAllisters to the crimes. Both are still open homicide cases. But I don't believe in coincidences."

Tension returned to Trent's shoulders, even stronger than before. He'd known these men were dead serious and lethal, but Zach only confirmed it. If those men captured them, he and Tessa would both soon be dead.

"What can you tell me about the murders?"

"The first was a delivery driver. One of the McAllister galleries was on his route. Name was Frank Webber. The other man worked at a bank. There's no direct correlation to the family, only that he played a game of golf with Walter McAllister once. Walter is Leo McAllister's uncle."

"The news just gets worse all the time," Trent said, his

gaze going to Tessa again. She faced the fire, unmoving except for occasionally sipping her drink. She was tough, but everything they knew was going to be tested before the end of this. "I may need more of your help, Zach."

"Of course. Anything."

Trent didn't know who else he could trust. He could call the local authorities, but he doubted they'd take them seriously. Plus, if Tessa's old boss was right, the rumor might be spreading around town that Tessa was one of the bad guys. He couldn't put her in that position. Since these guys had the ability to disguise themselves as the police, that also made him cautious.

He gave Zach a brief overview of the twelve hours since they'd last talked.

"Sounds as if you're in over your head," Zach said.

Trent glanced at the snow outside again. It continued to pile up, at least a foot deep. "Literally."

"Well, it just so happens I have two weeks between my old job and starting my new one. What do you want me to do?"

"I need you to find out what the police know about Tessa. She's been set up and now there's an APB out for her arrest. At this point, I'm not sure whom we can trust, not even local authorities. The more information I can be armed with, the better. The person behind this obviously has deep connections."

"I can do that."

"I need one more thing—for you to pick us up. The roads are slick. But we're trapped out here and, again, I don't want to call the police. The fewer people who know where we are, the better."

"Let me do a little research, make some phone calls. Then I'll check road conditions and head out there."

"Thanks, Zach. I appreciate it."

He hung up, grateful to know help was on the way. Trent only hoped they could stay safe until Zach arrived.

* * *

As soon as Tessa stood from her huddle of blankets on the floor, she regretted it. Pain shot up her leg. One glance at the bandages strapped around her calf caused her to squirm. A deep ache rushed through her muscles when she stepped on her foot.

"You shouldn't put too much weight on it," Trent said, reappearing and shoving a phone into his pocket.

The action caused her defenses to go back up. Who had Trent called? Was he hiding something? A niggle of distrust crept in. There was something he wasn't telling her.

She shoved away her doubts. Trent was on her side. There was no reason to doubt him.

Except that nearly everyone she'd trusted had let her down.

That thought caused a knot to lodge in her throat. Usually when people kept information from other people, it was because they were concealing something. What was Trent not telling her?

"I need to get moving." She raised her chin, knowing she couldn't depend on Trent fully. The idea was tempting but not logical.

Trent wrapped his hand around her arm, his expression firm. "You need to rest."

"But—"

"I'll keep an eye on things around here. You need rest. Save your strength for the battles ahead."

She wanted to argue, to be stubborn. But the truth was she couldn't stand much longer. Nor could she walk without help.

Begrudgingly, she sat down. She wouldn't admit it, but it felt good to get off her feet. What would feel even better were a long bath and some fresh clothes. Maybe a warm meal and some coffee. None of those things were possibilities right now, though. She had to be grateful for what she had—life, breath, a heartbeat and a chance at a brighter future.

She looked up, waiting for Trent to say something.

He didn't.

Not about the phone call, at least.

Instead, he said, "I'm going to look around here and see what I can find. We're going to need more supplies—in case we have to stay for a while and in case the men find us. We have to be prepared."

He was going to leave her alone. Her fear deepened. She knew she had to be a big girl; it was just that she felt so much more secure and protected when Trent was with her.

How could she question if he was trustworthy one minute and feel so safe with him the next? It didn't make sense, not even to her. She wished her emotions weren't such a tangled mess. She wished her past didn't dictate her reactions to people today. But that was the way life worked sometimes, whether she liked it or not. Keeping her distance from people had helped to keep her alive for the past several months. She wasn't sure if doing the same would keep her alive or kill her right now.

"Not to be a broken record, but you really should take it easy," Trent said, that edge of authority still staining his voice. It was as if he always knew exactly what he was doing and felt 100 percent confident in his choices. Must be nice.

Tessa grimaced as her leg ached again.

"Don't worry—I'm going to stay in this building, so I'll keep watch," he continued. "But if we're going to last here for very long, I'm going to need some more firewood—dry firewood—as well as some blankets and food."

She nodded.

There was no way Trent was in on this in some way... was there? Leo was conniving, brilliant and manipulative. He wouldn't have planted someone like Trent in her life, would he?

But that would be the perfect plan. Allow Tessa to trust Trent and believe he was on her side. Meanwhile, he would lead Tessa right into the den of lions—right to Leo.

She shook her head. No, that thought was crazy.

Yet it wouldn't leave her mind.

When Trent walked back into the main lodge area, he was surprised to see that Tessa had drifted to sleep. Good. She needed to rest.

He deposited the pieces of some old chairs he'd found onto the floor. He'd use this for firewood. With the flames blazing and strong, he went back and grabbed some cans of beef stew. They were about a year past the expiration date, but he'd check to see if they were still good because often canned goods lasted long past the date stamped on the lid.

He'd taken note of the entire lodge. Aside from the four doors located in this room, there were six other doors leading into the lodge. He blocked the rest of them with dressers. The furniture wouldn't hold back someone determined to get in, but at least it would slow them down or alert Trent that they were coming.

The two of them should be good here for a while. But as soon as the snow slowed, they should try to make a run for it. Staying in one place too long would be a bad idea. But he wasn't sure how fast Tessa could move with her leg injured as it was.

Something strange had passed through her gaze earlier—was it doubt? In him? He was going to mention his phone call to Zach, but he feared she'd ask too many questions. She was under enough stress without learning that the local police were also looking for her. He hoped Tessa trusted him enough to follow his lead.

Laurel had always told him that he expected people to have confidence in him easily. Maybe it was because of his training as a ranger—they'd had no choice but to trust each other.

It didn't matter if Tessa believed in him or not. His one goal right now was to keep her safe. Not to earn her friendship. Not to make her like him. Not to soothe her with platitudes.

Only to keep her alive.

Despite his determination, something twisted in his gut at the thought. He knew why. It was because there was a part of him that really liked Tessa, that wanted to get to know her better, that wanted to wipe away the worry from her gaze.

Just then, she opened her eyes and he realized he'd been staring at her.

Staring at the lovely lines on her soft face. At her hair as it ruffled across the blanket behind her and at her lips as they gently parted.

He hadn't felt this fascinated with someone since...well, since Laurel.

"I can't believe I fell asleep." She pulled a hair behind her ear self-consciously. "Again."

"Your body is telling you that you need rest."

He went to the fire again and added some pieces of broken furniture. Once the flames grew larger, he opened a can of stewed beef. He dumped it into a pot and placed it over the fire.

"Who'd you call earlier?" Tessa asked.

He startled a moment. "Just a friend."

"Which friend?"

She wasn't backing down. "A friend in law enforcement. I'm getting him to help us out."

Her eyes held a look of discernment. She was trying to measure whether he was telling the truth.

"You asked me to trust you, yet you obviously don't trust me. Why were you keeping that quiet?"

"I didn't want to share anything until I learned more."

"And? What did you learn?"

He let out a breath, stoked the fire once more and then settled back on the floor. "I learned that there are two suspicious deaths associated with the McAllister family."

"Who?"

"A delivery driver and someone who worked at a bank."

Tessa gasped. "Was his name Frank?"

Trent nodded. "I believe so. You know him?"

She squeezed the skin between her eyes, shoulders slumping. "Frank always made our deliveries. Every day. We talked quite a bit, and he was a lovely person. In his fifties, expecting his first grandchild, looking forward to taking a cruise. Of course, that was a year ago. When…?"

"About eight months ago."

"Around the time I left…" she muttered.

"Tessa, this probably didn't have anything to do with you. It was the master plan of a crazy killer."

"Maybe I should have warned him. Warned more people. Maybe I should have done more instead of running."

"Before you beat yourself up, I also heard that there was an anonymous call reported with information about the family."

She straightened. "Did the FBI actually research the tip I gave them?"

"Unfortunately, they couldn't find any solid evidence so the McAllisters have just been under surveillance."

Her shoulders slumped again. "I managed to copy all of the files off the gallery servers and then erase their contact information before I fled. But in my haste, I dropped the thumb drive where I'd saved the evidence."

"Don't beat yourself up. The authorities are still looking for proof so they can put these guys behind bars. But for now no one's talking and the paper trail has disappeared."

"That's not surprising. The McAllisters have power and

resources. They're good at covering their tracks. I didn't expect the cops to believe me anyway, not when Leo and his family are so active in the nonprofit community."

"Money and power definitely have reach. You'd be a fool to deny that. A lot of people can paint themselves as sheep when they're wolves."

"Biblical reference?" she questioned.

"Yes, definitely. It's refreshing to talk to someone who recognizes that."

"I might recognize it. I don't necessarily believe it, though."

"Why's that?" He stirred the stew, the savory scent of beef, potatoes and gravy rising up to meet him. He couldn't neglect food and sleep too long or he'd be useless.

"Up until a few days ago, I hadn't felt His presence in my life in a long time."

"You mean because bad things have happened?"

She shrugged. "You make it sound so simple. But maybe you're right. Maybe that's what my reasoning boils down to."

"Bad things happen because we live in a fallen world that's full of sin. The bad things are people's doing, not God's. But He can use them in our lives."

"I don't know. It certainly doesn't feel that way."

"Our relationship with Jesus was never supposed to be about feeling. That's a part of it. But emotions and feelings change. It's the same with every relationship in our lives. If we just depend on how we're feeling at the time, it will never last."

"You sound pretty smart."

"I've learned that lesson the hard way over the years. Believe me."

Something flashed through her gaze. Was it hope? Understanding?

Before he could identify it, he heard a crash.

FOURTEEN

Tessa jerked upright at the sound. *What was that?*

Trent was instantly on his feet, his stance showing the soldier he used to be, and the expression in his eyes so intense that she'd hate to be on the other side of the battle against him right now.

"Stay here," he ordered.

His tone left no room for argument.

She pulled the blankets more closely around her as she waited. What could that have been? It almost sounded as if a bomb had exploded. Had Leo's men found them?

Her gaze swung around. What if those men were out there now, watching her, ready to pounce?

She waited, each minute feeling like an hour.

Finally, movement caught her eye at the far end of the room. Her heart skipped a beat.

Trent. It was just Trent.

He strode toward her, a grim expression on his face. "Part of the roof collapsed in the east wing of the building."

Her heart slowed—until she realized how serious that could be, also. "What does that mean for us?"

He stirred the beef again. "Nothing. We have no choice but to stay here. The collapse happened in what looks like the oldest part of the structure. I guess it couldn't withstand the weight of the snow."

She glanced above her at the thick wooden beams arching across a vaulted ceiling. "I hope this part is stronger."

"We'll keep an eye on it." He spooned some food into her mug and then handed it to her. "Here, eat this."

She didn't argue. The first bite was hot and nearly tasteless, but she was so hungry that she didn't care.

As she glanced out the window, she saw the sun was beginning to set.

"We should both try to get some shut-eye."

"I've already rested some. How about if I keep watch for a while?"

He nodded, grabbed a blanket and settled on the couch across from her. "That sounds good. If you hear or see anything that's at all suspicious, wake me. Promise?"

She nodded. "I promise."

As soon as Trent drifted to sleep, she forced herself to stand. Her face scrunched in pain as she put weight on her leg. But she had to do this. She had to walk a bit, see for herself what was going on here at the lodge.

Each step caused an ache to pulsate through her, but she made herself keep going, keep moving. Finally, she reached the window. She already missed the warmth of the fireplace and her blankets. But she couldn't allow herself to become too comfortable.

She stared outside. The snow was already to the window. Tessa estimated about sixteen inches had fallen today. The roads would be impassable, which was both a comfort and worry. It meant Leo's men might not be able to reach them, but it also meant they might not be able to leave if they needed to.

Her conversation with Trent drifted back to her. He made sense. Maybe her faith in God should be more than something that changed based on her emotions.

The one thing she appreciated about Trent was that he didn't make promises based on emotions. He didn't manipulate. What she saw was what she got. She admired that, especially after being around Leo.

Just then, Trent muttered something. Tessa stepped closer and saw that he was still asleep. He was obviously having some kind of dream.

His shoulder jerked, as if he was fighting some kind of unseen force. He grunted again.

Tessa looked away, feeling as though she was being intrusive.

Just as she stepped back toward the window, Trent said something discernible.

"Laurel."

He'd said the name Laurel.

Who was Laurel, exactly? Was Trent's heart already taken?

How could Tessa have been so foolish? Of *course* someone like Trent would be taken. Here she'd been letting her feelings grow for a man who was unavailable. She should have known better.

More than ever she needed to stick to her plan: accept his help but keep her distance. Her emotions had been heightened; in the process, they'd grown out of control.

Experience should have taught her the danger of letting her emotions roam free. It was never a good idea. In fact, in the past it had only led to heartache.

Suddenly, she stepped back from the window as a chill washed over her.

She didn't know what had caused it. Her imagination? Caution over everything that had happened? Or was there real danger out there, getting closer and closer?

She wasn't sure.

But she decided to go back to the couch where she'd watch and wait…and try not to think about the handsome man who'd stuck by her through thick and thin.

Trent took the second shift, noticing as they switched roles that Tessa seemed a bit more distant than she had earlier. Maybe it was the lack of sleep. Maybe the stress of the situation was getting to her. He didn't know.

As she lay on the couch, he couldn't help but marvel at how peaceful she looked in the middle of all of this craziness.

Laurel had always looked so peaceful and hopeful. She'd been a kindergarten teacher, something she'd dreamed about since she was in elementary school herself. His heart still sank when he thought about how her life had been cut short.

He wouldn't let that happen to Tessa. He'd sacrifice his life if he had to in order to protect her.

He peered out one of the massive windows lining the lodge again. Only darkness stared back. Were the men out there? Were they watching?

His gut told him no. Not yet, at least. It was only a matter of time before they found them. As soon as it was daylight, Trent needed to check out the rest of the property and see if there were any resources here that could help them.

At least the snow had stopped. Forecasters had been correct. There was more than a foot piled up outside.

He glanced at his phone and briefly thought about calling Tessa's family to give them an update. But telling them that he'd found their daughter while he and Tessa were on the brink of so much danger didn't seem wise. Still, he knew her loved ones were waiting, still hoping, that Tessa would be okay. They'd lived with so many doubts and uncertainties for so long.

He'd wait, he decided. He wanted to hear back from Zach. He wanted to get somewhere safe and have a few more reassurances. Then he'd make the call.

"Hey," a groggy voice said.

He looked over and saw that Tessa was awake. His heart skipped a beat at her tousled hair and sleepy eyes. Even in this state, she was a vision, one of those natural beauties who needed little help to look good.

He glanced at his watch and saw that she'd gotten a few hours of shut-eye. It was better than nothing. "Morning."

"I feel as if I've been hit by a truck."

"Days like yesterday can do that to you."

"Has it really only been less than two days since all of this started? It feels like weeks."

"Hard to believe, isn't it?" He strode over to her and handed her some the last package of crackers. "Here you go. Eat up."

She didn't argue. Instead, she shivered, pulled the covers closer around her and then ripped the package open. "Anything new?"

He shook his head. "Sun should be coming up soon. I'll fix some hot water for us so we can stay hydrated. Then I'm going to head out."

"Head out?"

He nodded. "I need to see what else is out there. We won't get very far on foot, Tessa."

"So you're suggesting we cross-country ski instead?"

Her light tone made him smile. When he nodded at her leg, his smile faded. "Not with your injury."

"I'll be fine."

"Well, see if you say that after you put some weight on it."

She took a bite of her cracker then swallowed. "Can I ask you something?"

"Sure." Her tone indicated this was serious.

"How is my mom paying you? You've been working this case for a while. If you charge an hourly rate, I can only imagine how high the cost of your investigation is. I know my mom doesn't have that much money."

He didn't say anything for a moment.

"Please tell me Leo isn't helping?"

"Leo put up money as a reward."

She frowned. "Go figure. But that doesn't explain your fees."

"I'm waiving them."

Her eyes widened. "Really? But why?"

"Because I've grown rather fond of your family. I couldn't give up on them. I couldn't squeeze them dry for this case."

"That's...that's kind of you."

He shrugged. "Your mom has me over to eat about once a week. I've been invited to church with them, to birthday parties. They're starting to feel like my family."

A sentimental smile feathered across her lips. "That sounds like my family. But how are you managing to pay your bills?"

"I still receive some money from the army. Plus, I take on odd jobs here and there. Things that aren't really that interesting but that pay the bills. I have some savings."

"That's really kind of you, Trent. Thank you."

"Don't thank me yet. Not until we get out of this situation." He stood. "Speaking of which, I think I see some daylight peeking over that mountain. I'm going to go see what I can find."

"Be careful," she said softly.

"I will."

The snow was deep and cold outside. Trent sank in it up to his knees, which made the walk treacherous. He had little choice, though. In the first building he came to, he found a snowmobile. With some tinkering, he discovered it was still operational. He also found an old can of gas and filled it up. This could definitely come in handy later.

Throughout the rest of the building searches, he found a few more cans of food, some changes of clothes and more things he could use as firewood.

In the back of his mind, he thought about both the men

after them and the caved-in ceiling. By all appearances, Tessa was safe right now. The structure seemed sound. But he had to stay watchful.

Remaining in one of the old cabins, he checked his phone. No messages from Zach.

He rounded the back of the lodge on his way back. He wanted to make sure the building looked out.

What he saw froze him in his tracks.

There were footprints. Leading right to the back window and…to one of the doors.

Tessa mindlessly straightened blankets and stoked the fire and paced—in the name of physical therapy. At least that was what she told herself.

Really, she was anxiously waiting for Trent's return. What had he found? Anything? The results of his outing could mean the difference between hope or despair.

She was praying for hope.

As she paced to the window, she squirmed at the pain in her leg. The good news was that it wasn't broken. The bad was that the cut was deep and it would slow her down. Talk about bad timing.

As she stared outside, she thought about Trent spending time with her family. The realization was so bittersweet. She could easily see him fitting in.

And his kindness in taking on this case for little to no pay warmed her heart.

Then she remembered Laurel. It was best if she didn't let her heart go crazy and start daydreaming about what it would be like to hold Trent's hand or pretend he might care about her away from this crazy situation they were in. It had just been so long since she'd felt a connection with anyone. She realized she missed being part of a community, a tribe, a team.

Maybe there were people out there worth trusting.

Suddenly, she paused as a foreign sound teased her hearing. It had almost sounded like a footstep. Had Trent come back?

She swirled away from the window and scanned the room around her. It looked the same as always. Nothing suspicious.

If Trent had returned, he should be here any minute. He always used the same door down the hallway to keep the cold air in the room at bay.

She waited a few minutes, but he didn't appear.

Apprehension crept up her spine. If not Trent, then what was the sound?

The caved-in roof, she remembered.

Maybe that was what it was. Was more of the ceiling about to collapse on them? Or maybe the part that had already been destroyed was crumbling more?

No, she told herself. She could have been hearing things. After all, everything seemed silent right now.

Why couldn't Trent be back? She hated to admit it, but she felt much better when he was close by. Again, those crazy emotions of hers were leading her astray, causing her to toss back and forth between trust and distrust, dependence and independence.

She scanned the area behind her, which was the hallway leading to the old kitchen, according to what Trent had told her. Again, nothing looked out of place. What was going on?

Just as she reached for her gun, she heard the footstep again. She turned around just in time to hear something click beside her. A man stood there.

An evil grin spread across his face. "You didn't think you'd get away from us that easily, did you?"

At the sound of his heartless voice, her blood went cold.

FIFTEEN

Just as he feared—someone was inside with Tessa. Trent ducked behind the corner. How had the man found them? It wasn't important. All that mattered was figuring out how to get out of this situation. He'd worry about the other details once Tessa was safe.

Moving quietly, he crept inside, making sure to stay concealed and out of sight. From where he stood, he had a perfect view of everything that was happening. A man— he recognized him as one of the men who'd confronted them at Chris's house—stood in front of Tessa. He had two things that frightened any warmth right out of Trent: a gun and a diabolical smile.

"I radioed my other men," the man said, flaunting his Smith & Wesson in front of Tessa.

The man wanted to invoke fear; he enjoyed scaring other people. He was the kind of person Trent despised. It took everything in him to remain calm.

"They should be here any moment," the man continued. "The snow slowed us up. But all of this was just a matter of time. We never lose our guy—or girl. That's not going to change now."

"What do you want from me?" Tessa stared at the man, not fear in her eyes as much as anger. Her hands were braced on the couch behind her and she favored her unin-jured leg. But she wasn't shrinking. Trent could admire that.

"I'm just doing a job. Leo wants to handle you himself."

She leveled her gaze at the man. "I take it you're okay with a man beating up on a woman."

The man grinned, not even a speck of goodness or mercy in his eyes. "I'm okay with getting paid for a job I was hired to do. Well paid, at that."

"I hope there's enough money for you to live with your-self when this is all said and done."

His smile slipped some. "Enough talking. We just need to wait here until the rest of my guys arrive. Where's the man you came here with?"

"There was…an accident as we walked here. He didn't make it."

The man stared at Tessa a moment, as if trying to read her. "You don't seem too broken up about it."

She shrugged nonchalantly. "What can I say? We weren't close. He was hired to find me, just like you were. However, he was ten times the man you are. He'd never hurt a woman."

Her words warmed Trent, but only for a moment.

"Too bad he's not here now. He might have been able to help you out." He reached for her, his gun still drawn. "Now, I need to figure out what to do with you to bide my time. I can think of a few ideas."

Tessa gasped as the man squeezed her arm and pulled her toward him.

Fire coursed through Trent's blood. He drew his gun from his waistband and aimed. In one clean shot, Trent hit the man's shoulder. The man cried out in pain and dropped his gun. Tessa scrambled to retrieve the weapon, and she raised it toward her attacker, also.

Trent's heart slowed. But he knew the battle wasn't any-where near being won.

* * *

Tessa gasped for air as Trent grabbed her arm and pulled her away from the man. They'd tied him to a chair, knowing his friends would arrive soon enough to help him. In the meantime, he'd be indisposed.

Trent reached down and grabbed something from the ground. "Put this on."

She held up the puffy white snowsuit. "Where'd you find this?"

"One of the cabins. It's going to be cold where we're going."

She didn't ask any questions. At least it sounded as though he had a plan. That was more than she could say for herself. He pulled another coat on over his own and then pulled on a hat. He handed another to Tessa.

"When they find you, they're going to kill you," the man in the chair grumbled. His gaze looked haggard and every once in a while he moaned with pain. But he was still angry and determined.

"I'd worry about yourself right now," Trent said.

The man let out a deep growl before his face squeezed with pain.

"Now, come on," Trent said, turning his attention back to Tessa. "We've got to get out of here before the others arrive. We don't have much time."

She lifted a two-way radio that had been clipped to her attacker's belt and listened for a brief moment. "It sounds as if the rest of the guys are within eyesight of the lodge."

He nodded, as if impressed that she'd thought ahead enough to grab the device. "Good to know. This way we can stay a step ahead of them."

He grabbed her hand and pulled her outside. The cold air was brittle and frosty. It took Tessa's breath away for a moment. But she had no time to dwell on it. Trent pulled her forward and she let him. A few flakes from the treetops scattered downward and chilled her cheeks and eye-lashes even more.

The wind slapped her cheeks as they rushed through the snow. Of course, rushing through the snow was like rush-ing through quicksand. Each step tried to suction them to the ground. They trudged forward regardless.

Another building came into sight. Tessa hoped that was where they were headed, because her legs were becom-ing numb again. At least that meant she couldn't feel the throbbing ache from her wound.

"In here," Trent urged. He pulled her into the building.

Just as they stepped inside, the radio at her waist cack-led to life. "I see the building, Windwalker. What's the situation inside?"

Trent took the radio from her. "Targets are constrained. Waiting for help escorting them."

"Roger that. Should be there in less than five."

Trent and Tessa exchanged a look. They had to hurry.

"Come on," Trent urged. He climbed onto a…snow-mobile?

"Where did this come from?" Tessa asked, climbing on behind him with a touch of trepidation.

"It must have been left here when the resort closed down. I found some gas and finally got it hot-wired so it works again. All I know is that I'm not complaining. Hold on tight."

Her throat constricted at her nearness to Trent. "I am."

He took her hands and pulled them tauter around his waist. "Don't be shy."

Her cheeks heated but only for a minute. She didn't have time to dwell on the solid muscle beneath her hands or the broad back her cheek was pressed against. She had to focus on survival.

The radio crackled again. "Where are you, Windwalker? We're inside the building." A curse followed. They must have found their guy tied up.

Wasting no more time, Trent burst through the door of the garage. The vehicle hit the snow and sprinkled flakes around them. Any other time it would be amazing. Right now, it seemed like a blur.

Just as they sped down the slope, three men stepped from the building, guns in hand. Keeping one arm around Trent, Tessa reached into her waistband and pulled out the Glock. Using her best aim—which was difficult because of the speed and the movement—she took a shot. Even if it didn't hit them, maybe it would scare them off some and buy them a little more time.

Finally, they cleared the lodge. The men were no match for their speed on the snowmobile.

"Where are we going?" Tessa asked as reality set in.

"I have no idea."

"To the main road?"

"Too dangerous. They'll look for us there." He headed toward the woods instead.

"And this is going to be better? You know there are cliffs around the gorge here, right?"

"Now I do."

She sucked in a breath and closed her eyes. No, she couldn't afford to close her eyes. She stole a glance behind her instead. The men were still chasing them, coming on foot. It was good they weren't on the road—they'd likely be located much easier. But still, the thought of journeying into the white wilderness ahead of them was unnerving.

Trent swerved as a tree appeared in their path. The landscape became thicker and harder to manage. They had to slow down. And that meant that the guys chasing them had a better chance of catching up.

Just then, a bullet whizzed by, lodging itself in a nearby tree. Splinters of wood flew at them.

Tessa looked behind her. Their pursuers were no longer running. It was worse.

"They've got sniper rifles out!" she yelled.

As he turned again, a trail came into view. Perfect. At least this would make their journey easier and less treacherous.

Just as the thought entered her mind, another bullet whizzed by, narrowly missing them. She held on tighter to Trent as the trail became steeper.

The snowmobile slipped, but only for a moment. They whizzed away until the bullets could no longer reach them.

Thank You, Jesus.

Her relief was short-lived, as a fence appeared.

If they didn't slow down, they'd ram right into it the tall stone structure.

Trent swerved, trying to miss the wall in front of them. The snowmobile teetered, and he feared it might tip. Snow sprayed behind them at their sudden movement, and Trent's heart raced as he anticipated what would happen next.

They came mere inches from hitting the wall, from tipping over. Thankfully, the vehicle righted. He let out a breath of relief.

He didn't ease up on the accelerator but kept going. They didn't have any time to waste. But this wall, this fence, was going to be a problem. He wasn't sure if it stretched all the way around the resort or not. But somehow, they had to get off this property. Otherwise Leo's men would definitely find them, and Trent couldn't let that happen.

He followed the wall, hoping to find a gate. There had to be a service entrance around here somewhere that led to the main road.

The snowmobile hit a stump buried under a drift and the vehicle slowed. This was going to be tough. The terrain was too thick to be navigated easily by a snowmobile, but he was going to push the vehicle as hard as he could. He only hoped that the men chasing them didn't think ahead and search for a service entrance, also. If so, Trent and Tessa were on borrowed time.

Bingo! Just as he suspected, there was a gate up ahead. Now he prayed that it was unlocked or at least old and rusty so he could break through.

He slid to a stop and jumped off, instantly rattling the chain connecting the two wooden doors of the gate. It was old and rusty, yet still solid.

This wasn't good.

"Here, let me try," Tessa said.

She pulled out a cheap-looking multitool kit, similar to a Swiss Army knife, and began fiddling with the latch. He watched carefully, curious as to what she was doing and where she'd gotten the knife. Obviously, she was attempting to pick the lock. But why in the world did she think she could?

To Trent's surprise, the lock popped open. She jerked the chain down and pushed the gates open triumphantly.

"How...?" Trent started.

She shrugged as if it wasn't a big deal. "In addition to my self-defense and gun classes, I also learned how to pick locks. It seemed useful."

"The toolkit?"

"I found it in the glove compartment of the car. I slid it into my pocket before we abandoned the vehicle, just in case it came in handy. Looks as if it did."

"How fortuitous." Wasting no more time, Trent and Tessa climbed back onto the snowmobile and took off down the service road, grateful for the smoother surface. They'd make better time this way.

The cold air slapped him in the face and nearly took his

breath away. But he couldn't think about it now. All that mattered was getting away as fast as possible.

As he traveled he put together snippets of a plan in his mind. Hopefully he still had phone service, because he needed to call Zach and see if his friend could pick them up ASAP. Then they needed to enlist more help. Find evidence. Put an end to all this.

He kept his eyes open for a break in the trees. If he found one it could mean the highway was approaching. He hoped this back road had cut enough time off their travel that Leo's men wouldn't be able to catch up for a while.

As Tessa's arms tightened around him, he wondered if he was projecting his past onto her. Was that the reason he felt so determined to see this through? He knew he had an innate sense of justice. He wouldn't leave a woman stranded without help. But it wasn't just his nature. He knew that how he felt about Tessa ran deeper than that. Though they'd only known each other a couple of days, the stress of this situation had quickly deepened their bond.

A clearing appeared in the distance. That had to be the road leading from the ski resort. It was going to be slick from the snow, but he hoped it was still passable. The road crews probably hadn't made it this way yet, since the only thing up here was the abandoned resort.

He slowed, but only for a moment, as he reached the narrow stretch. He spotted no one approaching from either side, so he carefully maneuvered the snowmobile onto the asphalt there. Once he was steady on the street, he started away from the ski lodge.

This was a different road, he realized. They would have passed their abandoned car by now otherwise. Here, a river snaked far below, probably breathtaking in other circumstances. If he could only make it far enough that there was some sort of landmark where Zach could find them.

"Trent, they're behind us," Tessa said.

He glanced back and saw a car headed their way. The men were still far away, but that meant they only had a little time. Plus, they were running out of gas. He guessed they had five minutes max.

"Do you trust me?"

She hesitated before saying, "Yes."

"Then, we're going to have to jump. Okay?"

"Jump? Are you crazy?"

"It's our only choice. As soon as there's a good spot we've got to get off and hide."

"Okay." Her voice was stained with uncertainty.

He couldn't blame her. The possibility was daunting.

He saw just the place up ahead. It was a grove of trees they could duck behind. It would be perfect. But he had to time it just right.

As the area approached, he slowed slightly. On a mental count of three, he eased off the accelerator, swung his leg over the snowmobile and grabbed Tessa. They jumped into the embankment beside them.

He prayed the risk paid off.

SIXTEEN

Trent and Tessa rolled across the ground, tumbling over each other several times before coming to a stop. Snow cocooned them, burying them with cold, icy layers.

Tessa found herself nestled on top of Trent. Her eyes widened at their closeness. Or perhaps it was the snow, the exhilaration of what they'd done or the astonishment that they'd survived. Whatever it was, her heart beat out of control.

She had to get focused.

Laurel, she remembered. She had no right to be attracted to or having feelings for this man.

"Don't move!" Trent whispered, obviously unaffected.

She remained still, all too aware of his presence. Wanting to slide off. To run.

But instead she stayed still, willing herself to break their gaze. Instead, her eyes went to his lips.

Bad idea.

All she could think about was how they might feel against hers. Which she had no right to do. It didn't matter that she'd misread the bond between them. She had to put an end to this.

Instead, she stared at the snow, hoping Trent couldn't feel her heart thumping out of control against his chest.

Just then, she heard a crash.

The snowmobile had gone over the ledge.

Tessa prayed Trent's plan worked and that the men assumed Tessa and Trent had gone over the cliff, as well. If not, they were both goners.

The sound of a vehicle crunching through the snow shattered the silence around them. Leo's men. This was the moment of truth.

Would they be discovered?

"You're doing great," Trent whispered, his voice light in her ear and his breath soft and warm on her cheek.

She forced herself to keep her eyes focused on the snow. She feared Trent might see a glimpse of her attraction to him. And that was all it was—a moment of attraction. After Leo, she knew she was better off alone.

The vehicle slowed and finally there was a moment of silence. It had stopped, Tessa realized. Only feet from them.

Had they been spotted?

A car doors opened. Feet clomped on the packed snow on the road.

"The snow must have gotten the best of them," one of the men said. "It looks as if their snowmobile went down the embankment and into the river below. The tracks lead straight off the road. The river is still flowing, though. I must have carried everyone away."

Silence—except for some footsteps. Were the men lurking closer? Would they be discovered?

Trent pulled his arms tightly around her, as if he sensed her anxiety.

The cold was starting to get to her again, too. Though Trent was probably shielding her from the bulk of the frozen snow below, there was definitely a coat of white iciness around her. It was beginning to seep through her hair to tickle her neck.

They couldn't stay like this much longer.

"I'll send a crew farther downstream to look for their bodies," the man continued. "It was a big risk taking a vehicle like that out on this ice. Especially on roads like this."

Silence.

"You mean Grath? We found him, and one of our guys is taking him back to Virginia. We'll let your doctor look at him. People will ask too many questions otherwise."

Virginia. That was where Leo was still basing his operations. Wilmington Heights, maybe? Tessa stored away that information in case it came in handy later.

"All right. We'll clear the area and meet you. It looks as if this assignment is over. I know it's not the way you wanted it to end. But we got the same result."

Snow crunched again.

Tessa dared not breathe as she felt a shadow fall over her. The men were close—too close.

She continued to hold her breath, waiting to see what would happen next.

Finally, the shadow disappeared. Footsteps retreated. Car doors slammed.

A few minutes later, tires dug into snow and ice. The humming motor disappeared from earshot.

They were safe. At least for now, they were safe.

Trent gently prodded Tessa up, and they emerged from their snowy grave. Tessa glanced around. The men were gone. Thank goodness they were gone.

"I can't believe they didn't see us," Tessa said.

"Maybe that's because we have someone watching out for us."

She caught his gaze, surprised at the sincerity in his voice. "You mean God?"

He nodded. "Absolutely. I've seen Him answer prayers before."

She wiped the snow from her pants and jacket, unsure what to say except, "What now?"

"I'm calling my friend. I'm hoping he can pick us up—and soon." Trent gaze scanned the area around them. "In the meantime, we can't stand here. It's too dangerous, especially if those men come back to look at the crash site."

"Where do we go?"

He nodded up the hill. "There are some boulders up there. We should be able to take shelter behind there until we know for sure the coast is clear."

He took her hand and helped her up the incline, being mindful of her injured leg. Once they were settled behind the rock, he pulled his gloves off. His fingers were red, but he didn't seem to care. He pulled out his cell phone and dialed.

Tessa hardly heard him talk. The dampness was starting to trickle down her neck and into her clothing. She hoped—dare she say, prayed—that they wouldn't be out here too long.

When Trent hung up, he looked at her. "My friend is about twenty minutes away from the old ski lodge. He should be able to find us here. It's going to be okay, Tessa."

Something about the certainty in her voice brought her comfort. "What friend is that?"

"His name is Zach. We went to police academy together and worked on the force in Richmond for a while. He was a detective in Baltimore up until recently. He's one of the few people I actually trust."

He slipped his gloves back on and peered around the boulder.

"Do you see anything?" Tessa asked.

"Not yet. But we can't get too comfortable. How many men does this Leo guy have?"

"He can afford however many he wants. Money isn't an issue."

"It seems as though he has a whole army."

"For the right price, men will do anything." As she said

the words, despair bit at her. Leo had even betrayed her for the right price, hadn't he?

He squeezed her arm. "Not all men."

The look in Trent's eyes made her throat go dry. Maybe all men weren't like Leo. Trent had proved himself to be honorable. It was just that she had such a hard time believing in people. She'd been stabbed in the back, and the pain of that scar made her afraid to ever put her faith in someone again.

She dragged her gaze away. "That's good to know."

Trent saw a green SUV pull to the side of the road and the headlights flickered three times. It was Zach.

He was just in time. If he and Tessa were out here too much longer, there would be serious repercussions. The cold was biting, but it was the wind that nearly did them in. It blew down the mountainside, all the way through his jacket and layers of clothing.

"Come on." He led Tessa down the mountain, keeping one hand on her arm so she wouldn't lose her balance. Without wasting any time, they climbed into the back of the SUV. Heat filled the car, a welcome feeling after everything they'd been through.

"You two look terrible," Zach said.

"Good to see you, too," Trent said.

Zach flashed him a quick smile before turning serious. "I need to get you somewhere dry or, as my grandmother would say, you'll catch your death. I'm Zach, by the way," he told Tessa.

"Tessa," she said with a nod. Her teeth chattered together and her arms were drawn over her chest.

"Seat belts on. These roads are slick. Let's get out of here. I have the perfect place reserved."

Trent paused, waiting to see if Tessa needed help. It took some tugging, but she finally latched the belt in place.

He pulled the strap across his chest also and settled back, happy to have Zach with them.

Zach tossed something in the backseat. "I thought you might be hungry. There are some sandwiches in there. I also have some coffee up here. Probably not hot anymore, but at least warm."

Trent took a cup and handed it to Tessa. She slowly took a sip and closed her eyes with delight.

"This is just what I needed," she said. "Thank you."

Trent took his own cup. The drink was tepid, but it was just warm enough to lift his spirits for a moment.

"Any updates since we spoke last?" Zach asked, glancing in his rearview mirror.

Trent glanced at Tessa before launching into a brief update. When he finished, his friend shook his head. "It sounds as if you're lucky to be alive. Both of you. And these guys who are after you, they're no joke."

"You don't have to tell us that," Trent said.

He had the strangest desire to pull Tessa toward him. To keep her warm. Purely for survival, he told himself. But he knew there was more to it than that. There was something about her that drew him to her, that made him want to be close.

When she'd been so near him in the snow after they'd abandoned the snowmobile, he'd thought he'd seen a flicker of attraction in her eyes, also. He hadn't allowed himself to even think about another woman since Laurel. But maybe something was changing inside him.

As they ate their sandwiches, Tessa was surprisingly quiet. All of this was a lot to process. "What now?"

Trent sighed and shook his head. She asked that question a lot, and he wished he had a good answer to give her. "I'm not sure if we'll outrun Leo. So we need to think of a way to nail him."

"If we have internet, I'm pretty handy with a computer,"

Tessa said. "I can probably hack into their system and see if they have anything new on file. I won't be able to get to their hidden files, probably."

"You think you can pull some information from their site?" Trent asked. "Maybe enough info that we could go to the FBI?"

She nodded slowly. "I'm sure they have more firewalls in place now, especially after what happened last night. My biggest worry is that the minute I hack into their server, they'll be able to trace where the hack is coming from. I can try to redirect it, but I can't guarantee how long that will last."

"We can't risk that." He shook his head. "We can't keep running. There's got to be another way."

"Maybe after this, there won't be any more running. I mean, I can probably scramble it for a certain time period. It might be worth the risk."

He shook his head. "You're in no position to run anymore. You need to see a doctor."

She didn't argue. Instead, she lay her head against the window and closed her eyes.

Good. She needed rest.

So did Trent, but he would never admit it.

"I don't need to tell you how serious this is," Zach said.

"By no means," Trent said, leaning forward. "I've been chased and pursued more ways than I can count. This nearly makes those terrorists over in the Middle East look like amateurs."

"I'd say you're going above and beyond the call of duty when it comes to being a private eye."

He shrugged and glanced at Tessa again as her chest rose and fell evenly with slumber. "I can't leave her alone in this."

"No, you can't. I'm glad I can help. My contact with the CIA called me back, Trent. One of those murders that was loosely associated with the family? It was a banker who'd apparently made some dirty deals. It wasn't a nice murder. Not that murder ever is. But the scene…it was brutal."

Trent cringed. Not that the news surprised him. But the confirmation did shake him up. He didn't want that kind of suffering to happen to Tessa.

"Where's this place we're going?"

"One of my old friends from Smuggler's Cove is ex-CIA. He works for an organization called Iron Incorporated—they also go by Eyes—now. You heard of them?"

"The military contractors?"

"That's the one. He hooked me up with an old safe house operated by the agency. We should be out of harm's way there for a couple of days at least."

"Right now those men think we're dead," Trent said. "But they're looking for our bodies. When they discover we're not in that river, they'll resume their search for us."

"Maybe we'll have some answers by then."

"Maybe," Trent muttered. "We can only hope."

SEVENTEEN

When Tessa opened her eyes, a beautiful old Victorian house stood in front of her. She had to blink a couple of times to make sure she wasn't seeing things. Sure enough, it was like a real-life dollhouse. It was beautiful.

The place had turrets on both sides, siding that reminded her of gingerbread, multiple porches and even a corner gazebo with a swing. An inviting wreath swathed the blue front door and electric candles dotted the windows.

"Where are we?" Tessa asked, a touch of awe in her voice.

"It's where we're staying for the next couple of days," Trent said beside her.

Zach nodded. "Let's get you two inside. I'm sure a shower and some clean clothes sound good."

"Clean clothes?" Tessa questioned.

"I picked a few things up. Hope they're your size."

"I'm sure they will be fine."

As she climbed out she noticed the ache in her leg had returned. She'd probably have to have her wound looked at, as much as she didn't want to do that. She hoped she could hold off until this mess was done.

As always, Trent's hand went to her elbow. Did he think she wasn't steady on her feet? Was he just being a gentleman? She wasn't sure. She only knew that every time he touched her, waves of electricity coursed through her body.

They climbed the steps, Zach unlocked the door and they all slipped inside.

Before Tessa could even let her eyes explore her new surroundings, Zach directed her to a bathroom upstairs. "This one is all yours, Tessa. Trent, there's one downstairs you can use. I'll fix some dinner while you two get cleaned up."

Tessa didn't argue. As soon as the men retreated, she locked the bathroom door and took the warmest, most wonderful shower ever. It had never felt so good to wash all the grime away.

When she climbed out, she pulled back the bandage that Trent had wrapped around her leg. Blood had soaked through the gauze there and she knew she had to change it. She'd always been squeamish around blood.

As the deep gash on her leg came into view, her head spun. The cut was probably six inches long. And it was deep. Trent had put butterfly bandages across it, trying to seal it shut. She didn't see any signs of infection.

She found a bandage in the cabinet and then wrapped it up again. If this was the only scar she walked away with from this whole ordeal, she'd count herself fortunate.

She pulled on yoga pants, a long-sleeved turquoise T-shirt and fluffy socks with dogs on them. She dried her hair, wishing she had some makeup to cover up the circles under her eyes. But she had no room to complain, and she was thankful for what she'd been given.

She studied her reflection for a minute. This whole ordeal had taken a bigger toll on her than she'd expected. Her skin looked pale; her eyes had lost their glimmer.

Was she really going to let Leo do this to her? He could ruin a lot of the physical things in her life. But she'd let him ruin her inside, as well. She'd become a shell of the person she'd once been. That was giving someone a lot of power in her life.

Finally, Tessa stepped out of the steamy bathroom, not sure what to expect once she got downstairs.

Zach seemed nice enough and, if Trent trusted him, then certainly she could, too. He was tall, although not as tall as Trent, and he had blond hair with a slight curl to it. Inside the house, she'd caught a glimpse of blue eyes and dimpled cheeks.

What had Trent said? He was a detective somewhere?

She found the men downstairs, sitting at the breakfast bar and drinking coffee. They both got quiet when she walked in. Instead of feeling awkward, she slid onto the bench beside Trent. "Got any more of that java?"

"Coming right up," Zach said. He grabbed a mug and filled it for her.

Meanwhile, the scent of beef—steak, maybe?—sizzling on the stovetop made her stomach grumble. She was hungrier than she'd thought.

"About five more minutes until dinner is served," Zach said.

Tessa stole a glance at Trent. The man had always been striking. But right now, with his hair still glistening and the faint scent of soap emanating from him, her throat caught. He wore a long-sleeved black T-shirt that showed off his defined torso and a pair of dark-washed jeans. And despite everything they'd been through, he still looked alert.

By the time Zach set their food in front of them, Tessa was beyond hungry. She took the first bite of steak and it melted in her mouth.

"Where are you located out of now, Zach? Baltimore?" She tried to remember what Trent had mentioned.

Something flashed through his gaze so briefly that Tessa thought she'd imagined it. "I was there for a while. I've found that I actually like being the sheriff in a small town, though. It makes the people you're serving seem more real when you see them every day and know most of them by name."

She nodded, not pressing it. "I see. Well, thank you for all of your help today. I don't know what we would have done without you."

"I hear you're pretty resourceful," Zach said.

Tessa glanced at Trent. "What did you say?"

"You can shoot a gun like nobody's business and pick a lock. I might recruit you as one of my deputies soon."

She smiled, despite the grim situation. "I don't like being a victim. What can I say?"

"Being proactive is good." Zach suddenly stood. "Look, I don't want to cut this short, but it's getting late. Just leave the plates in the sink, and I'll get them later. I'm going to check all the windows and doors one more time and then turn in for the night."

"Thanks again," Tessa said.

He tilted his head, almost as if he had a hat on. "No problem. Night, you all."

As soon as he disappeared, Tessa felt of a touch of tension fill her. It wasn't that she was uncomfortable with Trent; she'd been around him enough to know that wasn't it. It was… She knew what it was. It was the fact that she was attracted to him. He made her feel jittery and unsure of herself and—

"So how are you doing really, Tessa?" Trent asked, turning toward her as they sat at the breakfast bar. A candle flickered between them and the lingering scent of coffee hung in the air. "You hanging in?"

She shrugged and leaned back, the wooden chair hard against her back. "I guess. What else can I do?"

"You want to go sit by the fire?" He nodded toward the other room where the warmth of the hearth beckoned.

"That sounds wonderful."

They walked into the living room. Tessa sat at one end of the couch and Trent draped a blanket over her before settling at the other end.

"Do you really think we're safe here?" Tessa asked. She didn't want to bring up the situation with Leo. She really didn't. She'd much rather pretend she was enjoying an evening with a handsome man. But that wasn't reality. Reality was that there were men trying to kill her and Trent's heart might already be taken.

"For a short time."

When he laid a hand on her leg, she drew in a deep breath.

"What? Your leg?" he asked.

She nodded, wishing she wasn't squinting with pain.

"Let me see it."

He peeled the blanket back and gently tugged up the leg of her yoga pants. "You bandaged it? You mind if I take a look?"

"Knock yourself out."

He gently unwrapped the gauze there and frowned. "I'd like to put some more medication on that, just to make sure it doesn't get infected."

Before she could insist she was okay and that he shouldn't fuss over her, he stood, disappeared and returned a few minutes with a first-aid kit. "A real one this time," he said with a small grin. Carefully, he took a towel and put it under her leg. "This is going to sting a little."

He poured some hydrogen peroxide over the wound. The liquid bubbled up, and she gritted her teeth at the sting.

"I know it's old-school to use this, but I've always thought it worked the best. Believe me—I've cleaned a lot of wounds in my day."

"As a ranger?" she asked, curious to know a bit more of his history.

"That's right."

"Why'd you get out?"

"It was time. I'd seen too much, felt too jaded, wanted to settle down." He patted the area around her wound dry and pulled out a tube of antibiotic ointment.

"So you became a police officer? Then a detective?"

He nodded again. "That's right. I did that for about eight years. Then I decided to go into business for myself."

"Why's that?"

His face went taut, and he began concentrating even more on dabbing her wound with ointment. "Long story. But I needed a change. Believe it or not, I'm usually a committed kind of guy. But sometimes you just can't ignore when changes need to take place in your life."

"I see." He didn't offer any more information, but, boy, did she want to know. What had happened to cause the sadness that crossed over his features? He wasn't willing to share, so she couldn't prod anymore, despite her curiosity.

Finally, he bandaged her wound, removed the towel and lowered her leg back onto the couch. He dropped the blanket over it and then settled back for a minute.

She felt she owed him something more than the bits and pieces of her life she'd shared. All he knew was that she'd dated a man who'd turned out to be a homicidal maniac. But there was so much more to the story.

She stared into the fire a moment, gathering her thoughts.

"There was a time I thought Leo walked on water," she started.

Her revelation seemed to startle him and he glanced her way, but said nothing.

"I was one of those girls who was really picky when it came to dating. I'd been out with guys before, but nothing really serious. I wanted to save everything for my one true love. Maybe I'd watched too many romantic movies. I don't know. But I didn't want to give my heart to someone if we weren't meant to be together forever." The memories came back stronger. "Then I met Leo. He swept me off my feet. I was working as the director at one of his art galleries. He was charismatic and handsome. He asked me out five times before I said yes."

"Five times? He didn't give up?"

"Leo isn't the type to give up." She cleared her throat. Leo had made that abundantly clear over the past few days, hadn't he? "Anyway, I finally said yes. I figured he'd try to impress me by taking me to a fancy restaurant and flaunting all of his successes. Instead, he took me on a picnic at a local park. We ate on a blanket, and he'd even made some sloppy sandwiches himself. I saw a different side of him that day. Maybe he wasn't the spoiled rich kid I thought he was. We were inseparable after that."

"It does sound like a whirlwind romance," Trent said.

"I literally thought he was the best thing that ever happened to me—until that day I caught him doing the arms deal. Then my eyes were truly opened to who he was. He'd been wooing me this whole time and keeping me distracted from everything happening right under my nose at the gallery. If I hadn't been so lovesick, I would have noticed that things weren't right. But I thought he could do no wrong."

"Love can be like that."

"In the blink of an eye, my life changed. I went from feeling like the happiest girl in the world to running for my life. Feeling betrayed. Feeling angry at myself for being so blind."

"It's not every day that someone's boyfriend is actually a terrorist in disguise. No one can really blame you."

"I blame me."

"Maybe you need to change that."

She stared at Trent moment. "You're right. I do. I was just thinking earlier that I'd let Leo have too much control in my life. That's a choice I made. I need to undo it."

Trent's admiration for Tessa grew. At first he'd thought she was a scared rabbit hiding in a little hole away from the rest of the world. But as the layers began to peel back, he'd realized that not only was she a survivor, but she was also protective of her loved ones.

She'd been hurt, but she'd also been prepared to face the consequences. Not many people he knew would take the initiative to learn how to use a gun, to pick a lock, to defend themselves.

As he stared at her now, the firelight dancing across her face, something squeezed in his heart. He wanted nothing more than to scoot closer, to touch her cheeks, to smooth away her hair.

He'd tried to extinguish his attraction to Tessa, but nothing he told himself seemed to work. No matter how he looked at it, Tessa was one of the most beautiful and intriguing women he'd ever met.

He saw the same look in her eyes—his feelings were mutual. Their emotions had grown quickly—a crazy situation like this could accelerate feelings. He had no doubt about that. But it almost felt as if there was something deeper between them that just a surge of attraction.

The fire dimmed, so he stood and stoked the flames a moment. When he sat down again, he was closer. Her legs draped over his lap.

"This seems surreal, doesn't it?" she said softly. "Being here. Everything that's happened. I just want to let you know that if we don't get out of here, I appreciate all you've done."

He glanced at her and saw a tear trickle down her cheek. "Don't say that. We'll survive this."

"I know what these men are capable of."

Before he could second-guess his decision, Trent scooted closer and pulled Tessa against his chest. She didn't resist; instead she rested there. They sat in silence, neither needing to say a word.

EIGHTEEN

"Where's Trent?" Tessa asked Zach the next morning.

"He went outside to get some more firewood," Zach said. "He's one of those hardworking guys. Always dependable."

"I've noticed that," Tessa said, sitting at the breakfast bar. She glanced outside and saw Trent gathering wood in the snow. Her heart warmed at the sight.

How had her feelings grown so quickly? She not only felt indebted toward the man, but she also felt an unmistakable bond.

"Look, he's still reeling from what happened with Laurel. I don't want to see him get hurt again," Zach said, lowering his voice.

"Laurel?" Her pulse spiked.

He paused, squinting with thought—and maybe some surprise. "He hasn't told you about her?"

Tessa shook her head.

"He will when he's ready. In the meantime, I just want him to be careful."

Tessa got the warning loud and clear. Zach was protective of his friend. Tessa had no intentions of hurting Trent. She wondered what his story was and, once and for all, who was Laurel?

She'd trusted him with her own story, and she had to

admit that it didn't feel good to know that Trent hadn't offered that same trust in her.

Just then, the back door opened and a gust of frigid air swept inside. Trent spotted Tessa and a smile tugged at his lips. "Good morning."

"Morning." Her return smile felt a little shy.

"I wanted to wait until you were both down here before I broke the bad news," Zach started, leaning against the kitchen counter, a new heaviness seeming to press on him.

Tessa instantly tensed in preparation for whatever he had to say. "Okay."

Trent sat beside her, and she found comfort in his mere presence.

"The bad news is that there's an APB out on Tessa," Zach said. "It's extended beyond Gideon's Hollow, beyond West Virginia and made it all the way to national law enforcement agencies. Someone reported that she was involved in a terrorism ring. Apparently, bomb-making materials were planted in the basement of the house she was staying in in West Virginia. She's a suspect in the explosion that took place at your cabin, Trent."

She gasped. "What?"

Zach nodded. "It's true. That makes a difficult situation even more difficult right now."

"That means the two of you could get in trouble, also. For being with me." Tessa's heart thudded with grief at the thought.

"You're being set up," Trent said, pulling off his gloves.

The grim lines on his face told the true story of what he was thinking, though: she had little chance of getting out of this situation. Either Leo killed her or she ended up in jail.

"Leo knows how to do it right," Tessa said. "What can I say? If they catch me, I'm dead. If the police find me, I'm locked up for life."

"I hate to continue with the bad news, but your face

is on the news right now, also," Zach continued. "It says you've been going by an alias."

She squeezed the skin between her eyes as despair tried to bite deep. Maybe she should just turn herself in. That might save a lot of people heartache, including Trent and Zach.

"Leo knows how to play a sick game," Tessa said. "He's managed to trap me, no matter which direction I try to run."

Trent squeezed her shoulder. "We'll get through this."

She shook her head. "You should just let me go out on my own right now. I've already caused you both enough grief and upheaval. This was never either one of your problems to begin with."

"We can't let you do that," Trent said. "We're in this together."

"But you have a choice. You can get out."

"I choose not to," Trent said, no room for argument in his voice.

"Same here," Zach said. "You need all the support you can get. You'll never survive this alone. Men like these… They'll just keep coming after you until you're destroyed."

"Besides, I have an idea," Trent said.

Tessa turned toward him, her full attention on him. "Okay."

"You said when you downloaded all the information, you dropped the jump drive, right?"

She nodded. "Yes. After I copied it, I deleted it from their server so they wouldn't have access to their contacts. Unfortunately, the information I hoped to take to the police also disappeared in my moment of klutziness."

"Where did you drop it?"

"One of the vents in the office building." Her eyes widened as she realized what he was getting at. "You want to see if it's still there?"

He nodded. "I do."

"And how do you propose to do that?"

"I'd like to dress like an HVAC guy and say I came to look at their system."

"That sounds risky."

"It's going to take some planning, but I think it's feasible. However, I will need some help."

"You know my hands are kind of tied here, Trent. After Baltimore, I can't exactly run around like a free agent anymore," Zach said.

Trent raised his hand. "I would never ask you to do that. No, I need you to stay here and keep an eye on Tessa." He shook his head as Tessa started to object. "I know that's not what you want to hear, but it wouldn't be wise to leave you alone. You know what these men are capable of."

She couldn't argue with that. "You can't do it alone, though, Trent. Maybe I can help—"

"That's out of the question. One glance at you and we'll be made."

She couldn't argue with that, either. "Then, who? Who will help?"

"I know some guys," Zach said.

Trent and Tessa turned toward him, waiting to hear what he had to say.

"You know Eyes, that private security firm I told you about? They do freelance work. My friend works for them now. He might be able to assist."

"Let's see what we can put together, then. Tessa, you remember anything about the HVAC company they used?"

"At the gallery they used Thomas and Sons. They had for years. It used to be that Tom or one of his boys would come out personally. Of course, now that it's grown in size, I'm sure they have various employees that they send out. I can't guarantee the gallery still uses them, but it's a good guess."

"Zach, why don't you get on the phone with your friends and see if they can offer any assistance. Explain that this is a matter of national security. I'll research this company and see about putting together a van, a uniform—basically a cover story."

"Absolutely."

Tessa tried to remember the details of the gallery. Trent would need that information if he sneaked inside. He'd need the names of contacts if he wanted to appear legit.

She could hack into their server and find out that information for sure.

But there were risks involved. She had to weigh everything before making a decision.

But the possibility that she could do more to help continued to linger in her mind.

Trent put the finishing touches on his plans for tomorrow and stood. Normally something like this would take at least a week to put together. But they were on the clock and needed to move fast. God must have been watching out for them, because they had been able to get everything they needed in place at lightning speed.

Tessa had been a huge help today. It was more than her knowledge; he actually found himself finding comfort in her presence. They worked surprisingly well as a team. It was when they were on opposite sides of the field that things got complicated.

He made some coffee, grabbed two mugs and carried them both into the living room, where Tessa sat. He extended one to her. "Thought you might need a drink to warm up."

Her bright smile in return was all the thanks he needed. "Sounds like just what I need."

He sat down beside her—probably closer than he should

have. He watched as she wrapped her hands around the mug, practically hugging it, and then she stared into the fire.

"I feel a little as though this is the calm before the storm," she said, glancing at him.

He let out a slow breath. "Maybe it is. But maybe after the storm has passed, this will be the norm and not the exception."

A light smile feathered across her face. "That would be nice. You seem so peaceful, even in the midst of all of this."

Suddenly, the weight on his shoulder seemed to press down harder. "I haven't always been like this. You asked me about why I became a PI?"

She nodded, a silent encouragement for him to continue.

"About three years ago, I put some pretty bad guys behind bars. They were gang members and responsible for the deaths of uncountable people. Mostly rival gang members, but there were a few who were simply innocent civilians who'd been caught in the cross fire. It was a really proud day for me."

"I can see why."

His shoulders became even heavier. "Unfortunately, my name wasn't kept hidden. It made the news. There were a few gang members that didn't go to jail—we didn't have any reason to hold them. I mean, you can't go to jail for being in a gang, only if you do illegal things while a part of it. Those men came after Laurel."

"Who's Laurel?"

"My fiancée."

All of Tessa's attention was suddenly focused on him. "Oh."

Even she seemed to sense that this story wasn't going anywhere pleasant. "I thought she was safe, but they found her. Before I could get to her, they put a bullet through her head."

"I'm so sorry."

He couldn't stop now or he'd never tell her the whole story. "I became obsessed with finding out who exactly had killed her. Made some bad decisions. Eventually they put me on desk duty. I reached one of the lowest points of my life. That's when my friend introduced me to Jesus, and I really found peace and purpose through that. I decided to become a PI so I could take on the cases that mattered the most to me."

"That makes sense. I know this probably doesn't mean much, but I'm so sorry, Trent." She put her hand on his biceps, her eyes an endless pool of compassion, kindness... and something more?

In a moment of decision, he leaned toward her. She didn't pull away. Slowly, certainly, he pressed his lips to hers. Emotions he hadn't felt in a long time hit him at full force.

"I hope you know not every guy is like Leo," he whispered.

Her eyes fluttered open, and a steady look of joy and trust filled them. "I know."

With that proclamation, he leaned toward her again, stealing another kiss. This one was longer, deeper and less tentative. He was enjoying being with Tessa a little too much.

He pulled away and stood. "We should probably say good-night. We need our rest for tomorrow."

"Good idea." He only prayed the hopeful feeling in his chest remained long after tomorrow was over.

Tessa couldn't deny the mix of exhilaration and fear that coursed through her. She didn't know where these feelings for Trent had come from or how they'd come on so fast. She felt a much deeper connection with him than she'd ever felt with...well, anyone. Even Leo.

And when she'd heard Trent talk about his fiancée, suddenly he made sense. His protectiveness made sense. His determination. His drive.

She didn't dare to tell him what she'd done earlier while he'd met with Zach. She'd sneaked upstairs and onto the internet. She'd hacked into Leo's server just long enough to confirm the name of the HVAC company, the lay of the building and the name of the new assistant at the gallery. She couldn't send Trent in without being certain.

She'd managed to scramble the servers, and it would be at least twenty-four hours before Leo's tech guys could trace where she was located. By that time, they'd have the information and could go to the FBI. She knew Trent wouldn't approve. But she'd done it for him. She'd own up to it once he got back.

She'd also looked for information that she could use against Leo, but his firewalls were too strong. He must have made them stronger after everything had happened with her. There was no way she could pull any new evidence from the reinforced system.

She'd thought about hacking into the system many times over the past eight months. But she knew she couldn't do that while she was living in West Virginia. It would have led Leo right to her. Plus, she'd had no one on her side. But now with Trent and Zach backing her up, maybe she had a fighting chance.

Trent…

Now, somehow, their lives were intertwined. But what happened when all of this was over? Would their lives ever return to normal? And what exactly was normal for Tessa? Would she actually be able to go home, to see her family? Could she look for a new job and start her life again?

The idea of all of this being over almost seemed too good to be true. There were so many things that could go wrong.

But for a moment—and just a moment—she dreamed

about what it would be like to actually put this behind her. To actually trust again. To believe in someone. To put her faith in God.

She closed her eyes. *Lord, I want that peace that Trent has. I want to trust. I want to be a rock that doesn't move in the middle of a storm, instead of being tossed by every hardship that comes my way. I want to get right with You again.*

When she opened her eyes again, she felt renewed. She was going to get through tomorrow, one way or another.

NINETEEN

Trent tugged on his uniform: blue pants and a button-up blue shirt with the name of the HVAC company—Thomas and Sons—proudly displayed on a label. He had to make sure everything was in place before he stepped inside the annals of the art gallery.

The McAllister Gallery was no mom-and-pop storefront. No, it was a grand building located in Arlington, and no expense had been spared. The exterior appeared to be marble and stone, the shrubs were well manicured and the entrance had a pricey-looking statue out front.

Trent slammed the door of his van. It was a plain, nondescript white one that could easily pass as one of the HVAC company's. He had the van for his PI work, and it had come in handy on more than one occasion. Thanks to an old friend, he'd also been able to collect some of the basic heating and air-conditioning supplies, including an anemometer to test airflow. He'd picked them up last night and gotten a rundown on HVAC basics.

Now it was time to put his plan into action. This was where the rubber met the road. This could blow everything open or end very poorly.

He prayed it was the former.

Adjusting the bag on his shoulder, he approached the

back door. Even the back of this place looked nice and well kept, with not a speck of dirt in sight.

He hit the back doorbell, a tremor of anxiety rushing through him. Some nerves were healthy, he reminded himself, especially in situations like this. A touch of fear kept a person sharp and alert; it helped the fight or flight kick in.

A trim woman wearing a stylish black business suit pulled the door open. She held a clipboard and pushed up her dark plastic-framed glasses when she spotted Trent. "Can I help you?"

"Ms. Clark, I'm here with Thomas and Sons HVAC. We had an appointment." It paid off that Tessa had done her research and discovered this woman's name. It lent credibility to him being here.

The woman tilted her head, studying him for a moment. "I don't recall an appointment."

"We come out twice a year to check out your system as part of your service plan. We scheduled this in advance, but our secretary, Barbara, should have called to confirm the appointment."

"Right, Barbara." That seemed to appease the woman a moment. She stepped back and allowed Trent inside.

Obstacle number one: check.

He only had about fifty more to get past before he could breathe easy again.

"You must be new. I haven't seen you before."

Trent flashed what he hoped was a charming smile. "I am. I've never been here before, but my girlfriend loves this place. I've been meaning to bring her here sometime."

He glanced around, hoping that he wouldn't see anyone he recognized—or anyone who recognized him, for that matter. Even with his hat on and the uniform covering him, there was little else he could do to conceal how he looked.

"Well, there's not much to see here behind the curtain except a lot of boxes and cleaning supplies." She spread her hand to showcase the back office area around them. "But beyond this area is fantastic. We feature some world-renowned artists, including Alejandro Gaurs."

She tucked a hair behind her ear. "Anyway, the thermostat is over there." She pointed to the wall next to an interior door.

"I'll need to check each of the vents, also." He raised the anemometer. "I run the meter over them so I can make sure they're running at full capacity. This harsh weather we've had already can overtax heating systems. It's better to discover it now than to wait until something goes wrong. Then you'll just have a lot of cold visitors to the gallery. No one wants that."

"Of course. No problem. Is that where you'd like to start?"

"That would be great."

"This way," Ms. Clark said to him.

Trent followed her out of the back office and into a hallway. Four doors were located there. The offices, he realized. This was exactly where he needed to be.

As he passed one of the doors, he heard someone talking on the other side. Two or three voices. All men. At least one seemed to have an accent. Could it be Leo and some of his cohorts?

Any relief he'd felt earlier disappeared. This could get sticky, and fast.

Ms. Clark opened the door. "This is my office. How about you start here?"

"Sounds great."

"I'm just going to step out to the restroom. I'll be right back."

"Sounds great." He walked over to the vent and held his meter over it.

As soon as she disappeared, he put his equipment down and quickly pulled up the vent.

If this didn't work, then Trent didn't know what they would do. This was their only lead and at times it seemed like their only chance.

He pulled out a flashlight and shone it down into the dark recesses of the vent.

He saw nothing.

Wasting no time, he reached his hand down into the metal shaft. He felt around carefully. If there was something down there, he didn't want to send it deeper into the duct.

Nothing.

He reached a little farther, knowing he was on borrowed time.

His fingers connected with something.

Could it be…?

His hand emerged from the vent. A flash drive was wedged between his fingers.

Bingo! The device had still been there, and Leo had been clueless about it the whole time.

Just as he slid it into his pocket, he heard movement behind him.

He turned in time to see Ms. Clark standing there, staring at him with obvious distrust. "What are you doing?" she demanded.

Trent had to think quickly.

Tessa was walking on eggshells. Her mind wouldn't stop racing as she thought about what Trent was doing at the moment. She paced the house, ran through scenarios in her mind, prayed.

It felt good to pray, especially since her life had been so absent of faith recently. Giving her cares to a higher being brought great comfort. But even with her renewed trust in God, there was still the human aspect of living—the fear that wanted to creep in, the uncertainty and the anxiety.

Lord, please watch over Trent.

Best she could tell, she'd gone onto Leo's server undetected last night. Trent was risking his life for her, and she wanted to do whatever she could to ensure his safety.

A small niggle of doubt still crept into her psyche, though. There were so many uncertainties, so many things she couldn't be sure about.

She allowed herself to dream for a moment about what life would be like without living under this kind of strain. Even more so, how much safer the world would be without a family like the McAllisters out there, smuggling out blueprints for weapons that would destroy lives. This whole thing was bigger than her. Bigger than her family. Bigger than the McAllisters, even.

With the right evidence, maybe the authorities would believe her. Maybe they would take her off the wanted list and actually take action against this powerful crime family.

Then there was a chance she and Trent could truly explore a relationship together. The idea of beginning something like that in the midst of all of this craziness seemed like a bad idea. Their emotions were just too heightened and enlarged.

Zach walked into the room at that moment.

"Did you hear anything?" Tessa asked, turning her full attention on him.

He shook his head. "Not yet. I wish we'd had more time and resources. We could have wired him or put a camera on him. But we couldn't do that. So we just wait instead."

"Do you really think this is going to work?" Tessa dared to ask. She wanted more than anything to believe that this was possible. But then the fear came. The fear of something happening to Trent, of being discovered, of Leo capturing her and exacting his torturous revenge.

"If anyone can do it, it's Trent. I know the stress right now is probably overwhelming, but all we can do is wait."

"I'd rather be doing something."

"The safest thing you can do right now is to stay right here. All we can do is trust that God is in control right now and that all things will work out the way they're supposed to."

"Even when the lives of millions of people are on the line," she whispered.

He squeezed her shoulder. "Even when the lives of millions are on the line. It's a tough world we live in, filled with hard stuff. Stuff that makes you sick and turns your stomach."

"So we cling to the unseen instead of what we see here in this world," Tessa said.

"Exactly." Zach settled against the wall. "You know, Trent is a great guy. He was devastated after what happened with Laurel. I didn't know if he'd ever fall in love again."

"He's not in love," Tessa was quick to say.

"Maybe not yet. But he's on his way. I can tell by the way he's acting. I'm really happy for him."

Tessa let his words sink in. Could he be telling the truth?

Even more so, this conversation made Tessa realize something else: against all odds, she was beginning to fall in love with Trent, too.

Trent stood and held up a wad of dust and dried leaves from the ficus tree nearby. "There was quite a bit of dust in this duct. I pulled the cover off so I could get a more accurate reading. Tell me, does it get cold in here often?"

The woman shifted. "I suppose I do always wear my sweater. I thought I was just cold natured."

He shook his head. "No, these vents need to be cleaned out. Of course, that's more than I can do today, but I'd guess some of the ductwork under the building may need to be touched up. The temperature in here should be sixty-eight, but it's only sixty-two."

She shivered at his words. "I'm glad I'm not going crazy. I always felt like a whiner when I brought up how chilly I was."

He tucked his meter back into pocket. "Don't worry. I'll have everything checked out. I'm going to have to come out with some help, though. This is more than a one-person job. It is covered by your warranty, so price shouldn't be an issue."

"Price usually doesn't matter with Mr. McAllister anyway, but that's good to know. It will be one less channel I have to go through, since there's no budget approval needed. When can we schedule you?"

"I'll have to get Barbara to give you a call back. I'll mention it to her when I get into the office."

"Thanks for coming in."

Trent's heart slowed for a minute. If he could just get out of here and into his van, he'd be home free. He'd take this information to his contact with the FBI, and then he'd pray that everything else fell into place.

He took a step into the hallway and balked. Leo McAllister stepped out of the office, two men behind him. Trent tugged his hat down lower, but made sure to keep his chin up. He couldn't afford to look guilty or bring any unnecessary attention to himself.

Leo didn't seem to see him. He continued to talk to the two men beside him as he walked down the hallway toward him. He did cast a look of approval at his secretary before mentioning something else about a shipment they had coming in.

He'd just taken one step past Leo when the man paused. "You're with the HVAC company?" Leo said.

Trent composed himself and turned halfway. The man

had talked to him before, but only once and only briefly. Still, there was a chance he might recognize Trent. "That's right. Just doing some maintenance."

Leo stared at him, something cold, hard and unreadable in his eyes.

Trent steadied his breathing. Had he been made?

TWENTY

Why hadn't Trent called yet?

Tessa continued pacing the living room. He'd been gone for three hours now. Certainly that was enough time to get in and out. So why hadn't he made contact?

Zach was talking to a former colleague on the phone, trying to ascertain the best person to hand over the information to once they had it.

This seemed like the longest day of Tessa's life.

Lord, please watch over him. Keep him safe.

She walked over to the window and peered outside, hoping to see Trent coming down the lane. Instead, she saw a yard covered with pristine snow.

It really was beautiful out here. Under different circumstances, there'd be so much to enjoy about being here. But at the moment it felt desolate and isolated and like a prison.

Much like what her life had felt like for the past year.

Desperate to keep her thoughts occupied, she began to review everything she would tell the authorities once Trent returned with the information. She would leave no detail out. She knew the names of associates, dates of business trips abroad, large sums of money that had been exchanged. Of course, all that meant nothing without proof.

When Trent returned—because he would return, she told herself—he would have that evidence to finally nail Leo.

Her gaze paused at something in the distance. She squinted, uncertain if she was seeing things. But down by the tree line, she thought she'd seen movement.

She shook her head. No, she must have been seeing things. She looked closer, stared harder, but all she saw was trees. Underbrush. Dark recesses.

If there had been movement, it was just the wind. Maybe a bird. It could even be a deer.

She was so used to living in fear.

But there was no way she could have been discovered here. She'd taken every precaution yesterday when she'd accessed those computer files. She'd redirected the server, made dummy locations, the works.

She stared at that spot in the distance again until finally her heart slowed. She was overreacting. She hoped her paranoia would soon become a distant memory.

"We've been having hot and cold spots. I'm glad you're here," Leo said.

As he walked away, Trent tried to relax. But when he heard the man's phone ring, his steps slowed.

"You're there now?" Leo said into the phone. "Perfect. Bring her to the location we discussed. We'll go from there."

Tessa? Was he talking about Tessa? There was no way she could have been discovered.

"Are you okay, sir?" Ms. Clark said.

He nodded and kept walking. Better not to draw any attention to himself. Besides, that wouldn't stop anything that was happening at the house. That would only delay him getting back to Tessa.

"So you'll be in touch?" the woman said.

He gave her an assuring smile. "Definitely."

"Great. Stay warm out there. I hear there's more snow coming."

He walked calmly back to the van, placed his supplies in the back and then climbed inside. To err on the side of caution, he started the van and pulled out of the parking lot. He stopped the next block down and pulled out his phone.

Zach picked up on the first ring. "What's going on?"

"Where's Tessa?"

"In the living room. Worrying. Why?"

"I think Leo's men know where she is."

"That's impossible."

"I don't know what happened, but I need you to be careful. Very careful. I'm on my way there now."

Before he hung up the phone, he heard a gunshot sound on the other end the line.

Tessa heard glass break at the other end of the house and her heartbeat ratcheted.

She didn't even take time to examine possible alternate causes for the noise. She only knew trouble was here.

The sound had come from the end of the house where Zach was staying.

She grabbed the gun from the table where she'd left it, held it near her chest and rushed toward the door. Moving slowly, carefully, she checked down the hallway. It looked clear.

She moved quietly down the corridor, clearing each room as she went. She knew where she needed to go: Zach's room, at the end of the hallway. She dreaded what she would find when she got there. In her heart, she already knew it wouldn't be good.

With trembling hands, she searched the second-to-last room. It was clear.

Finally, she approached the closed door to Zach's room.

Part of her wanted to run. To flee. To stick her head in the sand.

But she couldn't do that. Trent and Zach both had gone

out of their way to help her. She couldn't abandon either of them now.

It was silent on the other side of the doorway. That realization in itself sent a shudder through her.

Had a shot been fired through the window, hitting Zach and rendering him immobile? Or were there men inside, crouching and waiting to attack?

Drawing in a deep breath and trying to summon her courage, she held her gun in position and pushed the door open. To her dismay, she spotted Zach. He was on his knees. Hands behind his back. Blood trickled down his forehead and his shirt had red stains. He hadn't been shot—not yet. But the window was shattered behind him.

A man stood on the other side of him, a gun to Zach's forehead. Tessa recognized him as one of the men who'd been chasing them.

How had they been discovered? Was it because of the computer transmission? Had she led the men here? Had she invited death into this place of safety?

"Don't do it, Tessa," Zach said, his voice scratchy and low.

"Nice to see you could join us," the man said.

Three other men appeared in the room, all with guns in their hands. There was no way she could handle all of them. The moment she pulled the trigger, someone else with a gun would shoot her and then Zach. It was a no-win situation.

"How'd you find us?" she asked, her gaze flinging from Zach to the man holding the gun beside him.

"Did you think we wouldn't notice if someone got onto our server? We hired the best IT guys, just in case you tried to do something like that again. As soon as you logged in, we traced your location."

Her heart twisted with grief. This was her fault.

And what about Trent? Was he in danger now, too?

"What we can't figure out is why you logged on. Certainly you're smart enough to know we removed all of that information that was on there," the man continued.

She shrugged, trying to keep a cool head. "I have my reasons."

"Maybe you should start sharing." The man cocked the gun and shoved it into Zach's temple.

"No!" she shouted, fear pulsing through her. "He's done nothing wrong. I'm the one you want."

"Don't listen to them, Tessa," Zach said.

"This is my battle, Zach. Not yours. Not Trent's." She said the words with resignation. But she knew they were true. She couldn't live with herself if someone died because of her.

"Smart thinking," the man with the gun muttered. "Now put your weapon down."

Slowly, Tessa lowered it to the floor and then rose again with her hands in the air. "Let him go."

The man motioned to his thugs. Two of them grabbed Tessa and zip-tied her arms behind her with more than necessary roughness. She squirmed in discomfort.

This was it, she realized. The moment when she couldn't go back. The moment when she had to face her greatest fears.

Her eyes connected with Zach's and she saw the concern there. This wasn't what Trent would have wanted. But she had no other choice. No one else was going to get killed because of her.

The man in charge took the butt of his gun and slammed it into Zach's head. Tessa sucked in a quick breath, alarm rushing through her. As Zach's head slumped, she let out a moan.

She started to lunge toward him, but the man beside her jerked her back.

"Let's go," the man in charge said.

Tessa took one last fleeting glance at Zach before the men dragged her out the door and into a waiting SUV.

TWENTY-ONE

Trent drove faster than he should have. But he had to get to Tessa before Leo's men did. He'd tried calling Zach back, but there had been no answer. His blood pressure heightened to unhealthy levels as he imagined what might be happening.

He swerved into the driveway and saw an eerily calm house ahead. As he jumped from the driver's seat, he drew his gun. He crept around to the back of the house and saw the broken window.

That was when his fears were confirmed. Something bad had happened here.

He hurried to the back door, surveyed the area on the other side of the glass. It appeared to be clear. He quietly opened it and stepped inside.

Silence greeted him.

He had a feeling everyone was gone, but he still had to be careful.

At least in the kitchen, there was no evidence of a struggle. As he stepped into the dining room, he didn't see blood or broken furniture. But the twisted feeling remained in his gut.

He searched each room as he traveled down the hall.

That was when he spotted Zach.

His friend lay on the floor, his arms tied, a chair behind

him. Blood streamed from his forehead, his eye was swollen and he seemed to just be returning to consciousness.

Trent rushed toward him and untied his arms.

"They got her. I'm sorry," his friend croaked.

"We need to get you to a hospital."

"I'll be okay. We have to find her. They'll kill her, Trent."

Zach's words ignited something in him. His feelings for Tessa had grown quickly. But that didn't mean they were any less real. He couldn't lose someone else he was beginning to care about.

His thoughts flashed through his mind at an alarming rate. He was charged up and ready to find her. But where?

"I'm going with you." Zach pulled himself up with a wince.

"I can't ask you to do that."

"I'm not giving you a choice."

Trent accepted this with a quick nod. There was no time to argue. "Okay, let's go, then."

Trent's mind raced as he hurried to the van. Not the fastest vehicle, but it would have to work.

They climbed in, and as he cranked the engine, he turned toward Zach. "Tell me what you know."

"There were six of them. They all had guns. And they were unapologetic."

"Any hints on where they went?" He pulled onto the road.

"No idea."

Certainly they hadn't taken Tessa back to the gallery. But where else would they have taken her?

He thought back and remembered that address they'd found in the car they'd taken from the fake cops. Could they have taken her there? He didn't know, but he didn't have any other ideas at the moment.

"Can you pull up Wilmington Heights, Virginia, on your phone?" he asked Zach.

"I know where that is. Probably forty-five minutes from here. Why?"

"It's my best guess as to where they might have gone. We found an address in the car when those men impersonating police officers arrested us. How far do you think it is from the art gallery in DC?"

"Maybe fifteen minutes?"

The idea solidified in his mind. It was worth a shot.

He prayed he was right.

Tessa couldn't see where they were taking her. They'd thrown something over her head, a black bag of some sort. She was in the trunk, where she couldn't even hear their conversation, except for occasional laughter. These men were enjoying their job a little too much.

At first, she tried to pay attention to every bump, every turn. But after a while, she lost track. There were too many twists and turns, and she felt as if she'd been in the trunk for hours.

She steadied her breathing. How long had it been? An hour? Less? More?

She'd lost her sense of time.

The moment she stopped paying attention to the things she had control over was the moment panic started creeping in. That was when she started imagining seeing Leo again and thinking about what he might do with her.

He'd be angry. He'd had a long time to let his anger simmer, too. It had most likely only increased with time.

Think, Tessa. Think. Remain in control.

Where would they be taking her?

They were too smart to go to Leo's house, or any of his registered properties, for that matter.

Finally, the car rolled to a stop. Another surge of panic

started in her. Her heart raced as she prepared to face the unknown.

She felt the trunk open as a *whoosh* of air rushed inside. Then strong hands grabbed her and jerked her from the vehicle. Despite the fact that her legs felt like gelatin, she managed to stand.

Two men pulled her down a sidewalk. She couldn't walk fast enough to keep up. Then she heard a door open and she was shoved inside a building. They led her across a slick floor.

Pay attention, Tessa.

She could smell motor oil. Maybe cinnamon. Someone was talking in the distance.

The space was still cold, even though she was inside now.

Based on the echo of footsteps, she imagined the space to be open, airy and uncluttered.

Was she in a warehouse of some sort?

Finally, someone shoved her into a chair. She flinched as her back hit the wood there.

Then the bag over her head was snatched away.

She blinked at the bright light. Squinted at the men surrounding her. Squinted when she saw… Leo.

Trent pulled into the town of Wilmington Springs. He remembered the address Tessa had read to him. 123 Arnold Drive.

"Bad news," Zach said. "There is no 123 Arnold Drive."

"They had to use an address to register the car with the DMV."

"You know people fake documents like that all the time, right?"

Trent nodded, coming to a stop at a red light and resisting the urge to punch his steering wheel with frustration. "Yeah, I know."

"We've got to think. Maybe the address they chose has some kind of significance."

Trent racked his brain, trying to remember that conversation. "There was a name associated with it. Tom Tracy."

"I'll look him up and see if I can find out anything." Zach punched something into his phone. "What do you know? There is a Tom Tracy living in Wilmington Heights."

"Address?"

"Looks like it's 121 Arthur Avenue. It's so similar that no one would probably think twice about it if he was pulled over."

"Clever. Now tell me how to get there."

They zipped down the road, the tension between Trent's shoulders growing by the moment. He needed a plan for what he would do when he got there. Zach was too injured to help. Which left Trent pretty much on his own.

He had confidence in his abilities, but he had to be smart. One man against at least six—probably more—was a bad idea.

"Zach, I need you to call my friend with the FBI."

"You know they might arrest her, right?"

"I know. But without backup she'll be dead. I have hope that when they hear her story, they'll understand. I know Leo has planted evidence against Tessa. But there's a lot of proof here to convict Leo, too."

"Okay," Zach said, raising his phone to make the call.

Trent slowed as they pulled up to an aluminum-sided building in the distance. A chain-link fence, at least nine feet high, surrounded it, and there were no other structures around.

This looked like the perfect place for Leo and his men to plan their nefarious operations.

He pulled off the road and into the woods, hopefully where no one would spot them.

"Zach, if anything happens, I need you to turn this over to the authorities." Trent slid the jump drive into his friend's hand. At least if he and Tessa didn't make it out of this, Leo could still pay for his actions and they could save the lives of thousands of people by unveiling these terrorists and their plans.

"Trent, you should wait until backup gets here."

He shook his head. "I can't. Tessa could be in there. Waiting could mean losing her."

Zach stared at him a moment before letting out a breath. "Let's go, then."

"You're staying here. With this jump drive. You're not in a position to help me right now. I think you have some broken ribs and maybe even a concussion. The best thing you can do for me is to be a lookout."

Zach winced as if pain rushed through him again. Finally, he nodded. "Okay. Be careful, man. I'll be praying."

"Okay."

Trent stepped out, ready to save the woman he loved.

"Well, hello, my darling," Leo crooned, a wickedly charming smile on his face.

Tessa didn't even try to hold back her sneer. She jerked against the zip ties that kept her in her chair, knowing it would do no good. His face was not a welcome one.

He ran a finger down her jawline. "You left so abruptly all those months ago. I didn't have a chance to say goodbye."

Leo looked as slick as ever. He had thick blond hair, perfect teeth and tanned skin that looked as fake as his smile. His clothes were expensive, and he had cultured motions.

She pulled away from his touch. "That's because I never wanted to see you again."

"Well, you don't always get what you want, do you?" He dropped his hand back to his side.

"Why'd you bring me here?"

"Isn't that obvious? To make you pay."

"Just kill me," she seethed.

"That would be too easy."

"You just want to revel in your supposed brilliance."

The smile disappeared from his face. He slid his fingers to the base of her neck and tightened them. "You think you're so smart, don't you? What did you do with all of the information you stole from me?"

She tried to suck in a breath, but he squeezed out her ability to speak. She pushed back her panic, though. She wouldn't give him that satisfaction. Not yet.

"I don't have it," she croaked.

"Then, where is it?"

"It's gone."

"Do I need to do something to jolt your memory?" He leaned closer, his glare deepening.

How could she have ever thought he was handsome? He was conniving and selfish. "I couldn't let you kill innocent people. Thousands of them. Millions, maybe. There were things at stake more important than my safety."

He let go of her and coolly walked away, letting out a detached laugh. "I have to admit, you still impress me. Just like you did when we were engaged."

"That was my first mistake."

His laugh increased. "And you're still feisty. I feared you might lose some of your spirit. I always thought we were good together."

"You're delusional."

"We could still be good together, you know. We could forget all of this. Go and live our happy-ever-after together. What do you think?"

The thought turned her stomach. "I think you're crazy."

"Have it your way, then. My way was much more enjoyable." He paced in front of her and his gaze burned into her. "You did a better job hiding than I thought you would. I figured my men would find you the first week you were gone. There are so many means to track people nowadays after all."

"You were very clever, keeping tabs on my mom. I'm surprised she didn't see through you. The one thing I still don't understand is this—why? Why would you side with men who want to kill? Why would you go through all of this trouble?"

"Do you know what kind of money is available when you smuggle blueprints for weapons of mass destruction, drones and chemical agents?"

"But you're already rich."

"One can never have too much money," he said.

"This has to be about more than that." She simply couldn't fathom someone going to these extremes to obtain more cash. Then again, money had never had a big appeal for her like it did for some.

"Enough talking." He abruptly snapped back into homicidal-maniac mode. "I've thought long and hard about this. Bernard is going to help you understand what a waste of time and resources your betrayal has been. Bernard."

A man stepped forward. He didn't look as imposing as she might have thought. In fact, he appeared to be less than five feet tall. He was scrawny, with greasy hair and a receding hairline.

Then he flashed his knife.

Blood rushed through Tessa as she braced herself for whatever was about to come.

TWENTY-TWO

Trent managed to find an unlatched door. He stepped into a warehouse type of building that had been broken up into smaller spaces. The lights were dim and fluorescent, creating a subtle buzz.

He held his gun close as he gently closed the door behind him. He didn't see anyone, but he had to be careful.

Somewhere in the distance he heard murmuring.

What was this place used for? Was this where they ensured the artwork actually contained blueprints for top secret weapons? Was this place where all of the operations were based?

He didn't have time to ponder it now.

Footsteps came closer.

He pressed himself against the wall near the corner, his heart rate increasing with anticipation. Just as a man stepped toward the door, Trent brought the butt of his gun down on his head. With a moan, the man sank to the floor, out cold.

He grabbed the man's gun and slid it into the back of his waistband. One man down; how many more to go? He wished he knew.

Cautiously he moved forward. If Zach had called his contact with the FBI, then there was a possibility they could be here as soon as ten or fifteen minutes. That was good, because time was of the essence here.

He heard voices coming his way—at least two different people. He ducked into a room—a dark room with various boxes lined against the wall. And paintings. There were paintings in here.

He peered through the crack in the door and saw Leo passing.

"What are you going to do with her once we're done?" the other man asked.

"Dispose of her body," Leo said. "I'm thinking the ocean. Make it look like a suicide. With any luck, her body will be sucked out to sea and no one will ever find it."

"What about that man who's been traveling with her?"

"We can take care of him. He'll be tougher because of his connections with law enforcement. If he makes any accusations against us, we'll deny it. It's not as if he has any proof."

The men's voices faded, but the fire inside Trent grew. He had to get to Tessa. Now.

Once the hallway was silent again, he stepped out. He kept his steps light as he headed toward the opposite end of the building.

The voices he'd heard in the distance became louder. He was getting closer.

Finally, he paused outside a door.

A scream sounded inside.

Tessa.

That was Tessa.

He had to get to her.

When Tessa felt the knife prick the skin on her wrist and then saw the red blood appear, she couldn't stop the scream from surging out from her throat. She could try to be tough all she wanted, but pain was pain.

With a new faith in Christ, she wasn't afraid of death. However, the process of dying seemed terrifying. Besides, when she thought of her family, she had a reason to live. When she thought about Trent, she knew she wanted more than anything to explore what a relationship with him might be like.

Bernard smiled at her again. He was missing teeth and the few he had were brown or yellowed. Her arm ached after the first cut. She knew there was more to come.

Against her will, tears rushed to her eyes.

She fought against the restraints, trying to get away. She knew her effort was futile, but she didn't stop trying.

"Struggling will only make this more painful," Bernard said, displaying a crooked smile.

"It's too bad Leo isn't enough of a man to do this himself. He has to get you to do his dirty work."

Bernard chuckled. "I'll pass on the message. But until then, we have other business to attend to." He stepped closer.

A groan escaped her lips, belying her defiant tone.

Just as he lowered his knife toward the skin on her other arm, the door burst open.

In a flurry of events, she spotted Trent. His gun was raised. Quickly, he pulled the trigger, first hitting Bernard and then the other two men in the room. Each of them moaned with pain, clutching their shoulders or knees. Not lethal shots, but shots meant to hinder, to slow down their efforts. She could respect that.

A tear of joy cascaded down her cheek. Trent was here. Maybe she did have a reason to hope she might survive.

Moving quickly, he grabbed Bernard's knife and cut the ties around her arms. "Are you okay?" he asked, tenderness softening his voice.

She nodded. "Better now that you're here."

He glanced down at her arm and blanched.

As Bernard started to sit up, Trent slammed his fist against the man's head and he slumped back to the ground. "We've got to get out of here. Now."

She nodded, knowing better than to argue.

Trent pulled her out of the chair, glanced around and then walked toward the door. He scanned the hallway before leading her out. "You know another way to leave this place?"

"I was blindfolded. No idea."

He led her down the hallway. Footsteps and shouts sounded in the distance.

Tessa knew that with the gunfire, Leo would quickly discover what had happened. They didn't have much time.

They reached the end of the hallway. It was a dead end.

This wasn't good.

She looked up at Trent and saw the contemplation on his face. Finally, he pulled her into a room off the hallway and put a finger over his lips to signal silence. She froze, hardly able to breathe as she listened to the footsteps coming closer.

How many men had she seen? There were at least three or four more. Could Trent handle them on his own?

Now that they were on to the fact that Trent was here, it seemed unlikely. They were too outnumbered.

But she wouldn't give in to despair. There was no time for that.

"Where could they have gone?" a voice that clearly belonged to Leo exploded. "Find them. Now. Kill them when you do. I don't have time for any more of these games."

Trent's grip on her biceps tightened and he shoved her farther behind him. He had his gun in his hands.

"Check the rooms!"

Tessa's heart rate quickened.

Slowly, Trent leaned down and grabbed a metal doorstop from the floor. With measured movements, he tossed it down the hallway. The men turned toward the sound. When they did, Trent stepped out and fired.

Tessa gasped at the sound. Her ears would be ringing for days. If she lived that long.

He emerged into the hallway and kicked the men's guns out of the way. Tessa grabbed one and raised it.

They took a step down the hallway. Just then, a man stepped out behind Tessa. His arm went around her neck and, with one squeeze, her gun clattered to the floor.

Trent turned and spotted the beefy man who'd grabbed Tessa. He raised his gun.

"Let her go," he ordered.

"Put the gun down or I'll kill her," the man said.

"I'd do what he says," someone with a smooth voice said behind Trent.

Trent didn't have to look over his shoulder to know it was Leo speaking. His gut told him that the man had a gun pointed at him.

He took one last glance at Tessa, hoping she could read the apology in his eyes. Terror stained her gaze, clutching his heart with grief at the sight.

"Put the gun down," the man behind him said again.

"Don't do it, Trent," Tessa said, her voice raspy and strained.

"I don't have a choice."

"They'll...kill...you," she whispered.

"If I don't put this down, they'll kill you," he said. "I'm sorry I let you down."

Slowly, he raised his free hand and lowered the gun to the floor. He couldn't take the chance. But he didn't know how he was going to get out of this.

Leo strode closer. "Well, wasn't that a beautiful display of young love. You both just made my job easier. I thought I was going to have to track you down, too, but you showed up here. Now I don't have to. I like it when things are easy."

"You're not going to get away with this," Trent assured him.

Leo shrugged. "Sure I will. I always do. With money, you can get away with a lot of things. Everything is going to look like Tessa is behind it. I'll testify that I caught her using my business to do arms deals. I've even had some photos altered to show her meeting in the park with a member of a terrorist group. I always say, leave no stone unturned. It's why I'm so good at what I do. It's all in the details."

The man's cockiness set his nerves on edge.

Tessa gasped for air in the other man's grip. Blood from her wound dripped on the floor, and her face took on a pale hue.

"Let her go!" Trent said, desperate to reach her, to protect her.

Leo chuckled beside him. "I need to make her pay for what she did to me. Don't you understand that? Haven't your investigative skills come in handy at all?" He paced around him. "You're in love with her, aren't you?"

"I'm smart enough to know that love means not hurting or using or mistreating the object of your affection."

"Life is too short not to use people to your advantage." Leo's smile disappeared as he nodded toward the man holding Tessa. "Now finish the job."

Just as Leo said the words, he raised his gun at Trent.

As instinct kicked in, Trent swung his foot and knocked the gun from Leo's hands. Wasting no time, Trent grabbed the weapon and aimed it at Tessa's attacker. The bullet hit him in the throat. The shot was enough to loosen the man's hold on Tessa. She crumpled to the ground, crawling away from the man.

Just as the man reached for her, Trent took another shot, hitting his shoulder. The thug howled with pain.

When Trent turned back around, he saw that Leo had grabbed his gun again and was pointing it right at him.

He dived out of the way, knowing he probably wouldn't make it in time.

Tessa let out a cry and lunged toward Leo. She hit his knees just as he fired. The bullet veered past Trent, skimming the sleeve of his jacket.

"Freeze. FBI!" Four men appeared down the hallway.

Help was here. Help was finally here.

As soon as Leo and his men had been cleared from the building and taken into police custody, Tessa turned to Trent. She had so much she needed to say, but words didn't seem adequate at the moment. He'd saved her life, given her hope for the future and restored her faith in people. How could she show her gratitude for all of that?

She settled for "Thank you."

His hand covered her neck and jaw as he looked tenderly into her eyes. His look showed warmth and love and a depth of emotion that couldn't be faked. "You gave me a good scare."

"I know, but—"

Before she could finish her sentence, his lips covered hers. Time seemed to stand still around them. Everyone else disappeared. Memories of the atrocity that had occurred vanished. At the moment, it was just Trent and Tessa.

"I'd do anything for the woman I love," Trent whispered when they pulled away. "Anything. I hope you've realized that over the past several days."

Her heart raced at his proclamation. She wrapped her arms around his waist. "I love you, Trent. I never thought

I would be able to say that. But, against all the odds, here I am. I've never meant the words more."

"You two ready to give a statement?" the agent in charge asked behind them.

Trent kept his arm around Tessa as they turned toward the man.

"I'm ready to share everything I know," Tessa said. "Especially now that Leo is behind bars."

"We've had surveillance on Leo and his men for quite some time. I'm hoping that we have the evidence now to put him away for good."

"After we get done here, what do you say we go see your family?" Trent asked.

Warmth spread from her heart to the rest of her body. "I think that would be the most wonderful thing ever... especially with you by my side."

He smiled before kissing her forehead. "Then, let's get this over with."

EPILOGUE

Six months later

Tessa flipped off the TV after watching the evening news, and a satisfied smile washed across her face. She looked up at Trent, who sat beside her on the couch, and saw that he shared the same expression.

With a new sense of relief filling her, she threw her arms around him. "I can't believe it," she whispered. "This really is over."

His arms circled her waist. She still marveled at his strength—both physically and emotionally. He'd been her rock from the day they'd met, and she thanked God every day that their paths had crossed.

The news anchor had just announced what Tessa and Trent had already suspected would happen—Leo McAllister had accepted a plea deal. He'd be going away for a long time, as would the family's contact with the defense contractor. Not only that, but several weapon blueprints had been intercepted before they'd gotten into the wrong hands.

"You can finally get on with your life," Trent said, pulling back and looking her in the eye. There was an undeniable gleam of affection there. "We can finally get on with *our* lives."

Tessa smiled. She liked the sound of that. Ever since

Leo had been arrested, Trent had been at her side. He'd seen to it that he was her personal bodyguard until he was absolutely sure Leo was no longer a threat. And Tessa hadn't minded it one bit. She knew beyond a shadow of a doubt that Trent would do whatever he needed to in order to keep her safe. He'd proved that.

She'd never felt so loved or valued by a man before. Nor had she ever felt such an easy trust.

Not only that, but her mom and brother and sister and nieces and nephews were all back in her life. She'd been so happy to see them and catch up and hug them again.

She'd called Salem, also. He was just fine. Tessa had worried about him, worried that Leo might have tracked him down. Thankfully, that hadn't happened.

Life was falling into place again.

She leaned back into the couch. They were at Trent's house right now. Tessa was living with her mom until she started her new job. She was pleased that she'd soon be working for Trent. She'd be helping him with any cyber issues that popped up in the course of his PI work, as well as with coordinating some of his jobs. It wasn't necessarily something she'd seen herself doing, but she enjoyed organizing and coordinating. Even more, she loved working with Trent.

"Tessa?" Trent asked, his voice husky and serious.

She'd told him that she preferred to go by Tessa now. Theresa seemed too much like the person she used to be.

She glanced up at him, noting that there was a new expression in his eyes. She couldn't pinpoint what it was. Excitement? Nervousness? Mischief? "Yes?"

He rubbed his lips together before speaking. "I know the past six months have been a whirlwind. Totally unexpected and surprising and dangerous at times. But I need to ask you something."

She gripped his arms, hoping she never had to be without his embrace. She felt as though she could move mountains with him by her side. She sucked in a breath as she anticipated what he had to say. "Anything."

In one fluid movement, he was down on one knee. "Will you marry me?"

Her eyes widened with delight and surprise. That was when the ring in his hands came into focus. "Really?" She couldn't believe it—she hadn't been hearing things.

His eyes danced. "Really. You've turned my life upside down, Tessa. You made me realize I can love again, that there's life beyond tragedy. I know the circumstances that pulled us together were unconventional, but I'm so glad they led us to where we are today. I want to start a life with you."

"Me, too."

He smiled. "So what do you think? Will you do me the honor of becoming Mrs. Trent McCabe?"

She grinned so widely that it hurt. "Yes! I would be thrilled. Elated."

He laughed as he stood up, slid the ring on her finger and pulled her into a long hug. He twirled her around before putting her back firmly on her feet. Their gazes met, their faces only inches from each other. "I love you, Tessa Davidson."

"I love you, Trent McCabe."

And Tessa knew without a doubt that life had somehow worked out to bring her right to this very minute.

* * * * *

WE HOPE YOU
ENJOYED THIS

LOVE INSPIRED® SUSPENSE BOOK.

Discover more **heart-pounding** romances of **danger** and **faith** from the Love Inspired Suspense series.

Be sure to look for all six Love Inspired Suspense books every month.

Love Inspired. SUSPENSE

Annie was cleaning up the dishes when the phone rang. She
didn't recognize the number.

"Hello?"

"Annie, it's me."

Tyler.

Her estranged husband. The man she hadn't seen in two
years.

"Annie? You there?"

She shook her head. "Yes, I'm here. It's been a frazzling
day, Tyler. What do you want?"

A pause. "Something's happened last night, Annie. I can't
tell you everything, but the US Marshals are involved. I'm
being put into witness protection."

"Witness protection? Tyler, people in those programs have
to completely disappear."

In her mind, she heard Bethany ask when she would see
her daddy again.

"I know. It won't be forever. At least I hope it won't. I need to testify against someone. Maybe after that, I can go back to being me."

A sudden thought occurred to her. "Tyler, the reason you're going into witness protection... Would it affect me at all?"

"What do you mean?"

"Someone was following me today."

"Someone's following you?" Tyler exclaimed, horrified.

"You never answered. Could the man following me be related to what happened to you?"

"I don't know. Annie, I will call you back." He disconnected the call and went down the hall.

Marshal Mast was sitting at a laptop in an office at the back of the house. He glanced up from the screen as Tyler entered. "Something on your mind, Tyler?"

"I called my wife to tell her I was going into witness protection. She said she and my daughter were being followed today."

At this information, Jonathan Mast jumped to his feet. "Karl!"

Feet pounded in the hallway. Marshal Karl Adams entered the room at a brisk pace. "Jonathan? Did you need me?"

"Yes, I need you to make a trip for me. What's the address, Tyler?"

Tyler recited the address. Would Karl and Stacy get there in time? How he wished he could go with him...

Don't miss
Amish Haven by Dana R. Lynn,
available March 2019 wherever
Love Inspired® Suspense books and ebooks are sold.

www.LoveInspired.com

LISEXP0219